UPON THE MALABAR COAST

UPON THE MALABAR COAST

BY

PHILIP K ALLAN

ISBN-13: 9798744579487

Cover design by Christine Horner from original art by
Colin M Baxter
Edited by Dr Catherine Hanley

Dedication

To Patricia Kathleen Crimmin (1933 – 2020) scholar and teacher, who once planted a seed in a young student's mind

Acknowledgements

My Alexander Clay books start with my passion for the age of sail, which was first awakened when I discovered the works of C S Forester as a child, and later when I graduated to the novels of Patrick O'Brian. That interest was given some academic rigor when I studied the 18th century navy under Patricia Crimmin as part of my history degree at London University.

Many years later, I decided to leave my career in the motor industry to see if I could survive as a writer. I received the unconditional support and cheerful encouragement of my darling wife and two wonderful daughters. I first test my work to see if I have hit the mark with my family, and especially my wife Jan, whose input is invaluable.

One of the pleasures of my new career is the generous support and encouragement I continue to receive from fellow writers. In theory we are in competition, but you would never know it. When I have needed help, advice and support, I have received it from David Donachie, Bernard Cornwell, Marc Liebman, Jeffrey K Walker, Helen Hollick and Ian Drury. I have received particular support from my fellow age of sail writers Alaric Bond, creator of the Fighting Sail series of books and Chris Durbin, author of the Carlisle & Holbrooke Naval Adventures.

The production of *Upon the Malabar Coast* was the work of several hands. In particular I would like to thank Dr Cath Hanley for her excellent and thoughtful editing; Christine Horner from The Book Cover Whisperer for her design and the talented marine artist Colin M Baxter for his beautiful cover art. Readers interested in exploring Colin's work further can find his details at the back of this volume.

Although they were not directly involved in the production of this work, I will always be grateful to Michael James, and the team at Penmore Press, for having the faith in me to publish my first seven novels.

Cast of Main Characters

The Crew of the Frigate *Griffin*

Alexander Clay – Captain RN

George Taylor – First lieutenant
John Blake – Second lieutenant
Edward Preston – Third lieutenant
Thomas Macpherson – Lieutenant of marines

Jacob Armstrong – Sailing master
Richard Corbett – Surgeon
Charles Faulkner – Purser

Nathaniel Hutchinson – Boatswain

Able Sedgwick – Captain's coxswain

Sean O'Malley – Able seaman
Adam Trevan – Able seaman
Samuel Evans – Seaman

In Polwith

Ann Penrose – A young lady
Molly Trevan – Wife of Adam Trevan

In Lower Staverton

Lydia Clay – Wife of Alexander Clay
Francis and Elizabeth Clay – Their children

John Sutton – A naval commander, brother-in-law to Alexander Clay
Elizabeth (Betsey) Sutton – His wife, sister of Alexander Clay and author

In Travancore

Balarama Varma – Maharaja of Travancore
Velu Thampi – His chief minister or dalawa
Major Colin Macaulay – East India Company resident

Others

Guillaume Ropars – A French naval lieutenant
Nicholas Vansittart – A diplomat
Peter Rainier – Vice admiral commanding in the East Indies
Charles-Alexandre Durand, Comte de Linois – A French rear admiral

Contents

Prologue

Les Mouettes was one of the oldest taverns in the French port of Brest. Its ground floor was built from stone blocks that had been weathered smooth by countless Atlantic gales. Resting on this granite base, a half-timbered upper storey sagged outwards until it almost touched the building opposite. Between them ran a dark alley, a thin ribbon of wet cobbles. The lower end of the passageway opened on to the bustling stone quayside, where the sea slapped and fretted against the trading brigs and fishing boats moored along the waterfront. Higher up, past the inn door, the alley became a twisting tunnel, full of dank smells and whispering shadows where few honest citizens ever ventured.

On a chill evening in February 1803 a well-dressed young man in the uniform of a French naval lieutenant appeared at the harbour end of the alley. His coat was of thick broadcloth, his stockings were silk and silver buckles glinted on his shoes. He looked uncertainly up the narrow lane for a moment, a point of stillness against a backdrop of hurrying sailors and passing carts. Then he came to a decision, and with a last careful glance around him he approached Les Mouettes, holding the tails of his coat close and stepping around the worst of the puddles.

Once past the door of the tavern he found himself standing on the rush-covered floor of a low-ceilinged room. A few logs smouldered in a fireplace set in the wall off to one side, while ahead of him was a serving hatch through which a line of cider barrels could be seen. Most of the space was filled with plain oak tables and benches, some occupied by groups of men who regarded the smartly dressed arrival with frank astonishment. In the resulting silence the landlord wiped his hands on his apron and approached the lieutenant.

He gave a bow and indicated a line of booths deeper into the room. 'Your friend is waiting for you in the corner one, monsieur.'

'Thank you,' said the officer, advancing gratefully to escape the stares of the other customers.

The booth was candle-lit and intimate, with wooden partitions that reached up to the beamed ceiling overhead and curtains that could be drawn across the entrance. Two bench seats faced each other over a table on which was a scatter of playing cards, an open bottle and two glasses. Sitting in the corner was a solidly built civilian with dark eyes and long hair tied back with a ribbon.

'I had begun to wonder if you would be joining me this evening, Lieutenant Ropars,' said the civilian, gesturing for the officer to sit down. 'Would you care for a glass of this wine? It's barely passable, but the landlord assures me it is the best his cellar has to offer.'

'Thank you,' said the younger man, accepting a glass and gulping thirstily, while his companion gathered the cards together.

'What shall we play for tonight?' asked the civilian. 'Would twenty *sous* a point be too rich?'

'Not tonight,' said Ropars. 'I … I must tell you that I cannot pay you, sir. I have pleaded with my father for the money but he will not be moved.'

'I see,' said the man, pouring out more wine. 'That is indeed most unfortunate. I had assumed I was gaming with a fellow gentleman, who had some regard for the obligations of that rank.'

'I am a gentleman!' protested the officer. 'But I have never found myself in such a false position before. I have encountered a wretched run of luck. You must have marked how ill my cards have been in our encounters? I had thought that if I persisted in time the odds would move in my favour, as they inevitably should do in piquet.'

'And yet here we are,' said the civilian, consulting a tally in his pocketbook. 'You owe me over three hundred and fifty *livres*, that you tell me you cannot settle. What are you going to do?'

'I can pay you in time, sir,' offered the officer. 'I have my naval salary, and my allowance from my father. Perhaps I may be fortunate in the matter of prize money?'

'What prize money?' scoffed the man. 'France is at peace. I daresay it was only your father's influence that saw you appointed to a fine ship of the line like the *Marengo* at all. And from what I hear of the admiral, he will not long tolerate a rake among the officers of his flagship. No, I need a more certain way of recovering my losses than that.' He shuffled the pack with practised ease, the cards flowing through his hands. 'Could you not try the moneylenders?'

'It is widely known that the *Marengo* is fitting out for a distant voyage,' said Ropars. 'Not even those usurious bastards would take such a risk.'

'Is she now?' said his companion, continuing to shuffle. 'Where is she bound?'

'India, to restore our position there.'

The civilian placed the cards down on the table and made a note in his pocketbook. 'India, you say. That is interesting.'

'What are you doing?' queried Ropars, peering across the table.

'Reducing your debt to me by five *livres* to show my thanks for your candour,' said the man, holding the young lieutenant's gaze. 'Perhaps you do have a way of clearing your obligations after all. Tell me, will the *Marengo* sail alone, or in company?'

'What are you, some damned spy?' demanded the naval officer, rising to his feet and glaring at his companion.

'Come, come, Lieutenant, there is no call for such talk,' said the civilian. 'Sit down and have a little more wine. A spy indeed! Me, a fellow Breton? We are not even at war; besides, we are hardly speaking secrets here. You said yourself that even the moneylenders know your destination. No, I only seek to help you out of the false position you find yourself in, as a friend. You have a debt that will frankly ruin you if it remains unresolved, and I have some contacts in the mercantile community who will pay for such little scraps of tittle-tattle. It assists them with winning government contracts and the like. Nothing you say will be given to the enemies of France.'

'Do you swear it?'

'You have my word upon it,' said the man, holding his right hand across his heart. 'I will ask you for no indiscretions. Only to share in the discourse you might have with your brother officers around the wardroom table. I daresay before the evening is done, I may find myself in your debt, for a change. Now, you were about to tell me if the *Marengo* would form part of a squadron, I believe?'

It was very much later that Lieutenant Ropars left the inn, considerably less steady on his feet than when he had arrived. He chuckled to himself as he made his way down the alleyway and out on to an almost deserted quayside. Three hundred and fifty *livres* for a bit of gossip, he marvelled. Some fools are so easy to part from their money. He might have the luck of the devil with cards, but that man has a lot to learn when it comes to valuing information.

Ropars was still shaking his head in amazement as he approached the top of a flight of stone steps that led down to the water. At the bottom were a few wherry boats waiting to take late-night revellers out to their ships.

The moon had risen now, dusting the Rade de Brest with silver. He looked admiringly at the *Marengo*, moored out from the shore and held side on to him by the running tide. A few of her double row of gun ports were open to catch the breeze, squares of orange light in the dark side that faced him. Above her bulky hull masts soared high into the night sky, dwarfing those of the other vessels, the frigates, troop carriers and store ships, that lay around her. All of them were low in the water, heavy with the provisions they would need for their long voyage to India. And heavy with other, more surprising things; mysterious boxes and crates of tools and weapons. His companion had seemed particularly interested in all of that; goodness only knows why. No matter, decided Lieutenant Ropars with a belch. I can now depart with a clear conscience and my debts gone. Everything I told that idiot will soon be useless to his commercial friends. By the end of the week we will have departed.

With this pleasant thought he made his uncertain way down the steps, loudly calling for a boat as he went.

Chapter 1
The Sea

The *Little Sam* was the best-maintained fishing boat in the Cornish village of Polwith, as befitted a vessel operated by two former Royal Navy sailors. Their long service had engrained in them habits that were hard to shrug off. The hull had only to tap against the elm posts that lined the harbour wall for one of her owners to appear over the side, paintbrush in hand. Clutter and a degree of filth was the accepted norm on most of the other boats, but not on board the *Little Sam*. Within hours of returning to port her deck was scrubbed clean, her gear carefully stowed, and the brick-red sails on her twin masts were neatly gathered back into place. A few bemused fishermen passed by, shaking their heads at the gleaming vessel, but her proud owners seemed oblivious to them. They sat in companionable silence beside their precious boat, busy mending a driftnet.

They made a curious pair, for although they were dressed in similar loose shirts and baggy canvas trousers the two men could not have been more different. Adam Trevan was lean and wiry, with clear blue eyes and a blond pigtail dangling down his back. Able Sedgwick was larger and more solidly built, with black curly hair and sad, liquid brown eyes.

Trevan glanced up from his work, removed the clay pipe clamped between his teeth and called out to a group of boys as they ran along the top of the breakwater towards him in wild pursuit of a leather-covered ball. 'Have a care now, Silas Penhaligon, playing with that bladder here,' he cautioned. 'Your Ma will box your ears if she sees you risking a drowning, and I'll do the same if you spoils my paintwork. Able here might not be around next time you falls in.'

'All right,' said the youngster, picking up his ball and coming over to sit on the stone edge, his legs dangling above the water. His companions wandered over to join him, idling around the fringe of the group. 'Where did you learn to swim, Mr Sedgwick?' asked one of the boys, tapping at a bollard with the toe of his clog. 'Were it in the navy, like?'

'No lad, most tars don't hold with swimming,' rumbled the sailor in his deep bass. 'It were my uncle as taught me, back in Africa afore I were took. I were a fisherman there too, you know, but the boats be no more than hollowed out spars. They roll over easy in breakers, so you has to learn to swim sharp enough.'

'To get clear of all the crocodiloes?' supplemented Penhaligon, from his place on the wharf's edge. 'Like that wooden one you carved for me? Africa be thick with them buggers, I reckon.'

'Mind yer tongue, lad,' admonished Sedgwick. 'Buggers, indeed! Ain't a crocodile born for you to fear above your Ma, if she ever hears you using language like that. In fact, here she be now.' He raised his gaze and made to acknowledge someone further down the quay. The boy started around guiltily and Sedgwick pushed him in the back, grabbing him by his thin shoulders just before he fell. His cry of alarm was drowned by the laughter of his friends, delighting in the prank.

'Was there any crocodiloes when you fought at the Nile with Lord Nelson?' asked another boy. 'Coming to feast on the drowned?'

'If there were, I never saw none,' replied Trevan. 'Course it were dark and I were down on the gundeck, where you can't see aught. Able may have chanced to spot one from the quarterdeck.'

'Can't say I saw any. Plenty of Frogs, mind,' added Sedgwick, drawing another laugh from the boys.

'Did you see that great ship as took fire and blew up?' asked another boy.

'I did, and I also know when you lads be trying to fool us into yarning about war and the like,' said Trevan. 'Be off, and let us get on with mending this net.'

'Oh, can't you tell us one story?' pleaded Penhaligon.

'I might be slaking my thirst in the Blue Ship later,' offered Sedgwick. 'If you be there, I'll tell you how Adam and I near perished setting a wicked rebel ship ablaze. Now, away with you.'

The two men returned to their work, splicing and weaving in companionable silence, while the boys dashed off.

'You has a rare way with nippers, Able,' offered Trevan, after a bit. 'Our baby Kate fair worships you.'

'I likes them well enough,' agreed the big sailor. 'It makes a village proper homely, having them scampering around.'

'True, but most folk don't trouble to carve them toys or tell them yarns,' observed his companion. 'You never thought to have none yourself? Must be lonely in that cottage of yours.'

'I needs to be spliced first,' said his friend. 'Besides, maybe I likes nippers 'cause they don't judge me afore they knows me, like a few around here I could mention. Naming me Blackamoor or Turk when they think me out of earshot.'

'Don't you go biding what them tired old crones has to say,' urged Trevan. 'Most here see your worth and like you well enough. Besides, you be a bit of a catch, I reckon. Big handsome lad like you, with your letters an' all, your own cottage and a share in the *Little Sam* here. You should open your eyes a touch, and see what be around you.' He waved his clasp knife airily towards the village.

Sedgwick followed his friend's advice, and looked again at his adopted home. Polwith was set at the base of a narrow valley between lush green headlands. It had a settled air to it, as if it had been carved out of the grey bones of the land itself. Stone cottages squatted beneath their thatched roofs, tumbling down the slope towards the sea, where the little harbour sheltered within the curved embrace of its seawall. Wisps of smoke drifted upwards from chimneys into the clear spring air, while above it all was the church, a modest stone building set on a ledge in the hillside. Against the outer face of the breakwater the sea shifted restlessly, even on a calm day like this, calling gently to him. His friend was right, it was a lovely spot, an age away from where he had come from, but perhaps a place to make his own.

As he watched, he noticed a young woman walking down the cobbled lane that ran through the centre of the village. Her hair was wound up under a bonnet and she carried a basket swinging from one hand. She seemed to notice his attention and looked towards the two fishermen. Then she dropped her gaze and hurried on towards a big shed that stood above the village's little beach.

'Ain't that Ann Penrose?' he asked. 'Taking dinner down to her Pa.'

'Oh, is it?' said Trevan, with a vacant expression. 'Comely piece, ain't she? An' Old Penrose knows how to build a fine boat. Proper useful man to know, him.'

'You trying to match-make there, Adam, so as to get the

Little Sam careened on the cheap?' laughed his friend.

'No, Able. I'm just trying to show you what be in front of your face, lad. That poor girl's been making eyes at you since Michaelmas past.'

'Ann Penrose? Are you sure?'

'According to my Molly, who knows more about such things than you or I ever will. Any road, it be easy enough to find the truth of it. Try a bit of courting, and see how the wind be set.'

'I don't know, mate,' said the big sailor, twisting the net between his fists. 'She be proper lovely, an' all. Why would she want to take up with the likes of me?'

His friend erupted in laughter. 'Able Sedgwick, now I have seen it all! Be this the man as boarded a dozen Frog ships, cutlass in hand? Or faced down no end of lower deck bruisers? Can you truly be afeared by a wench with a pretty face? Look, there she goes! I can finish this here net. Just you go over and offer to carry her basket home. She'll set you right soon enough if she don't care for your company.'

A moment more of hesitation, and then Sedgwick got to his feet and brushed down his clothes with his hands. 'You be right, Adam. How do I look?'

'Like the finest man I ever served with,' said Trevan, waving him away. 'Now off you go before you miss your tide.'

Able hurried along the stone top of the breakwater towards the slim figure, noting how she glanced his way and shortened her step to allow him to catch up. 'Afternoon, miss,' he said, removing his hat. 'Might I carry your basket for you?'

'Now that it be empty?' she queried. 'Where was you when I was lugging it down the lane?'

'I suppose that be right, miss,' he said, scratching his head as he regarded the bare container.

'I'm only making game of you.' She smiled, passing it across. 'It be kind of you to offer, and I'd welcome your company. But only if you calls me Ann.'

'Oh, right you are, er … Ann,' he said, relief spreading across his face. 'Make free to call me Able.'

'Why thankee, kind sir,' she said, dropping a mock-curtsey.

They walked on up the lane, the basket handle lost in the sailor's fist, exchanging small talk about the doings of Polwith and its residents. Sedgwick was painfully aware of the listening village all around them, the open doorways on either side, the women sitting in the spring sunshine preparing food or mending clothes and the passers-by they met as they wound their way up towards the Penroses' house.

'Do you fancy a stroll up on the cliffs?' he suggested, as they reached the start of a path that led in that direction. 'Nice day like this, it'll be grand up there.'

'I daresay mother can spare me from my chores for a little while,' said Ann, looking at him directly with her dark eyes for a moment, before leading the way. It was the closest he had ever been to her, and he noticed what a pleasing almond shape they had.

'The village can be a touch close about sometimes,' he commented, as the path left the last house and continued up the hill. 'Especially where the affairs of others be concerned.'

'Ain't that the truth,' she chuckled. 'But I find it much improved. You should have seen it afore the peace, when all the menfolk was away with the navy. There were naught but women, nippers and grey-beards.'

They climbed higher up the path, Sedgwick giving her a hand over the harder parts, the touch of her cool fingers disturbing as they lay against his. When they reached the summit they stood overlooking the Channel, broad and calm in the spring sunshine, restless closer to as it broke and drew back against the base of the cliff. Out in the bay were a few fishing boats, their brown sails partly set as they drew their nets lazily through the water. Further out were several merchantmen, heading towards the wide Atlantic.

'Ah, the sea!' exclaimed Sedgwick, breathing deeply at the keen air as it tugged at his clothes. 'Ain't that an uncommon fine sight!'

She smiled with him, sharing in his pleasure. 'Lovely on a day such as this, but who would go to sea in a ship?' She indicated the departing merchantmen and shivered at the thought, pulling her shawl close. 'All that deep water, with no land in sight an' the weather getting up. No thankee!'

'It can be hard,' he agreed, 'Especially when it comes on to blow. Mind, the hardest time I saw was when we was sent into the Baltic back in the year one. Lord, but it were cold, even for the Danes and Swedes in the crew. Them sails was stiff as sheet lead, and the ropes froze like bars. But the nights were some'it else. Full of stars and queer ribbons of green light.'

'I almost envy you, Able, to have travelled and seen such things,' she said, sitting down on the grass. 'My lot won't be much beyond marrying a fisherman or serving in some big house, and we be one of the richer families in Polwith.'

'I have seen a bit of the world, but don't let my yarning fool you,' he said. 'Ninety-nine days in a hundred it be just routine in a man-o-war, same work, day after day.'

'What's it like then, living on one of them ships?' she asked.

'Much like a village, in truth,' he explained. 'There be all manner of folk packed cheek by jowl on the lower deck, good an' bad, kind and cruel. A deal more races on show, mind.

I don't stand out half so much. And then there be the officers, living separate in the stern, much as the squire does here. Lording over us an' fancying they know what the crew be about.'

'So, what were you, on this ship? One of the cruel and bad ones, I dare say!'

He smiled at her. 'Does that truly sound like me? I were the captain's coxswain, which be a proper important job on board, young lady, so show some respect to your betters, you hear? Officially you be in charge of the barge and its crew, but in truth you're there to see the captain knows what the crew be thinking, and the other way about, so waters be calm on board. I have much to thank the navy for, Ann, not least giving me my freedom.'

'Strange to think of the navy setting folk free. Around here the first we see of them is the press gangs, a-coming to take our menfolk away. I likes your talk of frost and stars an' the like well enough, but what of battles and death? We got our share of orphans and widows in the village, thanks to that navy of yours.'

'Aye, that ain't pretty,' he agreed. 'Battle can be cruel, and death don't come the way the ballads would have it, breathing your last with grieving shipmates all about.' He snapped his fingers. 'Folk can perish in the blink of an eye. My mate Rosie died in just such a fashion.'

'Poor man!' said Ann, shivering once more.

'You be cold, there?' asked Sedgwick, settling down beside her, and taking the opportunity to slide an arm around her shoulder. She moved nearer, enjoying the warmth of his closeness.

After a moment she spoke again. 'Rosie seems a curious name for a sailor.'

'We called him that to vex him. Rosso were his proper name, at least in the ship's books. Seemed to fit him like a glove, mind. He were the one as taught me my letters.'

'I had wondered where you could have come to learn them,' said Ann. 'My father holds such things important. He can't read much beyond his name, but he sent me and my sister over to Mistress Trinder's school in Falmouth when we was young. One or other of us reads to him of an evening. The Plymouth papers and books of learning, for the most part.'

'Well, that be a fine accomplishment,' enthused the sailor. 'I always reckoned there were more about you than a handsome face. You ever thought to use it to better yourself?'

'By doing what?' she smiled. 'Captain's coxswain, maybe?'

He laughed at this. 'Not that you wouldn't make a right fine one, but I were thinking more of teaching. I reckon this village could use a schoolhouse. Nippers would love being taught by you, and you'd be doing a sight more good in the world than as a lady's maid.'

'Now ain't you the forward one, Able Sedgwick!' she exclaimed. 'One stroll along the cliff tops, and you reckon to have my calling all planned out?'

'Was it just a walk in the sea air you was hoping for, Ann, when you let me carry your basket?' he retorted, his voice husky with longing.

'Perhaps a little more,' she conceded, turning her face towards his. She closed her eyes expectantly, but he didn't kiss her. After a moment she opened them again and was surprised to see sadness on his face. 'Whatever be the matter?' she asked.

'I does want to kiss you, Ann, more than anything, but I reckon it ain't fair to do so 'til you knows a little more of me,' he said, looking away, his arm slipping from around her. 'Life before the navy were hard as stone. Hell ain't some place in that book of the parson's, Ann, and I still feel the pain of it, inside like. I does truly admire you, but I wants you to understand me afore you gets in too deep. In case you'd sooner court another.'

'Oh, you lovely man!' she exclaimed, tears filling her eyes. 'Course you can tell me all about that, but not today. Just you put that arm back around me right now, and give me that kiss I be due.'

*****

The parsonage in the village of Lower Staverton was a solid Queen Anne house that stood next to the little parish church of St Dunstan. It was almost April and spring was in the air. Primroses had appeared on the roadsides and a haze of bluebells was carpeting the local woods. Birds flittered to and fro outside the parsonage's bay window under the gaze of Captain Alexander Clay's steel-grey eyes.

He was a tall, handsome man in his mid-thirties, with a head of chestnut hair. His body had once been lean and spare but a year of good living ashore was beginning to fill him out. His embroidered waistcoat felt considerably tighter then when he had first put it on after peace was declared, when his wife Lydia had urged him to lay aside the naval uniform he had worn since he was a teenager. He needed to get more exercise, he reflected, slipping his fingers between the buttons, but that was easier said than done. Some of his neighbours had tried to interest him in foxhunting, but Clay was a poor horseman, at far more danger to himself than any fox in a wild dash across country. Others had invited him to shoot on their land, but potting ducks with a fowling piece seemed poor sport for a man who had commanded a thirty-eight-gun frigate in battle so recently.

That was when his country was at war. Now Clay's day began with a substantial breakfast with his wife, interrupted by the bustling arrival of Master Francis, his sturdy three-year-old son, towing his tottering baby sister Elizabeth behind him. The time he spent with them each morning, playing on the floor, was the highlight of his day, but too soon they would be whisked away by their governess. In the afternoons he generally accompanied his wife on her social rounds, which today involved afternoon tea at the parsonage. The stroll here had been pleasant enough, accompanied by his sister Betsey and her husband, his close friend and fellow naval officer John Sutton. Little had he suspected that they were walking into an ambush as well planned as any the French had troubled him with.

The Reverend Charles Costain's wife, it transpired, was an avid reader of romantic novels and had recently discovered that the anonymous author of her favourite work was no less than Clay's sister. There Betsey sat, with her beaming hostess on one side and Lydia on the other, deep in a literary discussion, while Sutton stood nearby looking on admiringly at his talented wife. All of which left Clay by the bay window in the company of their host.

'They come here to collect moss, you know, Captain,' said the clergyman. 'To line their nests with.'

'I beg your pardon, sir,' said Clay, starting from his reverie. 'To whom are you referring?'

'The birds,' said the Reverend Costain, indicating where a robin was pecking at the stone path beyond the glass window. 'I have frequently shot them during this season of the year and found scraps of moss in their beaks.'

Clay regarded his host with incredulity. 'You shoot robins? Is there any sport in such a practice?'

'Oh, I don't do it for pleasure, Captain. The study of all birds has been an abiding passion of mine for many years.'

'Then why in all creation do you shoot them?'

'For the purposes of philosophical enquiry, of course,' said Costain. 'Much can be learned from the cadaver of a bird. Their stomach contents reveal their diet, their anatomy shows their habits and modes of movement, and their beaks in the spring attest to their preferred nesting materials. I do not shoot an excessive number. Never above two dozen a day. How else am I to advance my practical knowledge?'

'By observation, perhaps? I could lend you a naval spyglass if that would assist?'

'Oh, my dear Captain Clay,' chortled the clergyman. 'Such methods may have served in the days of Galileo, but this is 1803! Why should I not avail myself of powder and shot, now that you men of violence have chosen to stop hurling it at the French? Would you care to see my collection? Mrs Clay did mention the other day that you might be seeking some diversion, the peace having interrupted your naval career.'

'That is so, but I am not sure if shooting at robins …'

'Come, 'tis only through here,' continued Costain, moving towards a door in the far wall. 'I would be honoured to hear your opinion of it.'

Clay found himself being led out of the pleasant drawing room and into Costain's study. The buzz of animated conversation was shut off as the door closed behind him, and he found himself in an altogether more sinister place. The study was panelled in dark wood, with curtains drawn across the windows. In the gloom Clay found himself under the gaze of innumerable steely eyes glinting from the stuffed birds that lined every inch of wall space. Owls and hawks glared at him from behind glass domes. Large cases stood on the floor, or lined the shelves, all bursting with avian life frozen as if by a spell. Beside him was a mass of larks, many spreading their wings as if about to take flight. Next to it was a flock of thrushes all gaping in silent song, while on the tables were the corpses of other birds, pinned out in various states of dissection. The scent of embalming fluid wafted through the still air.

'God bless my soul!' exclaimed Clay. 'What an astonishing number of creatures! Why, it's a wonder that you have any time left to preach!'

'In truth my curate handles many of the day-to-day needs of the parish, permitting me to devote myself to my avian work.'

'And you killed all of these birds yourself?'

'Most of them,' smiled the clergyman, trying to look modest. 'I have been an industrious collector.'

'What becomes of their young, once you have shot the parents, I wonder,' mused his guest, the memory of a morning spent playing with his children still fresh.

'Oh, have no fear on their part,' said Costain, pulling open a shallow drawer, one of many in a cabinet. It was full of neatly labelled eggs.

'Remarkable,' said Clay, after a pause.

'I daresay you must have come across a wide variety of birds on your travels, Captain?'

'Plenty of parrots and the like, in the tropics, and seabirds sometimes follow the ship, often for days at a time.'

'Perhaps you could start such a collection yourself?'

'I am not sure that would be wise,' said Clay. 'The crew regard killing albatrosses as very unlucky. I did once rescue Captain Sutton from a remote atoll in the Indian Ocean that was quite covered in seabirds.'

'Did you indeed,' enthused Costain, massaging his

trigger finger thoughtfully. 'I wonder what kind they were?'

'Lord, I don't know. Shall we go and ask him for the particulars?' suggested his guest, moving back towards the door. 'It is a little close in here, I find.'

'Of course,' said the clergyman. 'The spirits of wine I use to preserve my specimens can prove a overpowering to those unaccustomed to its odour.'

'I am sure that is it,' said Clay, hastening out.

It came as a relief to step back into the drawing room, and find that the sun was still streaming in through the windows, and the few birds to have escaped the clergyman's attention were singing in the garden. Lydia glanced up as they came in, a look of concern on her face as she saw how pale her husband appeared.

'Are you all right, Alex?' she called.

'Perfectly, my dear,' he said. 'Mr Costain was just showing me his collection of cadavers, of which he has a great number.'

'Oh, Charles!' scolded Mrs Costain, 'and we are about to take tea.'

But before she could admonish her husband further, her maid came into the room and curtsied. 'Beg pardon, madam, but the gardener's lad has just run over from Rosehill Cottage with a message for the captain.'

'Are the children all right?' asked Lydia, rising from her place.

'He made no mention of them, Mrs Clay,' continued the servant. 'Only the captain has a visitor from London, come in a big carriage an' all, if you'll credit it.' She held out a tray towards Clay with a visiting card lying there.

The thick, embossed cream square felt familiar as Clay picked it up. 'What the devil can he want?' he exclaimed, looking at the name. 'And why must he always turn up unannounced?'

The Reverend Costain peered over his guest's shoulder. 'The Honourable Nicholas Vansittart, King's Counsel, and Member of Parliament for the Borough of Hastings,' he read. 'Why would a barrister be visiting you, sir?'

'Ain't he that fellow you sailed to the Baltic with, Alex?' asked Sutton. 'The diplomatic cove who was deep in with all the government's schemes?'

'The very same,' said Clay, pocketing the card. 'Mrs Costain, would you excuse me please? Thank you for your hospitality, but I must attend to this.' The other guests rose from their places but Clay waved them back down. 'Pray do not break up the party on my account. Betsey, Lydia, my dear, do stay. John can escort you home. Besides, the vicar here is agog to learn more about his time on Hope Island among all those seabirds.'

'Indeed,' enthused Costain, turning towards Sutton. 'They will have been boobies, I have no doubt. Did you chance to shoot any, sir?'

Clay slipped away, leaving his friend with the vicar, and strode through the village in the direction of his home. Lower Staverton was of modest size, and he was soon outside his house. Blocking much of his drive was a large carriage of lacquered black wood drawn by four bay horses. The uniformed coachman politely raised his hat to him as he squeezed past towards his front door. In his drawing room was a fashionably dressed man with short sandy hair and an aristocratic bearing.

He rose from his seat as Clay walked in. 'My dear Captain Clay, how inexpressibly pleased I am to see you once more. I do hope you are not offended by my calling around to see an old friend unannounced?'

'It does seem to be your way, Mr Vansittart,' said Clay, shaking his visitor's hand. 'May I offer you a drink?'

'A glass of madeira would be most welcome,' said his guest, resuming his seat. 'Forgive me, I pray, and do pass on my apologies to Mrs Clay for having summoned you away from a social gathering. It was impertinent of me, I know, but affairs of state, like those tides you naval chaps are so deuced fond of, wait for no man, what?'

'As it happens, you saved me from a rather disturbing encounter with our vicar, sir,' said his host, bringing over two glasses of wine. 'For a man of God, but he doesn't seem to hold much regard for members of the animal kingdom.'

'Oft the case with the clergy, in my experience,' observed Vansittart. 'My parson is so keen on riding to hounds that he wears his hunting clothes beneath his surplice during communion. Rattles through the service in double time, and has his groom waiting with his horse by the church door. But tell me, how are you finding the peace?'

Clay found the dark eyes he remembered so well from their previous time together appraising him over the rim of the wine glass. 'It does take time to adjust to, naturally, sir,' he conceded. 'I am enjoying the society of my family, after so much time spent apart. How about yourself? Still the diplomat?'

'Naturally. Someone needs to dissemble for our nation,' said Vansittart. 'And there is always a need to handle the more shadowy side of our relationships. Especially during a peace as uncertain as this one.'

'You believe it will end, I collect?'

'I know it for certain, for it is we who will end it. This peace was never meant to be more than a pause for two well-matched prize-fighters to draw breath. Boney is not cured of his desire to rule the world, and we'll be damned before we let him.

Even as we sit here, he is busy assembling flat-bottomed craft in every port and creek on the coast of Flanders. As a naval man, I am sure you appreciate that such preparations can have only one object in mind.'

'So it will be war again,' said Clay, sipping at his madeira. 'I have known little else for most of my life, of course.' He looked away for a moment and wondered how he felt at the prospect. Fear, naturally, and the cold dread at leaving Lydia and the children once more. But there was also no denying the tingle of excitement that he felt in the pit of his stomach. 'When will it begin?'

'Within a few months,' said his guest. 'Under the terms of the peace, the French are due to withdraw from the Ionian Islands, which they will decline to do, and we shall retaliate by not leaving Malta. That will provide sufficient cause. But what is exercising the government at present is not the situation here in Europe, but that in India.'

'India?' queried Clay. 'Why particularly there?'

'When war resumes, the navy will be required to blockade the coastline of Europe from Hamburg in the north to Venice in the south, in addition to keeping us safe from invasion, and protect our commerce from the cruisers of the enemy. How many ships do you suppose we will need to perform such tasks?'

'Lord knows,' said Clay. 'Two hundred ships of the line, and five or six hundred lesser vessels, I should imagine.'

'Close enough to the First Lord of the Admiralty's estimate,' said Vansittart. 'Can you imagine the cost of building and maintaining such a force? The greatest navy in human history? On top of paying the army and funding the allies we will need to defeat Napoleon on land. I tell you, Clay, the victor in the coming war will be the side with the largest purse, which is where India comes in. Our trade with the East is worth millions to the exchequer. We know it, and by Jove the Frogs do as well.'

'But John Company[1] control India, do they not?'

'At present, but only tenuously,' said the diplomat. 'They only directly rule Bengal, enclaves at Bombay and Madras, and a strip of the coast. The chief part consists of native states, many the size of European powers. Some are allies, but many fear us more than they admire us, and the French have not been idle during the peace. Offering military support here, a little honey there. Blackguarding us to any raja or sultan with ears to listen. No sooner do we stamp out a fire in one place, then another bit of heather goes up in flames elsewhere. I tell you hydras ain't in it.'

'And how, pray, does all that concern me, sir?' asked Clay.

'Last month I received word from one of my most reliable contacts in Brest. He's a royalist, of course, and a capital fellow, although I would not play cards with him for a peerage. He tells me that an expedition left Brest in the first week of March, consisting of a ship of the line, three frigates and sundry store ships, all bound for India under the command of Rear Admiral Linois.' Vansittart pulled a leather notebook from the inner pocket of his coat and consulted it. 'On board are all manner of warlike stores. Equipment, weapons, military advisers, almost two thousand troops. I tell you, Clay, the French are planning some sort of mischief, you mark my words.'

'Does your spy know their object?'

[1] John Company was the common nickname in the eighteenth century for the Honourable East India Company, which held the monopoly of Asian trade.

'He does not. He gained his information from some young popinjay he ensnared over a few hands of piquet. The fellow was too junior to know the particulars of the endeavour beyond its overall destination.'

'But that could mean much or little,' said Clay. 'They might be no more than reinforcements for the French garrison at Ille de France.'

'True, or they may be the promised help for some native ruler that will lead him into bloody rebellion against us. Which is why we need to follow them out to India so we may be on hand to thwart them before matters get out of hand.'

'We, Mr Vansittart?'

'I shall naturally need to be conveyed to the east, in a warship with sufficient resources to deal with any unpleasantness. The First Lord of the Admiralty suggested a large frigate, which put me in mind of our old *Griffin*. I naturally suggested you to his lordship as a suitable fellow to command her.'

'To sail to India?' exclaimed Clay. 'Goodness, when would we depart?'

'Not immediately. The ship in question is yet to be returned to service and I daresay you will want to gather together your people to restore her. The crew who accompanied us to the Baltic would be ideal. If any of them suspected the true nature of the, er … unpleasantness we had to deal with in St Petersburg, they have all shown admirable discretion in the subsequent years. Would that be possible?'

'The last I heard, Mr Taylor was driving his sister to distraction in a cottage that they share, so I daresay he will be game, and none of the other officers have resigned their commissions. Yes, I imagine they will all be willing to serve again, sir.'

'Even young Preston?' asked his guest. 'Did he ever marry the lovely Miss Hockley?'

'He did, and now commands one of her father's trading brigs, along with my former sailing master, Mr Armstrong. But to judge from his last letter to me, he finds the Baltic timber trade a deal less exciting than he had imagined. I believe I can answer for all my officers wishing to sail with me again, as will my former crew. Sailors have a way of finding out when a captain they desire to serve with is fitting out a ship. They all did handsomely in the matter of prize money during the last war, a subject of particular interest to most.'

'Gather your followers, then, and let us sail together once more,' said Vansittart, rubbing his hands together at the prospect. 'Assuming you desire to taste a little adventure, Captain?'

Clay rose from his chair and looked out into the garden. It was raining now, a light shower pattering against the glass. His son ran across the lawn, fleeing for the shelter of the house and squealing with delight. He would miss all this, he thought. The children, the safe quiet life here, Lydia's warm embrace in the night. But other forces were at work within him, forces that would not be denied. He also felt a deep longing to be at sea again. There it lay in his mind's eye, vast and blue, bounded by a silver horizon that hid only possibilities.

'I do believe that I am, sir,' he said, turning from the window. 'India is one of the few places that my wife has visited and I have not. She speaks very highly of its beauty.'

Chapter 2
Polwith

It was a wedding day in Polwith, and the routine of the little village followed a pattern that had been established for centuries. The night before the men had gathered to collect sand from the little beach by the harbour and had scattered it over the cobbles along the paths that the groom and bride would take from their homes to the lychgate of the church. Meanwhile, the women had worked late into the evening, transforming the interior of the building with flowers harvested from the surrounding countryside. They had cut baskets of bluebells from beneath the fruit trees in the orchards, picked sprigs of gorse from the hillsides above the village and gathered armfuls of delicate sea pinks from along the shore.

Once the sun was up the inhabitants dressed in their finery and gathered outside the dwellings of the happy couple. The women were outside the cottage of the Penrose family, set higher up the slope, and one of only a few buildings in the village to boast an upper storey. They all wore stiff white bonnets and neatly laundered aprons spread over the front of their coloured skirts. A few of the younger girls pressed their faces to the windows, in the hope of catching a glimpse of a blushing Ann in her blue wedding gown, but were quickly shooed away by her scandalised mother and aunts. The older women were content to enjoy the novel sensation of a day empty of chores and filled the time until the bride should appear with talk.

'What a grand day it be for them!' exclaimed Molly Trevan. 'When I married my Adam, it rained that much, near all the sand got washed back down to the shore.'

'Don't they say that be an ill omen?' asked Kate Pascow, a sour-faced woman who had always envied Molly her auburn curls. 'Rain on the wedding morn; a life ahead of toil and scorn.'

'Can't say as I've noticed any,' replied Molly. 'Toil, to be sure, but that be a woman's lot whatever the season. It worked out well enough for Adam and me. Besides, it would be a sad pass if rain brought ill luck, the amount we see hereabouts.'

'You sure about that?' persisted Kate. 'Weren't your Adam pressed into the navy just after you was hitched? He's barely been here these dozen years.'

'Aye, that be true enough,' conceded Molly. 'Been grand having him home the last twelvemonth, mind.'

'I hear war be a-coming again,' said another voice. 'They be busy as ants, fitting out ships in Plymouth, according to my John. I don't know how I shall manage if they press him.'

'War'll mean, they come take all our menfolk fast enough, your Adam included, Molly Trevan,' said Kate. 'Seafarers betwixt eighteen and fifty-five, that be what the law says. There'll be aught left but oldsters an' nippers once more. Ann Penrose best enjoy her Moor quick.'

The mood around the Penroses' front door chilled noticeably as this was digested. Barely a woman there didn't have a husband, father or son that would be affected. A few handkerchiefs appeared dabbing at eyes.

'Now this'll never do!' exclaimed Molly. 'It be Ann Penrose's wedding day, not her funeral! Let her have her joy without no talk of war or press gangs and let tomorrow take care of itself, I say.' Bonnets nodded in agreement at this from around the group, and a few weak smiles appeared on faces.

Old Widow Penhaligon, who was hard of hearing, spoke loudly into the silence. 'Will the heathen know how to behave in a Christian church?' she asked a neighbour. 'Him being naught but a savage, an' all?'

Some of the older ladies chuckled at this, the younger ones looked awkward, but Molly rounded on her, bending her trembling bonnet close so the widow would hear every word. 'Listen good, you shameless old goat, her husband's name be Able Sedgwick. A man who, among other kindnesses, saved your grandson Silas from a drowning. If I ever learn you called him a savage again, as God is my witness, I'll throw you into the harbour myself.'

Meanwhile, the men who might be of future interest to the Impressment Service had made their way to the groom's cottage, which stood on a quiet lane close to the harbour. Most wore embroidered shirts, tucked beneath waistcoats and hats decorated with coloured ribbons. Two of the younger members of the party had brought drums with which to process to the church with a suitable volume of noise.

At the appointed hour, the cottage door opened and Adam Trevan appeared. 'I be happy to say as the condemned man scoffed a hearty breakfast,' he announced, to a gale of laughter. 'So men of Polwith, I give'ee your groom!'

The crowd fell quiet at the sight of Able Sedgwick as he stepped out into the spring sunshine.

'Lord above, will you look at him?' exclaimed young Silas Penhaligon, dropping one of his drumsticks in disbelief.

Sedgwick's hair was washed and trimmed and his face closely shaved. He was dressed in a new linen shirt with a silk neckcloth settled around his throat. His waistcoat was richly embroidered, his coat was of fine blue broadcloth, and his buff-coloured trousers fitted his broad thighs close before disappearing into a pair of shiny boots. He drew on his gloves, clapped his hat on to his head and stood looking bashful on the top step before the hushed men.

'How does you reckon I looks, lads?' he asked.

'Heavens above, Able,' spluttered one of his neighbours. 'The squire his self ain't got no togs to match them 'uns! You looks a proper gent!'

'I feels a bit of a fool, in truth,' muttered the groom, tweaking at his cuff. 'There be a deal too many stays and straps in this lot for proper comfort, but Ann will have made a right effort, so I didn't want to put her to shame.'

'How's he come by such finery?' queried Amos the shepherd, in an aside to a neighbour. 'Ain't from landing pilchards, that be plain enough. He been smuggling?'

'Adam says he writ some manner of book a few year back, about being a slave an' all. Them Abolitionists line up to buy it, at two bob a time over Bristol way, if you'll credit it.'

'Aye,' whispered the man on the shepherd's other side. 'I heard her Pa was ag'in the wedding 'til Able took him to the Carne Bank in Falmouth and made the manager show him what he's got stowed away there. Old Penrose's eyes near fell out! That Midas feller ain't in it!'

Meanwhile Trevan was propelling his friend gently down the steps. 'Best be getting him up in front of the parson, lads,' he said to the crowd. 'Afore he changes his mind! Strike up them drums, nippers, and let's be shoving off.'

The two lads began to beat a steady tattoo on their instruments, and the men formed up in a solid phalanx around the groom, jostling and laughing as they set off. They slowly processed along the sand marked route, with many a bawdy call, or a song in guttural Cornish. Outside the Blue Ship tavern, which was about halfway to the church, a keg of cider had been set up with trays of pewter and horn flagons beside it.

'Just in case you lads be thirsting after all that clamour,' explained the landlord. 'Compliments of the groom, God help him!'

The men of the village, it seemed, were indeed in need of refreshment and crowded around the keg, while Trevan stood to one side looking out to sea.

Sedgwick came over to join him. 'Not thirsty, Adam?'

'Best not to touch it afore the service. That scrumpy has the kick of a plough horse, and I doesn't want to go messing things up afore you be spliced. But how are you doing? Need a little Hollander courage yourself?'

'I be calm enough,' said the groom. 'For I be certain of what I do this day, Adam. This past two months I've told Ann all there is to know of me.'

'Even them night terrors you sometimes have?'

'I did, although I don't recall telling you about them, brother?'

'You haven't,' said Trevan. 'But there ain't many secrets between Jacks as sling their hammocks from the same beam.'

'I suppose that must be so,' said Sedgwick. 'You never said aught?'

'Didn't figure there were aught as could be done about it.'

'Any road, I told her straight, and bless her, she ain't afeared one jot. And she's going to take forward my notion about a schoolhouse.'

'Aye, you got a good woman there,' confirmed his

friend. 'Kind as they come, according to my Molls, who knows a bit in that regard herself. Long may you sail in company.'

'Which will be as long as the navy leave us be,' said Sedgwick. 'When I were in Plymouth buying these here togs, the Sound were full of ships brought down from ordinary, including our old *Griffin*. Something be up, Adam, and sooner rather than later.'

'What be with the downcast faces!' exclaimed one of the revellers, pressing a mug of cider on each man. 'Much too late for turning aside now, Able, so best you sup up and face the fiddler!'

*****

His majesty's thirty-eight-gun frigate *Griffin* was starting to resemble a man-of-war at long last, now that eighteen-pounder cannon lined her sides once again. She had been warped out into the harbour, her freshly painted hull sitting above her reflection in the calm waters of Plymouth Sound, but there was still much to do. Her scowling figurehead should have been framed by four huge anchors, but only one had been delivered. Her lofty upper masts and the wide yards that marked her as a swift ship lay stacked on her skid beams waiting to be set up, and at least two feet of her gleaming new copper was proud of the water, proof of how empty her hold was.

Her main deck was cluttered with boxes, kegs and coils of rope, while sailors bustled to and fro around them. Nathaniel Hutchinson, the *Griffin*'s grizzled boatswain, was bellowing himself hoarse as he supervised the tricky business of bringing on board one of the frigate's anchor cables from a lighter alongside. The rope, a heavy serpent twenty inches thick and two hundred yards long, had to be drawn up over the rail and fed down, foot by foot, deep into the hull to be coiled in the semi dark of the cable tier.

In the middle of the deck stood George Taylor, the ship's harassed-looking first lieutenant, an iron-haired man of middle age with crows' feet fanning out from the corners of his anxious brown eyes. Standing in front of him were two sailors, one of medium build with a long dark pigtail, the other well over six feet and built like the prize-fighter he had once been. Both men held their tarpaulin hats in front of them, in the manner of those making a respectful request.

'So why do you and Evans here wish to borrow the launch, O'Malley?' asked Taylor. 'Until our cutter is delivered this afternoon it is the only large boat we have at our disposal.'

'To go to our old shipmate's wedding, sir,' explained the Irishman. ''Tis no more than a few leagues down the coast, and is happening this very day, so it is. Able Sedgwick himself, getting spliced to some Cornish wench, sweet Mary help him! An' your honour knows how long Evans and me have been shipmates of his.'

'And it would just be the pair of you going?' asked Taylor.

'Not exactly, sir, no. Your man is well liked among the lads, so there's a couple more as would wish to come.' He indicated a group of a dozen veteran sailors, watching on from a distance.

'A couple!' exclaimed Taylor. 'Why, they're the pick of my most experienced hands!'

'Aye, a better-liked man never served, sir,' explained O'Malley. 'With the wind set as she is at present, we can run down to Polwith easy as kiss my hand. We'll be there afore you know we've gone.'

'Hmm, that's as may be, but I still don't see why you can't go by land.'

'Ah, that might be unwise, sir,' said the Irishman, looking uneasy. 'You see if Big Sam an' I was to go ashore right now, you might not be seeing us for a while, on account of some fellers we trimmed a little, who seem awful sore about it.'

'Speak plain, O'Malley! What precisely have you been about?'

'Aye, tell Mr Taylor why there's another city I can't hang me bleeding hat in, Sean,' said Evans, folding his huge arms. 'I said we should never have taken up with sharps, but oh no! Fooling me into your bleeding schemes!'

'Well, how was I to know what fecking brandy tastes like?' protested his friend. 'It's not like I sup on it every day.'

'Am I to understand you have been involved in smuggling?' said Taylor, his brows knitting into a frown.

'As it happens, no, sir,' explained Evans. 'Turns out it were never more than watered-down gin, with a twist of backy in the keg to give it colour. Which were when things turned ill.'

The exasperated officer held up his hands. 'Spare me the sorry details, I pray! As it happens the captain did charge me with approaching Sedgwick and Trevan to see if they would volunteer to join the *Griffin*, along with any like-minded seamen in their village, so if you will bear that message for me you will be dealing with at least one of the matters I have to resolve. I daresay they may wish to enjoy the benefits of volunteering before they are pressed into the Channel Fleet.'

'Right you are, sir,' said O'Malley, replacing his hat with a grin. 'We'll return with a dozen of the finest Jacks in the place.'

'Very well, you may go. See that you give my best

regards to Sedgwick and his new bride, and that you return by eight bells in the forenoon watch tomorrow,' said Taylor. 'Not a moment later. Is that clear?'

'Aye aye, sir,' said O'Malley.

'Will Able not need a little more time afore coming on board, sir?' asked Evans. 'Him being newly spliced an' all?'

'I daresay he will,' mused Taylor. 'Tell both Trevan and him to send word by you if they want their former positions, and that they have a week to resolve their affairs before they report on board.'

*****

When Ann Penrose entered on the arm of her father an audible gasp ran around the little church. Not to be outdone by his new son-in-law, Mr Penrose had sent to Falmouth for cloth and employed several of the village's more able needleworkers to help his wife and daughters. Her dress was of pale blue satin, gathered into a high waist, and flowing in a train behind her. Her long dark hair was gathered up beneath a lace cap decorated with silver threads. In front of her she held a bouquet of wild flowers that matched those cascading down the ends of the pews. Ann was popular with the villagers who packed the church and many made free to share their opinions with their neighbours, particularly those who had enjoyed a second mug of cider outside the Blue Ship. Amos gave a long whistle of appreciation at much the same volume he used to summon his sheepdog Bess.

Sedgwick watched spellbound as she walked up the aisle towards him, her face colouring at all the attention, but her dark eyes steady on his. 'Ain't you a vision of loveliness, an' no mistake,' he muttered to her as she came up beside him.

'You've scrubbed up fair decent yourself,' she whispered back. 'I hardly recognised you, dressed all grand, like.'

'An' I weren't certain if you'd show up at all,' he replied. 'When we first walked out together, you told me how you didn't plan on wedding no fisherman.' She stifled a laugh at this and dug him in the ribs.

'Some decorum, if you please,' urged the Reverend Moon to his flock, hands raised. 'This be the house of the Lord, in case any of you had forgot.' When it was quiet once more, he began the ceremony.

Despite the urging of the clergyman, the wedding service proved to be a boisterous occasion. The hymns were sung lustily, with the more talented doing their best to drown out those relying on raw enthusiasm. Most were pleased with the union, and showed it in the warmth of their responses, while the villagers who disapproved had absented themselves altogether. When the sermon began to drag a little, those growing weary with the parson's droning could fortify themselves with the anticipation of the entertainment that was to follow. It was common knowledge that the bride's father had spent much of the last week clearing out his boatshed and getting his men to run up extra benches and trestles from spare lumber. Two whole sheep had been purchased from Amos, and would doubtless already have begun to be roasted down on the beach, while no fewer than four musicians had been engaged for the dancing. The weather was set fair and the guests were surely in for a treat.

With such visions playing in the congregation's mind, it was small wonder that the first gunshot passed almost unnoticed.

'Did any of 'ee hear that?' commented Amos, looking

around in alarm when the sound was repeated. 'Be that poachers after my flock?'

'In broad daylight?' queried his neighbour. 'Nay! It'll be the squire, potting conies up on the moor.'

'I, Able Sedgwick, take thee Ann Marian Grace Penrose to my wedded wife, to have and to hold, from this day forward, for better for worse, for richer …' Another shot caused the groom to falter for a moment, before pressing on.

'That weren't up on the moor,' announced Amos. 'T'was down by the shore. I best be going to have a peek.' He slipped out of his pew and walked quietly towards the door, accompanied by a few others.

'… until death us do part, according to God's holy ordinance; and thereto I plight thee my troth,' concluded Sedgwick, squaring his shoulders to the rising unease behind him.

'Now your part, Miss Penrose,' said the Reverend Moon. From somewhere beyond the thick stone walls came the rumble of angry shouting.

'I, Ann Marian Grace Penrose, take thee, Able Sedgwick …' the bride began. More and more of the congregation were getting to their feet now at the sound of running in the lane outside.

'What in all creation be going on?' demanded the clergyman.

In response Amos burst in through the doors. 'It be a bleeding press gang!' he exclaimed. 'The buggers have turned up bold as brass, sailing their launch straight into the port without so much as a by your leave! Couple of the lads is keeping them off with fowling pieces, but they seem mighty determined to land!'

'Carry on, Mr Moon, if you please,' said Sedgwick, a

steely look in his eye. 'If they takes me, so be it, but I'll be damned if them bastards are going to halt me from wedding my Ann.'

'Well said there, Able,' agreed Trevan. 'Just you press on, parson, and set a deal more sail an' all. Stowing some of them hymns might answer. I'll go an' help hold them off 'til you two be spliced all legal like.' He hurried down the aisle, followed by many of the male members of the congregation.

'Shall we barricade the church door, Adam?' asked one. 'Or perhaps them arses won't dare break in here?'

'They got a blunderbuss down at the Blue Ship,' suggested another. 'Shall I send for it?'

'No lads, ain't no call for killing,' said Trevan as they flooded outside. 'Fists and cudgels should answer with the numbers we have.'

'Have a care,' cautioned Amos. 'They be set on coming ashore, and one of them be a regular Goliath.'

Trevan paused in the middle of the little graveyard, and turned to him. 'This big sailor, he didn't speak as a Londoner, did he?'

'Well now, I wouldn't rightly know how one of them talks, but he did sound odd,' said the shepherd. 'Even stranger than them from Devon.'

Another shot rang out, accompanied by a roar of outrage echoing up on the breeze. 'Avast there! For the love of Sweet Jesus! Will yous fecking peasants quit your shooting, an' let a few honest Jacks come ashore?'

'Bless my soul!' exclaimed Trevan as he hastened down the cobbled street. 'I'd know that voice anywhere.'

*****

Upon the Malabar Coast

'Fearsome buggers, these Cornish,' remarked Evans later that day, once the sailors from the *Griffin* had been permitted to land and were installed at a table with restorative mugs of cider in front of them. 'Look at that!' he added holding up his hat and pushing a finger through the hole torn in the crown by a passing shot. 'Anyone would think we'd come to rape their women and steal their chink!'

'Rather than drink their grog and squeeze their wenches,' said O'Malley, with a leer. 'Adam says as how they marked us for the press, coming up from Plymouth like. Press gangs, I ask yous! Another fecking outrage you English have inflicted on the world.'

'Steady mate,' protested Evans. 'Everyone knows as the navy has to do it. How else can they defend our liberty from them wicked Frogs?'

The other sailors in the group nodded contentedly at this logic. 'Hear him!' urged Thomas Rodgers, a veteran who had been repeatedly pressed. ''Tis the right of every freeborn Englishman to be forced to serve.'

'But … but that makes no sense at all!' spluttered the Irishman. 'You're all like fecking slaves busy polishing up yer chains!'

'Come now, Sean,' urged the big Londoner. 'Let's not go spoil a shipmate's wedding day with your radical talk. Look around you! We're in for a decent night, I reckon.'

As dusk approached, the quayside at Polwith had been transformed. The doors at the front of the Penrose boat shed had been thrown open to reveal groaning tables of food and jars of cider. Bunting and oil lamps had been strung over a cleared area for dancing, and the hired musicians were starting to play. Much of the population of the village was there, from running children wild with excitement through to hunched elders dressed in crow-black sitting back from it all. From the beach came the glow of firelight accompanied by the smell of roasting mutton.

'It'll be a grand evening, for sure,' conceded the Irishman. 'Although if it was music Able was after, I'd have bought me fiddle from the barky. Your man is playing very ill, and that lad with the fife will have half the fecking dogs in the county here presently.'

'I daresay it'll sound better after another few of these,' said Evans, raising his mug. 'For my part, I never felt so bleeding proud. Fancy the lads naming their fishing boat after me. No buggers ever done aught like that on my part. Near brought a tear to me eye when I copped sight of it.'

'What you fecking talking about?' queried the Irishman.

'Why the only boat in the harbour as is kept naval fashion,' said the big Londoner, pointing across the water. 'Got to be theirs. I ain't no scholar, like, but I can mark me own bleeding name when I sees it.'

'Oh, you means the *Little Sam*,' exclaimed Rodgers. 'But weren't that lad of Adam's what passed named …'

'Course it be fecking you!' interrupted O'Malley, clashing tankards with his friend and kicking Rodgers foot under the table.

'*Little Sam*?' queried Evans, a puzzled frown forming. 'Why little? Coz the one bleeding thing I ain't is that, as every beam on the barky learns me quick enough.'

'No, that's how you knows it's you,' explained O'Malley. ''Tis wit, see. Like that big fecker Robin Hood bested.'

'Little John?' queried Rodgers.

'That must be it!' beamed the big sailor, catching Sedgwick's eye across the crowd and raising his tankard in salute. 'An' don't Able look trim in that rig?'

'Aye, an' that Ann's a comely piece, an' all,' observed the Irishman, looking over at where the couple were greeting late arrivals. 'Was there not talk of her having a sister?'

'Plenty of time for that,' said Evans, putting down his drink. 'But first I reckon we should get this bleeding night under way. Sean, you have a word with the players, the rest of you on yer feet. Who fancies a hornpipe?'

Soon the sailors from the *Griffin* had formed a double line across the dance floor, and the guests moved back to watch them. O'Malley called out the tune and they began to twirl and stamp out the steps of the dance. The song was a familiar one to the many former Royal Navy seamen in the crowd, and before long most had come forward to join in. Soon the space was crowded with a thicket of bodies, gracefully dancing, while those watching kept time with claps and shouts of appreciation.

'You look thoughtful, my lover,' said Ann, standing close within the arm of her new husband as they watched on. 'Penny for them?'

'Oh, I be a touch sad over them as ain't come tonight, Ann. Where be the squire and the vicar?'

'Now listen here, husband,' said Ann, twisting around to face him. 'Sir George made his fortune from sugar, so he'll not favour our match, and Parson Moon values his living too highly to go somewhere his betters shun. As for the others as stayed away, they ain't of no consequence to us this night. Besides, look at all them shipmates as are here.'

'And near paid for it with their lives,' agreed Sedgwick, watching the dancing sailors.

'Do you want to join them?' asked Ann.

'I suppose I does, in a manner of speaking,' he replied, his voice distant.

'I meant join in their dancing,' she said, looking at him curiously. 'What did you suppose me to have meant?'

He turned to face her, his big hands linked behind her waist. 'I thought you might have heard, Ann. The lads brought word from Captain Clay. Pipe wants Trevan and me to come serve on our old ship ag'in.'

'But … but you can't be thinking of doing such a thing!' she protested. 'With us barely wed, an' all?'

'It wouldn't be straight away. We'd not be needed on board for a week.'

'A week!' she exclaimed, tears welling up. 'Oh, that be right fine! Seven whole days of married life, afore you be gone for God only knows how long!'

'Oh, my darling,' said Sedgwick, pulling her close, in spite of her best attempts to push him away. 'If the choice were staying by your side, or the navy, I swear as I'd never leave. But that ain't how matters stand for us Jacks. It weren't the press gang today, but it'll be them for certain tomorrow. War be a-coming, Ann, and proper soon. Is that how you wants me to leave you? The door bust open in the night and me dragged away from your arms?'

'No, of course not, lover,' wept his bride, burying her face into his shoulder.

He rocked her in his embrace and murmured in her ear. 'When that happens, God only knows what hulk I'll wind up on. This way I gets to follow Pipe, the man I owe my freedom to, and to sail with shipmates as I can trust like brothers. An' them as volunteer get leave an' the like, especially ones as the Grunters know the measure of. O'Malley reckons it'll take a month or more to set all to rights on the old *Griffin*. Why, wives can even come stop on board while we be in port.'

'I've heard about the sort as do that, Able,' said Ann.

'Harlots and strumpets, for the most part, with barely a proper spouse among them.'

'So stay here, an' I'll come back as often as I may. That don't sound so bad, do it?'

She gazed out past the dancers towards the sea beyond, glowing amber in the last of the evening light. 'I knew this day would come, Able,' she sighed. 'Any women as weds a sailor knows that loneliness be upon the reverse of the coin. But it just be so quick. 'Tis our wedding day, for all love!'

'Aye, well, you can hang that on Boney an' his bleeding warmongering,' said Sedgwick. 'Now, take my kerchief and dry your eyes. Let tomorrow be. Tonight, I wants to dance, and to laugh, and to sup a little more grog than I ought.' He leaned close to her again. 'An' then I wants to take you back to our home. We got ourselves a whole week afore any of this'll happen, Ann. I daresay you'll be happy to push me out the door by then.'

She smiled at him through her despair, and he led her by the hand towards the light and the music; and, for good or ill, her future.

Chapter 3
Atlantic

It took more than a month before HMS *Griffin* was ready for sea. With each successive day Clay and his officers found themselves competing ever more fiercely for the dockyard's limited resources as the Sound around them filled with a growing fleet of warships being brought back into service. As April moved towards May, hefty ships of the line appeared, spreading along the rows of mooring buoys, their freshly painted sides lofty as sea cliffs. Delicate sloops and frigates, low and lean, clustered along the Tamar. The sound of men heaving on ropes and the steady beat of hammers was now almost constant as, like a beast slowly emerging from hibernation, the navy came to life once more.

Then, with a suddenness that surprised him, everything was signed for and stowed away on board, and the *Griffin* was ready to depart on her long voyage to India. The following afternoon, when the tide was flowing, she left her moorings, shook free her spotless new foretopsail and headed out into the green waters of the Channel. A small group of well-wishers had gathered on the Hoe in the lightly falling rain to see them off. Among them were Molly Trevan and Ann Sedgwick, holding fluttering kerchiefs aloft in the breeze, and wondering which of the little silhouettes dotted high in the rigging or lined up on the deck might be their husbands.

In the private parlour of the Dolphin Inn Lydia Clay was

also watching the frigate depart, protected from the rain by diamond panes of leaded glass and warmed by the coal fire in the grate. Standing on a low chair set in front of her was her son Francis, restless within her arms. He had heard her explain that the tiny blue and white figure by the frigate's wheel was his tall father, but it was hard for him to comprehend how that could be. Instead, he longed to return to the wooden top that lay abandoned on the floor nearby. As the ship rounded Rame Head and vanished from sight her grip loosened, but before he could jump down he became aware that she was crying.

'What's the matter, Mama?' he asked, looking intently at her wet cheeks.

'I'm just being silly, my dear,' she explained through her tears. 'Pray do not worry on my account.'

'Father will not be long gone, will he?' asked the boy, searching her face for reassurance.

'Oh, my angel, I fear that he will, for he is leaving on a great voyage to the Orient.' She pulled him close once more. 'You and baby Elizabeth will need to be very brave.'

A week later the *Griffin* was making good progress. She was out into the Atlantic, running southwards with the coast of Europe far below the horizon, driving onwards through the waves and trailing a foaming wake behind her. The wide ocean spread far on every side, barren of life save the occasional merchant ship or spouting whale. It was Sunday, a make-and-mend day of leisure for the crew, and the day when Clay entertained some of his officers to dinner. This early in the voyage the ship was blessed with fresh produce, and Harte, Clay's steward, had produced a large steak-and-ale pie accompanied by mounds of spring vegetables. Around the table the ring of dark-blue-coated officers moved their chairs in tighter as the food appeared, with only Vansittart's plum-coloured coat and Lieutenant Tom Macpherson's marine scarlet standing out in contrast.

'I see the accommodation on the *Griffin* is little improved since I was last on board,' remarked Vansittart, once everyone was eating. 'My room is still barely larger than a privy ashore.' He cast an envious eye over Clay's cabin, which ran across the full forty-foot beam of the frigate and was lit by daylight streaming in through its row of stern windows. 'You must have the benefit of every piece of window glass aboard, I collect, Captain.'

'I suppose that I do, sir, although only the empty glass by your plate need concern us at present,' joked Clay, turning to summon forward his servant. 'More wine here, if you please, Harte. But windows would not serve you at all down in the wardroom. It is frequently beneath the waves. Those in ships of the line have windows, but, alas, not frigates.'

'Yes, I did suggest such a superior ship for our journey to the First Lord, but he thought it excessive if the only object was to provide some fresh air and daylight for diplomats.'

'There is limitless air and light up on deck, sir,' suggested Jacob Armstrong, the frigate's bewigged sailing master, in his New England drawl. 'You need only stand watch with me at eight bells to benefit from it.'

'Too kind,' smiled the *Griffin*'s passenger. 'Perhaps when I am quite recovered from my *mal de mer*.'

'When do you suppose we will be at war, Mr Vansittart?' asked Edward Preston, the friendly looking young third lieutenant, pulling at the empty left sleeve of his coat.

'I daresay we may be already. If not, it will be no more than a matter of days. When I left London our ambassador in Paris had been given a public savaging by Boney over our continued presence in Malta. As soon as the fleet is manned, he will request his passports and we will declare war. Is the *Griffin* ready to fight?'

'I have never served on a newly commissioned king's ship that was better prepared, sir,' confirmed Taylor. 'Once word spread, we were quite inundated with returning Griffins, many bringing other fellow sailors with them, and every man jack of them a veteran. Powell the boatswain's mate came with a dozen volunteers. A few weeks of gun and sail drill and they will be ready to take on all comers.'

'That is good to learn,' said Vansittart. 'I believe I recollect Powell. A deuced big fellow with a face his mother would baulk at kissing, what?'

'He does have an unfortunate scar across one eye, but he is an excellent petty officer,' confirmed Clay. 'No, I have rarely seen a warship manned with such ease. Of course, the threat of a hot press will have helped. With all this talk of war, it's a case of better the devil they know.'

'If war is imminent, is there not a danger of our sailing ahead of intelligence that it has been declared and so being taken unawares by any Frenchman we fall in with?' asked Taylor.

'Treat 'em all as hostile, and you won't serve your king too ill,' suggested the diplomat.

'I believe we shall learn of a declaration of war on route, gentlemen, for we will need provisions as we go,' said Clay. 'We will touch at the Isles of Cape Verde and perhaps at St Helena too.'

'And may I say how reassuring it will be, when battle looms, to know I have all my old Baltic shipmates to keep me safe,' beamed Vansittart, looking around the table. 'A glass with you all!'

The toast was drunk, and as the wine was refilled

Vansittart turned to some of the officers who had not yet spoken. 'Was it terribly inconvenient for you gentlemen to rejoin the *Griffin*?' he asked.

'Not for me, sir,' said Macpherson, the commander of the frigate's marine contingent, and the proud owner of glossy black sideburns. 'I was on half pay back home in the Highlands when I received my recall. It came just after I attended a wee agricultural fair, where watching men trying to catch a hen with their teeth was the most amusing part. I have no regrets to serve once more.'

'Nor do I, in truth,' said John Blake, the fair-haired second lieutenant seated beside him. 'I was trying my hand as a portrait artist up in town, but found the whole business deuced frustrating.'

'Really?' queried his captain. 'But I understood you to have a passion for art, John. Anyone who has witnessed your work is always struck by how able you are.' He indicated the portrait of Lydia that hung on the bulkhead. 'The likeness of Mrs Clay you achieved is truly uncanny.'

'But that was the chief problem, sir,' said the painter. 'Most of my sitters were tradesmen's wives, or the favoured mistresses of gentlemen, all of whom found uncanny likeness to be a sad disappointment. Could I not make them a little slimmer? Or a touch more buxom and perhaps with a fairer countenance? Until by degrees my faithful representation became no such thing. I tell you, a deck of French privateersmen are more straightforward and honest in their dealings than most of my patrons.'

'Now we are all back on board our old *Griffin*, what is our object in travelling to the East, sir?' asked Preston, once the officers' laughter had faded.

'Principally we are at the disposal of Mr Vansittart once

more, to aid his diplomacy as we did in the Baltic,' explained Clay.

'To aid diplomacy,' repeated the diplomat. 'How delicately put! You mean to supply the fist that lies within the silk glove, what? Was it not Louis XIV who had *the final argument of kings* inscribed on all of his cannon? The truth of the matter, Mr Preston, is that our exact objective is unclear at present. Some weeks back a French naval squadron left Brest bound for India, supposedly to retake possession of their former enclave at Pondicherry. They must know that Admiral Rainier, who commands our naval forces in the East, will permit no such thing, which raises the interesting question as to what their true objective may be.'

'Do the enemy have many allies in India, sir?' asked Preston.

'Several of their generals are busy teaching the Marathas how to fight European style, which can only be a deuced bad thing,' said Vansittart. 'Of course, the French did have a notable friend in Tipu Sultan of Mysore, but General Wellesley gave his army a sound thrashing last year. Do you know, when they stormed his palace they found a large automaton of a tiger atop an Englishman. When they set it running, the beast repeatedly savaged its victim, growling all the while. Apparently Tipu would spend hours gloating over it.'

'If not the defeated Mysore, then what is Linois's object, sir?' asked the sailing master.

'I fear I have no answer to offer, Mr Armstrong,' said Vansittart. 'My sources are silent on that matter.'

'What force do they have at their disposal, sir?' asked Blake.

'Now there I can be more certain. A seventy-four named *Marengo*, three frigates, storeships and all manner of troops and warlike supplies. Sufficient to cause a deal of mischief, I am sure you will agree.'

'Linois is an excellent sailor,' added Clay. 'He commanded the French at the Battle of Algeciras when they gave a good account of themselves. They handled poor old Sir James Saumarez very roughly and captured the *Hannibal* when she ran aground.'

'We may not yet know what they are truly about, but whatever Linois has in mind we will need to thwart him,' said Vansittart. 'The East and its trade is vital for the financing of the war. This winter's China fleet alone will be worth eight million pounds when it leaves Canton. That is more than half the annual cost of the entire Royal Navy. We play for high stakes indeed, gentlemen.'

*****

'Land ho!' bellowed the lookout perched high on the royal yard. Blake looked towards the masthead, but the sun shone from directly behind the man. The *Griffin* was now deep in the tropics, with dazzling blue water all around. He stepped across the quarterdeck to change his angle, and as he left the shade of the mizzen topsail he immediately felt the white-hot power of the sun beating down on him.

'Where away, Pickford?' he called.

'Two points off the starboard bow, sir,' came the reply. 'Tops of some mountains and a wisp of cloud showing.'

'My respects to the captain, Mr Todd,' said Blake to the teenage midshipmen standing by the wheel, 'and land is in sight off the starboard bow.'

'Aye aye, sir,' said the youngster, scampering away. The news was not wholly unexpected, but after a month at sea the call from the masthead brought many of those off duty up on deck.

'Did I not say over breakfast that we would touch the Cape Verde isles this day, John,' enthused Armstrong as he came bustling across. He extended his telescope towards the horizon and considered the tiny dog tooth that broke the line where sky and sea touched. 'One of the lesser islands, I think, but still a pretty piece of navigation.'

'I give you joy of your landfall, Mr Armstrong,' said Clay. 'Have the ship put on the other tack, if you please, Mr Blake.'

'Aye aye, sir,' said the officer of the watch, touching his hat.

'Now, the Cape Verdes form an archipelago, I collect Mr Armstrong,' said Clay coming over to join his sailing master.

'Seven islands of note, sir,' explained the American. 'The others are all uninhabited. I fancy this one we are approaching is Maio, from its form, which means we need to pass to the south to arrive at the principal island of Santiago and Porto Praya, the capital.'

Clay watched the land mass grow into a brown cone of rock thrust up from out of the water. Through his telescope he saw steep cliffs dropping into a troubled sea, and slopes of rock dotted with scrub.

'Verde means green in Portuguese, does it not?'

'It does, but if you were expecting the lush islands of the West Indies, you will find these a sad disappointment, sir,' said Armstrong. 'Santiago is a little more pleasant, but the rest are volcanic with little rain. I fancy the name may have been chosen to beguile colonists into coming. Salt and fish are what they principally produce, unless your requirements run to rock and brimstone.'

'Then why were they occupied at all?' queried Clay. 'Surely the odd passing ship looking to replenish her water and buy some fruit cannot sustain them?'

'No, but the slave trade can, sir.' The American pointed away towards the east. 'Most of the Portuguese slavers who supply the Brasils operate from here. Africa is but a day's sailing away, and the islands suffer from none of the pestilence of that coast. No Yellow Jack or ague to concern them.'

'Delightful!' said his captain. 'Let us hope our visit will be touch and go, then. Long enough to take on provisions and we shall be on our way.'

Porto Praya was only a little more inviting than Armstrong had suggested. The harbour was a rocky bay scooped into the southern end of the island and dominated by looming peaks. The settlement itself was small, a collection of whitewashed houses with either terracotta or thatched roofs climbing up a slope towards a large church with twin towers. Dotted among the buildings, Clay could see some bushy green trees, while running beneath the town was a stretch of beach. It was lined with little fishing boats pulled up on the sand and nets strung out on poles to dry. In the bay were three other ships moored together, close under a headland topped by a stone fort. They were small and trim, with sleek hulls and tall masts. As the *Griffin* sailed towards the area reserved for visiting shipping the surrounding land cut off much of the sea breeze, and the temperature climbed quickly.

'Ready to pick up that mooring buoy, Mr Hutchinson?' roared Taylor towards the forecastle.

'Aye, sir,' replied the boatswain, raising his hat.

While the working life of the frigate carried on around him, Clay stood by the weather rail examining the town with his telescope. On the far side of the quarterdeck Vansittart stood with some of the officers, all eager for a sight of land after so many weeks at sea.

'What is that dreadful smell?' asked the diplomat, holding a lace handkerchief to his nose.

'That will be from those slavers, sir,' explained Preston, indicating the three ships moored upwind of the frigate.

'What, do they have negros in them?' exclaimed the diplomat. 'In this dreadful heat?'

'Mooring line on board!' bellowed Hutchinson.

'Helm up! Get the foretopsail off her!' continued the first lieutenant. From the forecastle lines of topmen rushed up the shrouds, urged on by the shouts of the petty officers.

'No, that is their odour when empty, sir,' replied Preston. 'No ship would choose to moor downwind of one with a full cargo.'

'Yet they are such handsome-looking craft,' continued Vansittart. 'Built for speed, I make no doubt.'

'Aye, to dash across the Atlantic without losing above a fifth of the poor wretches on board,' replied Preston. 'The sooner that abominable trade is stopped the better, in my view, sir.'

'I didn't have you marked as an Abolitionist, Mr Preston?'

'Mooring line secured, sir,' added the boatswain. The last scrap of sail was taken in, and the ship came to a halt, rocking gently in the stifling heat.

'Pass the word to Mr Rudgewick, if you please, Mr Taylor,' said Clay, lowering his telescope. 'Have him begin the salute.'

'Most in the navy are against the trade, sir,' explained Preston. 'Many have served with run slaves, and know what tolerable shipmates they can be. Take the captain's coxswain as a case in point.'

'That all sounds splendid, but I fear the naval interest in the House is sadly outnumbered by that of the sugar lobby,' said the diplomat. 'While that remains the case, Abolition shall have to wait.'

Preston's angry retort was masked by the first gun of the salute banging out, the sound booming back from the steep slopes around them. Each gun was responded to by the fort on top of the cliffs, the smell of powder smoke mingled with the stench of the slave ships.

'Boat putting out from the shore, sir,' reported Midshipman Todd as the echo of the last gun faded away.

'What colours is it showing?' asked Clay. 'Portuguese?'

'No, sir,' said the youngster. 'They look more like ours.'

'That will doubtless be Mr Moore, our consul in these parts,' said Vansittart, in response to Clay's look of enquiry. 'I know very little of him, but I wouldn't expect much, captain. He can hardly be a diplomat of the first rank and have been posted to a rathole like this, what?'

'Nevertheless, he needs to be met properly,' said Clay. 'Have him piped aboard in due form, Mr Taylor, and turn out the marines. I shall go and shift into my best coat. In this heat, God help me. Perhaps you would care to join me, Mr Vansittart?'

The visitor who waddled into Clay's cabin a little while later proved to be a short man who was fond of the pleasures of the table, to judge from the straining buttons on his distended waistcoat. Clay took in the lace of blue thread veins that radiated across Mr Moore's pendulous cheeks and the ruddy hue of his bulbous nose, and decided that he was fortunate to have caught his majesty's consul to the Cape Verde islands sufficiently early in the day for him to still be sober.

'Hector Moore, at your service, sir,' said the man, extending a large, moist-looking hand.

'I am pleased to make your acquaintance, Mr Moore,' said his host, shaking it briefly. 'My name is Alexander Clay, commanding his majesty's frigate *Griffin*, and this is the Honourable Nicholas Vansittart.'

'Delighted, I am sure,' smiled Vansittart, opting for a brief bow rather than accepting the proffered hand.

'I am honoured to make the acquaintance of such an august personage,' gushed Moore, returning the bow with as much depth as his frame permitted. 'Your reputation as a diplomat is justly celebrated, of course, sir. As is yours too, Captain Day,' he added hastily.

'Clay, Mr Moore, as in the raw material of pots,' corrected the captain. 'Might I offer you some refreshment? I generally take coffee at this hour, or perhaps you would prefer tea?'

'Too kind,' said Moore, 'but might I trouble you for something, er … more refreshing, as it were?'

'Harte, a pot of coffee for two, and a glass of wine for our guest.'

'That would be most acceptable,' said the consul, licking his lips, 'and pray forgive my mishearing your name, captain. I believe there may have been a noise on deck at the moment you gave it.'

'No matter,' said Clay. 'Do please be seated and give us what intelligence you have. We have been at sea this last month. Has war been declared with France?'

'It has, sir,' confirmed the consul, drawing aside the tails of his coat and smothering the seat of his chair. 'We received word from the enemy himself. A French man-of-war touched here not three days ago.'

'A man-of-war!' exclaimed Clay. 'What sort of warship, pray?'

'She was named the *Marseillois,* Captain. She stopped to renew her water, and then disappeared to the south. Capital wine this, although a deuced small glass, what? I don't suppose I might trouble you for a drop more?'

'What manner of ship was she?' continued Clay, after he had waved Harte forward with the decanter. 'Was she a privateer or French navy? Heading south from here we may well fall in with her. Indeed, it is my duty to attempt to do so, since we are now at war.'

'Oh, she was most assuredly a ship,' continued Moore, waving a hand in the air. 'With masts and sails and what-not.'

'But you must have observed more than that!' protested Clay. 'How many masts? What was her rating? How many guns did she carry? On how many decks?'

'Heavens above, I can't say as I counted them. I suppose she was much as this one, except where you have a buff-coloured stripe running along your side, hers was red. Does that help?'

Clay exchanged glances with Vansittart, who rolled his eyes before leaning towards their guest. 'A shrewd cove like you, Moore, will have all manner of contacts ashore with the Portuguese, I make no doubt?'

'Naturally, sir,' said the consul proudly.

'Capital, so perhaps you would oblige me and use them to find out a little more about this vessel. There are sure to be harbour records and the like, or I daresay those of a more nautical bent who made note of the particulars that we need. Such as the ones the captain just listed, along with where she was bound and even how much water she took on board. Be a good chap, and find all that out for us, eh?'

'Leave it with me,' said the consul, tapping the side of his nose.

'Now, as for the requirements of this ship, I need water, firewood and fresh provisions,' added Clay. 'Here is a list that my purser has drawn up. Do you envisage any difficulties?'

'They are familiar with supplying slavers here,' said Moore, waving his empty glass towards the group of ships visible through the stern windows. 'I daresay that can all be supplied, although not until the morning.'

'Not until the morning?' queried Clay. 'But you tell me that a French warship is only three days sailing from here. I must get after her without delay!'

'That's as may be, but today is the feast of their patron saint, Captain,' explained the consul. 'Papist nonsense, of course, but there you have it. Not a soul will stir to help you until the morning, and even then the port officials will be rising late. I suggest you let your crew enjoy the sundry amusements that will take place tonight and leave your supplies for the morrow. It will also serve for me to obtain the information you require.'

Chapter 4
Porto Praya

The *Griffin*'s launch pushed her way through the gentle waves until she grounded on Porto Praya's gradually shelving beach. The middle of the boat was full of sailors, all dressed in embroidered shirts and with their white duck trousers rolled high. As the bow slid to a halt on the sand, they waded delicately across the shallows, holding their best shoes aloft, and made their way towards the lights of the town. It was close to sunset and the evening sea breeze combined with the vanishing sun had drawn the temperature down from unbearably hot to unpleasantly warm. But this did little to dampen the enthusiasm of those about to enjoy some shore leave.

'Last boat will be at two bells in the mid watch, men,' cautioned the midshipman from the stern sheets as the boat backed oars and drew away from the beach. 'See that you aren't tardy.'

'Right you are, Mr Sweeny,' called O'Malley, with an airy wave. 'Fecking little Irish gob-shite, giving orders like an admiral when he's barely out of small clothes,' he added beneath his breath for the benefit of his companions.

'Sweeny's all right, Sean,' said Evans, leading the way up the beach towards the track that ran along the top. 'Now let's get cracking. According to Pedro in the afterguard, these dago fiestas are bleeding marvels. Awash with wine, and full of wenches randy as stoats.'

'I thought this be some manner of godly affair?' queried Trevan. 'A saint's day, or the like.'

'Oh, that's just a fecking excuse to riot,' said O'Malley. 'Some of the feast days back home see folk carousing for days.'

'Lead on then, Sean,' said Sedgwick. 'I'll be passing on them wenches, but I'll not say no to a jug of bishop.'

'All the more for you and me, Sam,' cackled the Irishman, digging his companion in the ribs.

The sailors plunged into the town and soon found themselves in a network of narrow, dusty alleyways. The buildings that crowded close were mostly poorly built, with peeling walls and dark windows and doors. Men wearing torn britches and children in rags stared at them as they passed, while a pair of stray mongrels crouched close to sniff at their heels. Every so often a shabby little courtyard of beaten earth opened on one side or another, where groups of women looked up from their cooking fires. The air was heavy with woodsmoke and the odour of grilling fish overlaying the acid smell from the open drains that lined their route.

'Bleeding marvel, he said,' muttered Evans. 'Wait 'til I catch up with Pedro.'

'I reckon we've just been and took the wrong channel,' said Trevan. 'There be a ruckus a going on here abouts, right enough, only it ain't in this part of town. Can't you hear drums and the like from away yonder?' The others paused to listen. Over the sounds of wailing children close at hand came the faint sound of music.

'Here, Sean,' said Evans. 'Why not ask that fellow there for a bearing.' He pointed to a heavily tanned man with a thick moustache who leant against the door frame of a nearby house, eyeing them suspiciously.

'Hey feller!' called O'Malley, starting an elaborate pantomime. 'Grogo? Scoffo? Jigo?'

The man stared at the Irishman for a moment, idly scratching at his thick pelt of chest hair before indicating the next side alley with his chin. Then he wagged a finger towards Sedgwick. '*Sem Mouros negros*!' he said to the others, before loudly spitting into the gutter.

'This way, you say?' said Sean, heading for the passageway he had indicated. 'Right you are then.'

'Friendly buggers, ain't they,' commented Evans. 'I wonder what he said?'

'I've heard that tone enough times to follow his meaning, whatever tongue be used,' said Sedgwick, grim-faced.

'Aye, I daresay that be true,' said Trevan. 'Pay the bastard no heed, brother.'

The new passageway cut across the seaward-facing slope of the town and soon began to widen. The houses became larger, and were now set back from the lane. Stone and terracotta began to replace whitewashed mud and thatch. Trees rose up among the dwellings, and flowering creepers clambered over the walls. Beneath their feet the beaten earth changed to cobbles and they emerged at last on to the main street that ran through the town.

It was fully dark now, but lanterns strung from ropes supplemented the lamplight spilling out from the buildings that lined a wide thoroughfare. The road was straight, rising from the sea up to a big church on the plateau at the top of the hill. The sides of the street were packed with a jostling throng of revellers, most of whom were locals with a sprinkling of the frigate's sailors among them. Coming down the hill towards them, like lava flowing from a volcano, was a torchlit procession. At its head was a noisy band of musicians, mainly drummers with the odd conch shell and flute adding to the din. Then came the painted statue of a female saint, wrapped about in flowing robes and borne aloft on a swaying platform. Finally, there was a long tail of noisy people, dressed in their finery and each carrying a spluttering torch.

'Why, 'tis the Virgin Mary,' exclaimed O'Malley, removing his hat as the statue approached. Some of the other Griffins in the crowd nearby did the same, many crossing themselves.

''Tis a papist idol dressed in the rags of the Beast, more like,' growled Owen Williams, a stout Welshman in the starboard watch known for the strength of his nonconformist views. He turned his back on the procession and crossed his arms.

'If yon likeness be Mary, why are the crowd all a hollering "Santa Isabel"?' queried Trevan.

'That'll just be dago for the virgin, to be sure,' said O'Malley. 'So, are they after drowning the poor wench in the sea?'

'Yes, to the sea,' agreed an excited man being swept past in the procession. 'We take her to the sea. Come too! But leave the slave behind.' He brandished his torch aloft with a grin and then was swept away by the throng.

'Did that bastard just call Able a slave?' queried Evans.

'It be all right, Sam,' said Sedgwick. 'Let's just go find ourselves a quiet grog shop and that mug of bishop. I needs a drink.'

The sailors pushed their way down a side street, until the crowd of revellers began to thin. O'Malley pointed to a shabby-looking building with lamplight and the sound of conversation spilling out from the interior.

'Here we fecking go, lads,' he enthused. 'Just our sort of tavern.'

The inn consisted of a single room with a stone floor. It was dimly lit by a few smoking lamps that hung above a scatter of benches and low wooden tables. Off to one side was a glowing wood fire on which a line of fish was grilling, the smoke slowly curling its way into the exposed underside of the low thatched roof. A man in a leather apron was filling a jug from one of a line of casks at the back of the room, while a serving girl in a torn skirt and grubby apron tended the fire. There were several groups of customers in the place, all of whom looked up as the sailors entered, and the sound of conversation died.

'God bless every fecking dago here,' announced O'Malley, with a friendly wave, and the sailors took their places around one of the tables. A few people acknowledged the new arrivals, and the three fishermen seated nearest to them returned to their game of cards.

The girl left the fire and came over to the table, wiping her hands on her apron and eyeing Sedgwick with disapproval. 'What you want, *Ingles*?' she asked.

'No need to look so fecking glum, colleen,' smiled O'Malley, patting his lap invitingly. 'Come take your ease with Sean, while we make up our mind.'

'You want whore, you find down by market,' she said, slapping away the hand that was encircling her waist. 'Food? Vino?'

'Wenches randy as stoats, my arse,' muttered the Irishman. 'Fecking Pedro!'

'A jug of your best vino, and a dish of them fishes, lass,' said Trevan. 'And a twist of baccy for my pipe, if you please.'

Just at that moment a large cockroach dropped on to the

middle of the table, and writhed there on its back. The girl leant forward and calmly swept it on to the floor. 'When dark, they come,' she explained, pointing upwards. The sailors followed her gesture to see that the dimly lit thatch was alive with scuttling movement.

'Er … maybe just the vino, love,' said Evans. 'I ain't feeling peckish no more.'

The wine proved to be both cheap and plentiful, and the sailors soon gave scant attention to the occasional falling insect. Even when one fell on Trevan's blond pigtail, normally his pride and joy, he merely shook it on to the floor and crushed it beneath his foot. The night was warm, and the sailors drank thirstily as jug followed jug.

'Right, I needs the bleeding heads,' announced Evans, rising to his feet. He sadly misjudged the height of the room, crashing into the thatch and dislodging a cascade of insects. Once the huge Londoner had brushed himself down, he made his way towards the low door in the rear of the building indicated by the serving girl. Outside was a small yard illuminated by a lantern hung on a nail. Evans searched around for a while and eventually found an open drain that ran behind a collection of empty casks. He looked for something more elaborate but finding nothing he stood astride the drain and fumbled open the buttoned flap on his trousers. As he relieved himself, he became aware that someone had followed him outside.

'You after the privy an' all, mate?' he asked the figure who stood lounging near the door. He was in shadow, with only the tip of his glowing cigar visible as he drew on it.

'No, *Ingles*, I want talk with you,' replied the stranger, pushing himself off the wall and into the light. He was heavily built and better dressed than most of those in the tavern. His britches disappeared into well-fitting leather seaboots, and his long coat was of heavy cloth. His hair hung loose, framing a swarthy face with narrow, dark eyes.

'Aye, an' who might you be?' said Evans, buttoning himself up and coming over.

'My name Oliveira, mate on the *Sao Vincente*,' he said. 'You see her when you come in, I think. Ship moored close to fort?'

'I certainly caught a bleeding whiff of her,' said Evans, folding his arms. 'So what are you to me?'

'My captain, he deal in slave,' explained Oliveira. 'Make good money. But price of savage from Africa is little compared with one who know civilised way. In Rio he footman, maybe butler. So how much for your negro?'

Evans suddenly felt very sober. 'What the fuck did you just say?' he snarled, his face contorted with rage.

'Careful, friend,' said the slaver, backing away. 'Only business. I make you good price. If you not owner, tell me who?'

'His owner? Why you dirty, slave-trading bastard!' Evans spat, advancing on the man. 'He's my bleeding mate, not some animal to be bargained over.' He pushed his left foot forward and raised his fists before his face. 'You need to learn some manners, proper sharp.' Oliveira slipped a hand inside his coat, and Evans sprang at him, before whatever Oliveira was reaching for could be drawn.

Even part drunk as he was, the Londoner was a formidable opponent. Most of those who fought him assumed from his lumbering size that he would be slow on his feet, but his years as a prize-fighter had left him surprisingly light and agile and still full of the tricks of the ring. He pretended to wind up the clumsy haymaker that his adversary might expect. The moment the slaver started to move out of its path he swapped to a darting left jab that caught the Portuguese sailor full in the face. With a roar of anger Oliveira swung a fist at Evans, who swayed aside and rewarded his opponent with a flurry of rapid blows to the body. He doubled over, winded and gasping for breath. Evans grabbed him by the hair, hauled him back upright, and reached under his coat for the concealed weapon.

'Going to bleeding stick me, were you?' he demanded, as he wrenched out a long dagger, and brandished it under Oliveira's nose. 'Now you listen good. I don't want no trouble with the traps here abouts, nor any from the Grunters on the barky for milling with a local. And I daresay you'd sooner I didn't slit your throat, like what you bleeding deserve. Am I right?'

'Yes,' groaned the slaver, a thin line of blood trickling from his nose.

'Good, so you bugger off now, and if I clap eyes on you again, I'll bleeding top you, understand?' He released his opponent's hair and flung the knife in the direction of the drain. Oliveira wiped the blood from his face with his sleeve, pulled his coat straight and stumbled away into the night. Evans watched him go and then returned into the tavern to rejoin his friends.

'Blimey, you did need the heads, and no mistake,' commented Trevan as he sat down. 'You be all right, Big Sam?'

'Aye, never better,' said Evans, pouring himself more wine and puffing out his cheeks. 'I were only jawing with one of the locals, an' he didn't half rattle on. Lord, but I could use a bleeding drink.'

'I reckon I saw the bloke you mean,' commented Sedgwick. 'Tough-looking Jack, sat over there. He's been a staring at me half the night. What did he want?'

'Beats me, mate,' said Evans, smiling at his friend. 'He were jabbering away about summat in dago. Any road, he's buggered off now, so nothing to concern us there.'

But Evans was wrong about Oliveira. A career of bullying sailors and intimidating unarmed slaves had left him ill prepared for his confrontation with an enraged ex-prize-fighter. The experience had been both new and deeply humiliating for him. As he stumbled away, his eyes blazed with fury. But as anger faded, the first mate's natural cunning returned. Perhaps there was a way to have his revenge on those sailors, he decided. He made his way up through the town until he found a narrow alley leading away from the main street. He entered slowly, searching the walls of the houses with care. Then he paused at one with a crude symbol painted beside the entrance. It was of a chalice with a snake winding around the stem, its tongue poised above the rim as if about to drink. He hammered on the door until it opened, and then slipped into the shadowy interior. A little while later he emerged, checked that the passageway was empty, and made his way back to the tavern. It didn't take long lounging among the empty barrels before the landlord came out.

'Senhor Oliveira!' he exclaimed, before staring at his battered face. 'Have you been attacked? The footpads must be getting bold to try their luck with you.'

'I am fine,' he snapped. 'Tell me, the *Ingles* sailors. Are they still inside?'

'Yes,' smiled the man. 'They drink like fishes, pay well and now Maria has put them straight, cause little trouble.'

'Good,' said Oliveira. He pulled out his purse, and counted some coins into his hand. 'How would you like to earn five *reals*?'

The tavern keeper watched the coins as they caught the

light. 'I would like that above all things,' he said. 'What is it that you want of me?'

'Next time they order wine, pour this into the jug,' said Oliveira, passing a vial over. 'You will need to add some sugar to mask the taste.'

'Is it poison?' The landlord's eyes widened with alarm and he crossed himself. 'I could never do such a thing, Senhor, not for any amount of money.'

'Relax, it is just a little something the natives use in the Americas. No one will die. I will be back in half an hour with some of the men from my ship. See that the tavern is clear by then. Do we have a deal?' He held out his hand, the heavy coins nestling together with a musical chink.

Avarice and alarm played across the landlord's face. Then he reached out and took the money. 'It will be done as you ask.'

*****

'Where's that fecking grog we ordered?' demanded O'Malley, leaning heavily on the table.

'You drink so much, the barrel, he is empty,' explained Maria. 'My father opens another.'

'Well, while we're becalmed, like, I reckon I took the wrong tack earlier,' the Irishman continued, offering his lap once more. 'Yous really are a handsome colleen. Are you sure you wouldn't like a little kiss, an' all? I don't bite, you knows?'

'It ain't the end with teeth as she's worried about, I reckon,' commented Evans.

'Maria!' called the landlord, indicating a fresh jug.

'Too late,' she sighed, drawing a hand across the Irishman's shoulders as she sashayed away. She returned with the jug, together with some sliced ham. 'From my father.'

'This pork be mighty dark,' said Trevan, eyeing it suspiciously. His face quickly cleared when he tried some. 'But it do have a pleasant savour, mind,' he added, helping himself to more.

'Aye, this bishop's a touch different, an' all,' said Sedgwick, sipping at the wine. 'Suppose that'll be the new barrel.'

The sailors continued to drink steadily, while the landlord worked his way around the tavern from table to table. It was only when the jug was almost empty that Trevan looked up and glanced around, blinking uncertainly. It took him a moment to register that everyone else had left.

'W … what t … time be it?' he asked.

'T … time for a … another of these f … feckers,' muttered O'Malley, holding up the earthenware jug.

Trevan watched it with a puzzled frown as the clay vessel ballooned and shrank before his eyes. 'Y … you holding h … her steady, th … there, Sean?'

'N … not s … sure as I wants no b … bleeding m … more,' mumbled Evans, trying to get to his feet. After a few uncertain attempts he sat back down, and opted to settle his head on his arms instead.

'I … d … don't f … feel so f … feck … good,' offered O'Malley, slumping back against the wall.

'H … how much g … grog we h … have?' asked Sedgwick, 'an' wh … why be the r … room a turn … turning.'

'T… this d …don't seem r … right,' said Trevan, lurching to his feet. He reached down to steady himself on the table, but the surface pivoted away from him and cups clattered on to the floor. He stood swaying for a moment, fixing his gaze on Maria and the landlord. Try as he might, he couldn't stop them from dividing and multiplying before his eyes, until the room was crowded with figures, all pressing around the table.

'Come *Ingles*,' said a voice. 'Our wine is strong, not like beer. We help you back to your ship.' Trevan felt hands pulling him away from the table and bundling him out of the door. Outside, the dark street lurched beneath him like a deck in a nasty cross sea, while overhead the stars wheeled around him. He tried to stand upright, but the effort was beyond him, so instead he flung an arm around the necks of the two strange figures that supported him, and allowed them to drag his feet across the cobbles and down towards the beach. Ahead of him was the figure of O'Malley, apparently passed out between two other men, while the curses in Portuguese behind him indicated where several more were struggling with the dead weight of Evans.

'T … thanks, l … lads,' he muttered, his chin dropping. 'M … much obliged …' If the two men supporting him heard, he missed their answer as he slid down into unconsciousness. He was back in a whaling boat again, although he hadn't been in one since before the last war. The boat was racing across a sea the colour of red wine, while he stood in the bow, one foot up on the thwart, and the solid ash shaft of his harpoon poised. He glanced back at the oarsmen, and noticed how poorly matched his crew was. Behind him the huge Evans had been paired with the diminutive Maria. Further back, O'Malley was cursing furiously at the statue of Santa Isabel resting on the bench next to him. She stood motionless, regarded the oar trailing in the water beside her with glass-eyed serenity. Then his attention returned to the chase, as the back of a whale broke the surface ahead, except that this whale was covered in a dark fuzz of body hair. As Trevan watched, the creature rolled under him to reveal a huge, strangely human face with cruel, penetrating eyes. Then it sent a jet of wine from its mouth towards him. 'Thar' she blows!' he spluttered, opening his eyes.

He was back on the darkened beach at Porto Praya, his face dripping with seawater. Standing over him was the bulky shape of Owen Williams, the launch's bailer in his hand, cross-lit by a lantern on the sand beside him. Trevan blinked to clear his eyes, and saw that the sand was dotted with returning sailors, some gathered around, others joking and skylarking. Beyond them he could hear the gentle waves lapping against the hull of the *Griffin*'s launch.

'Still a bit groggy, is it?' said the Welshman. 'Shall I be giving him another soaking, sir?'

'No, that will do, Williams. We don't want to drown the fellow.' The concerned face of Midshipman Sweeny replaced that of the grizzled Welshman. 'How are you feeling, Trevan?' he asked.

'Damned awful in truth, sir,' he groaned. He flinched as the lantern was raised to shine on him.

'You seemed to be having some manner of fit when we found you,' the officer continued. 'Do you think you can sit up?'

'Aye, maybe,' muttered the Cornishman, struggling upright. 'Oh! That weren't so clever, sir. Best you stand clear. I … I … reckon I be fit to puke.'

'That may be the best thing for you,' said Sweeny. 'Then we will take you back to the ship and get Mr Corbett to look you over. I am most uncertain about your eyes. Big as an owl's, they seem. You wait with him, Williams, while I go and see the others.'

Once Trevan had been gushingly sick in the shallows, he began to feel a little better. He splashed his face clean with sea water and attempted to stand properly, but the beach still reeled beneath him.

Williams grabbed him before he fell, and gently helped him to a place he could sit on the dry sand again. '’Tis not the sawbones as you need, but to mend your ways, boyo,' he offered. 'Satan hides at the foot of every bottle, look you.'

'I ain't truly drunk, Owen,' said Trevan, spitting to one side. 'Oh, I took enough to make merry, no doubt, but I've been raised on scrumpy since I were a nipper. No, I reckon that plate of pork the dago buggers gave us weren't right, to my way of thinking. Gave me some proper weird dreams, I can tell 'ee. Good of them to see us all back down here, mind.'

'Good, is it?' snorted Williams. 'That why they dumped the three of you down here in the dark, all hollering and fitting, like?'

'Be that right,' said Trevan, massaging his temples for a moment. Then he looked back at the sailor. 'Three?' he queried. 'You be putting me in that reckoning?'

'Aye. Evans and O'Malley are over there.'

'So where the hell be Able?'

Chapter 5
The Deserter

His majesty's consul to the Cape Verde islands had taken a full part in the evening's festivities, to judge from his bleary eyes and pale face as he was shown into Clay's cabin the following morning. 'Er, no madeira, I pray,' he muttered, in response to Clay's offer, 'but if I might trouble you for a dish of tea?'

'See to it, if you please, Harte,' said Clay, retaking his place beside Vansittart. 'Do be seated, I pray, Mr Moore.'

'Thank you, Captain,' he gasped, mopping his brow with a large calico handkerchief. 'You will be pleased to learn that I have the particulars you requested concerning the *Marseillois*.' He plunged the handkerchief back into the cavernous pocket on one side of his coat and drew out a notebook from the other side. Moistening a finger with his tongue, he worked his way through the pages until he found the place he sought. 'She is a frigate,' he announced, with an air of triumph.

'I never doubted it for an instant,' muttered Vansittart beneath his breath.

'A national ship of France, naturally, of thirty-six guns, eighteen-pounders in the main,' he continued. 'Commanded by a chap named Renaud. They took on water, firewood and fresh provisions. Although her destination was undeclared, I have been told that her sailing master visited several premises in the town, enquiring after guides and charts relating to the Cape of Good Hope and to the Malabar coast of India.' He snapped the book closed, and returned it to his pocket. 'Furthermore, I have arranged for Senhor Da Ribeiro to call on your purser this morning, Captain, to supply the provisions you requested for your ship. His name was Faulkner, was it not?'

'That is correct. Charles Faulkner.'

'You have done well, Mr Moore,' said Vansittart. 'I am impressed.'

'Much obliged, sir,' said Moore, bowing a little in his chair. 'Your good opinion is of inestimable value, particularly if shared with our masters at home, what? Cape Verde can be damnedably hot for a man of my constitution, and my repeated requests for another situation seem to have gone astray.'

'Thank you for your efforts, Mr Moore, but I fear I shall have to prevail on you to assist me further,' said Clay. 'One of my sailors went ashore last night and has now disappeared.'

'To have only one hand run might be considered by some a triumph, Captain,' said the consul. 'During the last war I had Royal Navy officers call on me quite in despair at having lost a dozen ratings in a single visit.'

'That will not answer in this case, Mr Moore,' said Clay. 'Sedgwick is certainly not the kind to desert. He is my personal coxswain, and a trusted and valued member of the crew.'

'In which case he will doubtless turn up presently, having recovered from all the mugs of bishop he has quaffed. The wine hereabouts is rather palatable, and very cheap.'

'I think not, for I suspect foul play. He was with three others, who were all found unconscious last night by one of my officers. My surgeon examined them and is convinced that they had been rendered insensible in some manner.'

'Give me the particulars, Captain, and I will do what I

can,' said Moore, dredging out his notebook once more, turning to a fresh page and drawing out a pencil.

'Thank you,' said Clay. 'His name is Able Sedgwick. He is a negro, a little above six feet in height, strongly built with well-formed limbs and a passing handsome countenance. Dressed as a sailor, obviously, but with only a short pigtail.'

'Did you say he is a negro, sir?' queried Moore, putting down his pencil.

'He is. What of it?'

'I do understand that it is considered fashionable in some quarters to have servants who are Blackamoors, but you must understand that finding such a man here, so close to the shores of Africa, will be very difficult,' said the consul. 'Why, much of the workforce on the islands are slaves. However, I am sure I can find a suitable replacement. I might even be persuaded to part with one of my own house slaves for a modest consideration.'

Clay felt his face tighten with rage. He rose to his feet, knocking his chair over as he did so. His hands bunch into fists as he leant across the desk, struggling to resist an urge to punch Moore on his bulbous nose. As he towered over him, he saw a look of terror in the consul's eyes. 'Sedgwick is a free man, and a valued shipmate who has served his king and his captain with great distinction,' he roared. 'I want him found!'

'Now sir, calm yourself, I beg of you,' cried the official, holding up his pudgy hands as if to ward off a blow. 'No need for such uncivil behaviour. If I have offended you with an ill-conceived suggestion, I am sorry for it. But you must understand the situation here. Once I tell the authorities of his race, they will be quite indifferent to his fate.'

'I want him found!' repeated Clay. 'A search instituted for him, enquiries made. Porto Praya is not above a modest town in size. You may tell the authorities that either they find him, or I shall blockade their little dung hole with the *Griffin* until they do!'

'Steady, Captain,' said Vansittart. 'Let us not be hasty. Portugal is neutral, and a longstanding friend of ours, and we have no authority for such an action. Concern yourself with the resupply of the ship and let me go ashore with Mr Moore here, and pay my respects to the governor. I know how you navy types thirst for action, but this strikes me as a case where a little diplomacy is called for, what?'

*****

When Sedgwick awoke, his first thought was that he was back on the *Griffin*, to judge from the gentle swaying motion of the deck. His head was sore and confused from the strange-coloured dreams that had filled his mind for the last few hours. It was dark where he lay and his limbs were stiff from the hard planking beneath him. Odd, he thought to himself, why aren't I in my hammock? Then his nostrils flared as they filled with a half-remembered smell, and he sat up quickly, immediately striking his head on the deck above. He cowered back down, terror gripping him as long-supressed memories flooded back. His eyes slowly adjusted to the dim light, revealing the empty deck, no more than a shelf, stretching away ahead of him towards the bow of the ship. Just overhead was the underside of the deck above, hemming him in like the lid of a coffin, the wood stained black with the excrement and filth that had soaked into it over the years.

But for Sedgwick the deck was far from empty. Before his eyes it began to fill with ghostly memories of the past. The heat and the filth; the constant sound of weeping and moaning;

row upon row of naked humanity all packed together like spoons in a drawer. Old and young, male and female, the living chained to the dead. He tried to turn on to his front to crawl away from the horror of it all, but found that his ankles were manacled to the planking, holding him on his side.

'Help!' he roared. 'Be anyone there? Help!' But his voice echoed back from the close walls about him, unanswered. How did I get here, he wondered, trying to force his mind to remember. They had been in a tavern, drinking wine and then the world had become distant and hazy. He recalled trying to stand up, and how the walls had seemed to tumble around him. Hands had gripped him and held him upright. Maria, the serving girl had been there, her face devoid of pity. Then he had been out in the street with the others, lights and stars turning about him. He remembered his friends being helped away, the slumped Evans needing four men to carry him. He had tried to stumble after them, but a cruel face had appeared in his way. 'No, you are mine,' the man had hissed. A hand gripping him around the upper arm, feeling the muscle; then fingers forcing his mouth open and probing at his teeth. The face again, smiling. 'Five *reals*, good price,' he had heard, before he had slid into a world of strange visions.

'Them bastards must have slipped me something,' he muttered. Now that he began to understand what had happened to him, he felt calmer. He breathed deeply for a while, driving back the panic that threatened to overwhelm him. 'Take control, Able,' he said aloud, the sound of his voice comforting in the dark and making him feel less alone. 'Right, you've been took by slavers, that's plain enough, so hollering won't answer any,' he continued. 'But it ain't the first time as that's happened, and after a deal of pain and toil you got free before, so I daresay as you can do it again. First, where be you? On a slave ship, for certain, but not at sea, to judge from the motion. So maybe you ain't left Porto Praya as yet, which is a comfort. Now, what else you got?'

He ran his hands down over himself, exploring the cramped dark. 'I still got all me togs bar shoes, but that don't matter any. I daresay they'll be hereabouts, tossed aside when they put me in irons.' Next he searched his pockets, all of which were empty. 'Well, that figures,' he sighed. 'My chink would be the first thing the thieving buggers will have took, an' it'd be too much to hope they'd have left me my knife.' Next he reached down to his ankles to explore the leg irons, hoping for a careless slip of some kind that would allow him to break free, but all was secure.

Despair threatened to overwhelm him once more as he lay there in the dark, fighting back tears of frustration. He reached out in the gloom until his fingers touched the inner skin of the ship. Through the thick timbers he could sense the sea, washing against the hull, and beyond it the moored frigate. Pipe will not abandon you, he told himself, nor will Adam or the others.

*****

The deck of the *Griffin* bustled with activity later that day as the crew, many of them the worse for wear, heaved on ropes or fetched and carried as the frigate prepared for the long run to India. It was hard work in the sweltering heat, in spite of the awnings that had been rigged to screen the men from the worst of the sun. The gratings over the main hatch had been removed on each layer of deck through the ship, allowing a large block and tackle to dip deep into her hold and pluck out her water casks. Each huge barrel was swung through the air, turning slowly, before being deposited in the longboat waiting on the water. Meanwhile, on the other side of the frigate several lighters nestled close. Here bundles of firewood and sacks of fresh provisions were being brought on board under the watchful eye of Charles Faulkner, the ship's aristocratic purser. Clay watched a goat struggling with the cargo net that enmeshed it as it was swayed aboard. For a brief moment the creature was at eye level with him up on the quarterdeck, and opened its pink mouth wide to let out a loud, plaintive bleat in his direction, much to the amusement of the hands.

'Pipe down there!' barked the petty officer in charge, as the goat began its descent towards the hatchway, and its brief time in the frigate's manger at the fore end of the lower deck. Not too much meat on that creature, thought Clay to himself, but it will make a pleasant change from salt beef and pork. A last survey of the deck was enough to show Clay that all was as it should be, and that between them Taylor and Hutchinson had the revictualling of the ship well in hand. He stepped across to the starboard rail, pulled out his telescope and looked over at the town.

The previous night Porto Praya had looked beautiful in the flattering dark. The lines of lanterns strung along the water front, the torchlit procession flowing down the main street to spread out along the shore and the gun salutes banging out from the fort had all been mirrored in the calm water of the bay. Now little of that magic remained. The beach was strewn with debris, the dusty streets were largely empty and the shabby buildings wavered in the heat beneath drooping palm trees. Where are you, Able, he asked himself as he searched. His gaze settled on two mongrels down by the shore as they busily squabbled over some titbit of rubbish in the shallows. Then he closed the telescope and began to pace the deck.

He needed to find Sedgwick quickly, he decided. Every moment the *Griffin* lay idle here the *Marseillois* would be getting further away from him, and yet how much confidence could he place in the Portuguese authorities? He knew from personal experience that Vansittart was an impressive and influential man, but if the governor showed the same indifference as Moore to the fate of a single black sailor, what then? He spun around at the quarterdeck rail and paced back towards the stern. Could he land Macpherson and his forty marines to search the place, he wondered, but then quickly dismissed the idea. Landing redcoats would spark a major diplomatic incident, and besides would surely end in ignominious failure. Why, there must be hundreds of soldiers garrisoning the fort alone, not to mention any militia in the town. He turned again in frustration, and continued his pacing.

'Boat putting out from the shore!' announced the midshipman of the watch. 'Our blue cutter, from the look of her, sir.'

Clay changed the line of his pacing into a curving arc that brought him up alongside the curly-haired youngster. 'Anyone in the stern sheets, Mr Todd?'

'I believe Mr Vansittart, sir,' replied the midshipman. 'I can see that pale blue coat he favours.'

'No sign of Sedgwick, then?'

'I am afraid not, sir,' said Todd, checking the boat once more with his telescope. 'That must be Young who has the bow oar. He's a deal slighter than Sedgwick.'

Clay waited for the cutter to sweep up beside the entry port and for the diplomat to make his uncertain way up the ship's side. After some clattering and a muffled oath he arrived, breathing heavily and bareheaded, followed shortly after by one of the boat crew carrying his hat and silver-topped cane. 'My thanks to you,' he said, accepting both and pulling his waistcoat straight. 'Deuced tricky, those steps,' he remarked as he came across to join the captain.

'I could order a boatswain's chair rigged for you in future, sir?' said Clay. 'We normally reserve them for ladies or bad weather, but if it saves you from a drowning?'

'I am glad to see my lubberly ways amuse you, Captain,' said Vansittart. 'But while Mr Preston can scamper on board with but one arm, there is little honour in your proposal. I come with mixed tidings, I fear.'

'You found the governor to be uncooperative?'

'On the contrary, he was most obliging in the assistance that he proposed. The town is to be ransacked by files of soldiers, generous rewards are to be offered and the more notorious ne'er-do-wells rounded up for questioning. In short, no effort will be spared to find your coxswain.'

'That all sounds very handsome,' said Clay. 'So where does the problem lie?'

'Because I suspect it all to be little more than cant,' said Vansittart. 'I know how to assess the worth of a fellow, and this one is a man of straw. He is quite in hock to the slave trade, which alone gives his little island purpose. I also count myself fortunate to have made his acquaintance so early in the day, for he and Moore are a well-matched pair. Had I called after luncheon I am most uncertain if I would had any sensible dialogue with him at all.'

'So what do you propose, sir?' asked Clay. 'That I abandon a valuable sailor who has never shown me anything but loyalty?'

'No, only that if you seek a resolution, you will need to shift for yourself,' said Vansittart. 'But I cannot sanction any action that threatens to cause a diplomatic issue, or to delay us over long.'

'I will not leave without Sedgwick,' said Clay, gripping the rail tightly as he stared towards the town.

'Then find a way, Captain, as you have always done before. But whatever it is, achieve your object quietly and do so swiftly. We are only at the start of our voyage. Now, I must go below and dispense with my coat and weskit before I expire from this heat.'

Clay remained staring at the town for several minutes after the diplomat had vanished, mulling over what to do. Then he came to a decision. He turned away from the rail. 'Mr Todd! My compliments to Mr Taylor, and would he have O'Malley, Evans and Trevan sent to my quarters if they have been released by Mr Corbett.'

'Aye aye, sir!'

Clay was seated at his desk in shirt-sleeves with all the window lights open behind him in the hope of some breeze when the three sailors were shown in by Harte. They shuffled into line in front of him, the huge Evans bracketed by the two smaller men.

'I trust I find you all somewhat recovered today?' asked Clay, thinking how pale they all looked, in spite of their many years at sea.

'Aye, much better, thankee kindly, sir,' said Trevan, knuckling his forehead to his captain. 'The doctor bled us all, and fed us a powerful draft as made us puke and shit worse than the plague. He says a few days of light duty and short commons will see us right ag'in.'

'Perhaps you would prefer to be seated?'

O'Malley had half-turned to pull up a chair, when Trevan exclaimed. 'Goodness no, sir! Not for all the tin in Cornwall. Us Jacks a sitting down with the likes of you? That wouldn't be proper, at all.'

'Very well,' said Clay. 'I asked you here to tell me what you recall from last night. I am most concerned to find what has become of Sedgwick.'

'In truth, I ain't sure as I can help much at all, sir,' said O'Malley. 'After we saw the feck … the procession we found ourselves a snug tavern, where we were after taking some wine, being a touch thirsty an' all. A little later something was slipped into our grog as gave us all manner of visions an' the like. Then some lads showed up, and took us down to the beach, and next thing I remember that feck … that puritan Williams was after pouring half the Atlantic over me, and Sedgwick had vanished like Fergus in the mist.'

'That be much the same as I recall, sir,' offered Trevan. 'I be proper worried on his account. Ain't like him to go a missing.'

'Quite so,' said Clay. 'Which is the strangest part of all. Did nothing untoward happened before then, to explain why these men sought you out? No altercation or disturbance? Did you give offence to anyone? Think, now, I beg. It might be very important.' He glanced across at the big Londoner, who looked troubled. 'Do you have something to say, Evans? Nothing ill will follow if you speak plain.'

'Your talk of fighting does put me in mind of this one thing as happened earlier, sir. Wasn't much of a mill, in truth, but it were over Able.'

'Go on.'

'See, I went to the privy, what were at the back of the tavern, sir, an' this flash-looking dago followed me out. Ill-favoured bloke, he were. Any road, he comes up to me, rattling on as how civilised blacks was worth a deal more in the Brazils than savages straight from the forest. I can't say as I caught his drift any, but then he came right out an' asked if I'd sell him Able, taking me for his owner. Well, I got a bit hot about that, him being a mate an' all, so I gave him a cuff for his troubles, which was wrong of me, sir. Then he made to stick me with his dirk, so I gave him a bit more tap, after which he were a touch more civil. Then off he scarpered, an' I thought no more upon it 'til now.'

'Why the feck didn't you say aught at the time?' exclaimed O'Malley, rounding on his friend.

'I'll ask the questions,' snapped Clay, glaring at the Irishman. 'And kindly mind your language and remember where you are.'

'Sorry, sir.'

'O'Malley does make a fair point,' said Clay, returning his attention to Evans. 'Why did you not warn Sedgwick of the danger he was in?'

'I didn't want to vex him, sir,' said Evans. 'Ever since we went ashore, them dagos had been looking down on him as if he were no more than a dog. I hadn't the heart to burden him with more, but if that were wrong, I'm proper sorry for it.'

'It's done now,' said the captain. 'No matter, for I declare we make progress at last. What can you recall of this slave trader? Did he tell you his name, or aught else about himself?'

'I reckon he may have, an' all, sir,' said Evans, rubbing his chin. 'I weren't thinking straight after that draft they slipped us, but I might be able to call it back to mind. Now, what were the name he gave?'

'Take your time, Evans,' said Clay, before directing his voice towards his day cabin, where he knew his steward would be listening. 'Harte!'

'Yes, sir,' said the servant, appearing with a cloth held

prominent in one hand and a half-polished brass lamp in the other.

'Kindly pass the word for Mr Todd.'

'Aye aye, sir.'

'It were some'it like Oliver, I reckon, sir,' pronounced Evans at last. 'He said he were mate of a ship.'

'I see, and did he name the vessel, per chance?'

'He did an' all, sir,' said the Londoner. 'Foreign name, of course. Sounded a bit like sour vinegar, or some such.'

There was a knock at the door, and the midshipman of the watch came in to join the line of sailors in front of the desk.

'Ah, Mr Todd,' said Clay. 'Was it you whom Mr Taylor sent to the masthead shortly after we arrived?'

'Yes, sir,' said the youngster, colouring slightly. 'On account of my having been tardy coming on deck at the change of the watch.'

'From where I daresay you must have had a splendid view of the town. Tell me, did you chance to see any compounds or stockades where slaves might be held?'

'No, sir. I can't say as I did.'

'Very well. And where, pray, is the longboat?'

'Just now returned with another hogshead, sir. Mr Hutchinson is having it transferred to the ship.' He pointed to the open skylight, where the deep bass of the boatswain could be heard berating one of the men.

'Handsomely there, you whoreson! If that cask be broke, I'll have you cleaning the heads 'til Lady Day next, MacDonald!'

'Splendid!' enthused Clay. 'When it takes the next barrel ashore, kindly see that it shapes its route to pass astern of those slave ships moored to leeward of us. Tell the officer in charge to note their names, without arousing undue attention.'

A little while later the longboat appeared from below the stern of the frigate with another big barrel filling the middle section and headed across the bay. In the stern sheets sat the dark-haired Midshipman Sweeny, with the tiller tucked under one arm and a slate and chalk on his lap. As he passed behind the first slaver Clay watched him raise a hand to acknowledge the friendly wave from one of the anchor watch, and then bend over the slate. A little while later the boat returned, sitting much lower beneath the weight of the full water cask. Time seemed to stand still for the three sailors under the thoughtful gaze of their captain. At last, there was a knock at the cabin door.

'Come in!' ordered Clay.

'Mr Sweeny's compliments, sir, and he has set down the names of the slave ships for you,' said Todd, handing the slate across the desk. Clay thanked him, glanced at the short list and then looked across at the sailors.

'Evans, this slaver of yours. Might it have been named the *Sao Vincente*?'

'That's it, sir!' exclaimed the Londoner. 'I said as how it were foreign, like.'

'Very well,' said Clay, rising to his feet. 'I believe I may know where our shipmate is to be found. Thank you for your assistance, and you may all return to your duties.'

Once he was alone, he walked across to the run of stern windows and looked at the slaver lying at her mooring. 'Are you truly so near, Able, my friend?' he murmured, framing the ship with his fingers. 'And how do I get you out of there without starting a war?'

*****

The moon was setting, its silver crescent yellowing as it

dropped behind the headland with its fort, leaving the night sky to the stars. A few lamps were alight in Porto Praya, amber eyes staring out over the calm waters of the bay. Then from one of the twin towers of the church on the summit a bell chimed out, the sound taken up aboard the moored ships in the bay.

'Four bells, sir,' whispered the first lieutenant, one of the dark shapes gathered around the *Griffin*'s wheel. 'Shall I have the boats manned?'

'With as little noise as possible, if you please, Mr Taylor,' replied Clay, and the officer slipped away. Moments later came the patter of bare feet across the deck and the whisper of orders. He turned to the other two figures that stood close by. 'Mr Blake, Mr Preston, do you have your parts well understood?'

'Yes, sir,' said Blake, the senior of the two. 'I am to come alongside the entry port and force my way aboard with the minimum of violence. My men will be armed, but only for show. Firearms are to be uncocked, and I have told them the first man to draw his cutlass without my say-so will have a dozen at the grating in the morning.'

'Very good, and what is your role in the enterprise, Mr Preston?'

'While Mr Blake is at the entry port, my men will come over the bow, sir, so should he meet excessive resistance, we can surprise those opposing him from the rear. Once the deck is secure, we will proceed to the search.'

'And have you considered how you gentlemen will deal with opposition?'

'Several of the party are familiar with pressing men from merchant ships, sir,' said Blake. 'John Powell and Josh Black have armed themselves with canvas coshes filled with sand, and assure me that once they silence the first man to protest, the rest will be meek as lambs.'

'You don't say,' said Clay, with a smile. The two petty officers Blake had named were among the toughest men on the frigate.

'But I doubt we will encounter much resistance, sir,' added Preston. 'A ship of that size, not expecting trouble, won't have above a handful of men posted as an anchor watch. We are hardly cutting out a warship.'

'Quite so, Mr Preston. Good luck to you both, then, and I will see you when you return.'

'Aye aye, sir,' said the officers, touching their hats before they vanished in the direction of the main deck. Clay went across to the rail, and stared out towards the men's target, the nearest of the row of slave ships. The night had grown darker, now that the moon had gone, leaving the waters of the bay a lake of pitch on which the hull of the *Sao Vincente* lay. On her deck the faint glow of lamps illuminated the base of her tall masts and rigging as it rose up, a spider's web against the stars, but the rest of the ship was dark.

Beneath him he heard the hiss of orders, a gentle rattle of oars, and two black shapes moved away from the *Griffin* and out into the bay on slightly diverging courses. They soon vanished altogether, leaving Clay with only his hearing to gauge their progress. An endless, impossibly long silence. Then a faint clatter from across the water, accompanied by a cry of protest, sharp in the night. The boarding of the *Sao Vincente* had begun.

*****

Sedgwick was awake when the frigate's boats reached the slaver. After hours of lying in the same position his side ached and his back and shoulders were on fire. To add to his discomfort, his clothes were damp and clammy where he had been forced to relieve himself and he now had a raging thirst. He tried to shift a little, to the limit of the iron grip on his ankles, and felt the pain ease a little, allowing him to return to his thoughts. He was trying to keep his spirits up by thinking of home. The sea hissing under the bow of the *Little Sam* as she fled across sunlit water towards the shore, her midships piled high with silver fish. Ann, beautiful, warm yielding Ann, smiling up at him from among the tousled sheets. But it was hard to hold back the advance of other darker memories. Of the savage beatings he had witnessed on the plantations, and the long cycle of endless labour that in time could reduce the strongest to zombie-like obedience. Was a return to that life really going to be his fate?

The onset of night had given the hold of the slave ship the utter darkness of a cavern. In place of light his world was filled with sound. From beyond the ship's side came the slap and suck of the little waves as they struck the hull, faint echoes of the Atlantic rollers beyond the headland. Through the deck beneath him he felt the creak and groan of the standing rigging as it took up and then released the colossal weight of masts and spars with each rock of the hull. Then there were other, closer sounds. The footfall and laughter of crewmen on the deck above him. The squeal and scampering of rats in the hold about him. He listened as one came running along the slave deck towards him, its tiny claws clicking against the planking until it stopped in amazement. He could almost sense it, whiskers alert, sniffing towards his face. He had only to reach out and touch it. Then he heard a fresh sound, a low voice, giving a familiar order in English from just beyond the skin of the hull.

'In oars, larboards,' it murmured. 'Hook on in the bow,

there.'

Sedgwick could sense the presence of the boat, close to where his head rested, sliding in over the dark water towards the slaver. He pushed his arms towards the ship's side, to knock on the wood and tell them where he was, but he could only brush it with his fingertips.

'I am here, Mr Blake,' he croaked weakly and the rat scampered away in alarm, leaving him alone once more.

Now there was a thud, from behind him, and more hissed orders. He felt the tremor of feet as they raced up the side. A cry of surprise, quickly stifled, from directly above him, and more feet pattering on the deck. Then the sound of a second rush of men, from somewhere forward.

'Secure those men, Powell,' came the voice again, louder now. 'Mr Preston, can your people attend to the crew in the forecastle? I'll make for the officers' quarters.'

Joy surged in Sedgwick's heart as he followed the boarding party's progress through the ship. He listened to the individual cries of surprise and anger of the crew, each one quickly stifled. He forced his dry throat into action, and after a few weak croaks found his voice at last.

'Ahoy there, Griffins!' he managed, rattling his leg irons against the deck for good measure. 'In the hold, Mr Blake! Mr Preston!'

In spite of his best efforts, it still seemed to take an age for the first beams of lamplight to play across the slave deck. 'Over here, shipmates,' he called out. 'I'm over here!'

At last the sound of approaching feet, running towards him. 'That you, Able?' asked Josh Black, the hulking captain of the foretop, his gruff voice for once threaded with emotion. A lantern was set down on the deck near Sedgwick's feet, blinding after so much dark. 'Bleeding hell, that be a tight spot the bastards have stowed you in!'

'Thank you for coming, Josh,' choked Sedgwick through his tears, the emotion of his rescue overwhelming him at last.

'Pipe weren't going to leave you, mate.' A rough hand against his leg, patting it. 'An' if it were up to us, them as done this would be pitched over the side, but orders is orders. Let's be getting you shifted afore they call out the garrison. Pass along that file there.'

'Have you found him, Black?' called Preston, from further off.

'Aye sir, but he be in leg irons. I can have them off him in time but the key would be right handy.'

Another lantern, and more approaching feet. The jingle of metal on metal. 'These were hanging by the hatchway. See if one fits,' ordered Blake. A number of fumbling attempts, and at last Sedgwick was free. Hands pulled him off the slave deck and into the central well of the hold, where he could stand upright, swaying at first, as if the *Sao Vincente* was at sea.

'How are you, Sedgwick?' asked Preston, his face creased with concern. 'Perhaps a drink of water will restore you?' He indicated a scuttlebutt that stood against the base of the main mast.

'Thank you, sir, but I'd sooner not drink here,' he replied. 'I can wait to be back on the barky. The quicker I can scrub the filth of this place off me, the better pleased I shall be.'

*****

Clay was having breakfast with Vansittart in the great cabin when his majesty's consul to the Cape Verde islands was shown in.

'Ah, Mr Moore,' said Clay, rising to greet him. 'You find us breaking our fast on some rather agreeable local fish hot from the pan. Would you care to join us? Harte, light along another plate there!'

'I have no time for food, sir!' exclaimed the flustered diplomat. 'The town is in uproar! The governor summoned me at dawn, for all love!'

'I had wondered what had got you from your bed so early in the day,' continued Clay. 'Take a seat at least, I pray, before you expire entirely, and tell me what has occasioned this commotion.'

The consul sat down heavily and leant his flushed face close. 'Do not presume to make game of me, Captain,' he warned. 'You know very well what has transpired. Men from this ship have committed an act of piracy this very night!'

'Piracy, you say?' said Clay, exchanging a glance with Vansittart. 'I don't believe I have the pleasure of understanding you at all. Whatever can you mean, Mr Moore?'

'I refer to the assault made by armed borders upon the *Sao Vincente*! Pray do not play the innocent with me, sir! You ordered the attack to recover this Blackamoor of yours. The one who was abducted.'

'Ah, I think I follow you,' smiled Clay. 'But perhaps I should commence by offering you an apology, for making such a fuss the other day. I was mistaken. It transpires that I do not have a sailor who has been abducted. It was a simple case of desertion.'

'Desertion!' queried Moore. 'Desertion! Whatever can you mean?'

'Oh, it is passing common in the navy,' continued Clay, helping himself to more breakfast. 'Why, you yourself suspected Sedgwick had simply run when I first raised his disappearance with you. As it turns out, you were right. Are you sure you will not try the fish? It is really very passable.'

'But … but your attack on the slave ship?' said Moore.

'What attack?' queried Clay, through a mouthful of food. 'I simply sent a party on board the *Sao Vincente* to search for my deserter, as I am quite entitled to do under Admiralty regulations. The rogue has been arrested and returned to this ship.'

'But you sent armed men! In the middle of the night!'

'With firm instructions to use the minimum of force. No one was hurt in the operation, were they?'

'But the governor is livid!' said Moore. 'He spoke of ordering the fort to fire upon you should you attempt to depart!'

'So, does the governor believe that this is not a simple case of desertion, then?' asked Clay. 'That rumours of a British seaman being illegally abducted by Portuguese subjects is true? Because that would be a very grave matter indeed. One requiring to be fully investigated by the governor, and the particulars reported to the governments in both London and Lisbon.'

'Er, well … I suppose …' spluttered Moore.

'Or perhaps he would prefer to accept that the matter is now closed?' said Clay, eyeing the consul over the rim of his coffee cup. 'I have made good my provisions and am anxious to depart in the wake of this Frenchman. Perhaps if you were to go and explain how matters lie, the governor might be persuaded not to fire on the *Griffin* when I leave? We wouldn't want such a trivial incident to start a war, would we?'

Once the consul had departed, Vansittart put down his coffee cup and slowly applauded his host. 'Bravo, my dear sir,' he said. 'I do declare we shall make a diplomat of you yet. A deserter, for all love! That was masterly done!'

Chapter 6
The Marseillois

The *Griffin* tried to leave Porto Praya with the same dignified military ceremony as when she had arrived, but her crew had other ideas. She exchanged salutes with the fort and began to gather pace as she headed towards the wide Atlantic. Regrettably the path she was obliged to take passed close to the *Sao Vincente*, and the sight of the slaver's crew lining the rail to watch them go proved too much for the Griffins. In spite of the best efforts of the petty officers to control them, a storm of jeers and obscene gestures were directed towards the slaver, including the exposure of buttocks from on her forecastle.

'Mr Harrison!' roared Taylor, his face red with embarrassment. 'Get those men back from the rail! I want the name of everyone involved in this shameful display!'

'Aye aye, sir,' replied the boatswain, bodily hauling sailors inboard by their pigtails. 'Fundaments away, you lot! You've had your fun.'

Clay decided to keep his telescope firmly to his eye and study the way ahead minutely while order was being restored. He doubted he would have been able to keep an entirely straight face, which would only make his first lieutenant's task harder. Only once the last boo had faded and he had composed himself to display the gravitas expected in a post captain did he close his telescope and look over the ship. Sailors were returning to their stations and order had largely been restored. The frigate rounded the headland with its brown rocky cliffs and as the first Atlantic wave rolled beneath the hull, Porto Praya vanished from sight. On the far side of the quarterdeck stood Sedgwick, staring back towards the island, his face unreadable.

'Now, Mr Armstrong, have you laid me off a course for the Cape?' asked Clay, turning to his sailing master.

'South-east by south, sir,' replied the American. He looked up towards the masthead pennant. 'This wind will serve us for now, although we shall meet the south-east trades in time.'

'And you hold that the *Marseillois* will have taken that course?'

'I reckon so, sir, if Mr Moore's intelligence is correct and she is bound for India. With no cause to be afeared of any pursuit, they'll take the straightest route to the Cape.'

'A stern chase is a long chase they say, Jacob, and the French have several days on us,' observed Clay. 'We need to crack on.'

'We do, sir.'

'Mr Taylor, do you have the men in hand?'

'Aye, sir,' replied the first lieutenant, coming over. 'I'll stop the worst offenders' grog for a week. I would have the others pumping out the bilges for the rest of the voyage but the *Griffin* leaks too little to occupy so many.'

'Punish the mooners and let the others be, George,' suggested his captain. 'In some ways their loyalty to a shipmate does them credit, and shows what a settled crew we have. That may count for much when we come up with the *Marseillois*. To which end, kindly set all topsails and topgallants.'

'Will she bear so much canvas, sir?' asked the first lieutenant, looking aloft and sucking in his cheeks. 'We might need preventer stays in this wind.'

'Make it so, Mr Taylor, if you judge it necessary, and let us get on.'

Sail after white sail blossomed on the tall masts of the frigate, and as each square of bulging canvas was sheeted home the angle of the deck increased further, until the ship seemed to be flying across the sea. Her bow crashed into each wave amid a plume of spray that flashed a brief rainbow into existence, while astern her boiling wake pointed back towards the scatter of volcanic domes that made up the nearest Cape Verde islands, shrinking with each passing mile.

'God bless my soul, the ship is leaning over like a deuced roof!' exclaimed Vansittart, coming up on deck to see what was happening. 'I was damned near rolled from my cot.'

'Splendid, isn't it, sir?' said Preston, who had taken over as officer of the watch. He swayed easily to each plunge of the ship, his telescope clasped beneath his lone arm. 'There are dolphins to be seen off the bow, if you care to go forward.'

'The Devil may take your dolphins,' grumbled the diplomat, as he clung with both hands to the binnacle. 'I merely came to enquire how long we shall be at such an inconvenient angle?'

'We press on in this fashion to close with the French, sir,' explained the officer. 'But they are far ahead. I doubt we shall come up with them for a week or so.'

'Ha ha! Hear him, will you!' laughed Vansittart. 'For a moment there, I took you to have said a week! I have missed your playful badinage, Mr Preston, but I see you still seek to make sport of an innocent lubber. Seriously now, how long do you suppose?'

'I wasn't making game of you, sir,' said the officer. 'Even if the French proceed with more regard for their spars and rigging than we do, it will take us that long to haul them in.

I can show you the position on a chart when I come below at the change of the watch.'

Vansittart regarded the lieutenant with horror, but, search as he might, there was no trace of humour in the younger man's face. 'A week,' he muttered, and his stomach gave a dry heave as the ship surged across a fresh roller. 'Tell me, Mr Preston, are you familiar with the writings of Doctor Johnson?'

'No, I can't say as I am, sir. Was he not that uncommonly learned cove?'

'The very same. He once said that no man would be a sailor who had contrivance enough to get himself into prison, because a ship was no more than a jail with the added chance of being drowned. I had never truly followed his reasoning. Until now, that is.'

*****

Lieutenant Preston was not quite correct in his prediction. The fifth day out from Porto Praya was a Sunday, which by long tradition was a make-and-mend day in the Royal Navy. Sail was reduced to minimise the number of men required to work the ship, which provided some relief for Vansittart's seasickness. After divine service and the captain's inspection tour of the frigate, most of the crew were released to spend their time as they pleased. It was a warm day, with the southeast trades blowing over the port bow as the *Griffin* beat her way across the broad ocean, all of which made for perfect drying weather. Most of the sailors had washed their clothes, filling the foremast with a bunting of flapping garments. Then they had unwound their long pigtails to wash their hair, and now sat around the forecastle enjoying the sunshine.

'Blimey, Able,' exclaimed Trevan, squeezing water

from the long golden tress that hung down across his chest. 'You be writing another of them books?'

'No, just summat for my Ann,' said the coxswain, looking up from a stack of papers. 'It be a sort of journal, like, telling her what I been doing, day by day. Pipe does the same for his wife, who finds it a comfort, so I thought to do the same. When we touch land, I'll send it back to her and start afresh, only I never got the chance to post this lot from the Cape Verdes.'

'That'd not be too clever if I had a bleeding missus,' observed Evans, looking up from the shirt he was repairing. 'Not sure she'd take kindly to reports of all the whoring and drinking.'

'It be more the little stuff I sets down, in truth,' explained Sedgwick. 'Strange goings on an' the like, so as she can share my world a little, rather than the grand stuff about battles an' India an' the like.'

'I hope you ain't been an' told her about drafts of poison, and slavers an' all?' warned Trevan. 'Coz if she be anything like my Molly, she'll be quite afeared enough on your part. Ain't no call to add to that burden.'

'In truth, I were stuck upon how much of that to set down,' reported Sedgwick. 'Perhaps none might be for the best.'

'I still hold we should have torched that fecking Sour Vinegar,' said O'Malley, combing the dark curls that flopped over his shoulders like those of a cavalier. 'That would have learned the devils.'

'I'd have found that Olive git and done for him, whatever the bleeding Grunters ordered,' said Evans. 'Only that fool of a sawbones wouldn't pass me fit to go.'

'Just as well you and Sean had no part in it then,' said

Sedgwick. 'Pipe be deeper than us all. Torch the ship and slay the crew, an' we'd have started a war.'

'I don't fecking get yous, at all,' exclaimed the Irishman. 'The buggers snatched you without so much as a by your leave. Why ain't you the one who's hot to be after paying them back in their coin?'

'Maybe once you been a slave, nothing surprises you no more,' sighed the coxswain. 'It be my lot, see. Not in the navy, perhaps, nor back home, but in Cape Verdes or in the Americas.'

'Fecking dagos,' muttered O'Malley.

'Why just dagos?' said the coxswain. 'I was took by English slavers every bit as cruel as that bastard Sam milled with. Londoners, Cornishmen, aye and Irishmen too, Sean O'Malley. Setting one slaver aflame won't answer, when there be a hundred more to take its place.'

'That be true enough, Able,' agreed Trevan, patting his friend's shoulder. 'Not sure what simple Jacks like us can do, mind, but Parson Moon back home reckons it'll not be long now afore them as favours Abolition will have their way. Until then, we best be keeping a weather eye over you.'

A companionable silence fell over the sailors and Sedgwick returned to his writing. He was disturbed by a burst of excitement from the group fishing on the starboard cathead, which prompted Evans to lay down his needlework and go and find out what had been caught. Trevan ran his fingers through his hair to check it was dry, and turned to O'Malley. 'Sean, you be going to tie my hair first, or shall I do yorn?'

'Mine first,' said the Irishman, settling down in front of his friend. 'This wind's after getting it in a fecking tangle faster than I can comb it out.'

Sedgwick looked up and noticed that the wind had

become fitful, first driving the frigate boldly on, and then fading amid a rattle of blocks and lines from above them. 'I ain't liking the look of this weather, lads,' he said, rising to his feet. 'Best be getting our togs down and stowed away.' Across the forecastle, sailors were looking towards the sky ahead and hurrying to recover their clothes.

Up on the quarterdeck Jacob Armstrong was officer of the watch. He felt the changing motion of the ship beneath his feet with a sensitivity born of long experience, and turned to the midshipman of the watch. 'Do you mark how indifferent this wind has become, Mr Todd?' he asked, scratching thoughtfully at his periwig.

'Aye, it comes and goes, sir,' came the answer. 'Do you suppose it will fail us altogether?'

'No, lad. We have long passed the Doldrums; besides, the sea shows no sign of growing calm. If anything, this swell becomes longer. I fear it is the dog before its master. We are in for a blow, or I am no seaman.'

He took the telescope from its place beside the wheel, which brought him close to the open skylight in the centre of the deck. A burst of laughter caught his attention and he glanced down to where Clay was entertaining those officers not on watch in the cabin below. The table was strewn with plates and half-full glasses of wine, while a flushed Vansittart leant forward from his place beside the captain as he entertained the company with a story. The American walked over to the back of the quarterdeck and made a careful survey of the horizon. Ahead of the ship, through the lines of rapidly vanishing washing, the sky was growing dark. As he watched, a tiny thread of lightning stabbed down and vanished. 'Mr Todd, give my compliments to the captain, and can you ask him to come on deck.'

'Aye aye, sir,' said the youngster.

Armstrong heard the flow of noisy conversation pause, followed by a scraping of chairs. Moments later Clay came up the companion ladder accompanied by Taylor. As soon as their heads cleared the deck, both officers were looking around them, sensing the change in the weather.

'Good afternoon to you, Mr Armstrong,' said Clay, returning the sailing master's salute. 'What seems amiss?'

'Good afternoon, sir. I am sorry for disturbing you, but I don't care for this weather.' He passed across the telescope. 'If you direct your gaze towards the south, you will see what I mean.'

What had just been a little darkness had grown into a hedge of lofty thunderheads. Clay took a moment to view it, and then passed the glass on to his first lieutenant. 'You did right to send for me, Jacob. Call all hands, and get the upper masts struck down on deck. Mr Taylor, will you take a party of men around and double breech the guns, and see to battening down the hatches. We are in for squally weather, gentlemen, I make no doubt.'

'Aye aye, sir.'

It was fortunate that the frigate had a veteran crew used to working together, because the storm came on with a speed that took the breath away. Almost with every glance it seemed closer, a boiling front of cloud above a darkening sea. Below it the air was streaked with rain. Urged on by the squealing boatswain's calls and the cries of the petty officers, the topmen rushed upwards, while the rest of the crew were organised on the deck beneath them. Soon the first of the upper yards were being swung through the air and down towards the deck, while other sailors began dismantling the standing rigging that supported the upper masts.

Upon the Malabar Coast

'It is a deuced remarkable sight, ain't it, Macpherson,' marvelled Vansittart to the commander of the *Griffin*'s marines. He raised the glass of wine he had brought on deck with him towards the swarm of activity aloft. 'Before I came to sea, I should never have imagined that all those poles and furlongs of rope and what-not, could be taken apart and reassembled out here on the ocean, but there you have your proof.'

'Aye, 'tis a spectacle that the mob at any fair back home would pay a joey each just to witness, sir,' agreed the Scotsman. 'Mind your head, there!' he added, steering the diplomat away from the mizzen royal yard, a long sausage of bundled sail and spar descending rapidly towards them at the angle of a spear. 'Perhaps we can more safely observe matters from the taffrail. Not that way, sir. It lies astern.'

Safely ensconced at the very rear of the quarterdeck, the two men had a fine view both of the vanishing upper masts of the frigate, and the wall of approaching storm, grumbling and churning as it grew across the sky.

'Why is all this commotion required, Lieutenant?' asked Vansittart, sipping at his wine. 'I mark the storm well enough, and deuced prodigious it appears, but surely we have taken in all bar a tiny scrap of sail?'

'I understand it to be a matter of windage, sir. Even stripped of sail, bare masts and their mass of rigging can prove quite substantial enough to be seized by the gale. Many an ill-prepared ship has been rolled over in just such a fashion. Why even Nelson suffered that indignity before the Nile, and was near drowned in consequence. The captain and Mr Taylor know what they are about, but if you have finished your wine, we should go below and leave them to it.'

Macpherson's confidence in Clay and his sea officers was not misplaced, but preparing the ship for what lay ahead was a close-run thing. No sooner had the last spar been lashed into place on deck then the first gust of wind blasted across the bow, snapping at the little triangle of storm jib that had been set and flapping at Clay's oilskins. The blue sea and sunny sky of earlier was only visible as a distant land far astern of them. In its place a canopy of billowing cloud closed in above the frigate, while the sea grew to shifting mounds of bottle green. Lightning crackled across the sky, followed an instant later by a deafening boom of thunder and hissing rain descended on the *Griffin.* Just in time she hauled her bow around up into the teeth of the wind to ride out the gale.

Now powerful waves swept down on them, lifting the bow up and up, and then releasing the frigate to surge down the reverse side amid a welter of white foam.

'Hold her thus, Amos,' yelled Clay to the veteran quartermaster at the wheel over the shriek of the wind through the mizzen shrouds.

'Aye aye, sir,' replied the sailor, not shifting his gaze from the few tiny scraps of sail the frigate was showing, a bare minimum to keep her steady.

Another flash of lightning forked overhead and the rain fell in curtains of water. Clay battled his way forward across a quarterdeck that was awash. It surged over the deck with each roll of the ship and poured from out of the scuppers in torrents. From the rail he could look down on to the main deck. Most of the watch were huddling for shelter beneath the gangways. Further forward the bow of the frigate was lost in the downpour, but he could feel from her motion that all seemed well. He turned away from the rail at the very moment that the wind suddenly veered around.

The steady torrent of air from ahead was replaced by a warm blast, like the breath of a monster, rushing in from the portside. It rolled the frigate over, so that he staggard across the deck. With a chorus of groans from the hull, the lee rail dipped under the waves.

'Up helm!' he roared. 'Mr Harrison, let fly the sheets!'

The pitch of the deck continued to increase as the wind pushed the hull over, until Clay had to cling to the rail just to stay on his feet. A pair of carronade balls from the shot garland broke free and bowled across the deck to vanish into the sea beneath him, and for a moment he wondered if Taylor had managed to double breech all of the guns before the storm had hit. For a moment the *Griffin* hung there, the blast of the wind in balance with her ponderous bulk. He held his breath and then he sensed the angle of the deck ease a little as either the rudder bit at last, or the wind backed a touch. Little by little she paid off, heaving herself back upright like a surfacing whale, water pouring from her deck, and Clay breathed again. His ship would live for a little longer.

'Mr Harrison! Reset sail,' he bellowed, one hand cupped around his mouth. An arm waved in acknowledgement from amid the swarm of figures picking themselves up on the forecastle. From the lee scuppers beside Clay a small bedraggled figure limped over, his usual shock of blond hair a dark mass plastered across his face. 'Mr Todd, did you miss your footing? Are you hurt?'

'A little battered, sir, and my h … hat went by the board,' the boy replied. 'Will the s … ship roll over again?'

'These tropical storms can be damnedably unpredictable, but I live in hope it has done its worst,' Clay said, leaning close to be heard. He reached out to grab the midshipman's sodden arm. 'I need you to find Mr Taylor for me. I want a report on any damage, and the carpenter to sound the well. Repeat what you are to do?'

'Find Mr Taylor for a r … report, and Chips to sound the well, s … sir.'

'Good lad. Make haste now.'

'Aye aye, sir.'

'By Jove, that was close,' shouted Clay, as he rejoined Armstrong by the wheel. 'That wind must have backed three points in as many seconds! I trust Harte was able to clear my table in time, or I shall be sadly wanting in crockery this voyage.'

'Aye, a most unchristian buffeting, but the old girl did well, sir,' replied the American, patting the top of the binnacle. 'That would have done for many a ship, yet I don't mark anything of note that carried away.'

Clay looked around his command, surging through the worst of the storm, but holding her solid bow to the huge waves, safe for now. The wind howled about him and spray and rain lashed at his face.

A small figure appeared at the top of the companion ladder and made its way over the streaming deck towards him. 'Mr Taylor's compliments, sir, and he says two hogsheads have broken free in the hold, which Mr Preston is leading a party of men to attend to, but otherwise no major damage, and that there is a foot of water in the well. Also the surgeon reports one of the waisters has a broken arm.'

'Very good, Mr Todd. Ask Mr Taylor to have the larboard pump manned, after which you have my permission to go shift out of those wet clothes.'

'Aye aye sir,' said the youngster, disappearing once more.

The storm blew on for the rest of that day, and into the night, but without any more dangerous shifts in the wind. Around midnight the lightning moved away towards the north and it finally stopped raining. The wind was still as strong, continuing to shriek through the rigging and rattling at the mass of yards and masts lashed among the ship's boats on the skid beams. Clay stayed on deck the whole time, as watch followed watch, until dawn found him grey with weariness and every limb aching from the battle just to stand upright amid the worst of the gale. But as the first glimmer of pink flushed the eastern horizon, the wind began to moderate.

Lieutenant Blake was officer of the watch now, and he sniffed at the air. 'The weather eases a touch, I fancy, sir,' he offered.

Clay stirred his tired mind to look about him. In the growing light the sea was still angry and green, streaked with white where the wind tore at the wave crests, but the motion of the deck under his feet did feel a little easier. He crossed to the mizzen shrouds and placed a hand on them. They hummed against his fingers as if alive, but the note they made had dropped below the banshee-shriek of the storm's height.

'I believe so, John,' he croaked, his voice spent from a night of shouting. 'If it continues to moderate, we may be able to relight the galley. Some hot food would be most welcome.'

'Amen to that, sir,' agreed Blake, coming over to join his captain by the rail. Together they looked out over the ocean.

'Our ship lost among the violence of the sea would make a fine subject for one of your pictures,' suggested the captain.

'There is certainly a nobility to a rough, empty ocean, I grant you, sir, but I had thought to save my canvases for India. I particularly desire to paint an elephant.'

Clay smiled at this, and then frowned. 'Not entirely empty, Mr Blake. What do you make of that?' He pointed out to sea. 'A cable length off, level with the main mast.'

Blake followed where his captain was pointing. Something solid and straight lay amid the curving waves. 'It looks like some manner of beam.' He turned to the midshipman of the watch. 'Mr Sweeny, my spy glass, if you please.'

In the field of the telescope, and helped by the growing light, there could be little doubt what it was. Blake could make out where the two sections overlapped at a crosstree, and the halo of dark shrouds that hung like weed all around. He even fancied he could see the broken remains of a yard and the splintered end where the mast had been snapped clean through. He passed the telescope to his captain.

'The upper mast of a large ship, for certain, sir,' he reported. 'Torn down with some violence.'

'So I thought,' said Clay, examining the spar. 'It would seem we were not the only ones roughly handled by this gale.'

*****

By noon the storm had passed. The sea was deep blue once more, rising and falling to a calmer rhythm, and the sun shone down on the *Griffin*. She had her upper masts back in place and was spreading pyramids of canvas to the steady wind again. All the minor damage the storm had caused had been put to rights during the morning, and she was ready to face whatever lay beyond the horizon.

'Sail ho!' yelled the lookout who stood high on the fore royal yard.

'Where away?' called Preston from his place by the wheel.

'A point to looard of the bow, sir,' came the reply.

'What do you make of her, Biden?'

There was a pause while the lookout considered matters.

'I ain't rightly sure, sir. A ship from the size of her, but rigged very ill. Barely moving an' all. We be hauling her in hand over fist.'

'My respects to the captain, Mr Todd, and can you let him know that a ship is in sight off the bow.'

'Aye aye, sir,' replied the midshipman, touching the brim of a borrowed hat at least half an inch too big for him.

Clay came quickly up from his cabin with his telescope in one hand, still chewing on a mouthful of luncheon. 'Is she in sight from the deck yet, Mr Preston?'

'Aye, I have her now, sir,' said the lieutenant. 'Just proud of the lee cathead. Biden could make little out from her rig, and in truth I can't either.'

Clay focused on the spot where a single, tall mast rose above the horizon. It carried the broad square of a topsail, a tiny panel of something more solid against the white sky, but little else beside.

'Up you go with a glass, Mr Todd, and tell us what you make of her.'

'Aye aye, sir,' replied the youngster, crossing to the main shrouds and cramming his hat on a little tighter.

The *Griffin* was sailing considerably faster than the strange ship and soon the hull appeared over the horizon. Preston balanced his telescope on the mizzen shrouds. 'She is a man-of-war, I fancy, sir, but she lies very low in the water. I can see her mizzen up to the top, but nothing above. Is she the Frenchman we seek?'

'Perhaps,' said Clay. 'If so, she is listing badly.' He tilted his head back and hailed the masthead. 'What do you make of her, Mr Todd?'

'She's a frigate, sir. Much the size of us, but sadly battered. Her main mast has gone. She looks to have been in battle recently.'

'With what enemy, sir?' queried Preston.

'I'll wager she has passed through the same storm that we have,' said Clay. 'We were only just ready in time, manned with prime hands as we are. Had we an indifferent crew we might well have shed a mast when that squall hit. Show our colours and hoist the current recognition signal.'

As the *Griffin* came closer more detail was visible. The ship's stern was covered with an old sail lashed tightly into place, and Clay could see the remains of her main mast, a stump crowned with splinters. Severed shrouds hung down from the mainchains to trail in the sea. Her hull was so low that waves washed against the closed gun ports spaced along her side.

'Has she responded to our signal, Mr Preston?' asked Clay, watching her with his telescope.

'No, sir. Not yet.'

'Nor will she. No need to clear the ship for action, but have the watch below turned up and the guns manned, if you please.'

'You think her the *Marseillois*, sir?' asked Preston as the boatswain's call rang through the ship and the first of the crew came pouring up on to the main deck.

'I do. Mr Moore was very uncertain in his description of the frigate that visited Porto Praya just before we did, but in one particular he was more secure. He said that she had a red strake on her side, just as this ship has.'

Both men stepped away as the crews of the carronades came running along the gangway to cluster around each of the big, squat cannons. Taylor appeared, buckling on his sword, followed by Tom Macpherson at the head of his marines.

'Where would you like my men deployed, sir?' he asked. 'Sharpshooters in the tops, or are we to board her?'

'Draw them up here on the quarterdeck for the moment, if you please,' replied Clay. 'I don't anticipate much opposition from a ship that can't open her gunports without foundering.'

'Deck there!' yelled Todd from the masthead. 'The enemy is showing French colours!'

'We have found our chase, I collect, sir,' said Taylor, looking across at the other ship. 'Just in time, if I am not mistaken, for she seems on the point of sinking.'

Now they could see the weak stream of water being thrown to leeward by the *Marseillois* pumps, and a row of faces lining her stern rail, watching their approach. One of them waved his hat above his head, but whether in defiance or welcome wasn't clear.

'Have the larboard side guns run out, if you please, Mr Preston,' said Clay. 'Let us show her we are in earnest.'

'Larboards! Up ports!' ordered Blake, from his place down on the main deck. 'Run out the guns! Handsomely there!'

There was a thunderous roar as the line of big eighteen-pounders slid out into the sunlight. In response to the *Griffin* baring her teeth, the small tricolour in the *Marseillois*'s rigging came tumbling down and she lumbered up into the wind, her few sails flapping noisily. Some of the gun crews cheered, but most looked at each other, bemused by the speed of their victory.

'Mr Preston, back topsails a cable to windward of her, if you please. Mr Blake, kindly secure the guns, and I'll have the boats in the water,' said Clay, issuing a volley of orders as the *Griffin* closed with her capture.

'Aye aye, sir.'

'Now, George, you had best go across and take possession of her. I am not sure what you will find, so have Tom and his marines with you. I'll have the surgeon, boatswain and the carpenter ready to follow, depending on what you require. I would sooner save her if possible, but I cannot be long delayed by her.'

'I understand, sir,' said Taylor, touching his hat. 'I had better take one of the Channel Islanders across with me, although I dare say their officers will speak passable English.'

Clay watched as the longboat pulled away from the side of the frigate, and headed over the stretch of blue ocean that separated the two ships, followed shortly after by one of the cutters with a further contingent of men. The middle of each boat was packed with a double line of marines, their scarlet coats contrasting pleasingly with the colour of the sea, the fixed bayonets on their muskets twinkling in the sun. When they arrived at the *Marseillois* they swarmed up the side and over the rail, now conveniently low to the water. Taylor approached the group of officers on the quarterdeck, and after a brief conversation was led below by a tall figure in a captain's uniform, while the marines herded those sailors on deck into a group. After a brief while Taylor reappeared, took a speaking trumpet from beside the wheel, and came over to the rail.

'*Griffin* ahoy!'

'Make your report, Mr Taylor,' bellowed Clay through a speaking trumpet of his own.

'It's no good, sir. The main deck is awash already, one pump is choked with ballast, the other cannot stem the flow, and the captain tells me almost all their fresh water is spoiled.'

'How far away is the nearest friendly port, Mr Armstrong?'

'Recife in Brazil is within eight hundred miles, sir. The island of St Helena is more distant but has the virtue of lying on our route.'

'Too far to tow that hulk, in any case,' mused Clay.

'Very well, let us do what we must. Mr Preston, have the orlop deck cleared to receive prisoners.'

'Er, for how many, sir?' asked the lieutenant.

'Not above three hundred, I should say.'

'Three hund— Aye aye, sir.'

'It will be closer than Noah's ark down there,' chuckled the sailing master.

'I shouldn't seek for too much amusement in the situation, Mr Armstrong. The wardroom will have to accommodate their officers.' Clay left the American pondering this while he turned back towards the prize. 'Very well, Mr Taylor. Kindly have the crew transferred across, and when the *Marseillois* is empty, set fire to her.'

*****

'May I present Captain Vincent de Saint-Genest, sir, of the *Marseillois*,' said Taylor, ushering a thin, spare figure into the cabin. Clay rose to greet the prisoner and found himself looking at a man as tall as himself and of much the same age, but there the similarity ended. The Frenchman regarded him with sunken, tired eyes, rimmed in red. His chin was black with stubble and his uniform was torn and filthy.

'I am sorry for the loss of your ship, Captain,' said Clay, as he shook his hand.

The Frenchman shrugged in response. 'I was obliged to surrender, monsieur. I had already thrown all my guns over the side, and both my magazines are quite inundated with water; besides, my men were in no condition to resist. As for my poor *Marseillois*, that is not your doing but the fault of the storm. If your men had not set her on fire, then the waves would have claimed her.'

'Mr Taylor and I had our frigate founder in the last war after we engaged with your *Argonaute*, so we have some understanding as to how you may be feeling. It is very hard to lose a ship, but the pain does pass in time. Be seated, I beg. A glass of wine?'

'*Merci*, Captain, that would be most welcome.'

'Would you be kind enough to share the particulars as to how the *Marseillois* came to be in the sad condition in which we found her?' asked Clay, when they were all seated. 'I ask for no intelligence as to your mission, of course.'

'I left France with a new crew, barely fifty of whom had ever been out of sight of land before,' explained Saint-Genest. 'The rest were all landsmen and boys. I started to drill them the moment we cleared Brest, but the weather was good for much of the voyage, which was no preparation for what lay ahead.'

'We say in our navy that calm seas make for poor sailors,' said Clay.

'That is all too true, monsieur. We were barely a week out from the Cape Verde islands when a fierce storm came up from the south. I did my best to prepare but we still had too much top hamper when it reached us. A gust caught us aback, rolling us over and breaking off the main mast. While we fought to cut it loose, my poor ship was dragged around by the wreckage until she was stern on to the waves.' Saint-Genest paused, fighting back his emotions, before turning his haunted eyes towards Clay. 'Have you ever been pooped, Captain?' he asked.

'Never, in truth.'

'It is terrible,' said the Frenchman. He pointed towards the run of window lights at the rear of the cabin. 'Glass and a few carvings?' he said. 'What can they do to resist the anger of the sea? Waves smashed straight into my ship, washing across the decks like the tide on a beach and pouring into the hold. Then the real battle began, pumping day and night, throwing everything we could over the side to lighten the ship. We did all this while still fighting the storm, and the knowledge that should we fail, there was no land within a thousand kilometres of us.'

'Terrible indeed,' said Clay quietly, and the three sailors were silent as they pictured the chaos that must have followed during that dark night.

Eventually Clay put his glass down and smiled at his prisoner. 'At least your men are safe now. Captain. If you have any questions to ask, pray do so.'

'May I know what the future holds for my crew?

'That is a large question which I can only answer in part. We are making for St Helena, where I shall disembark you and your men to the care of the garrison, after which I cannot say. But while you are on board this ship, I would be honoured if you would make free to dine with me in this cabin?'

'You are too kind,' said Saint-Genest, bowing in his seat.

'The only other requirement I have is for the names and details of your crew, so that we can send word of their fate to the authorities in France.'

'I have prepared the list here with the captain's assistance, sir,' said Taylor, passing across a sheaf of papers. 'In addition to the crew, the *Marseillois* carried a number of supernumeraries.'

Clay reached out for the list but found that his first lieutenant held on to it for a moment longer than was necessary, until his captain met his eyes.

'Thank you, Mr Taylor,' he said, rising to his feet. 'I shall see you later, Captain.'

The moment Clay was alone he scanned the list. 'Well, I'll be damned,' he muttered. 'Harte! My compliments to Mr Vansittart, and would you ask him to join me.'

'Always a pleasure to visit the echoing vastness of space afforded to a captain on board his ship,' said the diplomat, turning around in mock awe in the centre of the great cabin. 'Your carpenter is currently changing the tiny box that passes for my accommodation into one that I can share with Mr Taylor.'

'Only for a week or so, while we have so many prisoners to accommodate,' said Clay. 'But on the subject of prisoners, I wanted to discuss with you the list of persons we have captured.'

'Most diverting, I am sure,' muttered Vansittart, taking a seat.

'The surviving members of the crew form the bulk of the names, but we have also captured a number of civilians,' said Clay, leafing through the list. 'Sawyers, foundrymen, riggers, blacksmiths, carpenters, loftsmen, coppersmiths, augermen and shipwrights.'

'A fine list of trade persons,' said his guest, brushing some dust from the upper of his crossed legs. 'And what, pray is their significance?'

'The *Marseillois*, we may assume, has been sent to reinforce Admiral Linois's squadron that left Brest at the start of the year,' said Clay.

'Almost certainly.'

'Then perhaps these professions may shed some light on what his object may be,' said Clay, holding the list up.

'I am not sure that I follow, Captain,' said the diplomat.

'This list contains all the shipyard trades that you would require if you wished to construct a fleet of warships.'

Chapter 7
India

It was late September when the *Griffin* stood in towards the port of Bombay. She had left the crew of the *Marseillois* back on St Helena, an ocean and many thousands of long sea miles behind her. She had rounded the Cape of Good Hope in the midst of the antipodean winter, the slab of Table Mountain lost amid the roaring waves and veiled by rain squalls. Then she had entered the Indian Ocean and headed north, the weather growing steadily warmer and the sea acquiring a deeper note of sapphire with each successive week. Now the horizon in front of her was dominated by rolling hills, lush and green after the monsoon. At their feet lay the fortified city of Bombay on a long peninsula that ran out from the coast like a protective arm around a large sheltered bay.

The deck of the frigate thronged with every idler who could find an excuse to be there, all eager for a first glimpse of mysterious India. Up on the forecastle the few hands who had visited the country before spoke airily to their shipmates of snake charmers on every street corner and elephants as common as dray horses back home. On the quarterdeck all the telescopes were in use as the frigate's officers stared towards the land.

'Would that be a minaret, abaft the foremast, rising proud of those palm trees?' Preston asked Charles Faulkner, who had squeezed his way to a place at the rail beside him.

'Very like,' replied the purser, shading his eyes and

squinting in the bright sun. 'Perhaps if you might lend me your glass, Edward, I could confirm the matter?' He extended his hand towards his colleague, fingers flexing in anticipation.

'Presently, Charles, when I have completed my observations,' replied Preston. 'The city itself must open on to the bay, for it presents only walls and bastions to the world on this side.'

'I believe I can see the flag flying above Fort George and a quantity of shipping in the bay,' said Blake, from Faulkner's other side.

'That's a deal more than I can damned well see,' muttered the purser, looking peevishly from one lieutenant to the other.

Preston turned from the rail and lowered his telescope. 'Would you care to borrow my—'

'Much obliged,' snapped Faulkner, grabbing the instrument. Detail leapt closer as he swept the shore. Turbaned figures, stripped to the waist, working the fields with mattocks among the feathery palms. A pair of graceful women in brilliant-coloured saris, swaying down a track with brass water pots balanced on their heads. A queue of heavily laden carts drawn by humped bullocks waiting their turn to pass through a gate in the wall that surrounded the town. 'Truly fascinating!' he exclaimed. 'Why even the cattle are of a different character.'

'It will be good to feel some honest Christian soil beneath my feet at last,' commented Vansittart from further along the rail. 'Not that your society hasn't been agreeable this last half year, gentlemen, but a change is a rest, as they say.'

'Christian soil, sir?' queried Preston. 'I fear you may be adrift in your reckoning. Hindoo or Mohammedan soil is closer to the mark, I fancy.'

'What I chiefly crave is some fresh meat,' said Blake.

'We haven't had anything beyond salt beef and pork since we left Porto Praya. Last night I found myself dreaming it was Christmas, and that my father was carving a prodigiously large goose.'

'Och! A goose!' exclaimed Macpherson. 'I would trade my commission for such a feast.'

'Mr Faulkner, you will be going ashore to secure provisions for the frigate, I make no doubt?' asked Vansittart.

'I shall, sir. Just as soon as we are moored,' replied the purser.

'Then among your purchases, might you acquire a good-sized bird for the wardroom table, if they have geese in these parts? I will pay for it, and we can invite the captain to share our repast to mark our safe arrival.'

'Capital notion, sir,' enthused Faulkner. 'Most obliging of you. You may consider it done.'

In the time it had taken the wardroom to plan their next meal, the frigate had rounded Kolaba Point with its ruined fort and had entered the bay. The blue sea was behind them, replaced by brown water fed by two big rivers. It was crowded with shipping: big stately Indiamen, with striped sides as if they were warships; solid brigs with squared yards, moored beside delicate trading dhows with triangular lateen sails. Further along the shore lay Bombay, open to the sea on this side, with its bustling jetties and wharfs crowded with people among the stacked bales and mounds of sacks. The waterfront was dominated by a big square building, with the red and white striped flag of the East India Company rippling over it. Further off was Bombay Castle, a modern fortress and then the big squat mass of Fort George.

'Over there is a frigate and a two-decker with an admiral's duster at the forepeak, sir,' reported Taylor.

'That will be the *Trident*, sixty-four,' said Clay. 'Flagship of Admiral Rainer, who commands in the East Indies. You are acquainted with him, are you not, George?'

'I was fourth lieutenant under him back when he commanded the *Suffolk*, sir. He kept a prodigiously good table, as I recall.'

'Make ready to salute the flag then, Mr Taylor, if you please. Mr Vansittart, are you ready for us to report to the admiral?'

'I need only go below and shift into my better coat and collect some dispatches.'

'Send our number, and begin the salute, if you please, Mr Taylor.'

In a steady series of bangs the salute was fired, each one echoed by the *Trident*. Just as the final puff of smoke blew away towards the mainland, a row of flags broke out high on the two-decker's mizzen.

'Flag to *Griffin*. Welcome. Captain to report on board when convenient.'

'Clear away the barge!' roared Taylor, while Clay felt inside his full dress coat to check that his report on the voyage out and the dispatches he had brought from home were there. Reassured by the crackle of parchment against his fingers, he made his way towards the entry port. His barge crew were gathered in a line and were being checked over by Sedgwick. All were dressed in spotless white trousers and shirts, the seams decorated with green ribbons that matched the oar blades and coloured strake on the barge. On every head was a broad-brimmed straw hat with a ribbon around the crown on which *Griffin* was picked out in white letters.

'All well here, Sedgwick?' asked Clay.

'The lads may bring a little credit to the barky,' admitted

the coxswain grudgingly, 'so long as they don't row too ill. Shall we be away, sir?'

'We need to wait for Mr Vansittart.'

'It'll never do to be late, sir!' exclaimed Sedgwick. 'That admiral will have marked the boat is in the water, for certain. Abbott, Rodgers, go an' fetch the Hollander, the rest of you over the side.'

'Aye aye, cox.'

It was no more than a moment before Vansittart appeared, struggling into his coat between the two burly sailors. 'Unhand me, there!' he protested, looking from one to the other. 'Why this unseemly haste? Is the ship a fire, or about to sink?'

'Admirals can be touchy in my experience, if they feel they are being neglected, sir,' said Clay, gesturing towards the entry port, while keeping his face grave against the grin he felt tugging at his mouth.

'Five damned months it took to get here,' muttered the diplomat as he climbed down the frigate's side. 'One might think another five minutes to complete my toilet wouldn't signify.'

The moment Clay took his place in the stern sheets the barge was away, the crew bending their oars in their haste to make up for lost time as they arrowed towards the tall side of the *Trident*. Beyond her Clay could see a broad estuary disappearing to the east, the banks of the looping river quilted with little square fields between earth embankments and dotted with villages of brown thatched building. Further back were rolling, forest-covered hills, marked in places by cliffs and outcrops of brown rock.

'Do you know much about Admiral Rainer, then?' asked Vansittart, bringing him back to the present.

'Very little beyond his reputation, sir. Mr Taylor has

fond memories of his bounteous table, and I am aware that he has commanded in these waters for a good while.'

'More than a decade,' confirmed the diplomat. 'Even though this is a plum station that many covet, thanks to the unique opportunities the East offers to line one's own pocket, what?'

'So why has he proved so durable?'

'Because while he may have the appearance of a portly tavernkeeper, there are few men who understand the East better. He has the reputation of being a damned shrewd cove. We must attend to what he has to say, Captain.'

'Boat ahoy!' came the hail from the *Trident*.

'*Griffin*!' replied Sedgwick, holding three fingers aloft to confirm that a post captain was coming aboard. Moments later the barge swept up alongside. 'Easy all! Larboards, in oars. Clap on in the bow.'

Once the boat was nestled under the steps, Clay and Vansittart made their way up the side of the flagship.

*****

The victualling yard at Bombay was an odd mix of the strange and the familiar, decided Charles Faulkner, as he waited patiently by the open window in the superintendent's office. It was a modest affair when compared with the long wharfs and packed warehouses of Plymouth and Portsmouth, but the layout and buildings were much the same. On the far side of the stone-flagged courtyard he could see the dark interior of a cooperage, lit with glowing fire where barrel hoops were being heated. But in place of the leather-caped workers of home he could see turbaned Indians at work on a new hogshead. His view was then obscured by the broad, leathery side of an elephant as it shambled past pulling a cart under the urgings of a rider perched on the animal's neck.

'Not quite Deptford creek, Mr Faulkner, but you will find we are efficient enough in our way,' said the superintendent, coming in through the office door. He was a thin, spare man with a face burnt dark by the tropical sun which made his blue eyes piercing in contrast. 'My name is Bradshaw. Apologies for keeping you waiting.'

'No matter, Mr Bradshaw. In truth I was enjoying the diversion of so many new sights and sounds.'

'Most of those from home are similarly affected. It passes soon enough, mind. By the by, is that young lieutenant with you?' The superintendent indicated where a figure sat on a barrel, a sketch book on his knee, working furiously.

'He is, Mr Bradshaw. That is Mr Blake, second on my ship, and an artist of repute.'

'And is your friend content to remain outside?'

'Perfectly so. He is drawing one of your elephants, something he has desired to do since we left Plymouth Sound.'

'He should take care not to remain there too long. The sun hereabouts is prodigiously fierce, particularly for those unaccustomed to it. Now, what can I do for you?'

'I wish to indent for some fresh supplies,' said Faulkner. 'I have my requirements here.'

He passed across the list and Bradshaw surveyed it. 'Hmm, in the round I can supply all of your wants, so long as you are willing to accept substitutes in one or two cases.'

'Substitutes?' queried the purser.

'Beef, for example, is not to be had in these parts. The slaughtering of cattle enrages the Hindoos, and for much the same reason pork is also hard to come by. Mutton is what sailors chiefly consume in the Indies, unless you prefer buffalo?'

'Mutton will be fine. What other changes do you propose?'

'The ardent spirit of the East is arrack, which is passing similar to rum, and as for fresh provisions they will need to be of local source. Otherwise, I see no problems. I can send it all across by lighter first thing in the morning, if that will suit?'

'Much obliged Mr Bradshaw,' said Faulkner. 'I also need to purchase provisions for the wardroom and my captain. Would you be able to recommend a suitable chandler?'

'Hmm, let me think. I normally direct such enquiries towards Lloyd and Nicolson, but Mr Lloyd recently perished from the ague and Mr Nicolson is upcountry at present. But no matter, there are several reputable Persian merchants who can supply your wants in Bombay. The ones I have in mind have good contacts with the Portuguese in Goa. I make no doubt you will be wanting port wine and a pipe or two of madeira?'

'Among other requirements, yes,' confirmed the purser. 'Where might I find these merchants?'

Bradshaw rang a small brass bell on his desk. In response a clerk in a white robe came into the office. 'Sahib?'

'Ah, Ali, would you be so kind as to take Mr Faulkner to Nagpada Street and introduce him to Mr Godrej and Mr Morawalla with my compliments?'

'Thank you kindly, Mr Bradshaw,' said Faulkner standing up and collecting his hat. 'I will bid you a good day.'

Outside the purser collected his friend from his place on the barrel. 'Come along John, leave the oliphant be. We are off on an adventure, into the heart of the city proper. Ali here is to be our guide.'

The clerk gave a bow at his name and gestured towards the entrance to the yard, where sepoys in scarlet jackets stood guard with shouldered muskets. After they passed them, the two young officers were drawn into another world.

In the middle of the settlement was an open square, overlooked by many of the East India Company buildings that lined the waterfront. It was packed with a bazaar with row after row of little stalls, each under a sheltering canopy. The lanes between them bustled with people, while a kaleidoscope of sights whirled around the officers as they followed Ali across to the far side. Hawkers barked out the virtues of their wares, sliding from one language to another depending on the dress and look of a potential customer. One stall had open sacks heaped with brilliantly coloured spices that filled the air with their fragrance. The next had a wall of cages, each containing a live chicken blinking uncertainly at the world. Others had piles of fruit, glossy red mangoes beside hands of tiny yellow bananas, miniature versions of the huge plantains the officers were familiar with from the Caribbean. Noise, colour, smell and people crowded so close about them, that the officers felt overwhelmed. It was a relief when they left the market and followed their guide into a quieter lane.

'God bless my soul,' gasped Faulkner, mopping at his brow. 'That was packed tighter than the Pleasure Gardens of Vauxhall!'

'How I would love to try and paint it,' enthused Blake, 'But I doubt I have the skill for the undertaking. There is too much movement and bustle for any picture to capture.'

'Not so busy, Sahib,' corrected Ali. 'Now quiet. Just after dawn, when all is fresh. That is when most persons go. Street we want is this way.'

He shot off down another narrow lane and then abruptly turned in at an open doorway. Faulkner followed and found he was in a large shop, surrounded by boxes and bundles stacked against the walls. Behind a counter at the back was an arch leading through into a substantial warehouse. Two middle-aged men rose from some cushions on the floor and came across. Both were dressed in long robes of embroidered cloth. One man had a large beard covering much of his chest, while the other favoured a bristling moustache. Ali spoke in a rapid flow, in which only the officer's names, that of 'Sahib Bradshaw' and what sounded like a valiant stab at the name *Griffin* stood out.

Eventually he turned to the two Englishmen. 'This Mr Godrej,' he explained. The bearded man bowed low. 'And this Mr Morawalla.'

'May Guardian Yazad grant you long living,' offered his colleague, bowing in turn.

'Er, thank you kindly, sir,' said Faulkner, returning the bow. 'The same to you gentlemen, naturally.'

'Only Mr Morawalla speaks the English,' explained Ali. 'If all well, I go now?'

'By all means,' said Blake. 'Our thanks to you.' Ali touched his forehead and then his lips before he left them.

'How to help you gentling men?' asked Mr Morawalla, with a smile. Mr Godrej slipped behind the counter and drew a blank sheet of paper towards him. He then flipped open a brass inkwell shaped like a flaming pot and waited expectantly.

'I hoped that you might supply some provisions to my ship,' explained Faulkner. 'I have the particulars here.' He pulled a list from his coat pocket and passed it across.

Mr Morawalla studied the document politely for a moment, stroking his moustache all the while, and then returned it with a smile. 'Parsi, Arabic and Sanskrit I know, but not your English letters. So sorry. You can say for me?'

'Of course,' said Faulkner, recovering his list and

reading off the items. The process went reasonably smoothly, with only the occasional bit of pantomime required from the officers before Mr Morawalla smiled in recognition and barked out the Parsi name for his colleague to record.

‘So that is the candles,’ muttered Faulkner, scoring off another line. ‘Which just leaves the matter of the goose. We shall require a nice big one.’

‘Gooses? What is this gooses?’ queried the merchant.

‘Ah, let me see if I can show you,’ said the purser. After a moment of thought he extended his arm into the long neck of a bird, the fingers clenched towards Mr Morawalla, and he then pecked at him, emitting an angry hiss all the while. Mr Morawalla stepped back in alarm.

‘A cobra?’ queried Mr Godrej in Parsi to his colleague. ‘What can these barbarians want with a cobra?’

‘They are all quite mad,’ said his partner, in the same language. ‘Do not the Chinese eat of the snake? Perhaps they do as well?’ He watched the purser hiss and peck a little more, before inspiration came to him. ‘But wait! Perhaps he shows that he fears the snake! Ah, I think I may understand this gooses!’ He switched back to English. ‘You want mongoose?’

‘Moon goose?’ queried Faulkner, looking at his colleague. ‘That does sound right.’

‘I certainly know of a snow goose, and the domestic ones are chiefly white,’ observed Blake. ‘Perhaps their fowl are of a silvery colour?’

‘If that is what the creature is called hereabouts, Mr Morawalla, that is what we require,’ confirmed the purser. ‘A big plump one. Alive for preference.’

‘Yes, of course alive,’ said the merchant.

‘Perhaps it could be caged, like the chickens we passed in the market on the way here.’

'That would be prudent,' agreed Mr Morawalla. 'I can find for you. Some persons in the villages keep them to protect house.'

'Aye, a better watch keeper than a mastiff is your angry goose,' agreed Blake. 'As a boy I was taught that Rome was saved from the barbarians by the blighters making so much noise they awoke the citizenry.'

'The Romanie, they have mongoose also?' queried the merchant, with raised eyebrows. 'This I was not knowing. No matter. All you have asked for I can supply, sirs.'

*****

The great cabin of the *Trident* was unlike any admiral's quarters Clay had experienced. There was a herbal smell that he struggled to place, overlaying the usual shipboard odours of warm tar and bilge water. The oak planking underfoot was covered by richly patterned silk rugs and the furniture was elaborately carved from tropical woods. In one corner there was a substantial hookah pipe on a stand, the deck around it dominated by large cushions. In the opposite corner sat an immensely fat man behind a desk. From the décor, Clay had half-expected Rainer to be dressed in a turban and silk robes. It was something of a relief to find him dressed in an admiral's uniform with a periwig perched on his shaven head. He looked up from his work and studied the new arrivals with eyes made owlishly large by the round heavy-framed spectacles he wore.

'Welcome to the Orient, Captain,' he said, rising from his chair. 'I take it from your presence in these waters that we are at war with France once more?'

'We are indeed, sir,' said Clay, grasping the proffered hand. 'Although I only learned of it when I touched at the Cape

Verde islands. The declaration was made in May, just after we left Plymouth.'

'Not before time, if you ask me,' said Rainer. 'Although here in India the last war never truly ended, what with the damned French conspiring with every nabob with an ear for their lies. I take it this gentleman is the Honourable Nicholas Vansittart?'

'Delighted to make your acquaintance, Admiral,' said the diplomat, taking his hand.

'Yours too, sir. London told me I was to expect you. Do be seated, gentlemen.'

'I have my report on my journey out, sir,' said Clay, passing a bundle of envelopes across, 'together with dispatches from the Admiralty for you.'

'Always a pleasure to receive orders from home,' sighed Rainer. 'They are never less than six months out of date, of course, so seldom of any value, but their lordships still persist.'

'I was told that Boney was contemplating digging a canal across the desert when he was in Egypt,' said Vansittart. 'Regrettably we cut his little expedition there short, but perhaps we should have waited for him to complete the dashed thing. It might have proved useful, if only to expedite the mail.'

'You will find that we India hands rather enjoy the opportunities distance affords out here, Mr Vansittart,' smiled the admiral. 'With no prospect of seeking the counsel of our superiors, we are free to shift for ourselves. Would you excuse me while I peruse these?' he said, indicating the dispatches. 'Marshal, some refreshment for my guests.'

The admiral's steward slid a tray between the two men. 'A glass of madeira, sir? That is sugared mango in the bowl, while the biscuits are made with rice flour.'

Clay just took the madeira and sat back to sip at his drink, watching Rainer. Vansittart was right when he described him as resembling a portly tavernkeeper, but there was plainly more to him than met the eye. For one thing, he was reading through the dispatches at an astonishing rate, skimming each page before passing them to his clerk with a few whispered instructions.

The admiral had finished his reading long before his guests' glasses needed refilling. 'So you come here on the coat tails of Monsieur Linois?' he said, his eyes shrinking to normal size as he removed his spectacles to polish them with a silk handkerchief.

'Have you had contact with his squadron, Admiral?' asked Vansittart.

'Indeed,' said Rainer, putting his glasses back into place. 'I met with him in July, off Pondicherry. He came demanding the return of the fort and the French factory there. I had been expecting such a move on the part of the French, and had much of my fleet gathered to oppose him. He was quite within his rights, of course. The return was part of the peace treaty that ended the last war, but I'll be damned if we were going to turn the place over without a specific order from London.'

'What happened?' asked Vansittart. 'Was there a battle?'

'No need for such expedients,' said Rainer. 'I outnumbered him two to one, so instead he tried a typical French ruse. He invited me to breakfast on the morrow to resolve matters, and then slipped away during the night.'

'Might he attempt something against Pondicherry in your absence, sir?' suggested Clay. 'He has a considerable body of troops on board.'

'He might try, but I have left sufficient force on that coast to oppose such a move. No, I fancy he has some other object in mind. I had thought that he might try and intervene in the war that has broken out between John Company and the Marathas, but that is mainly an inland affair, and young Arthur Wellesley seems to have matters in hand. Dashed good general, by the way. The day Horse Guards sees sense and ships him home to fight the Frogs will be a sorry one for Boney.'

'If Linois cannot make a move on Pondicherry, or make a telling intervention in this war with the Mara-whatevers, what do you suppose he is about?' asked Vansittart.

'His squadron has only once been sighted, by a neutral merchantman close to their island of Reunion, but that was a month back. My nose tells me that they have been up to something, which brings me on to your report, Captain.' The admiral held up a page, as if in evidence. 'I must confess, I was intrigued by what you found on board this *Marseillois*.'

'Spare me all these dashed woodcutters again!' protested Vansittart. 'You naval coves seem obsessed with them.'

'You dismiss them at your peril, sir,' said Rainer. 'Consider, what purpose does it serve the enemy to send such artisans to India?'

'Why, to build ships, of course,' said the diplomat. 'Captain Clay explained it to me after we captured them, with some thoroughness, I might add.'

'To build ships, for sure. But why do so here?' continued Rainer, bringing a single podgy finger down on the top of his desk. 'Boney has shipyards enough already. Why, he controls half the ports in Europe! If it is building ships that he is after, he can surely accomplish it with far more ease at home. Why send valuable workers on a hazardous journey halfway around the world?'

'Lord only knows,' said Vansittart, his arms spread wide.

'Might it be the price of allegiance demanded by one of the native rulers hereabouts, sir?' asked Clay.

'Bravo, Captain,' beamed Rainer. 'I see your reputation in the service for sagacity is not misplaced. There is little that we Europeans have to offer the East by way of inducements. Certainly not wealth, for they have riches enough to pauper King Midas. But the one thing they all covet is our ascendancy in the matter of war, if only to give them the power to resist us. And a native state in possession of a fleet of modern warships would be a very grave matter indeed.'

'Then it is well that we took the *Marseillois*, and her troublesome cargo, what?' said Vansittart.

The two naval officers exchanged glances.

'A setback for the enemy, I don't doubt, but we cannot be so sanguine, sir,' said Rainer. 'To judge from the numbers that you captured, they were intended to reinforce an existing endeavour. No, I think the main part will have come out in the summer with Linois, in which case they have already been here for several months, passing on their skills and training up the natives. But if they have, they have been doing so in secret, for I have heard nothing of such activity.'

'So where are they, then?' demanded Vansittart.

'Now, let me consider,' said Rainer, rubbing at his temples. He glanced with longing towards the hookah pipe before opting to lean back in his protesting chair, lacing his fingers behind his large head. 'This sort of mischief making I would normally place at the door of Mysore or the Marathas, but General Wellesley defeated Tipu Sultan in short order a few years back, and is keeping the Marathas busy for now. Bengal and most of the states on the east coast John Company controls, which leaves somewhere on the Malabar coast, for sure, but who? Who?'

There was a moment of silence, and then Rainer's chair returned to all four legs with a thump. The large round eyes sparkled with pleasure. 'But of course! Travancore!'

'Travancore, sir?' queried Clay.

'Have you not heard of it?'

'Never, in truth. Where is it to be found, sir?'

'To the south of here,' explained Rainer. 'It is a substantial state with a deuced good army, trained up by the Dutch. Rich too, thanks to the trade in sandalwood, cloves and ivory. The previous ruler, Dharma Raja, was a solid ally of ours, but he passed away four years ago to be replaced by a boy named Balarama Varma. From all I hear, he is weak as a kitten. His chief minister Velu Thampi is the true power behind the throne.'

'And what makes you think that it might be these blighters?' asked Vansittart.

'Because it comes to my mind that this Velu Thampi approached us a few years back,' said Rainer. 'With some rot about a big coastal state like Travancore needing to have a modern navy, and asking for our help to set one up. We naturally refused the request. The last thing we need is a powerful native fleet, able to attack John Company ships at will. But they may well have approached the French with the same request, and found them altogether more accommodating.'

'I do believe the time has come for us to pay a visit to this young whippersnapper of a raja and remind him of his obligations to us,' said Vansittart.

'Yes, but be guided by the John Company resident there,' cautioned the admiral. 'Major Macauley is a shrewd cove. Poor chap spent two years imprisoned in Tipu Sultan's dungeon until Wellesley stormed the place and freed him, but he is an old India hand.'

'He sounds a touch more useful than that soak Moore in Porto Praya, sir,' commented Clay to Vansittart.

'I shall write to the governor-general in Calcutta and let him know what you are about,' continued Rainer. 'I fear I can offer you but little in the way of military support. The army are all tied up fighting the Marathas, and I must support them from the sea, in addition to guarding Pondicherry. You have the *Griffin*, of course, but in truth, this strikes me as a situation where persuasion may answer better than force.'

'London thought the same, hence my presence here,' said the diplomat, pulling one coat sleeve straight.

'Indeed, the orders you brought me are to afford you considerable latitude,' said Rainer. 'But I doubt that will come as a surprise to you.'

'I may have had a hand in their composition,' said Vansittart, with a modest smile.

'Very well,' said the admiral, rising to his feet and extending his hand. 'Then it only remains to wish you gentlemen good fortune and, if I may, some advice. Proceed with caution. We are overextended at present. The last thing we need is a fresh war on the Malabar coast.'

Chapter 8
Napoleon

When at sea, the wardroom of the *Griffin* was a dark, cramped little chamber. Set at the very stern of the frigate and tucked beneath the captain's quarters, it was only just above the waterline, which meant both of its stern ports, the only source of natural light, had to be kept securely bolted. Lined by tiny cabins, it was dominated by a table that ran the length of the space at which the officers spent much of their leisure time. But even when off duty, there was little escape from the workings of the ship. The base of the *Griffin*'s mizzen mast, thick as a mature ash tree, plunged through the centre of the room, transmitting the constant hum of taut rigging and straining canvas. Above the officers' heads the ship's tiller groaned and creaked as it was drawn to and fro with each turn of the wheel. And beyond the door was the throb of the lower deck, constant as a hive, where most of the frigate's two hundred and fifty crew slept and ate, laughed and cried, danced and sang.

But today the wardroom was transformed. The *Griffin* was safely moored in the sheltered waters of Bombay, which meant that both stern ports had been flung open to let in sunlight, a fresh sea breeze and the delightful view. The table sparkled with polished glassware and silver cutlery, borrowed from the captain's steward. Around the table sat the ship's officers, together with Vansittart and their captain, while behind each chair was a servant. There was already a lively conversation in progress, fuelled by wine that had been cooled to just below the temperature of blood by lowering the bottles over the side at dawn and leaving them beneath the water until required.

'Goodness, but it's hot,' said Preston, running a finger around his neckcloth.

'And we have the advantage of being upon the water,' said Blake. 'When Mr Faulkner and I ventured into the city yesterday it was warmer than Hades, but I confess I would not have missed it for the world. I found my first elephant!'

'I give you joy of your beast, John,' said Macpherson, his face almost a match for his marine tunic. 'A glass of wine with you, sir.'

'Given the conditions, I believe we might dispense with our coats without imperilling discipline, gentlemen,' suggested Clay.

'Hear him! Hear him!' roared the company in approval, and there was a general peeling off of broadcloth and unfastening of buttons.

When the officers were seated again in shirt-sleeves, the conversation resumed.

'I wish I could offer the prospect of some relief from the heat,' continued Clay, 'but Mr Taylor tells me that the southern end of the Malabar coast, where we are bound, is considerably hotter.'

'I fear that is so, sir,' agreed the first lieutenant. 'I only ventured there the once, some years back, but damnably hot is my recollection.'

'What sort of place is it, George?' asked Blake.

'If the heat don't vex you, rather agreeable. Green and lush as it comes, and very fertile, with plenty of stretches of sandy beaches.'

Upon the Malabar Coast

'The place we are bound for is named Travancore, a large native state that dominates the area,' explained Clay. 'They have generally been good friends to the British, particularly when we were fighting Mysore, their traditional enemy, but of late they seem to have been moving closer to the French.'

'Is that where Admiral Linois and his squadron will have gone?' asked Macpherson.

'Quite possibly,' confirmed Clay. 'At least that is the belief of Admiral Rainer. We leave in the morning to discover more, and put an end to any scheme of Boney's we may uncover.'

'Hear him!' agreed the company, rapping their fists on the table top. The noise blended into the sound of the door banging open and the entrance of Britton, the wardroom steward, at the head of a line of sailors bearing steaming dishes.

'A brace of roasted capons!' he announced, 'with rice an' all manner of greens.'

'So I see,' said Armstrong, peering into a dish of brazed ladyfingers. 'What, pray, are these?' he asked, holding one of the pods up for inspection.

'None too certain as to some of the stranger vittles, sir,' replied the steward, 'Many of which I ain't clapped eyes on afore today, but they seem wholesome enough.'

'How did you know their method of preparation?' queried Taylor.

'It were something of a poser, in truth, so I called in one of the lascars in the starboard watch, sir. Jamali Jim gave me a hand, in exchange for half a ration of baccy.'

'Well, it all smells delicious,' said Vansittart, as he accepted a plate loaded with food. 'But I was under the impression that we planned to feast on a goose? Did I not understood you to say that you had obtained one, Mr Faulkner?'

'As indeed I had,' said the purser. 'Mr Blake can bear witness. Yet when the boat of wardroom supplies arrived from Mr Morawalla, none was present, and I was obliged to send for these capons instead.'

'Have you been handing the wardroom's modest funds over to some cheating blackguard, Charles?' asked Taylor.

'But that's just it,' protested Faulkner. 'Mr Morawalla came recommended, and in every other respect his provisions are quite satisfactory, if a little unfamiliar.'

'I saw the whole episode,' supplemented Blake. 'Charles gave a passing imitation of the bird, and the chap claimed to know what he wanted. Even named it a moon goose.'

'No word of explanation, or substitute of any kind?' asked Vansittart.

'None, save a deuced odd-looking creature in a cage. Some manner of polecat, I believe.'

'How extraordinary!' exclaimed Clay.

Richard Corbett, the frigate's surgeon, leant forward in his seat and cleared his throat. 'I believe I may perceive the confusion here. The solution would appear to lie within the realms of natural philosophy. Tell me, Charles, was this creature somewhat larger than your regular polecat? With grey fur?'

'He was indeed.'

'And a long tail, perchance?'

'Precisely so.'

'Quick and lively in his motions?'

'Why you astound me, sir!' exclaimed Faulkner. 'The very creature. Can you identify it?'

'I believe Mr Blake's purchase is more commonly

known as a mongoose,' explained the surgeon, his eyes glittering with triumph behind his little round spectacles, not unlike those of the animal he had in mind. 'They are common in these parts, and much prized by the locals on account of their partiality for dispatching serpents. I understand they rely on astonishing speed to avoid the strike of their victims and the more venomous the opponent, the better pleased they seem.'

'A mongoose and not a moon goose, you say?' queried Blake. 'Now I reflect, that does seem to be how Mr Morawalla named it. We thought it to be but the local term for your regular goose.'

'It seems clear who the only regular goose present is,' muttered Vansittart to his neighbour.

'If you care to produce the creature, I can make a positive identification,' offered Corbett.

'Ah, that may be difficult,' confessed Faulkner.

'Difficult? How so?' asked Taylor. 'Where is the animal now?'

'I am not entirely sure,' confessed the purser. 'You see, it seemed rather an affectionate fellow, and the cage was quite small, so I let it out in my cabin. Only for a moment, to be sure, and at first it was perfectly docile. Then my servant chanced to open the door, whereupon it displayed all the rapidity of motion Mr Corbett spoke of. Vanished in an instant, and I have not laid eyes on it since.'

'You mean that it is loose in the ship?' said Taylor. 'A damned polecat, befouling my decks!'

'A damned mongoose befouling your decks,' corrected Macpherson, to general laughter.

'I believe that this Mr Morawalla may have done us all a considerable service, gentlemen,' said Corbett.

'How so, doctor?' asked Taylor.

'By sparing us from a most imprudent indulgence. Why, gorging on the unctuous fat of a goose in this heat would be most injurious to health. An ill-considered meal in the tropics can be quite as lethal as the bullet, you know. India is perilous enough without the need to add to those risks. We can count ourselves fortunate to have arrived in the dry season and avoided the worst of the local fevers.'

'We should attend to the doctor's words,' said Macpherson. 'I passed an agreeable wee time ashore this morning exploring Bombay with Mr Preston, when we chanced upon a cemetery reserved for Europeans, set just beyond the walls. Many of those there were shockingly young, and some graves were not without a gallows humour. One was inscribed *Mr Robert Townsend lies interned here, who intended to have gone home last year*. Perhaps that should be a warning to us all not to tarry.'

There was a general mutter of agreement to this, and several hands were pressed on to the wooden table top. Britton opened the door to the wardroom to fetch more wine, but no sooner was it ajar when a long, low creature about the size of a cat came in, dragging something in its jaws.

'Good heavens!' exclaimed Preston, who was at that end of the table. 'Is that the animal you spoke of, Charles?'

'What has it got with it?' queried Armstrong, as the officers pulled back their chairs to better observe the new arrival. Unperturbed, the mongoose continued to pull a large ship's rat across the deck until it arrived in front of Faulkner. There was an audible thump as the twitching rodent was dropped between his buckled shoes. The mongoose then backed away, regarded him with its beady eyes for a moment and then began to clean its whiskers.

'God bless my soul!' exclaimed the purser.

‘Do you know, Charles,’ said Blake, placing an arm around his friend’s shoulders. ‘I believe your goose may prove to be a most valuable addition to the ship’s company.’

*****

Upon the Malabar Coast

It was almost seven hundred miles from Bombay to Trivandrum, the capital of Travancore, and the steady south-easterly that blew was dead foul for the whole journey. As a result, the *Griffin* was forced to beat far out into the Indian Ocean to make any progress. More than three weeks had passed before the frigate stood in towards the coast of India once more. The rounded summits of the Western Ghats appeared first, their slopes made purple by the distance. Then they were joined by the lush plains and forested hills that lay at their feet. The frigate turned on to a course that ran parallel to the Malabar coast as she approached her destination. She sailed across a sea of dazzling blue that intensified to topaz where it touched the white sand of the shore, backed by a wall of lush green. But this was no empty jungle. The land teemed with life. Close in, the water was dotted with fishing boats, manned by bearded men and young boys with bare, spindly legs, casting their nets from poles. On the coast, amid the swaying palms, were villages of thatched huts, each surrounded by a clutch of paddy fields.

‘Deck there!’ yelled the lookout. ‘I believe I can see the city!’

‘A creditable landfall, Mr Armstrong,’ said Clay, focusing ahead of the frigate. After a while the white stone tops of several temples, thick with carved figures rose like pyramids above the trees while on a hill further inland he could see a fortified palace. ‘A large settlement, but little in the way of port facilities, I collect?’

'That's right, sir,' said the sailing master. 'There is an inlet above the city mentioned in the directions. It will serve for our boats, but it is too shallow for a ship like the *Griffin*. Most of the trade passes through Cochin, up the coast. There is good holding ground to anchor off that point ahead.'

'Make it so, Mr Armstrong, but have Mr Harrison back the anchor,' ordered Clay. 'I don't want us driven ashore should the wind get up.'

'Aye aye, sir.'

As the frigate sailed on, the coastline was changing subtly. The green trees and fields thinned, to be replaced by more and more buildings, while the sky above the settlement was streaked by the smoke of cooking fires and dotted by wheeling birds. The beach gave way just above the city to a small estuary, where a river wound its way inland. The side nearest the city was lined with precarious-looking jetties growing out from the bank with small boats clustered around them. On the opposite bank women, their saris hitched high, stood in the shallows slapping wet clothes in the water or beating them against rocks.

'Up into the wind, there!' ordered Armstrong. 'Back the topsail! Anchor away, Mr Harrison!'

The frigate swept around, her sails volleying and flapping. The moment she began to slip backwards, her best bower plunged over the side and with a roar the cable ran out through her hawse hole. Overhead her topmen raced aloft to gather in her sails.

'Anchor's holding!' announced Harrison as the last scrap of canvas vanished and the *Griffin* was at rest once more. As the shipboard noise died away it was replaced by the sound of the nearby city. A low grumbling, the aggregate hum of unseen thousands going about their business, overlayed by the occasional sharper sound – the shrill ring of a temple bell or the steady clang of a hammer on an anvil.

'Boat putting out from the shore, sir!' reported Todd. 'I can see a man in a scarlet tunic seated in the stern sheets.'

'That will be the John Company resident here,' said Clay. 'Kindly have him received with suitable honours, Mr Armstrong, and pass the word for Mr Vansittart to join me.'

Major Colin Macaulay proved to be a lean, iron-haired Scotsman with a brisk, no-nonsense air.

'No thank you, Captain,' he said, in response to Clay's offer of a glass of wine. 'My father was a minister in the Kirk, and raised his sons in a spirit of temperance. I find it a sound principle of particular value here in the East, where too many of our race find solace in drink.'

'Splendid,' muttered Vansittart beneath his breath. 'A teetotaller.'

'Admiral Rainer sent word that you would be visiting our wee backwater,' continued the Scot, 'and for once a courier on land outpaced a ship upon the ocean. How might I assist you gentlemen?'

'Have any French vessels touched here of late?'

'The admiral wrote of a powerful enemy squadron, which certainly hasn't been seen here, but a frigate together with two storeships did arrive some months ago. They landed a delegation that visited the maharaja, after which they left, heading north.'

'Do you know what was discussed?' asked Vansittart.

'I was told it was only a courtesy visit, which I doubt to be true, but I have been unable to obtain a definitive account of what was said. My palace contacts have become somewhat reticent of late, which is a worrying sign.'

'Any notion as to where the enemy ships were bound,

Major?' asked Clay.

'None, if fear, although the Company's representative in Cochin, which is at the northern end of the Malabar coast, reports that they did not touch there. This shore is a curious one. It presents a front of sandy beach and forest to the sea, but behind it there are hidden lagoons, inlets and estuaries aplenty, where an armada could lie concealed. You might have passed them on your way here, and been none the wiser.'

'How would you characterise our relations with the local government?' asked Vansittart.

'Had you asked me a year back, I would have said very good,' said the major. 'The traditional enemy of Travancore is Mysore. Tipu Sultan attacked them back in ninety-five and we came to their aid. Then they fought with us when General Wellesley invaded Mysore. The Travancore army is very good. Their sepoys have been trained to fight European style. But of late, I have detected a cooling of relations. It started following the death of my old friend Dharma Raja, and his son replacing him on the throne.'

'There is no better foundation for an alliance than a shared foe,' said Vansittart. 'But once that foe is defeated, the reasons for the friendship oft come to be questioned, I find.'

'Aye, and John Company can be a demanding friend,' said Macaulay. 'Our protection comes at the price of a monopoly on trade. Many leading families here fondly remember the profits they used to make playing Dutch merchants off against Arabs, or the Portuguese against the French.'

'Ah, trade,' said Vansittart. 'So often the fly in the diplomatic ointment. Still, it pays for all, so cannot be set aside. Very well, the sooner we meet up with this young maharaja, the better. When can it be arranged?'

'Court etiquette requires me to first present you to Velu Thampi, the dalawa, or chief minister, but in reality, he will be the more important person for you to become acquainted with. The maharaja is but a lad, and a none too bright one at that. It is the dalawa who is the true power behind the throne. I have arranged an audience with him for this evening. Will that answer?'

'Splendidly so,' said Vansittart. 'Did you have anything else to add, Captain?'

'Only a request for assistance from the major,' said Clay. 'Could you direct my first lieutenant and my carpenter to the leading timber merchant hereabouts. I hear that the local teak wood is every bit as good as oak, and I have a pair of frames in need of attention.'

'By all means,' said Macaulay. 'I shall send the particulars across to you. Until later, gentlemen.'

*****

'I still ain't sure what manner of fecking beast Napoleon is,' said O'Malley, 'but I've never met with his equal as a ratter. Five already this day, an' that last one was the size of a puppy! I tell you, the kitties back in Ireland will be out on the parish when word of these feckers reaches home.' He scratched the mongoose on the top of his head and Napoleon closed his eyes with pleasure and let out a low growl.

'Aye, the purser be a content man, an' all, now them vermin ain't feasting on his provisions,' said Sedgwick, looking up from his writing. 'I heard him crowing about it to the other Grunters, as if bringing him aboard weren't a blunder at all.'

''Tis not just vittles rats scoff,' cautioned Trevan, who was sat opposite him. 'The old *Levant* near foundered in the last war, after they ate through her bottom.'

'You'll not let them feckers drown Uncle Sean, will you Nappy?' said O'Malley to the mongoose, in a tone generally reserved for indulging an infant.

The other sailors exchanged glances.

'That's as may be, Uncle Sean, but we all said as how he weren't to be let up on the mess table where we eats our bleeding scoff,' said Evans, picking up Napoleon and returning him to the deck. 'Besides, we don't want to miss the launch for the shore, unless you'd sooner skip the grog shops and bawdy houses for a quiet night in with yer new mate?'

'Haven't I been ready this last hour, at all?' said O'Malley, standing up and clapping on his hat. 'Jamali Jim was telling me the wenches hereabouts know tricks as would make a Jezebel blush, all on account of some local whoring manual named the Cunning Suitor.'

Bombay may have been crowded, but the streets of Trivandrum made that little settlement seem abandoned. From the moment the sailors stepped ashore at the stone jetty in the inlet they were absorbed into a world that saturated every sense. It was uncomfortably warm on the *Griffin*, but in the airless heart of the city the sun beat down, baking the walls of the buildings until they were hot to the touch. The smell was almost overpowering, with the stench of open sewers and packed humanity laced with spice and incense. And it was much more colourful than the sailors had expected, painted with a pallet of fire. Saris of pink and yellow, turbans of red and amber, the walls of the buildings painted in saffron, blood red or deep scarlet. The noise was deafening too, as crowds of hawkers competed with the pleas of beggars. But above all, the sheer number of people amazed even men used to the packed lower deck of a frigate and all seemed enthralled by the new arrivals.

Upon the Malabar Coast

'Why does every bleeder need to stare so,' asked Evans, conscious of the hundreds of unblinking eyes on him. 'An' it don't answer to stare back, neither.'

'I doubt they sees many giants hereabouts,' said Trevan. 'Let's face it, Sam, you be a good foot taller than most of them.'

'What a place,' muttered O'Malley. 'Fecking temples galore, but is there a grog shop where an honest man can slake his thirst? Let's try down here.'

The Irishman led them off down a narrow street, which at least had the virtue of being shady. Ground floor shops opened on to the road, each one piled high with bolts of cloth, while the windows above were guarded with carved screens that let in air but concealed the residents from prying eyes. The sailors advanced with difficulty, shouldered their way through the crowds of customers haggling noisily over swaths of brightly decorated calico and muslin.

'Perfect, Sean,' said Evans. 'If it were a new frock as we were after. A touch light on bleeding grog shops, mind.'

'Well, why don't yous try fecking leading, for a change,' suggested O'Malley.

'Right you are,' said Evans, pushing his way to the front. 'I reckon we've come too far from that creek. Next left should sort it. I got a nose for a tavern, me.'

But the big Londoner's nose was sadly off today, for the road he selected was lined with spice merchants. Down both sides of the way were bulging sacks of perfumed cardamon pods, heaped peppercorns and dried chillies, like frozen flames.

'This is fecking ridiculous,' moaned O'Malley.

'Aye, no taverns, nor so much as a glimpse of a bawdy house,' said Evans. 'No wonder suitors need to be so bleeding cunning.'

'Look there!' said Trevan, pointing ahead. A man

wearing the hat and long coat of a European came out of a side street fifty yards further down the road and turned to walk away from them.

'Quick! Let's follow, before we lose the fecker in the crowd!' exclaimed the Irishman. 'Christian like that, he's sure to be on his way for a glass of summat.'

The sailors made their way down the crowded street, keeping pace with the stranger but failing to close with him. After a while, he took another turning, down a less busy thoroughfare that led towards the edge of the city. The road grew wider and less well maintained, and the nature of the buildings around them changed too. The grander merchants' houses and temples gave way to thatched, single-storey dwellings clustered around courtyards of beaten earth where children played and chickens scratched. They passed a two-wheeled cart, piled high with reeds, drawn by a pair of spindly bullocks with humped shoulders. Still the man pressed on, neither turning aside nor slowing his pace.

'There'll be a mug of grog at the end of this, or I'm a Dutchman,' enthused O'Malley.

'But who do you reckon he is?' asked Sedgwick.

'Don't know,' said Evans. 'Shall we catch him up and ask, like?'

Sedgwick shook his head, continuing to watch the stranger. 'No, I ain't sure as that's wise. Look at the cut of his coat? That don't look quite right to me. Foreign like? Let's hang back for now.'

A high wall appeared, lining one side of the road and pierced by a gate halfway along it. The man reached the entrance and immediately turned in, waving in acknowledgement to a turbaned guard armed with a heavy stave and an ancient-looking scimitar hanging from his belt.

'What manner of tavern be it as has a tipstaff at the door?' queried Trevan.

'Or has a bleeding wall about it, for that matter,' added Evans.

As the sailors approached the compound they began to smell smoke in the air, while from behind the wall came the sound of beating hammers and shouted orders.

'Shall we be after heading back into town?' suggested O'Malley, but Sedgwick carried on, moving slowly. Just before the start of the wall there was a narrow passageway that ran back from the road at a right angle. 'Down here lads,' he urged.

'I ain't sure as we'll find no inns this way, Able,' said Evans, peering down the alleyway, 'or were it the local footpads you was after?'

'Neither, Sam,' said his friend, assessing the height of the wall beside them. 'I don't like the look of that bloke we been following. Ain't you fought with enough Frogs to know when you sees one? Adam, you be the lightest of us. With a foot on my shoulder and another on Sam's here, do you reckon you could take a peek into that compound?'

'Why'd he be after doing that?' queried O'Malley. 'There's a fecking gate just around the corner.'

'Coz I'd rather not be seen poking around, like,' replied the coxswain.

'But it be all right if they clap eyes on me?' queried Trevan.

'Keep your head low, and no one'll mark you, Adam. Let us get set, and up you goes.'

For a trained topman like Trevan, scrambling up on to his friends' shoulders was an easy task. He removed his hat and dropped it down to O'Malley, and then slowly raised his head.

'It be some manner of foundry, I reckon,' he whispered.

'There be mounds of charcoal and ash, pigs of iron in a stack, and a shed with a chimney puffing out smoke like Lucifer's pit.'

'What of that bloke we followed?' asked Sedgwick.

'He be with a couple more dressed much the same. Foreigners for certain, the way they be waving their arms about, along with a gaggle of locals, all looking over summat.'

'Any idea what it be?' asked Sedgwick.

'Hard to tell, with them all in the way, like,' reported Trevan. 'Smokin' hot it be, mind. Now they be giving it a slap with a sledgehammer, as you can most likely hear.' The deep ring of struck iron rang out in the warm air.

'Can you see what it be?' asked Sedgwick.

'Aye, do tell,' supplemented Evans. 'Before your bleeding boot wears an 'ole in me best shirt.'

'In a moment like,' said the spy. 'Now they be starting to move away I can see a shaft an— Well, I never did! What are they wanting one of them for?'

'What is it, Adam?' asked Sedgwick. 'What have you seen?'

'It be an anchor, with flukes an' all. A mighty big one. Every bit the size of our best bower.'

Chapter 9
Travancore

The landing stage reserved for visitors to the palace was easy to spot, even in the fading twilight. Broad white stone steps rose from out of the water of the inlet, lit with torches that flickered and smoked in the muggy air. As Clay's barge approached, Major Macaulay, resplendent in his full dress regimentals, stepped forward from beside another man to greet them.

'Handsomely,' hissed Sedgwick to the crew, aware of the many eyes on them from the crowded bank. 'Easy there!' The sailors stopped pulling as one, their dripping oars held poised over the water in a pleasing fan, like the wings of a bird. 'In oars, starboard side,' ordered the coxswain, and the barge came to a rest against the bank. Vansittart and Clay stepped out.

'Good evening gentlemen,' said Macaulay, shaking each by the hand. 'Your boat crew make a very creditable showing, Captain.'

'Thank you. They have been with me some years now.'

'Upon my soul, it is still damnedably hot, Major, even though the sun has set,' grumbled Vansittart, fanning at the air with his hand. 'Does it ever grow tolerable in these parts?'

'Aye, it does, in time,' said the resident. 'The first three years are the worst, after which one becomes accustomed to it. May I present the court chamberlain to you?'

He indicated an imposing man with a neat black beard.

He wore an elaborately embroidered tunic, held in place by a wide green sash, and a glittering brooch sparkled from the front of his turban. He listened attentively to the resident's explanation of the visitors, bowing gravely to each when their names appeared from Macaulay's flow of Malayalam.

'Many welcoming, Sahibs,' he said at length, before indicating the palace, a distant cluster of lights on a hill above the city. 'We now go?'

'That place seems rather distant, Major,' observed Vansittart, slapping at a mosquito that had found his neck. 'Are we expected to proceed on foot, or does the maharaja's hospitality run as far as a carriage?'

'I believe you may find the transport he offers to be surprisingly lavish, sir,' said Macaulay. 'Pray follow the chamberlain.'

The bearded man led them past a blue-coated sepoy guard, who saluted with a collective stamp of boots and slap of muskets that would not have disgraced the *Griffin*'s contingent of marines. Out on the quayside two big elephants stood quietly waiting for them. Little more than their broad feet and domed heads were visible beneath the trailing square caparisons draped over them. Each animal had thrusting tusks decorated with bronze bands, a mahout sitting astride their necks, and a square howdah perched high on their backs. The few visible patches of each elephants' skin were elaborately painted with swirling patterns. A deep brown eye blinked at them from the heart of a thick coil of white on the nearest animal.

'God bless my soul!' exclaimed Vansittart. 'Are we to ride in them, like Hannibal in his pomp? I think I might have preferred to walk!'

'The representative of the king can hardly appear on foot like a dusty beggar at the gate,' said Macaulay. 'I will travel with the chamberlain on the lead animal and you will go with the captain on the second. Ah, here come the ladders.'

'And is this form of transportation wholly safe?' asked the diplomat, poised with one buckled shoe on the first rung of the ladder.

'Perfectly so, as long as we encounter no low gateways, sir. I find the motion of the beasts very pleasant, although in some it can induce a wee bit of nausea.'

'Sea sickness,' muttered Vansittart as he climbed the ladder. 'Again.'

Once he was settled on the cushions inside the howdah, Clay found himself thoroughly enjoying the novel experience. The elephant's padding footfalls were almost silent, while the gentle, swinging motion was much more pleasant than that of riding a horse. He didn't find the height of the elephant alarming. It was certainly much less than the *Griffin*'s quarterdeck stood above the water, for example, but he was still sufficiently elevated to have a splendid view of the passing city. As the elephant left the riverbank he found he could see over a perimeter wall and into the compound of a passing temple, where rows of devotees were washing themselves in a huge tank of dark water covered with floating orange flowers. Then the road began to climb through a quarter with narrower streets. It was fully dark and he was level with the first-floor rooms of the passing houses, where orange light spilt out from screened windows and half-guessed shadowy figures moved about inside.

After a while they left the city behind. Now there were stands of dark trees between patches of open fields. A high rampart studded with square towers appeared beside them and the elephants turned on to a bridge that crossed the moat and up to a big gate. There were more sepoys here, who drew aside to let them pass. On the far side the elephant swayed to a halt in response to a barked order from the mahout. A ladder was propped up against the side of the howdah, and Clay descended, followed more slowly by Vansittart. They were in a large courtyard, surrounded on every side by palatial buildings. There were more torches here, together with lamplight spilling out from doorways and windows. Immediately in front of them was a broad flight of stairs leading up to an imposing entrance. Macaulay went to climb the steps, but the chamberlain stopped him.

'Please to follow, Sahibs,' he said, motioning them towards a much smaller door. As they crossed the courtyard, he gave a supplementary explanation to the major.

'It seems your wish to see the maharaja is to be granted, gentlemen,' said the Scot. 'Both he and his chief minister, the dalawa, await us in the pleasure gardens. Have a care what you say. The dalawa speaks excellent English, and the father insisted on the wee lad learning some too.'

The sepoys guarding the entrance saluted stiffly and they entered a corridor decorated with elaborately patterned floor tiles. There were carved doors on each side, but the chamberlain led them on to the end of the passageway where there was a spiral ramp leading upwards. They passed through another guarded door and out on to a high garden terrace. Clay found that the city lay beneath them, a carpet of light that stretched out to the dark ocean beyond. Paths of little white stones led away in different directions, lined with small trees and shrubs. The night air was full of the sound of tinkling fountains and the rustle of the sea breeze among the leaves. Clay felt immediately a little cooler as he followed the chamberlain towards a patch of light in the heart of the garden. This proved to be coming from a raised pavilion with open sides and lit with coloured lamps. More lights studded the nearby trees like glowing fruit. Inside was a throne on a dais, with arms shaped like standing elephants in which sat a thin, rather bored-looking youngster. He wore a long tunic over his white trousers and a turban decorated with a spray of exotic feathers. In front of him was a western-style table laid out for a meal, while next to the boy stood a tall man in his late thirties with a bristling moustache curling across his face. His clothes were less elaborate than the boy's, but still magnificent.

As they approached, he stepped forward with a smile. 'Major Macaulay, welcome,' he said. 'Are these the two gentlemen you wanted to present?'

'They are, your excellency. Might I name the Honourable Nicholas Vansittart, who comes here as a representative of King George, and Captain Clay of His Majesty's frigate *Griffin.* This is his excellency Velu Thampi, Dalawa of Travancore.'

'Delighted to make your acquaintance, excellency,' said Vansittart, bowing low while slipping a hand into his coat. 'May I present my credentials?'

'Of course,' said the dalawa, glancing briefly at the papers the diplomat had given him, before returning them. 'May I present you to the maharaja?' he said, indicating the boy. He spoke rapidly in Malayalam and the boy received each man's bow with a smile.

'I thought we might meet here, for a change,' resumed the chief minister, indicating the terrace around them. 'Our ancestors resisted the Moghuls for centuries, but were not above adopting a few ideas from them, not least the delights of a garden. I understand you gentlemen are new to our lands, so I thought you might find here more comfortable.'

'Most obliged, sir,' said Vansittart. 'It is an inspired

choice.'

'Of course you might find the climate more agreeable if you were to lay aside all that wool you English wear in favour of our lighter garb,' continued the dalawa, indicating the heavy broadcloth of Clay's full dress coat.

The maharaja followed where his chief minister had indicated and saw the gold disc that hung near Clay's throat catch the light. He leant forward in his throne and pointed, while asking something to the dalawa.

'His Majesty would like to know what the medal you wear signifies, Captain?' translated his chief minister.

'This one was given to all the captains present at Lord Nelson's victory at the Battle of the Nile, your majesty,' said Clay. 'Would you care to see it more closely?' He lifted the ribbon over his neck and advanced on the throne without waiting to be asked. The dalawa seemed annoyed by his presumption but the maharaja reached out to take the medal with a smile of pleasure.

He examined it with interest. 'Gold, yes?'

'For captains, yes,' said Clay. 'Officers received ones made from silver and the men's were struck from bronze.'

'I remember when word of that battle came to India,' said the dalawa. 'The maharaja's father, Dharma Raja, ordered a week of celebrations, knowing that it meant the French could no longer come overland to India to aid his enemy Tipu Sultan.'

'A glorious victory for both our nations, excellency,' said Vansittart. 'And proof that if we stand together, we can defeat any foe.'

The chief minister bowed in acknowledgement and then indicated the table. 'Shall we take a little refreshment while we talk?'

The maharaja was plainly quite hungry, hopping down

from the throne to take his place at the head of the table with little regal gravitas. Once he was installed, the other guests arranged themselves around him.

'For your convenience, we will eat western style, although the food is classic Travancore.' The chamberlain clapped his hands in the direction of the palace, and a line of attendants appeared, bearing large dishes of food. There were curries of fish, chicken and lamb; lentil and pumpkin dahl, piles of crispy rice cakes and spiced vegetables, and a volcanic cone of rice that required two men to carry.

'A little of the mutton stew with rice would be agreeable,' said Vansittart, pointing to the nearest curry.

'An excellent choice, sir,' enthused the dalawa, taking the same. 'It is the chef's finest dish.'

'Is it, by Jove,' said the diplomat. Once everyone had been served, he shovelled a large forkful into his mouth. Vansittart's facial expression changed abruptly, from good humour to first surprise and then alarm.

'My dear, sir, are you quite well?' asked Macaulay.

'See him!' laughed the maharaja delightedly. 'Very funny face!'

'The dish may prove a little strong for those unfamiliar with our food,' observed the dalawa, calmly chewing on his own mouthful. 'Perhaps it has too much chilli?'

'Ch … illy?' gasped Vansittart. 'By n … no means. Deuced hot and peppery, I should say. Like sucking on a red-hot poker.'

'No, chillies. The plants from the Americas,' explained the chief minister. 'The Portuguese brought them here in the time of my grandfather, and now we use them in most of our food.'

'V … very interesting,' choked the diplomat, fanning

at his open mouth. 'Might I trouble you for a glass of water?'

'I cannot permit that,' said the chief minister, barking a rapid instruction to one of the attendants. 'Only a yoghurt drink will truly provide relief. Water serves to make matters worse. Captain Clay, are you inconvenienced by the food?'

'By no means, excellency, but then I have encountered the chilli plant before. I served in the Caribbean on several occasions and am used to made dishes such as Trinidad Pepper Pot.'

'Is there any food that Mr Vansittart may try without hazard, excellency?' asked Macaulay.

'Of course. Chamberlain, a fresh plate and some plain rice and dahl for our guest.'

'Much obliged, I am sure,' said the diplomat, nursing his yoghurt drink close.

The maharaja looked on expectantly, but when his principal guest showed no signs of pulling any fresh faces for his amusement, he pointed at Clay and rattled off something to his chief minister.

'My master would like to know a little more of this Battle of the Nile, Captain,' he explained. 'Speak freely, I beg, and I will translate for his majesty.'

'By all means,' said Clay, smiling at the boy. 'It was fought on a dark night, hot like this one, off the coast of Egypt, your majesty. The two fleets were well matched in numbers, although the French had some ships of a superior size. The enemy had moored in a line one behind the next, close in to the shore. But they were not so close that some of our ships could not pass between theirs and the land, which proved to be their undoing. We were able to take each of theirs between two of ours, and so proceeded down the line, until by dawn the victory was won.' He spoke casually of the battle, keeping his account brief and light, but his face became grim as his mind filled with the horror of that night. The crashing broadsides in the dark, the stubborn French resistance, the enemy flagship blazing like a torch before blowing up and the rain of debris and worse that engulfed his ship. And the grey dawn that followed, revealing a bay dotted with bodies floating among the wreckage.

'Why you sad?' asked the youngster, rocking his head from side to side, the feathers on his turban emphasising the movement.

'Because a battle is always terrible, even when it is a victory, your majesty.'

'Although perhaps not as terrible as a defeat, eh, Captain,' said the dalawa. 'In Trancore we have a more positive view of battle, for ours is a nation forged by war. I know that Major Macaulay is familiar with our history, but might it interest you and Mr Vansittart?'

'Very much so, excellency,' said Clay.

'The maharaja's grandfather, Raja Varma, inherited a tiny kingdom called Venad, just up the coast from here. It was one of many little states in this part of India. Early in his reign the Dutch came across the sea in their great ships and landed an army to seize his lands. But they had sadly misjudged him, for although young, Raja Varma was a talented warrior. His little army defeated the Dutch, driving them off and capturing their leader Admiral De Lannoy. He pleaded for his life, offering his knowledge in exchange. He served his new master well, training his soldiers to fight European style, with muskets and artillery, and building ships for him to dominate the Malabar coast. The armies of his neighbours were no match for his newly trained sepoys, and he quickly conquered all of this area as far as Mysore in the north. When he died, his son consolidated his conquests into the Travancore you see today, and recently passed that inheritance on to my master.' The men looked across at the current ruler, who was experimentally jabbing the palm of one hand with a fork held in the other.

'He sounds like a splendid fellow,' said Vansittart. 'I understand from the major that your army remains a formidable force, and proved most valuable in our recent common victory over Mysore.'

'Indeed so,' said the dalawa, bowing in his chair. 'And now our ally sends a representative from the Court of St James to visit us here. How is it that Travancore might be of service to you?'

'Our mutual enemies, the French, have sent powerful forces into these waters, under Admiral Linois,' said the diplomat. 'Doubtless they are here to cause mischief. I was sent to warn our friends of their presence.'

'That is most kind of you,' said the chief minister.

'Although my intelligence is not unexpected, I think, excellency,' continued Vansittart. 'The major tells me they have already visited here. Were they received at court?'

'Only to learn of what silver-tongued promises Napoleon might offer my master, for our better understanding of a mutual enemy.'

'That was thoughtful of you, excellency. So what was the nature of their offer?'

'Oh, it was an absurd idea,' said the dalawa, waving a hand dismissively. 'Some help with the building of warships, for the better protection of his majesty's possessions.'

'Absurd, of course, excellency,' agreed Vansittart, 'And yet oddly specific as well. How strange of Linois, to come all this way with such a particular offer, without some hope that it would be viewed favourably?'

'Perhaps they simply looked at the map. My master

rules a trading country with a long coast. What could be more natural for him than to desire a few ships to protect those shores?'

'But he has the protection of such a fleet, though he may not be able to view it, excellency,' said Vansittart, pointing towards the ocean, glittering in the distance beneath the stars. 'It lies out there, beyond the horizon. Like those ships the captain spoke of that fought off the coast of Egypt and whose victory was justly celebrated here. Thanks to the wisdom of his father, his majesty is in alliance with the greatest maritime power the world has ever seen. His advisers would do well to consider that, before forsaking such friends for the blandishments of a few Frenchmen.'

'My dear, sir,' protested the chief minister. 'What do you accuse my master of?'

'I accuse no one, excellency. I only seek reassurance from a friend. Am I to understand from the strength of your denial that they have received no encouragement?'

'Of course!'

'And that no warships are being constructed under the supervision of the French?'

'Your enemies are my enemies, sir,' said the dalawa, placing a hand across his heart. 'They will never be welcome here.'

'That is reassuring to hear, excellency,' said Vansittart. 'My government will be gratified to learn that they have such good friends, and that any French forces that chance to be here are certainly not present with your approval.'

'Indeed,' smiled the dalawa with his mouth. His dark eyes remained fixed on the diplomat. 'Shall we see if the next course is more to your liking, Mr Vansittart?'

The rest of dinner passed comfortably enough.

Vansittart was a good raconteur, and now the business of the evening was concluded he used his full fund of anecdotes to amuse the company. The dalawa proved to be a courteous host, while Clay helped to keep the young maharaja's attention with further tales of his various battles, each detail faithfully translated by Major Macaulay. The guests eventually left the palace close to midnight with many pledges of eternal friendship between their countries. Back in the courtyard they mounted the two patient elephants that had brought them and made their swaying return trip down the hillside towards the city.

From the parapet at the edge of the garden terrace the dalawa watched them go. He stood lost in thought, stroking his moustache with one of his manicured hands. After a while the chamberlain reappeared and stood a respectful distance behind the chief minister.

'Has that imbecile gone to bed?' asked the dalawa.

'His majesty has retired to his chambers, excellency. Was the evening satisfactory?'

'It was much as the French predicted. The English poking their noses in where they are not required. Oh, they smile at us and name us allies and friends, but in reality, we are no more than a dog to them. Free to roam, but only as far as the leash permits.'

'Would a French master be an improvement, excellency? The late maharaja didn't believe so.'

'What need has Trancore for any master?' spat the dalawa, his face contorted with rage. 'There were philosophers living in the cities of this coast when these barbarians still dressed in skins! The impertinence of these men! Why should Travancore not have a navy, just as she has an army?'

'Because the English are masters of the sea, and will not

give that up lightly, excellency.'

'Then that is where we must grow strong too. We must continue to take the French help, learn their skills and forge our own path. The real question is what to do now? These men guess too much.' The chief minister began to pace across the garden, his head bowed and his hands clasped behind him.

With a look of alarm, the chamberlain fell in step beside him. 'This Vansittart has letters of introduction from the English king, excellency,' he warned. 'He cannot be touched!'

'Hmmm. Perhaps not,' said the dalawa. 'Although he does all the talking, he is not the one to truly fear, I sense.'

'Not Sahib Macaulay, excellency?'

'No, this Captain Clay is the one who intrigues me. He knows a good deal more than he says. Did you not mark how deftly he ingratiated himself with the brat? He could be trouble. It would be most valuable if he was removed from the picture.'

'The murder of a British officer could cause us dreadful problems, excellency,' cautioned the chamberlain.

'Who speaks of murder?' said the dalawa. 'These foreigners, fresh out from home, fall prey to accidents all the time, my friend. India is a very dangerous place. I leave the details up to you, but it should present little difficulty to one of your tame Thuggees. You and I move rooms most nights, but the captain of a ship is always to be found in the same place.'

*****

Before returning to the *Griffin*, Clay and Vansittart went to Macaulay's residence, a large house set back from the road behind a high stone wall and guarded by Company sepoys in scarlet tunics.

'That blackguard is playing us false, of course,'

announced Vansittart, accepting a drink in the major's study, his shoes resting on a huge tiger skin that sprawled across the polished floor. 'Really, the notion that the French would make such efforts, without firm encouragement! Does he take us for fools? No, he struck me as a man caught in the act of betrayal, vigorously protesting his innocence. All that clasping of hands over his heart, I ask you! Do you not agree, Major?'

'Aye, I do, sir,' said Macaulay. 'But I also caution you. The dalawa is a dangerous man when vexed. Did you note that when you asked outright about the French building ships he gave us some gammon about our enemies being his, rather than deny it. He is surely up to mischief, but we need proof of his betrayal before we can expose it.'

Vansittart waved his hand towards Clay. 'Tell him, Captain.'

'I am quite persuaded that something is up,' said Clay. 'For one thing we are not dealing with some notional intrigue of the enemy that will come to fruition in the future. The French are building at least one warship as we sit here. Do you recall I asked you for the particulars of a local timber merchant when we arrived?'

'Indeed, you spoke of your frames, whatever they might be, sir.'

'A most necessary part of a ship, I assure you. But while I do have some concerns over the *Griffin*'s hull, my principal object was to find out the state of the local timber supply.'

'And what did you discover?' asked Macaulay.

'That stocks of large balks of seasoned lumber are quite exhausted. Strange that, in an area so heavily forested.'

'That is certainly suggestive, Captain, but it is hardly proof.'

'True, but then some of my men on shore leave earlier

today report that they followed a gentleman they believe to be French to an iron foundry on the edge of the city, where an anchor suitable for a fifth-rate had recently been forged.'

'Hear him!' exclaimed Vansittart. 'What have you to say about matters now, Major?'

'That if I confront the dalawa with such tales, he will dismiss them out of hand, sir. He will say that the timber shortage is due to the renovation of one of the city temples, and that the anchor is destined for a merchant vessel of some kind. He will then look pained, and wonder why a friend is making so much of wee trifles.'

'Can we not speak with the maharaja, or is he party to this treachery?' asked Clay.

'That will not answer, sir,' said Macaulay. 'I doubt if he knows much about this. He lacks the ability to dissemble and even if he did know, he fears the dalawa more than us. No, what we need is something definite to confront the blighters with.'

'Then let us find where this deuced ship is being constructed, what?' suggested Vansittart. 'How hard can that be? A stroll along the river in London, and you can't fail to stumble over a dozen shipyards?'

'You forget the nature of the coast here,' warned Macaulay. 'Hundreds of miles, much of it thickly forested, with inlets a plenty. You could spend an age searching and yet find nothing.'

'But we need not search it all,' said Clay. 'A bower anchor of that size weighs forty or fifty hundredweight. No smith this side of Bedlam would choose to produce it at any great distance from the ship that requires it.'

'You think the construction site is close?' said Vansittart.

'Of course. The dalawa even told us where to search.'

'He did?' exclaimed Macaulay.

Vansittart sat deeper in his chair and smiled at the naval officer. 'Pray enlighten those of us too dull to keep up with you, Clay.'

'It will lie within the borders of this small kingdom the grandfather inherited. Venad, I think he named it.'

'Let me get my atlas,' said the resident, pulling a large leather-bound volume from a shelf. 'While you explain why you are so certain.'

'He said this Dutch admiral they captured also built them warships, which helped Venad to overwhelm their neighbours,' continued Clay. 'That would have required slipways and other facilities, doubtless long abandoned but probably still serviceable. The French will not rebuild afresh what already exists. Indeed, it was probably the knowledge of what was achieved in the past that gave the dalawa the whole notion of rebuilding a navy.'

'Ah, here we have it,' said Macaulay, spreading out the atlas on his desk. 'A map of the coast made by the Portuguese at the time. The border of Venad is set down as just to the north of here, and the whole extends no more than forty miles or so up the coast.'

Clay came over and considered the map for a moment, and then pointed to a spreading inlet shaped a little like a hand. 'There, that place marked Kollam. Sheltered waters with ready access to the sea. That is where I would begin my search.'

Vansittart came across and glanced at the map too. 'Splendid notion, Captain. And what will you do if you are right?'

'Sail in directly and put an end to matters,' said Clay. 'We are at war with France, and the dalawa was quite clear that any French forces on their soil are not present with their approval.'

'And what if they have the protection of the maharaja's forces?' asked the diplomat.

'Then we will at least know where we stand,' said Macaulay. 'But I doubt if you will find any but Frenchmen. The dalawa is too shrewd to permit himself to be so thoroughly compromised.'

'Excellent,' enthused Vansittart. 'Then we have a plan. I am all for diplomacy, but this strikes me as a case where force may well prove to be for the best. Present them with a *fait accompli*. I am rather looking forward to our next meeting with him.'

Chapter 10
Kollam

The *Griffin*'s bell rang out later that night, stirring Sam Holden, one of her two master's mates, into action. At sea, only the sailing master or one of the naval lieutenants stood watch, but at anchor, with the ship safe, the officers and most of the crew were allowed to enjoy a full night of sleep. This was a moment of rare responsibility for the young man. For once, he was in sole charge of the frigate's small anchor watch, and he took his role seriously. He left his place by the wheel, clasped his hands behind him in faithful imitation of one of those officers and set off on his rounds.

He was surrounded by creaking night as the ship rocked gently in the swell. He carefully side-stepped the many obstacles in his path on the upper deck, checking that each lookout was alert and at his place, and that none of the navigation lights high in the rigging had blown out. He ended his circuit back by the wheel, where he sighted over the compass binnacle towards the looming bulk of one of Travancore's temples. Content that the *Griffin* hadn't dragged her anchor in the half hour since he last checked, he stepped over to the ship's side and looked out at the water.

It had been a quiet night so far, he reflected. The captain had returned from the shore just as Holden was coming on watch, but had long since vanished below deck. Once the barge had been lashed back into place on the skid beams, and the boat crew had gone to their hammocks, there had been little to disturb him. The wind had dropped to a whisper and the dark sea had an oily calm to it. From the city came a stream of little fishing boats, like fireflies emerging from a nest. Each one had a lamp glowing on a pole projecting over its bow, every point of light paired with its reflection. Some were content to drift with the gentle breeze, others rowed, hastening out to sea to claim the best spots. Soon the cloud of lights were all around the frigate, dividing into two streams to pass her. It will be dawn in a few hours, he decided, and the end of my watch. The young man's thoughts turned to the breakfast he would have, and his stomach groaned in expectation as he left the rail.

It was a shame that the master's mate chose to look away at that moment, for he missed the only noteworthy occurrence of his watch, although he would have needed astonishing perception to spot it. One of the fishing boats had stopped level with the frigate's stern quarter. The men at the oars continued to row in faithful imitation of those around them, but they had twisted their blades edge-on to the water so that the boat remained stationary. Another man, naked save for a thin rope draped around him with a hook at one end, slipped over the side as smooth as an otter. His dark skin and sleek black hair were close to invisible. One of the oarsmen handed him a sack filled with coconut husks that rode high in the water, several lengths of bamboo and then, more gingerly, a heavy-looking leather bag. The naked man settled the bamboo on top of the sack, looped the bag around his neck and set off towards the *Griffin*. He pushed the husks in front of him, using it as a buoyancy aid. With its help he moved through the water with barely a splash.

He reached the cave of night where the ship's counter curved out over his head and the sea slopped at the huge rudder.

Nine feet above him was the frigate's name, picked out across the counter. A foot higher was the great cabin's window lights, open to catch what night air there was. In the shadow beneath the counter the man worked quickly. He fitted the lengths of bamboo together and then slotted the thin metal hook into one end. Using his sack to stay afloat, he gently raised the pole like a trembling periscope up towards one of the windows. It took three patient attempts before the hook dropped over the frame with barely a sound. He discarded the bamboo pole and gave the thin rope a tug. Satisfied that it was holding, he began to climb using a series of knots spaced along it, the leather sack swinging from his neck. Slowly he emerged dripping from the sea and made his way upwards.

At the top the man paused with his head just proud of the open window. In the faint light from a pair of shuttered lanterns he could see into the big cabin. Near to him was a desk, with a dining table and chairs beyond it. On each side was the hefty bulk of an eighteen-pounder cannon. Lifting himself a little higher, he was able to see the two doors in the bulkhead in front of him. One was closed but the other was ajar. From the cabin beyond he could hear the rhythmic breathing of someone deeply asleep. When the man was certain that the cabin was empty, he pushed his way through the open window. Then he froze, his heart beating as he sensed that eyes were on him. He inched his head around until he found himself looking at a painted image on the wall. It was a beautiful lady, in a long swirling dress, with eyes that stared deep into his. The woman's long dark hair and piercing gaze were oddly reminiscent of the goddess he served.

'Kali?' he whispered, bowing his head in submission. He paused for a moment and considered the path he would need to take to the sleeping man, right beneath those burning eyes.

For a moment he hesitated, and then came to a decision. He took the bag from around his neck, the wet leather coiling and knotting in his hands, and teased open the mouth. Holding it at arm's length, he gently dropped the contents on to the hard deck.

There was a heavy thump followed by an angry hiss. Then a long snake with faint white bands looped across the floor in the direction of the open door. With a grunt of satisfaction, the man slipped back out of the window and into the night.

*****

Lieutenant Ropar of the French seventy-four *Marengo* stood in the shade of a cluster of palm trees and looked over his command, the first independent one of his career. The temporary gun battery had been placed at the very end of the low spit of land that separated the inlet at Kollam from the ocean beyond. It consisted of a wooden platform built on level ground by the ship's carpenters, protected by a wall made from palm trunks, sand and earth; high enough – and, he hoped, thick enough – to protect his men from bombardment from the sea. Lined up on the platform were four big eighteen-pounder cannons removed from the *Marengo*'s upper battery and brought here with colossal effort, each one aligned with a gap in the earthwork embrasure. He idly held out a hand towards the breech of the nearest one and sensed the heat radiating from the dark metal. My God, but it's hot, he thought. Even this close to the end of the day.

He glanced behind him to where the gun crews lay dozing in the shade or quietly played dice on an upturned bucket. Further back, amid the trees, were the shelters the men had built from canvas and rope with the ingenuity of seamen. One for him, another for the petty officers, and a large mess tent for the men. Standing on its own was the powder magazine, a more solid structure of wood and mud with an armed guard at the entrance. For two months, this has been our home, reflected Ropar, with no prospect of our being relieved until the *Marengo* should return. No wonder the men look so bored.

The clang of a hammer on an iron ring echoed across the brown water from the far side of the inlet to signal the end of another working day. The crowds of Indian labourers clustered around the mud slipways started to gather up their tools and leave the two half-built frigates for another night. One was little more than a dozen frames rising up from its keel like the ribcage of a huge skeleton, but the second had much of its hull planking in place and was clearly recognisable as the warship it would soon become. The chattering shipyard workers began to file off down a track that ran away from the yard, leaving their French supervisors in groups among the piles of timber, discussing the day's progress. By sunset there would only be a few watchkeepers left, and he would have the inlet to himself once more.

He turned away to glance over the shipyard's second line of defence. This was a large ship's cable, thick as a man's torso. The near end was secured around the base of a huge tree close by the battery, while the far end was bent around a group of palm trees on the other side of the entrance. The cable was weighted down with nets of rocks attached along its length which kept it dipped just beneath the surface of the water. Even the ends were barely visible where they crossed the little beach. Under its own weight the cable had worked its way down into the sand, and more had been heaped by the wind against one side. An attacker determined enough to brave the fire of his guns and force a way into the inlet would be in for a nasty surprise, concluded the lieutenant. All I need is someone foolish enough to try.

Satisfied that all was as it should be, he turned his attention out to sea, searching the ocean for any sign of the enemy. There were fishing boats, of course, from the village further along the beach. They were making their way home as the sun drew near to the horizon. He could hear the men on the nearest one calling to a rival in their sing-song language as they set their little triangle of tattered sail. The availability of fresh fish was the one advantage of being posted here, he reminded himself. Yesterday he had dined on a local lobster, a strange spiny creature with almost no claws when compared with those of his home in Brittany, but still quite delicious. Anyway, there was no threat there, he concluded, looking further out.

He saw the sails immediately, two curves of pink just proud of the horizon, almost aligned with the low sun. 'Duval!' he barked to one of the dice players. 'Bring me my spy glass!'

'Here it is, monsieur,' said the petty officer, hurrying over. 'What have you seen?'

'Sails, far out at sea,' said the lieutenant. 'A ship for certain.' He focused on the horizon for a moment and sighed. 'But no more than a passing trading brig, I think,' he concluded, handing the telescope across to his deputy.

'Yes, only two masts, monsieur,' confirmed Duval. 'They have vanished into the setting sun now, but they were not on a course to close with us. Probably bound for Cochin or Goa.'

'Keep watching,' ordered Ropars. 'It may not be the English this time but one day it will be.'

'You think so, monsieur?' queried the petty officer. 'Some of the Indian workers say they kicked over a hornet's nest when they attacked the Marathas, and will be tied up fighting them for years.'

'What you and I think matters very little, Duval. Admiral Linois was quite certain. The English will attack the shipyard here. All his plans depend on it. Keep an eye on that brig, and if there is any change, let me know. I shall be in my quarters.'

*****

'What, pray, was the captain's object it taking down the larger part of our rearmost mast?' asked Vansittart, waving an arm towards the frigate's curious rig. Her fore and main masts soared like spires, almost two hundred feet into the warm evening air, while her mizzen rose no higher than its fighting top, a platform that sat like a stork's nest on top of a chimney, a mere fifty feet above them.

'Why, he seeks to confound the enemy, sir,' explained Armstrong. 'By changing our appearance to that of a two-masted vessel, and therefore like to be harmless. We have only to keep our lower masts and hull beneath the horizon for the ruse to answer. Now we can observe the land from our remaining mastheads without raising excessive suspicion.' He indicated the pair of officers posted on the main royal yard. Vansittart could see that Blake had a telescope trained towards the east, while Midshipman Sweeny struggled to control the flapping pages of a notebook in which he was trying to record the lieutenant's observations.

'Are all two-masted ships innocent, then?' asked the diplomat.

'Chiefly they are, sir. Trading brigs and the like, although there are brigs that are warships, and merchantmen with three masts, so it is by no means a gospel rule,' conceded the American. 'But our course is also suggestive of innocence. We do not close with the land, and any watcher will have seen us proceed on our way to the north, before it is quite dark. The captain has timed our appearance with some care.'

'He has?' queried Vansittart, 'it is certainly a pleasant evening, I grant you.'

'Evening is the perfect time to observe a west-facing coast,' explained Preston, who stood near to them. 'Mark the setting sun. It illuminates it splendidly, while blinding those attempting to study us.'

'And depending on what has been observed, you and Lieutenant Macpherson will go ashore to discover more later, I collect?'

'Aye, that we shall, sir,' said Preston, grinning at the prospect. 'To which end, I need to see the armourer about issuing weapons to the launch crew. Would you excuse me?'

Vansittart watched the young lieutenant depart. 'Will his want of an arm not inconvenience him, Mr Armstrong?' he asked.

The American chuckled at this. 'Who would you send in his place, sir? Mr Taylor? A worthy man, I don't doubt, but a little long in the tooth for creeping around in the dark. Or me perhaps?' he added, running a hand across his ample belly.

'I was thinking of Mr Blake.'

'Mr Preston is the more lithe and agile; besides, he has carried out such reconnaissance before. Macpherson will see that he comes to no harm,' said the sailing master, before stiffening to attention as Clay's head appeared as he came up the quarterdeck ladderway.

'Good evening, gentlemen,' said the captain, looking around to see that all was well. He started when he saw the mongoose stretched out across the top of the capstan dozing in the last of the sun. 'Has that creature been given the licence of the quarterdeck?' he asked.

'With good reason, sir,' said Armstrong. 'He is presently held in some esteem by your officers. On top of his heroics in your defence, there is now the small matter of a successful wager we had with the gunroom over how many rats he could slay in a single day. He must be fatigued by all his efforts. Shall I have him removed?'

Clay regarded the animal and noticed the pair of dark eyes staring back at him. 'No, leave him for now,' he concluded. 'It is true, I do owe him much. I daresay that snake came on board among all the provision we loaded in Travancore, but how it found its way into my quarters is a mystery.'

'Did you see the fight?' asked Vansittart.

'Slept through the whole affair, sir,' said Clay. 'It was only when Yates arrived with my shaving water that we discovered Napoleon breaking his fast on raw serpent. Harte showed the remains to Jamali Jim who positively blanched at the sight. Apparently, that viper was a deal more venomous than any cobra. But we have weightier matters to consider.' He cupped a hand next to his mouth and hailed the masthead. 'How do your observations proceed, Mr Blake?' he asked. The mongoose beside him raised his head for a moment, as if he too was interested in the response, before settling back on the warm wood.

'Just concluding matters now, sir,' replied Blake. 'The light is fading, in any event.'

'You mean to attack tonight, Captain?' asked Vansittart.

'No, the tide and light will not serve, sir,' said Clay. 'Ideally, we need dark for our approach, some moonlight for the attack and a running tide to bear us out again. Wednesday next suits best. Tonight is for learning more of the challenges we may face. Edward and Tom will lead a small party ashore to see how the land lies, their faces blackened with soot from the galley chimney.'

'Will they, by Jove?' chuckled the diplomat. 'What a fine pair of sweeps they shall make!'

'They shall, unless John has marked all,' said Clay, watching his second lieutenant slide down the backstay and come along the gangway towards them. 'What have you seen from aloft, Mr Blake?'

'Little above the general layout, sir,' reported the officer. 'There is a deuced lot of trees on this coast, which serves to conceal much.'

'Could you see anything of note?' asked Clay.

'I could, sir. Would you like me to show you?'

'I do, but more importantly we need Mr Preston and Mr Macpherson to hear what you have to report. Pass the word for them, if you please, Mr Todd.'

'Aye aye sir,' said the midshipman of the watch.

When the two officers arrived, Blake opened his notebook on the part of the capstan head not occupied by mongoose, and the others gathered around. Napoleon sniffed tentatively towards the book, and then returned to his dozing. 'Mr Sweeny has laid out a general plan of the area, sir. The coast is straight, as you see, with good sand beaches and little sign of any reefs that need concern us. There is a native village about a mile to the north of the inlet and sign of a more substantial settlement inland. The approach seems clear of obstructions, but it might be best if the launch crew take a lead with them to check the depth of water.'

'Agreed, although I daresay it is deep enough,' said

Clay. 'The French would hardly build ships in a place they could not sail them out from.'

'I will see one is stowed aboard sir,' said Preston. 'We can drag it rather than cast it, so as not to alert any watchers with an excess of splashing.'

'That will do admirably,' said Clay. 'Pray continue, Mr Blake.'

'The entrance to the inlet is perhaps fifty yards across, and it immediately widens into a lagoon so that each side of the opening is a finger of land with water all about it, sir. On the north side some manner of earthwork has been thrown up. I could see a rampart of freshly turned dirt, and perhaps some tents further into the trees. The other side seems undefended, but it is hard to be certain from out here.'

'My lads will take a wee peek at it, sir,' said Macpherson.

'Fine, but I don't want the enemy forewarned, Tom,' said Clay. 'No sentries found with their throats open in the morning.'

'I'll keep the boys in hand, sir. Have no fear.'

'Once through the entrance, the lagoon splits into two main parts, sir,' continued Blake. 'The southern one looks to be shallow and stagnant, with rafts of vegetation upon the surface and trees pressing close. The northern arm is altogether more substantial. Deep and free flowing, fed by a good-sized river and the far bank has been cleared of forest. Two slipways here, both occupied with ships under construction, with plenty of lumber ready to hand. Further back from the water I could see sheds and tents and I fancy I glimpsed a road that has been driven inland through the trees.'

'And what of the enemy?' asked Clay. 'Besides the earthworks?'

'A multitude of workers close about the ships, of course,' said Blake. 'All departing for the night, but no other sign, sir.'

'No warships? Or encampments of soldiers?'

'None that I saw, sir.'

'I wonder why?' mused Clay, tapping the book. 'A valuable site with so little protection? No matter, perhaps we shall learn more tonight. How will you approach the enterprise, gentlemen?'

'I would have Mr Preston come ashore between this village and the entrance,' said Macpherson, pointing at the sketch map. 'He can land me and my men, and we can approach this wee earthwork under the cover of the trees.'

'Once the marines are ashore, I will survey the entrance, and see if there are any defences Mr Blake has missed to the south, sir,' said Preston. 'After which I return to take off Tom and his Lobsters. Back again in half a watch at most, and the enemy none the wiser.'

'Make it so,' said Clay, looking around him. The sun had set, leaving a flush of pink across the far horizon, and the sky above was growing dark. 'Let us wait for it to be full night, and then we shall stand in for the shore. Have your men assembled and ready to depart at four bells in the first watch, gentlemen.'

'Aye aye, sir.'

*****

A week later, and another day of patient waiting with little to report was now drawing to a close, reflected Lieutenant Ropars to himself, as he sat in his tent. An oil lamp hung over the table, illuminating the open logbook before him. Some welcome sea breeze threaded its way through the flap of the tent, stirring his damp shirt and bringing with it the salt tang of the ocean. He paused to listen to the Indian night outside. The crump and hiss of waves upon the nearby beach. The cough and tramp of the sentries posted by the guns. The palms, rustling in the wind and over all the drone of an infinite universe of insects. All sounded well, he decided, as he returned to his journal.

The trouble is finding something new to report, he decided, as he leafed his way through the previous entries. At least at sea there had been some variety. The *Marengo*'s changing location, the weather, other ships sighted, the various training evolutions as the captain strove to work up her crew. In the days after they had first landed there had been constructing their little battery and exploring the area, but now each day was the same. Dawn inspection of the men, scrubbing down the gun platform, breakfast, exercising with the eighteen-pounders, beach patrol, dinner, sleep, repeat. Waiting for something to happen, while watching the ships on the far side of the inlet taking shape.

No, not every day the same, he decided, as he came upon an entry from last week. “Brig sighted at six twenty, bearing west by south, course north-north-east, range twenty kilometres,” he read. A little further down he had written “sentries reported sound of movement to the north. Patrol of four men sent to investigate. Nothing suspicious found.” Ropars stroked the side of his face with the feathery end of his quill for a moment as he re-read the entry. Probably no connection between them, he concluded, and dipped his pen into the inkwell to begin writing today’s entry. He had got no further than the date when a voice called from just outside the tent.

‘Monsieur?’

Upon the Malabar Coast

'What is it, Duval?'

'Sorry to disturb you, but one of the lookouts thinks he may have seen something,' reported the petty officer. 'It is Gaudin, who is generally steady, monsieur.'

'Very well, I will come,' said Ropars, raising his journal to his lips and blowing on the wet ink. Lucky that I hadn't completed the day's entry, he decided. Perhaps I will have something more interesting to report at last.

The ink dried quickly in the warm air. He pulled on his coat, picked up his hat and sword and closed the shutters on the lantern. When he first stepped out of the tent he could see nothing, so dark was the night. He waited a moment for his eyes to adjust, until he was aware of faint light shining through the trees. There were clear patches of star-speckled sky between the clouds overhead, and a silver glow behind the hills to the east. Somewhere over the plains of India the moon was rising. Once he could see the curved trunks of the palms around him, he picked his way towards the gun platform, stumbling a little on the uneven ground.

'Over here, monsieur,' said the voice of Duval, one of the shadowy figures grouped around the gun closest to the sea. Either his eyes had continued to adjust, or the light was growing, he decided, as the pale lines of cross belts resolved out of the night on some of the figures.

'What have you seen, Gaudin?' asked Ropars, guessing he must be one of the men.

Starlight winked off polished brass as a telescope was held towards him, and one of the cross-belted men pointed out to sea. 'I think I can see the loom of a ship, monsieur,' said the sailor. 'It's some way out, showing no lights. In that direction.'

Ropars focused the night glass and began a patient search. At first he saw nothing more than a sea of black pitch, veined with a little grey where starlight touched the crests of the waves. He tried again, more slowly this time, and then he paused. A black shape, darker than the sea. Could it be a ship, he wondered? He searched above it and saw a ghostly swath of grey, where a backed topsail should be. 'Duval, go and wake the men,' he ordered, continuing to watch. 'Quietly now, and have the guns manned.'

'Yes, monsieur.'

The more Ropars stared at the shape, the more convinced he became that it was a ship. He could see the occasional hint of grey light as waves slopped against the bow. It looked to be large, he decided. A frigate at least. And it was positioned just where he might expect an attacker to lie, waiting for the right moment to turn and run down towards the entrance to the inlet. Around him he heard the sounds of the guns being manned. The rattle of rammers and buckets as the crews assembled. The deep rumble of gun trucks on the planking as the men tested the tackles. Duval clanking down a shuttered lantern beside each gun to give the men a little light to work by. Then Ropars smelt the sulphurous tang of burning slow match drifting on the air.

'The guns are ready, monsieur,' reported Duval beside him.

He looked around to see the battery transformed. It was fully manned by sailors, lit from below by the lamps, some swatting at the clouds of insects drawn to the light. Each gun captain had a smouldering linstock in his hand, the tip a glowing eye in the night. 'Good. Have them run out,' ordered Ropars. While the guns were hauled into place he returned to the shape out at sea. It was still there, perhaps three kilometres away, he decided.

'Quoins out,' he ordered, and the angle of each gun

barrel slowly changed to their maximum elevation.

'Is she there, monsieur?' asked Duval.

'Yes, still waiting,' replied the lieutenant. Waiting, he repeated to himself. Waiting. For what? Surely not for his men to complete their preparations? For the moon to rise above the hills, perhaps? Or for something else?

'Duval?'

'Yes, monsieur?'

'How many men are guarding the rear of the battery?'

'The rear?' queried the petty officer. 'But only the village lies in that direction.'

'How many!' repeated Ropars, lowering his telescope.

'Er, well, there are a couple of men on the beach, and another on the path—'

The crack of a musket sounded, sharp and close in the night, accompanied by a cry of alarm.

'*Merde*!' yelled Ropars, spinning around. 'To arms! The enemy is here already!'

*****

The *Griffin* had spent the day out at sea, carefully waiting beneath the horizon, while her crew prepared for the night ahead. Her forty marines and the party of sailors who would accompany them ashore practised manning the boats. Files of soldiers crept down the ship's side as quietly as their heavy boots and creaking leather equipment would permit. They had almost succeeded when the last in the line, an awkward lanky figure, allowed his musket to slide from his shoulder. It crashed down into the longboat, narrowly avoiding those below and bringing forth an outraged yell from Corporal Edwards.

Those who would remain on board the frigate were busy too. Armstrong made a careful survey of the chart, planning the best approach for the ship to take. The gun crews checked over their equipment and brought up extra rounds of canister from the gunner's store, ready for their part in the battle. Hutchinson supervised the hanging of battle lanterns between the cannon to give the men enough light to work by.

As the sun set behind them and the long shadow of the *Griffin*'s masts pointed across the darkening water towards the shore, the frigate began to close with the land, towing her boats behind her in a row like a mother with ducklings. The black line of the Western Ghats appeared first, a looming wall on the horizon. Then the coastal plain rose from the water, dotted with light clusters where the various villages lay. Armstrong stood beside the wheel conning the frigate with quiet instructions to the helm.

'Can you manage without the binnacle lit, Jacob?' asked Clay, 'There is such a confusion of lights on shore.'

'I can manage tolerably enough, thank you, sir,' said the big American. 'A summit in the hills above our destination aligns tolerably with the entrance to the inlet. I have it as a mark to steer by.'

Clay stared towards the line of hills, fretted like the teeth of a saw, and wondered which of the many possibilities the sailing master was using, but after years together he had learned to trust in Armstrong's uncanny ability as a pilot. Instead, he crossed to the rail and looked down at the sea. A thin line of green phosphorescence tumbled along the frigate's side beneath him before vanishing into the wake. He watched it idly for a while, his mind running through the plan for the attack, searching for any flaws. Although his thoughts were elsewhere, he was conscious of the ship around him. From the main deck came the murmur of voices and the clank of equipment as the shore parties assembled. The vibrating mizzen shrouds beside him spoke of topmen rushing aloft to take in sail, until the frigate would only have her foretopsail set. Clay glanced towards the shore, surprised how close it had grown. He heard some hoarsely whispered orders, and the ship came up into the wind. Then he became aware of figures approaching him.

One cleared his throat. 'It's an hour from moonrise, sir,' said Taylor. He indicated the two officers who stood beside him. 'The shore party are ready to depart.'

'Has every man his package of combustibles?' asked Clay, voicing the last thing he had been worrying about.

'Aye, they do, sir,' confirmed Macpherson. 'A tar-soaked rag and a length of slow match, all wrapped in an oilskin to keep it dry. The gunner issued them earlier.'

'And you have a lantern for making the signal, Mr Preston? Three flashes, then two, repeated until I acknowledge?'

'Sedgwick has it in his care, sir,' said the lieutenant.

'Then God speed to you both, and we shall meet again in the inlet,' said Clay, grabbing each man by the hand.

'Thank you, sir,' muttered the two officers, before turning away to depart. Clay listened to the sound of the men taking their places in the boats. Preston's party of seamen did so with barely a murmur, apart from a muffled oath and the rattle of an oar as it was slotted into place. The marines were a little noisier, but there was no repetition of the dropped musket to warn those ashore. He watched the beetle-like shapes, pools of greater dark, as they pulled away from the ship's side and vanished into the night.

'And now we wait, sir,' said his first lieutenant.

'Indeed we do, Mr Taylor,' said his captain.

Chapter 11
Attack

'Row steady, lads,' hissed Sedgwick, as one of the crew missed his stroke, the oar foaming through the water with a swirl of phosphorescence. 'It be no bleeding race.'

Preston sat next to the coxswain and stared towards the beach, a pale line backed by a black fringe of trees. Off to one side was the fishing village, its few points of light a useful mark to steer by. Then he caught the first sound of waves breaking and hissing on the sand.

'We are close,' he whispered. 'The tide is still making, but with this wind the surf should not prove troubling.'

'Aye aye, sir,' grunted Sedgwick. A few more strokes and the nature of the sea changed. The surface rose into modest waves, rolling up from behind and bearing them forward. 'Put yer backs into it now,' the coxswain ordered. 'Handsomely there!'

The boat surged through the crest, and tipped forward down the slope of water. Out of the corner of his eye Preston saw the dark shape of the longboat in a welter of white as it too arrived on the shore. A rush, the catch of sand under the keel, and the launch grated to a halt.

'Over the side, lads!' ordered Sedgwick, and the men tumbled out into the shallows. Preston swung his legs into the warm water and, holding his pistol above his head, waded ashore to join the growing crowd of dark shapes.

'Marines to me,' came the voice of Corporal Edwards from off to one side.

'*Griffins* here,' said Midshipman Todd, his voice a full octave higher.

'Sedgwick, see the boat handlers know what they are about,' said Preston, to the bulky figure next to him. 'They are to follow us, towing the boats through the shallows.'

'Aye aye, sir.'

Sedgwick was replaced by a much smaller figure. 'Shore party formed up and ready, sir,' it squeaked excitedly.

'Speak softly, Mr Todd,' said Preston. 'But my thanks for that. Rejoin your men and await my order to proceed. And see that each man has his white armband in place.'

The midshipman turned away and Macpherson came over. 'My lads are ready. I've sent a couple of pickets ahead to scout the way. When they report back, I submit we can advance.'

'Excellent, Tom,' said Preston. 'If all is clear, I would sooner follow the beach. It gives no prospect of losing our way.' It was too dark for him to see, but he guessed the Scotsman was stroking his sideburns, as he always did to aid thought.

'Aye, that would be grand, sir,' said the marine. 'If it proves to be unguarded, which would be fortunate indeed. But for my men's final approach I would sooner be among the trees for the purposes of surprise.'

'As you will. Who did you send out to reconnoitre?'

'Three men I saved from Plymouth Assizes,' said the marine. 'Two poachers and a notorious footpad. 'Tis wonderful what accomplished scouts such men make. And here comes their first report. Yes, Corporal?'

'Two Frog pickets on the beach, sir, a furlong shy of the battery. Baker has his eye on 'em. Otherwise, the way seems clear.'

'Can they be silenced?' asked Preston.

'Oh aye, sir,' replied Edwards. 'Easy as kiss my hand. They're sat under a tree attending very little to their duties. One has even lit his pipe. Shall I see it done?'

'If you please, Corporal. I shall follow with the rest of the men,' said Macpherson.

'Aye aye, sir.'

Edwards vanished into the night and the rest of the shore party quietly followed him. Macpherson led the way at the head of his men, Preston following with his party of sailors. Lagging behind came the boats.

Had it not been for the anticipation of action ahead, deep in the pit of his stomach, Preston would have enjoyed the walk. The air was warm and balmy with a gentle breeze blowing in his face. Under his feet the sand was soft and yielding. To one side the sea spread away from him beneath the stars, while on the other side were the trees, impenetrable and dark, full of the hum of insects and the stirring of palm fronds. As he walked, he began to notice more detail. The sand seemed to glimmer a little whiter, and the column of marines ahead of him now showed their pale cross belts where none had been visible earlier, although their scarlet coats were still funeral black. He looked around and noticed that the tops of the palm trees to his left were silhouetted against the sky.

'Moonrise be on the way, sir,' murmured Sedgwick from over his shoulder. 'I hopes we reach this Frog battery afore long.'

Another dozen paces and then Macpherson's soft voice came from ahead. 'Marines will halt.'

'Easy there,' hissed Preston, bringing his own party to a stop. 'Sedgwick, see the men stay together, and above all quiet. I am going ahead with Mr Todd.'

'Aye aye, sir.'

When he reached the head of the line Macpherson was standing beside Edwards, talking quietly with two other marines. A third soldier was crouched down, pushing a naked bayonet into the sand to clean it. The soldiers stepped back as Preston approached, touching their hats.

'What is the situation, Tom?'

'The way ahead is clear,' whispered Macpherson, indicating the patch of shade cast by a large palm tree. In the gloom beneath it were two huddled shapes and a discarded musket on the sand. 'You can see the entrance to the inlet from here,' continued the Scot.

Preston followed where the Scotsman pointed. Less than two hundred yards ahead the beach curved inland to vanish behind the trees. There was a wide gap of calm sea before the pale sand resumed again on the far side. 'I can see light, among the trees,' he whispered, pointing towards a faint orange glow in the distance.

'Aye, and I fancy I heard the sound of guns being manned earlier,' replied Macpherson, his mouth close to his colleague's ear. 'We must make haste, for it grows lighter by the minute. I even caught the loom of the *Griffin* away yonder in the offing.'

Preston looked quickly around. Behind the marines was his party, the tall Evans the only recognisable figure among the shorter men. Trailing behind he could see the boats, dark against the surf. We shall need those once the battery is taken, he reminded himself.

'Very well, take your men into the trees,' he ordered. 'With the beach on this side and the inlet on the other the way should be easy to follow. I will advance along the shore.'

'Corporal, have the men drawn up in loose order,' said Macpherson. 'They may fix bayonets.'

'Aye aye, sir.'

'And I submit you keep your men's pace down, Edward, so that we fall upon the enemy as one,' said the Scotsman. 'Remember yours is the easier path.'

Sound advice, Preston decided as he led his men forward, but also hard to follow. For one thing, Macpherson's men were advancing in silence, making it impossible to judge their progress among the trees. For another, marines trained for hours to march at a set rate, while his sailors spent much of their lives being urged to do any task as quickly as possible, with a rope's end the reward for slacking. Try as he might, the forward pressure from those around him seemed to sweep him along like the current in a river. 'Steady!' he hissed, as the men began to overtake him, but in his chest the pounding of his heart urged him on. A faint rim of moon had risen above the hills, sending a few shafts of light into the trees. He began to see more signs of the enemy. The ghostly glimmer of a canvas tent, a flash of movement as someone crossed an open patch of ground. The chink of equipment and the glow of light from among the guns in the battery. 'Steady,' he repeated, in a whisper. Almost before he realised it, he had arrived at the French end of the beach.

He only realised how far ahead of the marines his men had strayed when he glimpsed a flash of light behind him. He spun round as the sharp bang of the musket rang out, at least fifty yards back. A warning cry in French was quickly cut short. Then he heard the clear sound of Macpherson, farther back in the trees. 'Marines will advance at the double!' he shouted.

What should I do? Preston wondered. Let the marines draw level to launch the combined attack as Macpherson had wanted? Or go now, before the enemy saw them out here in the moonlight? The sailors shifted uneasily, looking towards him for direction while he struggled to decide. Think, Edward, think, he urged, ignoring their faces. For a moment he slid back in time. He was young Midshipman Preston once more, with both his arms and the smooth face of a girl. He was having dinner in the cabin of a smaller ship, on the eve of going into action. Faces crowded around him here too, but their attention was towards the captain, who was offering him advice. 'In battle, Edward,' Clay was saying, 'you will face hard choices. The men will look to you for leadership, and there will be no superior to defer to. When uncertain what to do, always chose to act rather than delay. It is the bold, decisive opponent whom an enemy fears the most.'

Back on the beach again, Lieutenant Preston drew his sword. 'Sedgwick, stay close. The rest of you, follow me. Griffins away!' he ordered, and set off toward the trees, with a charging mob at his heels.

After the beach it was dark beneath the canopy of leaves, like a gloomy hall filled with tree-trunk columns. Ahead he could glimpse the waters of the inlet, a shimmering mirror under the moon. The flash and bang of a pair of muskets briefly lit up the night, showing where a ragged line of French sailors were firing towards the approaching marines from cover. In the second flash, Preston saw the nearest Frenchman swing his musket towards the new arrivals and settle his aim on him. Then it was dark again. He ducked behind a tree just as the gun went off. He felt the bullet smack into the palm trunk and smelt the long gush of smoke as it rushed past him. Then he was away once more, dashing at his opponent, his sword extended before him.

A flicker of moonlight on a steel edge alerted him to the

thrust of a bayonet. He struck it aside with his sword and then hacked at the man with the curious, side on technique he had adopted after he lost his arm. The man parried the blow, but then fell to the sweep of a cutlass as Sedgwick appeared beside him. Preston glanced around, searching for a fresh opponent, but the wood was full of dark struggling figures, the white armbands worn by the Griffins invisible. A shadowy pair crashed towards him, one much larger than his retreating opponent. 'Evans?' queried Preston.

'Aye, sir!' responded the giant, through gritted teeth, and the lieutenant dispatched his adversary with a rapid thrust of his sword.

The flash from a nearby pistol illuminated the battered face of O'Malley, blood trickling from his nose, locked in a desperate fight with a bear of a man in a checked shirt. Each sailor had seized the other by the wrist, and they were wheeling around in a strange dance. Evans leapt forward and deftly tripped the Frenchman, finishing him with a savage hack from his cutlass as the man crashed down among the leaf litter.

'Cheers, Sam,' panted the Irishman. 'That fecker had a grip like a miser on a penny, and was all for butting me to death.'

'Steady, marines,' called the voice of Macpherson, close now. 'Be certain before you fire!' A wall of cross-belted figures resolved from out of the trees from Preston's left.

'Griffins!' shouted Preston. 'Call out your names and show your armbands, so the marines may mark friend from foe!' A chorus of names hastily rang out amid the clashes and cries of the melee. And then the fighting ebbed away as the remaining French broke off and retreated towards the guns, dragging their wounded with them and leaving the ground strewn with slumped bodies.

'Sedgwick, open that lantern a little and shine it on my uniform,' ordered Preston. As the gleam of light fell on the lieutenant he called out. 'Griffins! To me!'

From out of the night they came, some with light wounds, others supporting groaning shipmates. Midshipman Todd was the last to appear, a light in his eye and a spent pistol thrust in his waistband.

'Reorder the men, Corporal Edwards, and see every piece is loaded,' said Macpherson's voice. Moments later the unruffled Scot appeared through the trees. 'Well met, Edward. My lads barely had a fight once your men appeared to take the enemy in the flank.'

Preston stuck the point of his sword into the ground to accept the Scotsman's groping hand. 'You're welcome, Tom,' he said, trying to read any irony in the marine's words. Was he really interpreting his mad, ill-timed charge as a skilfully thought-out plan? Or perhaps Clay was right. When in doubt, act. He plucked his sword from the ground and squatted down to look ahead through the trees. In the glow of the battery's lanterns, Preston could see one of the guns, a bare fifty yards away and uselessly pointing out to sea. The earthwork around it protected it well from all sides save the back, the direction he would attack from. He heard the sound of French voices barking orders, and several figures passed in front of the lamp.

'They can reorder themselves as they choose, but we have them,' enthused Macpherson, kneeling down beside him. 'Caught with water on three sides and us on the fourth. Like rats in a barn when the terriers are at the door.'

'Or perhaps the mongooses?' suggested Preston, standing upright.

'Aye, perhaps so,' chuckled the marine, rising beside him.

'The men are ready to advance again, sir,' called the voice of Edwards.

'Thank you, Corporal,' said Macpherson, serious again. 'I submit it will be best for your men to fall in behind mine, Edward. That way I can be certain that naught but the enemy lie in my path.'

'Very well, Tom. Carry on.'

Preston watched as the marines resumed their advance. From ahead a steady fire began, as some of the French sailors fancied they saw an opponent, the shots smacking their way through the foliage. A cry rang out from off to one side as one ball found its mark, but the soldiers tramped on in silence until they reached the edge of the trees. Then a barked order from Macpherson, and every musket swung up to a shoulder and settled on the French defenders. In their midst was a petty officer, loudly urging his men to resist, but even before the marines had fired, Preston could see defenders edging away. The volley crashed out from point blank range, sending a rolling cloud of gun smoke coiling up into the moonlight. A moment of shocked calm, and then the cries of the wounded filled the night.

'Marines will charge,' ordered Macpherson, pointing the way with his claymore before striding forward. His men gave a cheer and surged after him into the dispersing smoke.

'Up and at them, Griffins,' yelled Preston, and his men followed the marines into the battery.

The deadly volley had done most of their work for them. Several dead and badly wounded lay among the big cannons, while other defenders had thrown aside their weapons and run down into the shallows, where they were being rounded up by jubilant marines. But there were still a few knots of resistance. Preston had to duck under a sweeping blow from a rammer wielded by one determined survivor. Sedgwick was close beside him and finished the off-balance Frenchman with his cutlass. Further off, a French officer was holding a last band of men together beside the end-most cannon.

Preston rushed over to join the mixed group of marines and sailors surrounding them. 'Surrender, monsieur!' he urged. 'Save your men! Please, you can do no more, and they are too brave to die like this.'

The young officer glared at him, his eyes narrow with rage, and then he seemed to become calm, as he absorbed the growing mass of men at Preston's back. Emotions played across his face, and then he barked out an order. His men laid down their weapons and the officer reversed his sword and held it out.

Preston accepted it once he had sheathed his own. 'You were taken by surprise in the night, monsieur. There is no shame is such a defeat. You and your men fought very courageously.'

The French officer gave him a bitter look and kicked out at the wheel of a nearby gun. 'Surprised, Lieutenant?' he queried. 'By no means. I had been warned that you would come.'

Strange man, thought Preston to himself, and then dismissed the officer from his mind. There was still much for him to do this night. The moon had risen high above the distant hills now, bathing the inlet in light. Out at sea he could see the *Griffin* clearly. The big frigate was broadside on to him, its guns run out and waiting. His men milled around the battery, unsure what to do next, while down in the shallows he could see the boats arriving along the beach. On the far side of the inlet were the two ships under construction, their bare wood white against a backdrop of dark forest. There were cries of alarm from those posted to guard them drifting across the water. Flaming torches had appeared further back amid the trees, and he could hear the sound of a distant drum.

'Sedgwick, signal to the ship that all is well, and they can enter safely,' he ordered.

'Have a care with that lantern, though,' commented Macpherson, coming over to join his colleague. 'There are abandoned charges aplenty around these guns.' He pointed to where three cylindrical canvas bags had been stacked against the front of the gun emplacement.

'Aye aye, sir,' said the sailor, moving away to a position from where he would be visible out at sea.

'Have your men secured the prisoners yet, Tom?'

'Corporal Edwards has it in hand,' confirmed the marine, pointing to where a huddle of seated figures sat dejectedly on the beach within a ring of marines.

'Good,' said Preston. 'Mr Todd, go and hurry forward those boats. We shall need them presently to cross to the shipyard. Then you can attend to the wounded here.'

'Aye aye, sir,' said the youngster.

'The barky has acknowledge the signal, sir,' reported Sedgwick, returning to his side.

Preston looked out to sea, where the frigate was swinging towards the shore and starting to sail for the mouth of the inlet. 'Sedgwick, have the men follow me,' he ordered. 'Come, Tom, let us find the best place to enjoy the fireworks,' he said.

'Aye, I shall. A warship firing at night is a fine spectacle. It makes the fireworks at Vauxhall seem dull indeed. Do you remember the Nile, Edward?'

'As if it was yesterday,' said Preston, as the two officers strolled down to the water's edge. They had not gone far from the battery when they came to a strange bank running across their path with sand heaped up against it.

'Curious,' said Macpherson, pushing it with his foot. 'It seems very solid. Running from up among those trees and vanishing into the water. What the devil can it be?'

Preston felt cold dread grip his heart. He dropped to his feet and swept at the sand with his arm. The woven hemp bands of a huge rope appeared. 'Damnation! It's a bloody anchor cable, laid across the inlet!' He turned to the group of sailors trailing along behind him with Sedgwick at their head. 'You men! Here! Now!'

The sailors broke into a run and gathered around the officers.

'Mother of God, that's fecking big!' exclaimed O'Malley.

'All of you, use your knives, cutlasses, whatever you have! It must be cut before the ship reaches us!'

The sailors needed no further urging, and set to sawing and stabbing at the tough fibres, while Preston stepped back and forced himself to think. He looked back at the frigate, swelling in size as she gathered pace towards him. Hitting an un-yielding barrier like the cable would do terrible damage. Her solid bow might survive the impact but the sudden halt would bring down her foremast at least, leaving her crippled.

'Corporal Edwards!' roared Macpherson. 'Six men here, at the double!'

'Trevan, follow the cable up into those trees,' ordered Preston. 'Swiftly now. See if it can easily be cast off.'

'Aye aye, sir.'

Preston looked back at the *Griffin*. She was forging through the water, her tall masts stretching high against the star-filled sky and her big square topsail driving her on. 'Faster there! Faster!' he urged. There were grunts from the labouring men, but the cable was as thick as a tree trunk, and the bright scar they had cut in the top was barely a few inches deep.

'An axe would serve better, sir,' growled one of the men. Preston considered this, but he knew his men hadn't brought one and searching in the dark for a French axe would take much too long. 'It need not be cut clean through,' he encouraged. 'Just sufficient for it to part on impact.' The marines Macpherson had called for ran up and began sawing and stabbing with their bayonets.

Macpherson pulled Preston away and leant close. 'This will not answer, sir. The men's progress is much too slow.' He indicated the looming presence behind them. They could hear the splash of her wake and creak of her rigging now.

'Sedgwick, go and signal to her again,' ordered Preston.

'I can try, sir, but we only agreed a sign for come on. I ain't got one for hold off,' said the coxswain.

'Any better suggestions, Tom?' asked Preston, at his wits' end.

Macpherson looked at the lantern that Sedgwick was frantically flashing towards the approaching ship, and something came back to him. 'By Jove, I think I just might! Have the men excavate a hole beneath the cable. I will return directly.'

'But what …' began Preston.

'Just dig, man!' yelled the Scotsman over his shoulder as he ran towards the captured battery.

It occurred to Preston that this was the first time he had seen the ever-calm marine break into a run, even when charging the enemy. 'This had better be good, Tom,' he muttered, as he turned to the labouring sailors. 'Belay cutting,' he ordered, 'and start digging under the cable.'

Upon the Malabar Coast

*****

Clay was beginning to feel as if he had spent days standing on the quarterdeck of the *Griffin* looking through his night glass at the Malabar coast. Yet, stare as he might, little seemed to have changed since the ship's boats had vanished. A faint glow of light had appeared, close to where the battery must be, but everything else remained the same. The grey line of beach still lay between the restless sea and those forbidding trees, but there was no sign yet of any attack. He lowered the telescope and rubbed some moisture from his eye with his sleeve and then stopped. Something had changed. The deck at his feet was now pale grey, streaked with a cat's cradle of lines where the shadow of the mizzen rigging fell on it. He looked back towards the shore. The top edge of the Western Ghats was surely more distinct against a paler sky. As he watched the faintest rim of silver, no more than the paring from a fingernail, rose above a hill. He reached for his pocket watch to check the time and then stopped. He knew very well what time the moon rose. It was the hour he had selected for the attack to begin.

'Five bells, sir,' said Taylor from the rail beside him. 'Let us hope that Mr Preston and his men are in position, for the enemy will be able to mark us out here presently.'

'Is everything ready, George?'

'It is, sir,' confirmed the first lieutenant, indicating the gun crews of the quarterdeck carronades as they sat around their weapons. 'The ship is cleared for action and Mr Blake has the main battery loaded and run out, sir. Ball, with canister to hand to dissuade any Frenchmen present from emerging from the forest to protect their ships.'

'That may very well prove our chief part,' said Clay. 'To drive back the enemy and allow Mr Preston's men to inflict the gravest injury. And the anchor?'

'Mr Harrison has it cockbill, up and down and ready to drop with a spring to bend on it, if required.'

'Thank you,' said Clay. He returned to examining the coast with his night glass, just in time to see a flash of red somewhere among the trees. Moments later the faint pop of a musket sounded over the gentle mumble of the surf. 'Ah, things begin at last.'

Now there were more flashes, prickling in the night as the fight intensified, this time in a fresh place, and Clay fancied he could hear cries amid the sound of gunfire. Then the shooting petered out, well short of the battery, and both men watched, tense and alert.

'Pray God they have not been repulsed, sir,' said Taylor. Clay said nothing, as he tried to pierce the dark and see what was happening. More firing now, desultory and close to the battery, followed by the stab of light and crack of a massed volley.

'Ah, that is decidedly better,' said Clay. 'Our marines, I don't doubt.' A few more flashes, and what sounded like a cheer. Both men waited, expectantly, watching the mouth of the inlet. The faint sound of a drum banged out from further away. An endless pause, and then the orange glow of a lantern held aloft. The light was cut off as something, perhaps a hat, was held in front of it. Three flashes, then two, repeated.

'That's the signal that the battery is in our hands, sir,' said Taylor.

'Yes, kindly acknowledge and put the ship before the wind. Make haste, if you please. I don't like the sound of that drum. Let us enter this inlet and do our worst before the enemy are fully roused.'

The broad span of the frigate's foretopsail yard was

hauled around, and as it caught the wind the *Griffin* began to move through the water.

'Helm's answering, sir!' reported the quartermaster, rolling the wheel between his hands.

'Come two points more to larboard,' ordered Armstrong. 'Steer for the centre of the channel.'

'Two points and plum middle, aye sir.'

The entrance to the inlet was clear to see, wide beneath the moon, with the last of the tide flooding into it. Beyond, Clay could see the estuary, a broad expanse of silver, with the two half-built ships on the far side. They lay on their mud slipways, angled towards the water, encased with scaffolding and lit with a few flaming torches. Stacks of wood dotted the ground around them in neat pyramids.

'The French battery is coming up on this side, sir,' reported Taylor.

Clay glanced across at the four big muzzles poking out towards him from the wall of heaped earth and felled logs that protected them. They had been sited with care, he decided, able to make life very uncomfortable to an attacker. The *Griffin* was close now, about to enter the channel. He could see the swarm of figures all around the guns, some waving at the approaching ship, and he thought he could hear raised voices. One with a lantern, presumably Sedgwick, was flashing it repeatedly. As Clay looked down on the scene a feeling of unease settled on him. It was strange for experienced officers like Macpherson and Preston to allow such ill-discipline. 'Is the way ahead quite clear, Mr Armstrong?' he asked.

'Perfectly so, sir,' confirmed the sailing master. 'The entrance is a deal wider than Pompey.'

'Very well. Carry on.'

*****

'Digging like fecking badgers, is it?' grumbled O'Malley, as he cast handfuls of loose sand and earth aside.

'Silence and make haste!' urged Preston, standing over the men.

'How much dirt we got to shift, sir?' asked Evans. He indicated the low chamber under the cable that had been scooped out already, large enough to make a snug den for a fox.

'In truth, I am not certain,' said Preston looking around to see where the marine officer had gone. 'Dig was the most instruction I got.'

'Here comes the man himself, sir.' O'Malley pointed to where the officer was running over the sand towards them, a heavy-looking cylinder tucked under each arm.

'Ain't that powder for the guns?' asked Evans.

'Six pounds of coarse grain is the charge for them long eighteens,' confirmed O'Malley. 'I hope your man doesn't stumble.'

'Quick, place these in the hole!' gasped the marine as he came up. He shoved one bag into each sailor's hands. 'Quickly now. The rest of you, take cover.'

'You're going to blow the cable up?' marvelled Preston.

'Have you a better solution, Edward?'

Preston looked at the *Griffin*. She was very close. Sailors and marines had begun waving in alarm at her, but still she came on, heading straight down the centre of the channel towards the hidden cable, barely two hundred yards ahead. 'No, Tom. Let us hope your idea will serve.'

'Did you bring slow match for a fuse, sir?' asked O'Malley, kneeling by the cable and holding out his hand.

'No time for such niceties,' said Macpherson. 'Just see

that the end of one of the charges is visible above ground.' He pulled his pistol from the officer's sash tied about his waist and began to pace back across the sand. 'Everyone! Get clear! Lie down among the trees, but well back! Go now!'

The sailors and marines fled, leaving the two officers alone.

'Tom, I beg you!' urged Preston, walking beside him. 'At least retreat behind the parapet of the battery.'

'Nay laddie 'tis too far,' said the Scotsman, cocking his pistol. 'I cannot hazard a miss. Twenty yards will have to serve. Beyond that no pistol is true.'

'The blast …'

'… will go chiefly upwards, as is the wont with explosions. Now go!'

'But Tom—'

'Run!' yelled Macpherson, pushing him away. 'Tis now or never! Get into cover. Away!'

Preston stumbled back to the battery. The frigate was level with him, a wall of oak, her long side an endless row of guns, rolling past him as she bore down on the cable. He looked at where Macpherson knelt on the sand, the pistol held before his face like a duellist as he calmed himself for the shot. He glanced once at the ship, then extended his arm and settled his aim on the bulging end of the charge bag. Then he pulled the trigger.

Chapter 12
Fire

Clay chanced to be looking directly at the crouching figure on the beach when the pistol fired. His attention had been drawn by all the others scattering away from him. He had barely time to register the flash before the bullet struck home. The blast roared out and a spreading ball of smoke rose upwards. The frigate was some distance out, but he still felt the explosion buffeting him in the chest. Moments later fragments pattered down into the water alongside, while just ahead of the *Griffin* a huge serpent slithered across the sand and into the water like a crocodile taking fright. Something banged and rumbled against the hull beneath him and then the frigate was through into the wide inlet beyond.

'What in all creation was that?' asked Taylor, coming to join him. 'Have they got one of the captured guns in action?'

'No, for it was away from the battery,' said Clay, peering behind him at the milling figures on the beach. 'It looked more like a charge going off, to my ear. I trust that our men are all right.'

'Amen to that,' said Taylor. 'I hope Mr Preston will yet be able to play his part? We need him to cross to the yard and set fire to those ships.'

'We touched an obstruction of some kind just after, sir,' added Armstrong, from his other side.

'I am not sure what it was, sir,' said Taylor. 'Perhaps

only a sunken log, but I would be more content if we had a good man posted on the lead line.'

'Make it so, Mr Taylor,' said Clay, looking back towards the entrance. He could make little out from the milling figures, but at least there were no further explosions. 'As for that blast, I don't understand it at all. There is something strange afoot on shore.' He left the side with a shake of his head. 'No matter, all will be explained in due course. We must attend to our own part of the enterprise, and trust the others do the same.'

The push of the tide was almost spent and the frigate glided across a pool of water towards the half-built ships on the far side. They towered over the sheds and piles of lumber scattered around them, their naked wood glimmering in the darkness. They would have made two fine frigates, reflected Clay, once completed and fitted out. Too bad that they would never leave this estuary.

Up in the forechains a sailor made his first cast of the lead, the splosh of the heavy weight sounding clearly over the gentle sound of the frigate sailing forward. 'By the deep, eight!' he called as the line became vertical.

'Enough water to float a first-rate, sir,' commented Taylor. 'They have sited their yard well.'

'Good,' said Clay. 'The deeper the water, the closer we will be able to come to our object.'

The frigate stood on, a thing of beauty beneath the flattering moon.

'By the mark, seven!' called the leadsman.

'Pray bring us in just there, Mr Armstrong,' ordered the captain, pointing in the direction he wanted. 'Anchor no more than a half cable from the shore.'

'Aye aye, sir,' said the American. 'Bring her up a point, quartermaster.'

'A point, aye, sir.'

The drum continued to beat, somewhere deep in the forest. Clay examined the yard carefully with his night glass, although the moonlight was quite bright enough for him to see by. He could pick out about twenty figures watching his approach, standing close around the ships. More figures were emerging from the woods, but most looked to be civilian workers, who would probably flee the moment the frigate opened fire, he decided. Where were the soldiers, who might offer some resistance when Preston's men arrived to complete their night's work?

'And a half, five!' offered the leadsman.

A flash from the shore, followed by the report of a musket. Clay had no idea where the bullet went. Even a target the size of the *Griffin* must be hard to hit at that distance, he concluded. But there was no range at which her sides, made from eight inches of seasoned oak, had much to fear from a musket ball. The defiant shot prompted more of the watchkeepers to try their luck. Flashes dotted the shore, each one accompanied by a tongue of fire and a ball of drifting grey smoke.

'By the mark, five!'

A slap sounded from somewhere above Clay's head, evidence that the range had come down to the point where one marksman at least had found his target. As if that was a long-awaited signal, the frigate came to life.

'Wheel hard over!' ordered Armstrong. 'Mr Harrison, let go the anchor!'

'Aye aye, sir!'

The *Griffin* creaked slowly around, turning up into the wind. She slowed quickly and there was an explosion of water from beneath the bow as the anchor smashed into the calm lagoon. The big topsail flapped lazily and then settled back against the foremast, pushing the frigate backwards until she snubbed up against the pull of her anchor chain.

'Forecastle men away!' yelled the boatswain, and a swarm of sailors ran up the shrouds to take in sail. The *Griffin* swung around her anchor until she was broadside on to the shore. Within moments she was transformed from a ship sailing under the stars to a floating battery full of dark menace. All across the little shipyard, figures began backing away.

'Mr Taylor, I'll have that spring fitted to the anchor chain directly, if you please,' ordered Clay.

'Aye aye, sir.'

'Mr Blake, are the starboard guns ready?' asked Clay, striding to the front of the quarterdeck and looking down.

The lieutenant stood at the base of the main mast, his usual place when his guns were in action. 'Loaded and run out sir. You have only to give the word.' He indicated the long row of big eighteen-pounders that stretched away down the side of the deck, each one with its crew clustered around it, lit by the orange glow of the battle lanterns that hung between them.

'Very well, said Clay. 'You may open fire.'

'Aye aye, sir,' said Blake. 'Aim, low, Starboards! The nearest ship is your mark!'

A moment more of calm as the gun captains made their final adjustments, the hum and croak of insects from the nearby forest suddenly clear, and then the frigate fired a full broadside. Tongues of flame roared out from the side, and for an instant night was day. Clay could see every detail of the two ships etched out in orange and black. Then a grey wall, thick as fog, billowed up, hiding the scene. The ship heeled over as her cannons ran back on board, each muzzle emitting a curl of smoke, and the gun crews raced to reload their pieces.

'Independent fire!' ordered Blake. 'Hit it again, lads!'

The smoke began to clear a little, although the quarterdeck carronades around Clay were barking out steadily, adding fresh gushes of their own. The more complete of the two ships was closest to the *Griffin.* He could see several holes punched into her curved side and some of the scaffolding holding her up had collapsed. As he watched, the first of the guns to be reloaded fired again and a nearby mound of timber partly collapsed as the shot struck home. With steady intensity the frigate pounded away, sending ball after heavy ball bounding through the little shipyard. Shelters collapsed, cut pieces of lumber were scattered and splinters flew from the frigates under construction. The few watch keepers who hadn't fled were hiding from the barrage. He could just see the turbaned head of one unfortunate as he cowered in the bottom of a saw pit close to the shore that was directly in line with one of the quarterdeck carronades.

Clay turned as a sailor came running along the companionway from the forecastle. 'Mr Harrison's compliments, and our boats have put off from the captured battery, sir,' he reported.

'Thank you, Hobbs,' said Clay. He went to the far side of the ship and trained his glass back across the inlet. The longboat and launch had left the shadow of the trees and were out on the water, each one packed with men. 'Mr Sweeny,' called Clay. 'Kindly go and find Mr Taylor and ask him how the spring is coming along, with my compliments.'

'Aye aye, sir,' said the midshipman, dashing for the companion ladder.

'Tell me, Mr Armstrong, is it me or is that infernal drum sounding louder?'

The sailing master cocked his head to listen beyond the

roar of cannon fire, now almost continuous as it rolled up and down the side of the ship. 'I believe it is, sir.'

Both men returned to the side of the frigate facing the shipyard and looked in the direction of the trees.

'There, sir!' exclaimed the American, pointing towards the dirt road that ran away into the woods.

Clay caught sight of rhythmical movement on the shadowy trail. There was the silver glint from polished metal and the flutter of something pale close to the head of whatever was approaching. 'A column of troops, Mr Armstrong?' he asked.

'For certain, sir. And I fancy that's the white portion of a tricolour we can see at the head.'

As the column came nearer, figures in loose order appeared along the edge of the trees. A chain of flashes banged out and shots pattered through the rigging like rain drops on leaves. One musket ball struck the muzzle of a carronade, leaving a smear of silver. Another smashed a window in the stern.

'Mr Taylor!' roared Clay down the quarterdeck grating. 'Where is my spring?'

'Just being wound around the capstan, sir,' replied the first lieutenant, his face appearing under Clay's feet through the grid of squares. 'A moment more, that is all.'

'Very well.' Clay drew out his whistle and blew a blast.

'Ceasefire there!' yelled Blake, and the guns fell silent across the frigate.

'Mr Armstrong, kindly hail the boats and tell Mr Preston to hold back for the present, until we have dealt with these soldiers.'

'Aye aye, sir,' replied the American, pulling the speaking trumpet from its becket and striding towards the bow.

'Mr Blake! We have a column of troops approaching and skirmishers in the fringe of the wood. I'll have the ship pulled around presently, when I shall need them dealt with before Mr Preston's men can land.'

'Aye aye sir,' said the lieutenant. 'Canister now! Load with canister, starboards.'

Clay watched as the big copper cylinders were rolled towards each weapon, the hundreds of musket balls they contained chinking as they turned. From beneath his feet he heard the capstan clank as the spring was wound in, and he felt the frigate turn a little against the push of wind and tide.

'Mr Taylor's compliments, sir, and the spring is ready,' reported Midshipman Sweeny.

'Thank you. Kindly ask Mr Taylor to have it drawn in until the guns can bear on the forest.'

'Aye aye, sir.'

There was a cry of pain from the main deck as one shot at least found its mark through a port lid. The capstan was clanking regularly as it turned, twisting the *Griffin* steadily around. The firing from the trees seemed to intensify as the frigate presented an ever-larger target, inch by inch. Clay could now hear the regular tock of bullets striking the side of the hull. He looked across the devastated shipyard to where the head of the column of troops was emerging from the trees. There seemed to be hundreds of soldiers running to left and right as the column transformed into a line of men under the barked urging of their officers.

'Shakoes and gaiters, sir,' commented Armstrong beside him. 'And it is a tricolour. These are no sepoys.'

'Yes, French regulars, from the look of them,' agreed Clay. He paused as one of the quarterdeck gun crew spun away from the rail, clutching his arm and cursing loudly. 'Half a battalion?'

'Of that order, sir,' said Armstrong, contemplating the growing line of soldiers. 'Poor bastards. Unless they can swim, they have little to trouble us with.'

This thought seemed to be occurring to some of the soldiers as the frigate continued to turn, presenting an ever-lengthening line of cannon. The skirmishers' rate of fire was faltering and Clay fancied he could see the odd head glancing back towards the comfort of the woods.

As the frigate completed its turn there was a blare of orders, the drum resumed its beat and the soldiers began to advance towards them. Progress was difficult, the unwieldy line parting and reforming to navigate each obstacle in its path, with much fussing from officers and sergeants. Clay selected the point at which he would open fire with care. It needed to be comfortably within canister range of the frigate's eighteen-pounders, but sufficiently distant that any volley of musketry from the soldiers would not trouble them. He selected an open-sided building with a partly collapsed roof of palm leaves as his mark. Coiled rope and a stack of bales could be seen spilling out from it. He waited for the French line to tramp their way level with it. 'Mr Blake, you may open fire!' he ordered.

'Aye aye, sir!'

Another gush of flame in the night. The sound of this broadside was different, the deep throated roar of the guns overlayed by a hornet-whine as each cannon spat out a long cone of musket balls. Once again the shipyard was cloaked with smoke, concealing the damage the broadside had caused, but there was no mistaking the chorus of cries from the wounded, lost somewhere in the fog. As the sea breeze thinned the clouds, the line of troops gradually reappeared, broken into islands of untouched men divided by channels of tumbled carnage torn into their ranks. Most stood dumbstruck, despite the urging of their officers. Then the drum struck up again, and the soldiers moved forward once more, compressing together into a shorter line as they closed the gaps torn in their ranks.

'I reckon them buggers be in range of the smashers, sir,' offered the petty officer in charge of the quarterdeck carronades.

'Very well, Jarvis, see what you can do,' said Clay.

It was long range for canister fire from the stumpy carronades, but Clay saw a few more men drop as they banged out. It might help to unsettle the enemy while the main armament was reloading, he decided. There was an order and the line came to a halt. Clay could see the officer in charge, standing close to the flag with a small drummer boy beside him. Moonlight flashed from the drawn sword in his hand. In a smooth movement, the look of the line changed as each soldier twisted around so they were side on to the frigate. Another order, and every musket came up to a shoulder, trained towards the *Griffin*. Clay felt an overwhelming urge to throw himself flat on the deck. He gripped the rail in front of him with a maniac's strength while he awaited the volley. It crashed out, a thin line of fire in the night amid fresh clouds of smoke. Bullets thudded into the ship's side or whined past him. A halliard parted and swung out in front of him and one of the crew of the aft carronade fell back, blood pouring down his face.

'Get him below to the surgeon,' ordered Clay, unclasping the rail and rubbing life back into his hands. Now the soldiers were all reloading, tearing open cartridges with their teeth and working their ramrods. There was an ominous rumble from beneath his feet as the long row of eighteen-pounders re-emerged.

Clay sensed the line was faltering. He had been in

enough sea fights to recognise the moment when the balance of a battle was tipping one way. There were little ripples of movement in the ranks. He could see one man frozen in horror with his ramrod poised halfway out of his musket, while the soldier next to him pressed on loading with frantic speed. Or there was the slightly pleading note that had entered into the tone of the shouted orders. Then the *Griffin* fired again.

When the smoke cleared the line had disintegrated completely. Where it had once been was marked by fallen bodies, a high tide mark strewn across the ground. Those who had survived the blast of canister were retreating back towards the woods, some running for their lives, others pulling wounded comrades back. The blast from one of the frigate's guns must have caught the colour party. Clay could see the little pile of bodies, draped in the tattered flag, the drum discarded beside them. After a moment the watch keeper in the sawpit took his opportunity to flee. Clay felt sick at the level of destruction, mixed with anger. His hand trembled as he pulled out his whistle again. Who sent men with muskets to fight against the heavy cannon of a warship out on the water? The whistle blast wavered a little, and the guns fell silent once more.

'Mr Blake, have the men pitch the odd ball into the trees to deter the enemy from returning,' he ordered. 'But have a care not to endanger our shore party.'

'Aye aye, sir.'

'Mr Armstrong, tell Mr Preston it is safe for him to proceed. Half an hour to set his fires, no more, and then I want to be clear of this damned place.'

'Aye aye, sir. I fancy the tide is starting to ebb. It will serve to bear us out when the time comes.'

*****

After the explosion, Preston was the first across the beach, his arm held in an arch above his head against the sand and stones tumbling down. Macpherson lay on his back, a wisp of smoke rising from the pistol gripped in his hand. The front of his tunic was blackened and his battered hat had been torn from his head. 'Tom!' yelled Preston, leaning over the prostrate figure. Then, 'Bring water! Now!'

There was a rumble from beneath the surface of the channel as the deep keel of the frigate brushed over the sinking cable. Preston looked that way and saw Clay staring back at him, a look of confusion on his face. Then the *Griffin* was through, her wide carved stern sliding away from him, and he returned his attention to his friend. 'Tom, can you hear me?' he asked, cradling the Scotsman's head. Macpherson's face was filthy with powder smoke and one of his sideburns had vanished, along with a strip of hair.

'Here you go, sir,' said Sedgwick, appearing beside him with a marine's water canteen. 'How he be doing?'

'Out cold, I think,' said Preston.

Sedgwick pushed his fingers against Macpherson's neck. 'His ticker be going, sir, a bit faint but steady like.' He wetted his neck cloth and wiped at the marine's face, producing a groan as he touched one of his burns and the eyes flickered. 'D … did … sh … ship … through?' he croaked.

'Thank God for that,' said Preston. 'Yes, the *Griffin* got through, you mad bastard.'

Macpherson stared past Preston's shoulder for a moment. 'Wh … who's there?'

'Its me, Tom. Edward,' said the officer, waving his hand across the marine's eyeline.

'I don't reckon as he can hear owt, sir,' explained

Sedgwick. 'My lugholes be still ringing, an' I was a deal further back than the lieutenant. Leave him with me, and I'll see him shifted over to somewhere he can rest. The captain be needing you on the far side of that creek.'

Preston took one more look at Macpherson, who had closed his eyes again, his head resting against the big coxswain's thigh. 'That's right,' he said, rising to his feet, and wiping his eyes on his sleeve. 'Take care of him for me, please.'

'He'll be fine, sir,' said the coxswain, waving over a pair of marines standing close by. 'I saw a camp bed in one of them tents we passed. These two Lobsters will help see him shifted.'

Preston nodded and then walked away, forcing his mind to release the image of Macpherson. From the other side of the inlet came the pop of musket fire. He looked that way and saw the *Griffin* approaching the far shore. Time to finish this night's work, he decided. 'Corporal Edwards!' he called.

'Yes, sir,' said the soldier, coming over.

'Mr Macpherson is wounded. You will need to lead the marines. Guard the prisoners and secure the perimeter of the battery. I'll leave Mr Todd in command.'

'Aye, aye, sir,' said Edwards. 'Is the lieutenant badly hurt?'

'I am not sure, in truth. Sedgwick has him in his care, but I must go now.'

'Yes, sir. Leave it to me.'

'Mr Todd! Take command here, if you please. I shall leave you ten men and the marines. You must tend to the wounded, see that the guns are spiked and rig the magazine for demolition. Oh, and be ready to depart when the ship returns for you.'

'Eh, yes sir. I mean, aye aye, sir,' said the youngster

nervously.

'You'll be fine, lad,' said Preston, leaning close. 'Corporal Edwards and Sedgwick are very steady, and both are here to aid you. Wounded, then guns, and then lay a trail in the magazine. Is that clear?'

'Aye aye, sir.'

'I'll take the others in the long boat and launch. Good luck!'

Preston collected the shuttered lantern from Sedgwick and then gathered the rest of the shore party together down by the boats. He took some time to check they all still had the package of inflammables they had been issued back on the frigate, seemingly a lifetime ago. Then he waited while they had all reloaded their firearms. 'I'll take the longboat. Black, you take command of the launch,' he announced, when all was ready.

'Aye aye, sir,' growled the petty officer. He raised his musket in acknowledgement, the weapon like a toy in his huge grip.

'Good. Follow my lead. Let us depart.'

The men clattered aboard and the two boats slid out on to the water, their crews rowing easily as they headed across the inlet. In the bow of the longboat was Trevan, keeping time with O'Malley and Evans on the bench in front of him. It was a lovely night, warm and calm, with only the rattle of a distant drum and the bang of musket fire from ahead to remind the men that they were still in the midst of battle.

'What's all that fecking shooting about, Adam?' hissed O'Malley.

The Cornishman glanced over his shoulder and slightly mistimed his next stroke.

'Eyes in the boat there!' ordered Preston. His next

words were lost as a broadside roared out, filling the night with fire.

The men rowed on across the water with their backs to the growing fury of the frigate's bombardment, each blast steadily louder, each wash of furnace light shining brighter. The steady beat of the drum continued, growing in volume. Trevan wrinkled his nose a little as the first trace of gun smoke coiled across the water. 'Brimstone, or I ain't smelt it afore,' he whispered, leaning forward. 'Pipe be burning a deal of powder. We be close lads.'

'Boat ahoy!' came a hail.

'Easy there!' ordered Preston, before raising his hand to form a half cup close to his mouth. '*Griffin*! he yelled. 'What is it, Mr Armstrong?'

'You're ordered to rest on your oars and not to land,' replied the ship's master. 'A body of the enemy are coming on very bold. Mr Blake will disperse them presently.'

The two boats drifted side by side, turning slowly as the flow from the river pushed against the tide. There was another blast of gunfire, accompanied by the cries of the wounded, and then the devastated little shipyard came into view. One of the flaring torches had been knocked into a pile of discarded wood pieces, and a small blaze had started, lighting up the high stern post and clawing ribs of the nearest partly built ship. Further back, gun smoke trailed like river mist between the buildings. There was the *Griffin*, bow on to them, the black lines of her rigging a cage for the moon, anchored just off the bank. Confronting the big ship was a frail line of soldiers, their wounded strewn on the ground behind them.

'What the feck are them Frogs about?' protested O'Malley. 'Muskets will never answer against broadsides!'

'Poor bleeders,' agreed Evans. 'Might as well toss

pebbles at a whale.'

The soldiers fired a single volley, the sound sharp and thin, after the throaty roar of the frigate's eighteen-pounders. It was received without any apparent effect. Evans could see the tall figure of Clay standing among the carronade crews of the quarterdeck. Then the *Griffin* fired back, and the line was no more.

'Mr Preston!' came a shout across the water.

'Yes, Mr Armstrong?'

'You may proceed now, but make haste. The captain wishes to be off directly, before the French can rally.'

'Aye aye, sir,' said Preston. 'Get underway,' he ordered to the coxswain. 'Head for that landing stage over there.'

As the boats rattled alongside the little wooden jetty, the *Griffin* began a desultory fire, sending single balls crashing into the treeline. Preston led the crowd of sailors as they clambered out of the boats and cautiously entered the abandoned yard. The hull of the more complete ship rose up above them, massive and immovable, propped up on its slipway. It seemed solid and as indestructible as a cliff, despite the holes punched into the planking by the *Griffin*'s bombardment.

'Plenty of chips and lumber lying here,' mused Preston, looking around him. 'And we can use thatch from those shelters. Black, take your men over to the other ship and get a brace of fires started hard against the keel. Keep loading on more wood once they are alight.'

'Aye aye, sir,' said the petty officer, knuckling his forehead before heading off with the launch crew at his heels.

'O'Malley, take half a dozen musket men and skirmish into the yard a little. Keep a weather eye on the French. You can use your combustibles on any promising targets, but your chief object is to warn us should the enemy rally. They are little threat to the ship, but we are another matter entirely.'

'Right yous are, sir,' said the Irishman, selecting five men to follow him.

'The rest of you, with me,' ordered Preston. He opened the shutter on his lantern and strode into the dark cave formed by the swelling outward curve of the hull above his head. He had to crouch low to reach the keel and then began searching for a suitable place. The sailors looked at one another, and then up at the poorly supported and damaged hull. A puff of breeze made it rock, with a groan of protest from the remaining props. With considerable reluctance, the braver members of the party followed their officer into its shadow.

'Let us set a fire here,' said Preston, scoring a cross with his heel on a dry-looking spot. 'Thatch and small stuff first, then wood. Swiftly now, lads.'

*****

O'Malley's little party spread out into scattered pairs and advanced into the abandoned shipyard, their pace slowing as the sound of their fellow Griffins faded behind them. Piles of stacked timber loomed over them. Black sawpits gaped suddenly at their feet, while the thatch of shattered buildings flapped in the breeze like the wings of dark birds closing in around them. From somewhere ahead came the moans and cries of wounded French soldiers, punctuated by the flash and roar of the *Griffin* firing. Soon they found their pace slowing until they were creeping forward, as if picking their way through the castle of a slumbering ogre.

'Bleeding hell,' whispered Evans. 'It don't make no sense but this place gives me the creeps. I'd sooner a bunch of Frogs jumped out than it be as empty as this.'

'Not me, Sam,' replied Trevan. 'I've had my fill of slaughter this night. I ain't got the heart for it after seeing all them soldiers fall. It be them poor souls a-wailing as is spooking you.'

Evans paused to listen to the wounded for a moment and then carried on, pushing his way down the narrow gap between two buildings. The first of the fires had been lit behind them by their shipmates, sending their long shadows streaking ahead in the flickering light.

Beside him Trevan wrinkled his nose. 'Summat be burning,' he whispered.

'Aye, well ain't that what we're bleeding here for?' replied Evans.

'No, Sam, it be that.' Trevan stepped a few paces forward and stooped down to pick up a smouldering torch, lying where it had been abandoned when its bearer fled. He knocked off the ash and blew the glowing end back into life. A few little flames blossomed from the blackened tip. 'Here, we can use this to set a fire, Sam,' he said. 'Like what Preston said we ought to.'

Evans looked around him, and pointed to a building ahead, walled with overlapping planking that had escaped the worst of the bombardment. 'How about over there?'

The two men crept up to the entrance until one stood on either side. The interior was dark and forbidding.

'In you go, mate,' whispered Evans. 'Don't worry, I've got yer back.'

'Oh aye? Much obliged, I'm sure. And why be it me as goes first?'

'Coz you've got the bleeding torch, ain't you?' explained the Londoner, nodding at the flaming brand in his friend's hand.

'That be soon mended,' said Trevan, holding the torch out.

'All right. We'll go in together. Come on.'

In the flickering light the interior was filled with mysterious crates and bundles, interspersed by deep pools of shadow.

'Right, this lot should burn a bleeding treat,' said Evans, propping his musket up against the wall and drawing out his cutlass. He used the blade to lever open the nearest crate. 'Best check these ain't filled with powder or grenadoes, afore we sets the place alight.'

'Right you be,' agreed Trevan, laying the torch aside and starting on another box.

'I ain't sure as this will answer,' said Evans, holding up a thick sheet of orange metal. 'Don't suppose copper sheathing burns any?'

'Not at all,' confirmed his friend, lifting some long copper bolts from another box. 'Nor will the fixings. There be anything better?' He dropped them back into the box with a clang and then suddenly froze, aware that he was being watched. 'Sam!' he hissed.

Evans turned to see the glitter of torchlight on the edge of a weapon as a figure leapt from hiding towards the Cornishman. Quick as a flash, he launched the copper plate across the room, striking the figure on the shoulder. The blow knocked the attacker off course, allowing Trevan to sidestep the clumsy blow from the short sword. As his assailant staggered past him he pushed the figure hard in the back, his momentum crashing him into the wall. With a high-pitched yelp of pain, the sword clattered down and Trevan stamped his foot on the blade. His attacker reeled away, crying out and tucking his bruised hand under one arm to comfort it.

'Why, he ain't naught but a nipper!' exclaimed Evans. 'Dressed mighty odd, mind. I've seen less braid on an admiral.'

The boy was no more than twelve or thirteen, his face streaked with tears. He had lost his hat, but his heavily decorated military tunic was magnificent, in spite of a long tear in one sleeve, and the smears of powder smoke and dirt spread across the rest.

'You reckon he be the drummer boy of them soldiers?' asked Trevan. 'Our Lobsters always use little shavers.' He pointed to the boy, and pantomimed beating a drum. After a moment of wide-eyed terror, the boy nodded briefly. Trevan laid aside his cutlass and smiled at the lad. 'We ain't going to harm you any,' he said, pointing towards the door. 'Away you go, nipper.'

Evans stepped back from the entrance, and the boy took a few faltering steps towards it, his pace quickening to a run as he vanished into the night. 'Poor bastard,' said the Londoner with a shake of his head. 'Come on, let's see about this fire.'

The sailors searched more of the building until Trevan spotted a group of small barrels. He prised out the bung on one, and a pungent smell filled the air. 'Here we goes,' he announced. 'Some firkins of best Stockholm tar.'

Trevan open several of the barrels and tipped them over so the thick tar dribbled out to form a growing puddle. Then he gathered up the crate lids they had pulled off and piled them on top. Evans used the butt of his musket to batter planking free from the walls to add to the pile.

'That'll burn right well,' enthused Trevan, stepping back. He pulled out his pack of combustibles and lit it with the torch. Once it had spluttered into life, he thrust it in among the wood, and then threw the torch on for good measure. The result was almost immediate. A column of flames reared up, spitting and hissing. It grew alarmingly, the trunk of fire quickly branching outwards as it met the thatch roof above, filling the space with heat and thick black smoke. The two sailors retreated quickly, stumbling to the entrance and out into the night.

The yard outside had been transformed. Many more fires had been started and columns of swirling sparks rose up from close to the dark mass of the half-built ships. The crackle of burning timber and the smell of wood smoke came from all sides. Overlooking the scene was the solid mass of the *Griffin*, lit by the flickering light. But few blazes were a match for the building the two sailors had just left. For a moment only smoke and wavering heat seeped out through the thatch. Then, with a roar, the roof collapsed, releasing a torrent of flame upwards. The heat was unbearable, driving both men back.

'Bleeding hell, Adam!' exclaimed Evans. 'How much of that tar was there?'

'Oh, a good dozen of them barrels, maybe more. I reckon they'll be seeing that the other side of Bombay.'

Fanned by the flames, the blaze began to lick at the next shelter along, while fragments of burning thatch whirled away across the yard. Then both men heard a chorus of cries from downwind of the blaze.

'Who be that a hollering so?' asked Trevan.

'No bleeding idea … Hang on. Ain't all them soldiers as copped it up ahead?'

The sailors exchanged glances and then set off, skirting the monstrous fire they had created. On the far side the ground was littered with wounded French, lying among the dead. Rearing over them was the wall of flames from the blaze. Both sailors quickly slung their muskets and began pulling the nearest men clear.

The task proved difficult. The ground was littered with discarded equipment and burning fragments from the building. Most of the wounded who were able to drag themselves clear had done so, leaving only the badly hurt, many of whom were little more than dead weight. Others tried to resist when they realised the identity of their rescuers. One, a fiercely moustached sergeant, managed to pull free his long bayonet from its scabbard and lunged weakly at Trevan.

'Easy there, mate,' protested Evans, knocking the weapon aside. 'We ain't here to harm you any.'

The job was barely started when cutting through the sound of crackling fire came several blasts of a whistle.

'Time to scarper,' said Evans. 'That's the recall.'

'Hold up a moment,' said Trevan. 'Them two over there needs shifting first, else they be in for a broiling.'

'All right, but then we shove off.'

The first soldier was so badly hurt he needed to be carried with care. By the time they had returned for the next one the whistle was blowing again.

O'Malley appeared, waving frantically at them. 'What the feck are yous about!' he protested. 'Your man's been blowing his call fit to burst, and you two are playing at being sawbones!'

'These bleeders are like to be roasted if we leaves them,' protested Evans.

'So will you be if those feckers catch you,' said O'Malley, pointing towards the trees. Small groups of soldiers were emerging into the firelight and running from one piece of cover to the next. Several of the *Griffin*'s guns fired together and another wood pile was scattered across the ground, but still the soldiers came on. One group was heading towards them, with a small figure in a braid-covered tunic at their head.

'Ungrateful little bleeder!' muttered Evans, as O'Malley pushed him on his way. Trevan gave a last look at the wounded and then followed his friends as they slipped away back to the boats.

Chapter 13
The *Curlew*

Clay sat at his desk in his open shirt and britches, working at his report on the Kollam inlet attack. The *Griffin* was at sea once more, sailing south. All the window lights at the rear of the cabin were open to the breeze, as were the gun ports on both sides. He had only to tilt his head a little to be able to see the Malabar coast, a strip of bright green against the blue. Clay caught sight of the portrait of his wife looking down on him and felt a pang of longing. It was well over half a year since he had seen her, and would be as much again before he was home once more. Why had he been in such a perishing hurry to leave her when that damned diplomat had come to call?

The clearing of a throat recalled him to the present. 'My apologies, Mr Vansittart, my thoughts had wandered. Pray, where had we got to in the account?'

'I was expressing a hope that you would give due weight to Tom's role in the affair,' said the damned diplomat.

'Precisely so,' said the captain, returning to his rough draft. 'Let me find what I had set down. Ah, I have it. "No report of the action would be complete without mention of the exemplary initiative and considerable courage displayed by Lieutenant Thomas Macpherson of the marines. Using powder from the battery, he destroyed the cable positioned across the path of HM vessel that I have the honour to command. This was achieved at some hazard to that officer, but I am happy to report that though he was much scorched in setting fire to the train, his eyes are now safe and his hearing restored." Is that tolerably put?' asked Clay, looking up from the paper. 'I take it that is still the case? The patient hasn't had a relapse?'

'Have no concerns on his account. They must breed them tough in the Highlands. He presently lies insensible in his cot, snoring fit to wake the dead, thanks to the good doctor's tincture of laudanum. He is no longer black as a Moor, although his whiskers will be a sad loss to the wardroom, of course. But I take it your request for assistance with your dispatch was not just occasioned by a desire to see Tom treated well?'

'No indeed, it is the next part that I needed your advice with,' said Clay, brushing at his own sideburn with the feathered end of his pen.

'In what regard?' asked Vansittart. 'If it is the particulars you seek, I was with Mr Corbett attending to the wounded down in the cockpit, so my view of the affair was rather limited. Apart from noting the gratifyingly small number of casualties, I can have little to add.'

'It was more in the diplomatic line that I sought your counsel. An account of the action is quickly done, but I am troubled by how to present it. We were in neutral waters, after all, without the express permission of Travancore. Should the matter be enquired upon, this report might be a key document.'

'Oh, I wouldn't trouble yourself about that,' said Vansittart, holding out his glass for Harte to refill. 'The Company's treaty with them permits the pursuit of bandits and rebels on to their territory, which can be stretched to include a nation we are at war with, such as France. Matters might have become troublesome if you had encountered any of the maharaja's forces, but Macaulay was correct in his view that we should only find regular French troops there. The dalawa is too shrewd a cove to allow himself to be compromised in such a way.'

'That is a relief, sir,' said Clay. 'I find all this intrigue and politicking very little to my taste. Give me a straightforward enemy to go at, I say. How do you suppose the chief minister will react when he learns of the destruction to his ships?'

'How would you respond, Captain?'

'I believe that I would be deuced angry at the thwarting of a long-cherished plan,' said Clay. 'I would be unable to deny all knowledge, for we have captured too many prisoners from the *Marengo*'s shore party for that. War or grovelling apology seem the only options, and the chap we met don't seem the apologising type.'

'Ah, there speaks the up-and-at-them, military man in you,' said Vansittart, pointing accusingly at him with his glass. 'But we both know that you are a deeper cove than that. This whole affair reminds me of an acquaintance who had his coxswain taken by slavers in a friendly port. After a deal of anger at the offence, he elected to take back his man by force. A "*fait accompli*," as the French would have it. When challenged over his actions, he explained them as the simple recovery of a deserter. I have no doubt that both sides understood perfectly what had happened, but chose not to make a major issue over what was, when the dust settled, the matter of a single sailor.'

Clay laughed at this. 'And that is what you expect awaits us at Trivandrum?'

'Of course. In private the chief minister will gnash his teeth and rend his clothes, but in public he will express surprise at the audacity of the French, deny all knowledge of their actions and will probably thank us for punishing their impertinence with such vigour.'

'So that will be that?' said Clay. 'Both sides aware of the offence, yet studiously maintaining the pretence of friendship?'

'For the present, but rest assured that such treachery will not go unpunished. Once this Wellesley fellow has dealt with the Mahrattas, and the company's army is free to descend on the Travancore border, Major Macaulay will be in a position to suggest to the young maharaja that he stands in need of fresh counsel. The dalawa will be moved aside, and a noble with a greater appreciation of his country's obligations will take his place. Rather less thunderous than the broadsides of your ship, but quite as effective. It is called diplomacy, dear sir.'

'I cannot wait to see his countenance when you meet him,' chuckled Clay.

'Actually, I think it might be best if Macaulay and I handle the interview. The dalawa may smile and preen to us, but in his black heart he will be furious at the person responsible for this. I owe it to Mrs Clay to return you to her in one piece. We cannot rely on Napoleon to always be on hand.'

'Napoleon?' queried Clay, looking towards the window seat, where the mongoose was dozing on the most sun-kissed of the locker cushions. 'Do you mean to say that … that snake …'

'Oh, I have no proof, but a venomous serpent in one's cabin late at night is certainly suggestive,' said Vansittart. 'Assassination has long been an accepted part of statecraft in these lands, and the locals have had many centuries to perfect the art. I daresay you recall the ability in that regard of my former valet Rankin?'

'God bless my soul!' said Clay, shaking his head. 'And I imagined that only the actions of the French need concern me.'

After a moment he pulled his chain letter to his wife towards him and made a note. 'I had best amend my correspondence to Lydia. It might be for the best if I was not to mention the snake at all.'

*****

It took less than a day for the *Griffin* to return to Trivandrum. It was late in the afternoon as the frigate turned in towards the shore, picking her way through fishing boats to her place in the roadstead. The familiar temples and haze of cooking smoke rose up from behind a beach thronged with people enjoying the approach of evening. All this was familiar. What was new was the Royal Navy cutter that bobbed at anchor. She was a trim little craft, flush-decked with sleek lines and a long bowsprit thrusting out ahead of her. The moment the frigate was within signalling range, a stream of flags rose up to the top of her single mast.

'She is the *Curlew*, six-gun cutter, Lieutenant Abraham Hummer, sir,' reported the midshipman of the watch.

'Make the correct response, if you please, Mr Todd,' said Clay.

'I'll have the topgallants off her, Mr Harrison,' roared Armstrong from his place by the wheel.

'Aye aye, sir!'

A flood of seamen rushed aloft, the vibration of their collective feet making the image tremble a little in Clay's telescope as he stood by the mizzen shrouds to study the new arrival. More flags ran up the cutter's halliard.

'*Curlew* is signalling again, sir,' said Todd. "Have dispatches on board".'

'Thank you. Signal for her commander to come across

once we are at anchor, if you please.'

'Aye aye, sir.'

Vansittart was standing by the rail beside Clay, dressed in an immaculate pale grey coat which contrasted pleasingly with the dusky pink of his waistcoat. 'I take it that all these little flags you are waving at each other will not delay my trip ashore, Captain?' he said. 'I am most anxious to be the first to bring tidings of our little victory to the Travancore court, and I need to consult with Major Macaulay first.'

'No messenger on a horse can outpace the *Griffin* with a following wind, sir, but I will see that Sedgwick has the barge in the water the moment the anchor is let go. I daresay the *Curlew* has brought word from Admiral Rainer and perchance a little post from home, if we are fortunate. Maybe the admiral has encountered Linois's squadron. In any event, I need to attend to it.'

'Hard over, quartermaster, bring her up into the wind,' added Armstrong. 'Mr Harrison! Let go the anchor!'

'Aye aye, sir!'

'Good luck, sir,' said Clay, shaking Vansittart's hand. 'Give my regards to the major.'

'I will,' said the diplomat, clapping on his hat and making his way towards the entry port.

'Boat putting out from the *Curlew*, sir,' reported the midshipman of the watch, keeping an eye on the cutter in spite of all the bustle on deck around him.

'Thank you,' said Clay. 'Mr Armstrong, have Lieutenant Hummer sent below when he arrives and kindly inform the crew that if they have any letters to send home, now is their moment.'

'Aye aye, sir.'

Lieutenant Hummer proved to be a tall, gangly young

man with a face framed by curly ginger wisps to mark where his sideburns would one day grow. The obvious care he had taken over his appearance was partly undone by the extent to which he had outgrown his uniform jacket, giving an impression that was all elbows and knees.

'My apologies, sir,' he said. 'I was but sixteen when I joined the East Indies squadron, and naval broadcloth is hard to obtain hereabouts.'

'No matter, Lieutenant,' said Clay. 'I well remember the issue of uniforms on a foreign station when I was a rapidly growing midshipman. Do take a seat. You have dispatches for me, I understand?'

'From the admiral,' confirmed Hummer, passing over a thick canvas package.

Clay felt the hard musket balls included in every naval dispatch roll beneath his fingers as he took it. They were there to guarantee the letter would sink if thrown overboard to avoid capture. He checked the seal was intact and picked up his penknife to slit open the package before remembering his manners. 'Pray excuse me while I read these, Lieutenant,' he said. 'Would you care for some refreshment?'

'That would be most welcome, sir.'

'Harte! Some wine for my guest.'

Hummer accepted the glass, exposing several inches of wrist as he did so, and settled back in his chair while his host read his correspondence.

'General Wellesley has won another victory, I collect?' said Clay, looking up from the sheaf of papers.

'Yes, it occurred back in September, sir. He gave the Marathas a sound thrashing at the town of Assaye. He's a deuced clever chap, by all accounts. For a soldier.'

'But the campaign is not concluded, it seems,' said

Clay, reading on. 'The admiral is still required to support the general's forces?'

'For all of the forthcoming winter, sir.'

Clay read on to the end of the dispatch and then dropped it on to his desk. 'And what of the French? Still no word of Admiral Linois and his ships?'

'Not on this coast, sir,' said Hummer. 'Nor at Reunion. The admiral is most concerned. He did hope that you might have encountered them.'

'So he writes in his letter. Last night I captured two dozen men from Linois's flagship that he had put ashore to man a small gun emplacement, but that is all. And they claim not to have been in communication with him for some months.' Clay rose to his feet and began to pace. Hummer put down his glass hastily and started to get up too, but Clay waved him back. 'Pray do not trouble yourself, Lieutenant. It is a habit of mine. I find that walking helps me to think with greater clarity.'

Hummer watched the captain stride backwards and forwards across the width of the cabin in front of the window lights. Clay was obviously familiar with the route, which lay between two beams, so that he only had to tilt his head a little forward to prevent it striking the deck overhead, while his about turns as he reached the quarter galley on each side could be made entirely unconsciously. Backwards and forwards Clay paced, and backwards and forwards the young lieutenant's eyes followed him, until his gaze chanced upon a fur cap that lay abandoned on one of the locker cushions. Strange, thought the commander of the *Curlew*. Why would anyone wear fur in the tropics? 'God bless my soul!' he exclaimed. 'It moved!'

Clay came to a halt midstride and looked around in surprise. 'I beg pardon?'

The fur cap got to its feet, stretched languidly and

regarded the young man, who now found a second pair of puzzled eyes on him. 'Your pardon sir, but I took your mongoose for a hat,' he explained. 'It is a mongoose, is it not? I have only seen one fleetingly before, near Madras.'

'He is, according to my surgeon,' explained Clay. 'He came on board in place of a goose, for reasons I will not weary you with. The crew have taken him to heart, naming him Napoleon, on account of his being both small of stature yet surprisingly fierce. I will own he is a curious addition to the company of a king's ship. He is an affectionate fellow, unless you are a rat, when he is the very devil.'

'I trust I did not break into your thoughts at a delicate stage, sir,' said Hummer.

'I was considering Pondicherry when you cried out,' said Clay, resuming his place behind his desk.

'The French settlement near Madras?'

'The very same. Admiral Rainer told me that Linois tried to reclaim it when he first arrived here from Europe. Fortunately he was on hand to thwart the attempt. Perhaps Linois will try again, while the admiral is distracted?'

'He might, sir,' conceded the lieutenant. 'But word of such a move has not reached us. Should he try, he will find the place well garrisoned and Captain Warren on station with two of the line and a frigate.'

'Then what the hell is he about!' exclaimed Clay, listing options finger by finger. 'He isn't at Reunion, according to this dispatch. Nor is he annoying Admiral Rainer's support for General Wellesley in the north. We have seen no sign of him here upon the Malabar coast save the little shore party we encountered, which only leaves Pondicherry, yet you tell me he has not moved on there! Where can he be?'

'Perhaps he has returned to Europe, sir?'

'No, that will not answer,' said Clay. 'He left during the peace. If simply conveying soldiers and shipwrights was his mission, they could have been sent on merchantmen. Besides, a single ship of the line and a handful of frigates will count for nothing in the balance of power in Europe, while in these waters it is a force to be reckoned with. No, he is still here, waiting for his moment.' Clay was quiet, staring past the young officer at the bulkhead behind him.

Hummer felt an overwhelming desire to turn in his chair, but instead sat patiently.

'It will come to me, in time,' sighed Clay at last. 'In the meanwhile, you will have to wait here until the morrow. I shall have some letters for you to take back for me, once Mr Vansittart has completed his interview with the authorities in Travancore.'

'Aye aye, sir.'

'Which means you can dine with me tonight,' said Clay, with a smile. 'I would dearly like to know a little more about India. My wife spent some time in Bengal during the last war and speaks with great fondness for the country. For my part, I have only been on shore once.'

'I will be happy to oblige, sir,' said Hummer. 'In exchange, it is always a pleasure to hear word from home, and I would gladly learn more about your action last night.'

'Then I shall be sure to include Lieutenants Preston and Macpherson of the marines in the party, so long as he has recovered sufficiently from his wounds. They are the true heroes of that encounter. Shall we say six bells in the dog watch?'

*****

It was a pleasant gathering in the great cabin of the frigate later that evening. The *Griffin*'s officers were a friendly group, well used to each other after the long years that they had served together, and they did their best to welcome the awkward young commander of the *Curlew* into their midst. The sole exception among the animated crowd was Thomas Macpherson. Clay watched him with concern, wondering to what extent his reserved manner might be the residual effects of all the laudanum he had been given, or whether it was caused by his appearance. Clay had only ever seen the Scotsman immaculately turned out, and it was hard to recognise his friend in the battered dinner guest sitting at his table. His face appeared lopsided, thanks to its one surviving sideburn, and gleamed with all the grease applied to his more tender burns. But the marine seemed content enough, quietly sipping his wine and listening while the others pressed their guest about life in India.

'I've seen a little of the country, gentlemen,' conceded Hummer. 'During the monsoon, the fleet generally keeps to port, which gives us the chance of some leave.'

'What do you make of the place?' asked Blake.

'Well, for a start it ain't a single place at all. It's the size of Europe, with as many races, tongues and religions as you care to mention. Each region is different. Some have mountains, other parts are flat, while still more have forests that stretch for miles. And in every respect, it is more than one imagines possible.'

'How do you mean, Lieutenant?' asked Clay.

'Our cities are crowded, but theirs are positively teeming. Our poor are wretched, theirs are destitute. Our nobles are wealthy, but here they have riches beyond imagination. Everything is more extreme than one is accustomed to. The food is spicier, the noise more penetrating, the colours more brilliant, the heat fiercer, the rain more torrential. I sometimes wonder how dull home shall seem after living here for a few years.'

The young officer's burst of eloquence had run its course, leaving him red faced with embarrassment and the rest of the group quiet.

It was Blake who broke the silence. 'A glass of wine with you, sir,' he said, smiling across the table. 'You move me with the fervour of your account. I rather envy your having explored such a land. What pictures I might paint had I done likewise!'

'You are an artist, sir?'

'I daub a little,' said Blake modestly, indicating where the portrait of Lydia Clay smiled down on them from the bulkhead.

'Aye, and don't we know it,' offered Vansittart, with a wink to the others. 'When he's in full flow there ain't enough scent in Piccadilly to quite mask the stench of turpentine in the wardroom.'

'I believe the hunting hereabouts is very diverting, with all manner of game,' said Faulkner, who had been brought up on his father's considerable estate.

'There is indeed, sir,' said Hummer. 'At Madras you will find three separate packs of hounds, all brought out from home, although most favour sport with a more local flavour. Pig-sticking is very popular, particularly among the company's cavalry regiments.'

'Pig-sticking?' queried Armstrong. 'What in all creation might that be?'

'The hunting of wild boar from horseback with a lance,' explained their guest. 'Beaters drive the hogs from cover, while the hunters await them like so many knights errant. I have only observed it, but it seems devilishly exciting, especially as a large tusker is quite capable of turning about and bowling over a horse with a brisk charge.'

'That sounds a trifle hazardous to me,' said Faulkner. 'I enjoy riding to hounds, but at least foxes don't turn on you, what?'

'But I have wearied you enough with talk of India,' said Hummer. 'Pray tell me of your attack last night, sir?'

'I was but a bystander,' said Clay. 'Mr Preston and Mr Macpherson, would you oblige?'

'Shall I proceed, Tom?' asked Preston, speaking close to his neighbour's ear.

'By all means,' said the marine, his voice louder than was strictly necessary.

Preston gave his account to a captivated audience. Most knew their part in the night well, but not the whole. When he reached the end, he turned to his neighbour. 'Tom here was the true hero. I thought him lost at one stage, but the devil looks after his own, it seems.' He placed his arm around his friend's shoulders.

'Hear him,' said Armstrong, drumming his hand on the table top. 'A glass of wine with you, Tom.'

'Thank you,' said Macpherson, once Preston had nudged him and pointed towards the sailing master. He managed to drain his drink with a little difficulty, in spite of the back thumping being administered by Blake on his other side. The faces around the table were flushed with pleasure and wine, all save their host, who was staring thoughtfully over their heads.

'And how was word of all this destruction received in Travancore, Mr Vansittart?' asked Taylor.

'That is perhaps the strangest part of the whole affair,' said the diplomat, leaning back in his chair to reveal an expanse of pink waistcoat. 'There is little doubting the genuine anger felt by their chief minister at the ruin of his ambition to command a fleet of warships, but I formed the distinct impression that his rage was chiefly directed towards the French. Major Macaulay thought the same.'

'Small wonder,' said Blake, with satisfaction. 'If they were charged with the protection of the shipyard, then they did a damnedably poor job of it. Four cannon and a stretch of rope won't answer against a determined assault, and throwing companies of infantry into the path of my guns was never going to mend matters. It was as if they had no expectation of an attack.'

'They knew we were coming, right enough,' said Preston. 'Why, that naval lieutenant we captured said as much.'

'Really?' queried Taylor. 'When did you have occasion to converse with him?'

'It was when he yielded the battery to me. He was upset, so I said some words to comfort him, to the effect that he had fought bravely, and that there was no dishonour in his surrender.'

'And what did he say, Edward?' asked Clay, leaning forward in his seat. 'His precise words, if you can call them to mind.'

'Eh, well, I was somewhat distracted with securing our position, but it was a clear denial of my suggestion that he had been taken by surprise. He maintained he had been warned that we would come. I considered it so much gammon at the time, but now I think on it, he spoke more in frustration than bravado.

What with prisoners to secure and the shipyard still to destroy, I gave it little thought. I trust I have not done wrong, sir?'

The others looked at Clay, whose face had an air of triumph. 'Why of course!' he exclaimed, bring his fist down on the table.

'Sir?' repeated Preston.

'It has been vexing me all day,' continued their host. 'As I wrote my dispatch this afternoon, and as I listened just then to your excellent account, Mr Preston. The one question that truly matters. Why did our attack last night encounter so little opposition? Linois has the resources of his entire fleet to call on, yet what did we encounter? It is as Mr Blake said, a few dozen sailors and some files of soldiers. Why?'

'Perhaps they placed an excess of reliance on the ship's cable?' offered Armstrong.

'It was a well-conceived trap that might have ended ill for us had Tom not had his wits about him, but I hold myself at fault for not anticipating it,' said Clay. 'An arranged signal to wait and the *Griffin* would have remained in the offing till it was cut in a more conventional manner. I don't think that is it, Jacob.'

'Perhaps the enemy did not expect our attack, sir?' offered Taylor.

'That will not answer either. Mr Preston has just told us that the officer he captured had been warned we would come. No, there is a much more compelling explanation.'

'Which is?' asked Vansittart.

'Linois failed to defend it properly because he cares not a jot about a muddy creek on the Malabar coast!' he exclaimed. 'Even the dalawa knows it, which is why his annoyance was directed at the French, sir.'

'But that makes no sense,' protested the diplomat. 'Why

set up this shipyard, and then fail to protect it?'

'Because it holds our attention here,' said Clay. 'While his true objective lies elsewhere.'

'Which is?' repeated the diplomat.

'Why did the government send us to these waters, sir? It was the very first thing you spoke of when you visited me last spring. The Eastern trade, of course! In this very cabin you told of how the China fleet alone would pay for half the navy. Eight million sterling, you said it was worth.'

'Eight million last year, when we were at peace,' said Vansittart. 'This year its cargo will be worth more.'

'That will be Linois's true object, depend upon it,' said Clay. 'This China fleet is an annual convoy, is it not, Lieutenant?'

'It is, sir. It generally leaves the Pearl River at the turn of the year,' explained Hummer. 'A dozen East Indiamen and a like number of lesser merchantmen.'

'And what escort do they have?' asked Taylor.

'Only a company brig for the first part of the voyage, sir. The arrangements were put in place while we were yet at peace, and East Indiamen are sufficiently well armed to deal with any Malay pirates bold enough to chance their arm in the South China seas. Once they reach Madras, they will rendezvous with a more substantial escort provided by the admiral to see them through to the Atlantic.'

'There is the French plan, gentlemen,' said Clay. 'To meet with this convoy before it is properly protected, and land a most telling blow. How swiftly can you take word to Admiral Rainer, Lieutenant?'

'Give me your dispatch, and the *Curlew* can depart within the hour,' said Hummer.

'Then perhaps we yet have time? mused Clay. 'It is only

just November.'

'In truth we may already be too late, sir. My cutter is fast, but first I must reach Admiral Rainer, and Bombay lies in quite the wrong direction.'

'You must go in any event, to warn him,' said Clay, 'but in the meanwhile the swiftest aid that can be sent is this ship. What if we depart immediately?'

'If you make a fast passage it will still be a good two months to reach Canton, sir,' said Hummer.

'Nearer to three if the winds prove contrary, sir,' explained Armstrong. 'Which they will for some of the passage, in this season. I fear the China fleet will have left long before we arrive.'

'Then we must meet with them coming the other way,' said Clay. 'Where do you suggest, Lieutenant?'

'In the Straits of Malacca,' said Hummer, without hesitation. 'Between the Malay peninsula and the island of Sumatra. All trade with China passes that way. We know it and so do the French.'

'Then that is where we must go,' said Clay. 'Now for the dispatch you are to take. Harte! Pass the word for my clerk, and light along some coffee.'

'Aye aye, sir.'

'Mr Vansittart, is your correspondence complete?'

'It is, Captain, and already with your clerk. If you will indulge me with a boat to take a message ashore to inform Major Macaulay of our departure, then I am content to go when you wish.'

'Splendid!' said Clay, turning to his guests. 'A thousand apologies, gentlemen. What must you think of me? We have barely passed the second remove, and here I am breaking up our little gathering. Lay the blame where it lies, at the feet of the

French, and remember that injury when we fall in with Admiral Linois.'

There was a rumble of approval at this from around the table, and a few calls of 'Damnation to him!'

'No matter, sir,' said Preston, rising to his feet. 'In any event, Tom here stands in need of his bed to be quite restored when we next must call on him.'

'And I must see to the ship,' said Taylor, emptying his glass. 'As must the other sea officers here.'

'While I need to lay off a course for us to follow,' said Armstrong.

'Make it so, gentlemen,' said Clay, rising to his feet. 'There is not a moment to lose.'

Chapter 14
In the Straits of Malacca

The New Year had come and gone as the *Griffin* beat her way across the Indian Ocean in her race to reach the China fleet before the French should find them. In January they had rounded the huge island of Sumatra, a full thousand miles of forested hills lying across their path, to finally enter the long Straits of Malacca. And then, as so often happens at sea, calm. Long days beneath the tropical sun, patrolling backwards and forwards, waiting.

Jacob Armstrong was officer of the watch. He stood in the modest patch of shade provided by the mizzen topsail and mopped at his brow. Nearby the noon navigation class was being helped with their observations by his deputy, the ever-patient Sam Holden.

'Now have a care, Mr Todd,' urged the master's mate. 'You'll be needing to use all of them smoked glass plates with a sun as fierce as this 'un.'

'Well, I have all my plates deployed and find I now cannot locate the sun at all,' protested Sweeny, swinging the bar of his sextant backwards and forwards in frustration.

'That is because the sun here has a greater altitude than you will be familiar with,' said Armstrong, pointing a finger upwards, as if about to bless the class. 'It is directly over the mastheads, for we lie close upon the equator. Remember what I taught you. Perform the hardest part first. Find your sun and then seek to bring her down to the horizon.'

The sun was indeed high above the frigate, a molten orb that beat down on them. The planking of the deck was bleached white in its light, the tar in the seams soft and blistered, emitting wafts of resinous scent.

'Dear me, no, Mr Sweeny, that can't be right,' exclaimed Holden, inspecting a proffered slate with his pupil's calculations chalked across it. 'That would place us deep in the forests of Siam! Make your sighting again, and attend to what you are about this time, rather than skylarking with Mr Todd.'

Armstrong cleared his throat before favouring the youngsters with a frown of disapproval and they settled down to perform the calculation again. 'Report any cases of truancy to me, if you please, Mr Holden.'

'Aye, aye, sir,' said the master's mate. 'Now, just you watch me close with my sextant, Mr Sweeny.'

Armstrong left the class and moved under the larger area of shade offered by an old staysail that had been suspended above the leeside of the quarterdeck as an awning. Beneath it sat Blake, with a paint-daubed smock pulled over his uniform, working at an easel propped against one of the carronades. Beside him sat Macpherson in shirt-sleeves, looking a little more like his old self. The raw part of his face had returned to a healthier colour, and a strip of dark stubble showed where a replacement sideburn was forming.

The American came up behind the officers to see how the painting was advancing. 'Why, you are making good progress, John!' he exclaimed. 'What a magnificent elephant. It is the one you saw at work in Bombay, I collect?'

'And has seldom mentioned above eight or nine times a day thereafter,' added Macpherson.

'The very same, and if I have permitted my enthusiasm

for the noble beast to run on a trifle, I shall proffer no apology. When one has desired to see such a marvel for so long, a little excitement is permitted.'

Armstrong continued to study the painting. 'Pray tell me, are the ears not a trifle small, I wonder?'

The artist turned around and glared at him. 'Are elephants common in New England, Jacob?' he asked.

'They are not, in truth,' conceded the sailing master. 'But I have seen various illustrations of them. As a child I had a print of one on my nursery wall.'

'And were these elephants of the African or Indian variety?'

'There is a difference?'

'Most assuredly,' snorted Blake. 'Principally in the matter of ears! I devoted some care to measuring the proportions of this animal when I made my preliminary sketches, and can assure you that the size of these ears is perfection.'

'Then I stand corrected, John,' said Armstrong, patting his shoulder to mollify him.

'If it is any consolation, I too thought the ears a wee bit meagre, and received a similar lecture for my pains,' said Macpherson.

'On the subject of ears, yours seem to be fully restored, Tom?' observed Armstrong.

'Aye, the last of the ringing past a while back now.'

'No longer needing to yell to address you across the wardroom table is a comfort,' said Blake, adding paint with unnecessary vigour to his canvas.

'Sail ho!' yelled the lookout perched on the fore royal mast.

Armstrong stepped out from under the awning and

shaded his eyes with one hand as he stared aloft. 'What do you make of her, Dawson?' he called.

'No more than one of them pirate skiffs, sir,' came the reply. 'Beg pardon, there be a brace of the buggers. Just appearing beyond that island, a point off the larboard beam.'

Armstrong crossed the deck, picking up a telescope from its place beside the binnacle as he did so. The island had steep cliffs on the side facing him, topped by dense jungle. As he looked, the first parao slid into view, sleek as a shark. It was long and low with an outrigger along each side. Large triangles of sail rose from its twin masts, and its narrow hull was packed with crew. Behind the first parao a second appeared, slightly smaller, with a dirty red hull.

Armstrong turned to the midshipman of the watch. 'My compliments to the captain and tell him that two pirate ships are in sight.'

'Pirates!' exclaimed the youngster, his eyes opening wide at the thought. 'Er, I meant aye aye, sir,' he continued, turning quickly away in response to the American's frown.

'We have found ourselves a brace of Malay buccaneers, I collect, Mr Armstrong?' asked Clay as he came up the companion ladder to join the officer of the watch.

'Yes, sir. Doubtless in hopes we may be a lucrative merchantman. See how they begin to circle towards us.'

The two ships skimmed across the water with barely any wake, heading to windward of the *Griffin*. 'They are truly beautiful craft, are they not, Jacob. Very fast, even in these light airs.'

'They are, sir, although your parao cannot keep the sea should it blow above a capful of wind, which is why they stay so close to land. Dangerous if they can surprise and board you, mind. That leading one must have sixty men on board, everyone a bloodthirsty Mohammedan eager to slit a few Christian throats.'

'Then we must teach them that we are not to be trifled with. Kindly show them a gun, Mr Armstrong.'

'Aye aye, sir.'

It took no more than a few minutes to clear away one of the frigate's eighteen-pounders. The deep boom of the cannon echoed out, sending a cloud of white birds up from the island. Clay watched as the ball skimmed between the two pirate ships, raising a chain of splashes from the surface. The effect on the paraos was almost instant. Turbaned heads bobbed in agitation, and the leader came sweeping around, reversing its course as it sped away closely pursued by its companion.

'Very wise,' said the American with satisfaction. 'Those hulls are little more than eggshell thick. Shall I put the ship about, sir?'

'If you please, Mr Armstrong,' said Clay. 'Perhaps we will sight the China fleet on this tack? If Mr Hummer was correct in his reckoning, they should appear presently.'

'Aye, let us hope so, for tacking to and fro day after day grows wearisome, does it not, sir?'

'Some would count us fortunate, Jacob. Many a frigate on blockade patrols the same patch of sea for months, without glimpsing anything as diverting as Malay pirates.'

Clay stayed on deck as the watch was called and the frigate swung around on to her new course, back towards the coast of Sumatra over the horizon. Astern the two paraos vanished back behind their little island.

'Deck there! Sail ho!' yelled Dawson again, a few minutes later.

'More pirates?' queried Armstrong with the speaking trumpet.

Dawson continued to stare for a moment. 'No, sir! 'Tis a regular topgallant, with perhaps a second behind it. Them be coming up from the south'ard!'

'The right direction for the China fleet, sir,' offered Blake, wiping his hands clean on a rag as he came over.

'Or for Admiral Linois's squadron, if they have been watering at Batavia,' added Clay.

'Mr Todd!' said the sailing master, holding out a telescope. 'You have the keenest eyes. Give your sextant to Mr Holden and away aloft with you.'

'Aye aye, sir,' grinned the youngster, delighted to be released from the agonies of trigonomical navigation.

'Put the ship about, if you please, Mr Armstrong,' said Clay. 'Let us close with them.'

'Aye aye, sir.'

The *Griffin* turned once more on to a new course, a thing of towering beauty in the bright sunshine with her columns of white sails and water foaming along her black and buff hull. Soon the first little topsail Dawson had seen lifting above the horizon multiplied as more and more ships were reported by Todd and the lookout.

'So, the China fleet at last, it would seem,' said Clay, examining the new arrivals with his telescope. Coming towards him was a long line of stately East Indiamen, with a small armed brig a mile to windward of them. To leeward was a second, more motley string of a dozen smaller merchant ships, boasting a variety of different rigs. Most had British colours but among them Clay could pick out at least one Portuguese flag and possibly a ragged-looking Swedish one.

'They make a brave show, do they not, sir,' said Blake. 'Fifteen – no, sixteen – East Indiamen, every one as big as a sixty-four. They keep station well, too.'

'Aye, were it not for the John Company gridirons they fly, you might almost think them warships, sir,' added Taylor, from Clay's other side. 'The little brig must be the escort Mr Hummer mentioned. Was it named the *Ganges*?'

'Will you look at the lead ship, now?' exclaimed Armstrong. 'Topping it the admiral, with that commodore's pennant at the peak. These Company nabobs do fancy themselves.'

Clay stood among his officers and lowered his telescope, a frown of concentration on his brow. It was true, with their twin broad white stripes and lofty sides, the East Indiamen might indeed be confused for warships, even if behind most of the gunports was nothing more offensive than a bale of silk or a crate of porcelain. Those flags were a giveaway, of course, with their red and white stripes, but then a flag could be changed.

'What armament do they carry, Mr Taylor?' he asked.

'As little as they need to repel a determined privateer, sir,' said the first lieutenant. 'They are commanded by merchant captains who well understand that each ton of armament is one less ton of tea, at three shillings a pound when unloaded at home. That is the way the Company reckons matters. They might have fifteen to twenty cannon a side, most of which will be twelve- or six-pounders at best, with half a dozen carronades on the upper decks.'

'Not much to pit against the thirty-six-pounders on the *Marengo*,' mused Clay, continuing to stare at the approaching fleet. Then he glanced at Blake, as if noticing for the first time his painting smock.

'What are you thinking of, sir?' asked Taylor, recognising the look in his captain's eyes.

'Mr Blake's unconventional attire put me in mind of our

last time in the Indies, when he used his considerable talent to make our warships resemble an East Indiaman, to lure those French frigates to their doom.'

'I remember it well, sir,' said Armstrong. 'High canvas sides, wooden props and a deal of paint, I collect.'

'You present it as little more than the backdrop at some travelling show,' complained Blake. 'An effective *trompe l'oeil* requires considerable work, I'll have you know.'

'But how will that answer here, sir?' persisted Taylor. 'Surely we already have a multitude of vulnerable targets to encourage the French, and far too few genuine warships to oppose them.'

'Quite so, George,' said Clay. 'I believe a signal should be visible now. Kindly make our number and ask whoever's broad pennant that is to come on board, together with the commander of the *Ganges*. When they arrive, pray bring them below along with Mr Blake, who I trust will be wearing the king's uniform once more. I shall go to my quarters and give matters some thought.'

'Aye aye, sir.'

*****

The two men whom Taylor escorted into Clay's cabin a little while later were a contrasting pair. One was a solid-looking man in his early fifties, his silver hair in marked contrast to his dark eyebrows. His face was deeply tanned, testament to long years spent in the tropics. The other was a spare, hesitant young man with pale eyes and thin hair. Both wore the elaborate naval uniforms of the Honourable East India Company, although when it came to glittering braid the older man outdid his colleague by a wide margin.

'Nathaniel Dance, at your service, sir,' said the senior of the two, firmly grasping Clay's proffered hand. 'Captain of the *Earl Camden* and senior officer of this year's China fleet. This gentleman is Lieutenant George Cumpston of the Company's armed brig *Ganges*.'

'Delighted to make your acquaintance, gentlemen,' said their host. 'My name is Alexander Clay. My first lieutenant you will have met, while this gentleman is Lieutenant Blake. Would you care to be seated? Harte, some refreshments for our guests.'

'Capital drop of madeira, that,' exclaimed Dance, quickly emptying his glass, and twiddling it by the stem in hope of a refill. 'My last case ran out a month back.'

Clay nodded to Harte. 'Your convoy seems even more numerous than was reported to me back in India, Captain?'

'Some more Indiamen were awaiting us in the Pearl River, and various country ships arrived desirous of our protection. We even have one from Botany Bay.'

'And did you have a safe passage from Canton, Captain?' he asked.

'Moderately so,' conceded Dance. 'Plenty of deuced pirates, of course, hopeful of making their village's fortune, but Cumpston here held the bulk of them back without need for us to waste too much powder on the blighters.' He turned his keen gaze on Clay. 'But the most noteworthy event occurred this day. I was surprised to find a king's ship in these waters. Admiral Rainer told me not to expect any escort before Madras. To what do we owe the pleasure?'

'What do you believe the current position to be between France and Britain, Captain?'

'We were at peace when my ships left Madras, but then word from Europe takes a good four months to reach India, and then as long again to follow us to Canton. Have matters changed?'

'War was declared last May,' explained Clay.

'Then it is good to have your protection, sir, although I take it since we are to be escorted by a single frigate, the danger is not excessive?'

Clay exchanged glances with Taylor before responding. 'Not exactly, Captain. The French Admiral Linois is currently in these waters and I believe intent on attacking your ships.'

'An admiral, you say? Does that mean he commands a fleet?'

'A squadron, certainly. A seventy-four and perhaps three other warships.'

Dance's jaw dropped open. 'A ship of the line!' he exclaimed. 'Is Rainer mad? What the hell is he thinking of, sending a single frigate to protect us?'

'In fairness to Admiral Rainer, I came to your aid under my own initiative,' explained Clay. 'I have, of course, sent word to him by the swiftest means and I am sure that more substantial reinforcements will be on their way.'

'And in the meantime, how do you propose we proceed?'

'We must continue on your planned route,' said Clay. 'That is where we will be sought by any ships sent for our protection.'

'Except that your Admiral Linois will also be seeking us in those same waters. Will we not simply fall into his lap?'

'That is a distinct possibility,' conceded Clay. 'Which is why we must be prepared to counter it. Tell me, Lieutenant Cumpston, how is your brig armed?'

'Fourteen six-pounders and a pair of larger carronades on the quarterdeck, sir,' said the young officer, blushing slightly as the attention focused on him.

'Six-pounders!' muttered Taylor. 'Against the scantlings of the *Marengo*? Why, they'll bounce off like hailstones!'

'They have served us tolerably so far this voyage, sir,' protested the commander of the *Ganges*.

Clay held up a hand. 'Every material contribution has a value. What of the East Indiamen? They carry guns, do they not?'

'Aye, but only in a modest way,' said Dance, running a hand through his hair. 'My *Earl Camden* is the best armed. She has thirty-six guns. Long twelves and carronades on the upper deck for the most part, but she is not designed to give battle in earnest. Her sides are thin compared with a warship and her timbers too frail for sustained punishment. And of course, we all lack the men for serious combat. What is the complement of the *Griffin*, pray?

'Two hundred and fifty, sir,' said Taylor.

'All trained veterans, I don't doubt. By comparison I have a crew of a hundred and forty, most of whom are lascars and Chinamen. Would you have me stand toe to toe with this *Marengo* you speak of? I ask you, sir!'

'You mistake my intentions,' said Clay. 'It is clear there will only be one victor if the enemy should close with us. We must make them wary of doing so.'

'And how, pray do you intend to achieve that?'

'Why, by means of a ruse,' explained Clay. 'I was told your fleet would have a dozen East Indiamen, and live in hope that a similar report will have reached the enemy.'

'Twelve or sixteen? It hardly signifies …'

'Hear me out, I pray. Which three of your ships are the best armed?'

'Let me see,' said Dance, stroking his chin. 'I should

say my *Earl*, for one, and the *Royal George* next and then I would choose the *Warley*. Captain Wilson is a former king's officer, so her people are better trained than most.'

'Very well, let us make it so,' said Clay, jotting the names down. 'Now, to remedy the want of men, could the other East Indiamen spare a dozen hands each to bolster the crews of those three? Sending over the better-trained quarter gunners, any former man-of-war's men and the like?'

'No sea captain willingly gives up his best men on the eve of action, but let us assume they can be persuaded to do so.'

'Good,' muttered Clay, making more notes. 'We can spare half a dozen men for each of the three, under a good petty officer to provide some training and stiffen resistance. Could we do that much, Mr Taylor? Without impairing our ability to fight?'

'The loss of eighteen hands will play Old Harry with my watch list,' said Taylor, 'but I daresay I shall manage.'

'So, we now have three ships crewed with closer to two hundred men each, ready to make some semblance of resistance. Next, they are to sail as a separate squadron, all flying blue ensigns to match that of the *Griffin*. Admiral Rainer is vice admiral of the blue, and Linois has already encountered some of his ships when he first arrived in these waters. That will give the impression of a powerful naval escort.'

'You think?' queried Dance. 'Will they not appear as what they are? Three merchantmen flying false colours?'

'They might, which is where we must rely on the services of Mr Blake. Kindly join me at the stern window lights and look over the convoy, John. Tell us how you might make three of these East Indiamen seem superior to the rest. Pray aim at simplicity. With Linois in the offing, time is not our friend.'

The others watched as the lieutenant looked along the

line of ships, each one almost a copy of those around it, tugging at one ear.

'Tell me, Mr Taylor,' said Dance in an aside. 'Is your Mr Blake some sort of conjurer or illusionist?'

'In a manner of speaking he is, sir,' whispered the first lieutenant. 'He is an artist.'

'Do you have black and yellow or buff paint on your ships, sir?' asked Blake, turning from the window.

'Paint?' queried Dance. 'I can't say that I am overfamiliar with the contents of my boatswain's store, but I daresay we have.'

'Mr Harrison can supply more if required,' said Taylor.

'What are the particulars of your plan, Mr Blake?' asked Clay.

'The overall size of the ships cannot change, of course, so they must appear further from the viewer to seem bigger. I would reduce the size of their ensigns, say an eighth smaller than the others. Then I would adjust the two strakes painted along the ship's sides. Make those of the three pretend warships a hand's width thinner above and below, and the rest make wider by the same amount. And see that they are painted in buff, the *Ganges* too, to match the *Griffin*. That might do it.'

'Is that it?' protested Dance, folding his arms. 'The sum total of protection his majesty's navy has to offer? The loan of eighteen men and a fresh paint scheme, against the might of this French squadron. Why stop there? Why not repaint all sixteen Indiamen and pass ourselves off as the Channel Fleet!'

'No, because the illusion requires the contrast …' began Blake, but Clay cut in.

'The plan will only answer if it plays on our enemy's fears. It is not defeat we seek to inflict on him, only deception. Think as he might do. Ten thousand miles from home, in waters where his little squadron is heavily outnumbered by the Royal Navy …'

'If only,' scoffed Dance.

'Heavily outnumbered,' continued Clay, 'with few facilities to repair battle damage. His fear is that he will find the China fleet well protected. It is on that we play. Three of the line and two lesser ships is just the escort he fears. The moment he approaches, we must sail boldly towards him in a spirited manner. Promptitude and firmness, that is what we must show, and let my ship do the bulk of any fighting.'

Dance looked at Clay for a long time, mulling over all he had heard. Then he reached across the desk to shake his host's hand once more. 'I admire your confidence in the face of such odds. I shall speak with my fellow captains in council, and put your proposals to them.'

'You cannot simply direct them?' asked Clay.

'Lord, no. This is the Honourable East India Company, not the bloody navy! Each master is solely responsible for his ship and cargo. But if my opinion carries any sway, you may rest assured it will be on the side of your advice, in every particular.'

'Thank you, and will they follow your recommendation?'

'If you were any other, Clay I would have my doubts,' said Dance, rising to his feet. 'But they know of your reputation from the last war, both as a fighting captain and for winning through against the odds. When I tell them it is your plan, I daresay they will go along with it. Good day to you, sir.'

*****

The main deck of the *Earl Camden* differed from that

of the *Griffin* in several important respects. For one thing, there was the clutter between the guns. When the frigate was in action the whole gun deck was swept clear, with even Clay's furniture and the bulkheads of his cabin packed up and taken down to the hold. By contrast, here mysterious piles of crates and boxes lashed down under canvas covers crowded close. They stood in mounds between the guns, isolating each weapon from its neighbour. Then the cannon themselves were different. They were smaller than the eighteen-pounders the frigate carried and their thin gun barrels lacked any nicknames painted across them by their proud crews. But they also looked dusty and seldom used. The daily gun drill on board the *Griffin* meant that every bit of both cannon and equipment was oiled and worn by constant handling. The ash-shafts of the rammers were smooth to the touch, the rope of the gun tackles had a soft flexibility to it, the gun trucks fitted into ruts worn in the deck.

'Has this ever been fired?' queried Evans, bending over the breech and dipping a finger into the touchhole. It emerged streaked with rust. 'That'll be a nay, then.'

'These fecking wheels ain't seen grease of late,' added O'Malley, who had stooped down to examine the carriage. He turned towards one of the prospective gun crew, a Chinese sailor with a long queue down his back. 'You … haveo … tubo… of galley slusho?' he intoned slowly.

'Sorry mate, we only just got enough for the bleeding rigging blocks,' the seaman replied, in an accent that was more Shoreditch than Shanghai. He jerked a thumb towards the rest of the gun crew, all of whom were Indian. 'You don't get much animal fat on a John Company barky, what with half these bleeders not touching pig, and others kowtowing to cattle.'

'Where … what… the feck …' spluttered the Irishman, amid the laughter of his colleagues.

'Jack Wang's the name. They shipped me over from the *Bombay Castle*, on account of my six years in the Channel Fleet. That were on the old *Repulse*,' he explained. 'And I agree, that bleeding gun ain't been fired for a while.'

Fletcher, the veteran petty officer in charge of the Griffins, interjected at this stage. 'Sorry to break this all up, ladies, but what was you expecting O'Malley, the *Sovereign of the* bleeding *Seas*? It's a gun, of sorts, so live with it. Just you and Evans start teaching this lot how to rattle it about as might harm a Frenchman. An' make Wang here the gun captain.'

'Right you are, Mr Fletcher,' said O'Malley, touching his forehead. 'Fecking arsehole,' he added under his breath as the petty officer marched out of range to see how training was going on the next gun in line. 'Now lads, we'll start with some dumb show. Who's after using the rammer?'

Between them Evans and O'Malley allocated the crew out to the various roles around the gun. Those with some experience or better English were given the more crucial tasks of loader, rammer and handspike men, while the others were spread out along the gun tackles. Then the two sailors did their best to explain each man's job, together with the more obvious dangers of naval gunnery.

'Always give the barrel a wet swab before loading the charge, lads,' said Evans, one huge arm draped across the shoulders of the rammer man, the other around the designated loader. 'You'll find all manner of glowing crap gets left when she fires. Shove a bag of powder down amid that lot, and you can kiss goodbye to your fin.' He drew one hand into his shirt sleeve, leaving only his index finger bent in a hook to emphasise the point to his wide-eyed students.

'When your man shouts "clear", look to yer feet,' cautioned O'Malley to the men on the gun tackles. 'When it fires, that fecker'll run back faster than the Dublin Mail, and it weighs much the same.'

When everyone had been briefed and pushed into place, O'Malley surveyed his charges. 'Right we are,' he announced, clasping his hands together. 'Up ports!' he ordered. Nothing. A sea of blank faces looked back at him.

'It'll be a chilly day in hell afore these lascars can fire three broadsides in two bleeding minutes,' commented Evans.

'Let me try, mate,' said Wang, from his position behind the gun. He let fly a volley of pidgin English, in which the words 'up' and 'port' were clearly discernible, and the man with the rammer leapt into action. The hatch opened wide to reveal a square of sunlit sea.

'But that's what I fecking said!' protested O'Malley. 'Never mind. Run her up, lads, and watch your feet! Go on! Pull!'

The twelve-pounder was dragged across the deck, its wheels squealing in protest, and out into the sunlight. Training the crew of the *Earl Camden* had begun.

Chapter 15
The *Berceau*

Rear Admiral Charles-Alexandre Léon Durand, Comte de Linois, stood beside the rail letting the warm breeze flap at the tails of his coat. He was a handsome man in his early forties, with a prominent nose and long brown hair that he wore gathered with a neat ribbon at the nape of his neck. He was on the broad quarterdeck of the *Marengo*, the long lines of planking stretching away like the floor of a ballroom.

Off to leeward he could see the second most powerful ship in his command, the solid-looking forty-gun frigate *Belle-Poule,* on a parallel course and occasionally spilling wind from her foretopsail to maintain her position exactly ten miles from him. Bruilhac was an excellent officer, he reminded himself. When the time came, he could rely on him to fight well. Another ten miles to windward, visible to the *Belle-Poule* but over the horizon for him, would be the second of his frigates, the thirty-six-gun *Sémillante.* Her captain, Motard, was a grizzled veteran in his fifties. A good sailor, but one who has been defeated by the Royal Navy twice before, reflected the admiral. I must remember that. It may make him cautious in battle. Beyond her would be the last ship in the chain, the little twenty-two-gun corvette *Berceau.* He didn't know much about her young commander, Halgan, other than that he had an uncle high up in the *Ministère de la Marine* in Paris. This may be the New France, considered Linois with a smile, but good connections were still what counted for an aspiring naval officer.

'You seem thoughtful, monsieur le comte,' said Captain Vrignaud, the commander of the *Marengo*, coming to join him.

'I was just thinking about the squadron,' Linois replied. 'I know Bruilhac by reputation, and you of course, Joseph, but not the other two.'

'Should it come to a fight, it will be the *Belle-Poule* and my *Marengo* that will do most of the work, monsieur. But I understood that this China fleet was almost unprotected? Surely we have only to show them our seventy-four cannons, and the merchants and civilians on board will scramble over each other to haul down their colours?'

'Seventy cannons, mon ami,' corrected Linois. 'You forget the four we left with Lieutenant Ropars back in Tranancore. A sad loss to the ship, I fear, although my quarters are so much more spacious without them.'

'Yes, I hope he will still be there when we return for him,' said Vrignaud.

'If he is, then my ruse will have been for nothing, Captain. In war, as in the kitchen, you cannot make cake without breaking eggs.'

'You think the English will have attacked him, monsieur?'

'To fight an enemy, you must first understand him,' explained the admiral. 'The Royal Navy have enjoyed a century of success by always attacking, whatever the odds. It is what makes them such dangerous opponents, but it can also be their weakness. I captured their *Hannibal* in the last war because her commander was so eager to close with me he ran his ship aground. We must treat our enemy as the matador does a bull. Flash a cloth to make him charge towards the inconsequential, and then attack him where he least expects. Young Ropars and those ships were my red cape.'

'Will your plan work, monsieur?'

'I think so, as long as the China fleet arrives before the bull realises that he has been fooled,' said Linois with a smile. 'We can do little more than we are at present. I have the squadron spread like a net. We just need something to swim into it.'

Both men looked around as a midshipman began to chalk down numbers on his slate. 'What is happening, Lieutenant?' asked Vrignaud to the officer of the watch.

'The *Belle-Poule* is signalling, monsieur,' said the officer.

'Masthead! Is there anything in sight?'

'Non, mon capitaine! Just the *Belle-Poule* and a glimpse of the *Sémillante* on the horizon.'

'*Belle-Poule* is repeating a message from further up the line, monsieur,' reported the midshipman, coming over and saluting smartly. '*Berceau* to flag. Fleet in sight bearing north by west.'

'Thank you,' said Linois with a smile. 'At last! Have the ship put about, Captain, and order the squadron to close on the *Berceau*.'

*****

Clay and Vansittart were sitting opposite each other, sipping at their wine, when Harte reversed his way through the cabin door bearing a large dish.

'Keeping the table clear, if you please, sirs, this here dish being hotter than brimstone!' he announced as he approached. Clay hastily removed the decanter from the inviting gap between the two place settings and his servant banged the dish down in its place with a sigh of relief.

'Why, 'tis a veritable sea pie!' exclaimed Vansittart, as Harte broke through the crust of crushed biscuit pastry to release a delicious cloud of steam. 'You have no idea how happy that makes me.'

'Where did the fish come from, Harte?' asked Clay.

'Compliments of your coxswain, sir,' explained the steward, loading up their plates. 'Him and Trevan was line fishing from the lee cathead last night. They lowered a lantern to just above the briny, and caught a deal more joeys than they reckoned on. No idea what manner of fish they be, but the wardroom had their pie at eight bells, and found it very tasty.'

'They did indeed,' said the diplomat, forking out his portion to let it cool. 'I was forced to absent myself while they did so, knowing I was to dine with you, but it was a sore trial. And here is my just reward!' He shovelled a fork-load in to his mouth and closed his eyes with pleasure. 'Delicious! There is truly nothing like a few months of salt meat, day after day to make a man crave a change.'

'I give you joy of your pie, sir,' smiled Clay, raising his glass to his guest.

'So tell me, how does training proceed on board the John Company ships?' asked Vansittart, pointing to the stern windows where the *Earl Camden* filled the view with a tumbling bow wave crowned by her figurehead of a large red-faced man in a horsehair wig. Behind her could be seen the upper masts of the other two selected East Indiamen, each ship a cable length from the one in front. Off to leeward was the rest of the convoy in two further lines.

'Tolerably well, sir,' replied Clay. 'I hope that their gunners will not be called on, but if required they can now put on a creditable show. We at least look the part of a squadron of ships protecting their charges.'

'Will it answer, do you suppose?' wondered Vansittart.

'If we handle ourselves as if we are the superior side, that will do much to persuade the French, sir,' said Clay. 'My chief concern is in the matter of signalling.'

'Signalling?' queried his guest.

'Indeed. It will never do for a humble frigate to be seen issuing orders to three ships of the line. That will alert a deep cove like Linois directly. No, the flow of signals must seem to come in the other direction, and though I have agreed with Dance what most of our tactics are to be, I am most uncertain of his ability to make the correct signals in a timely manner.'

'Could you not station yourself on board his ship?'

'Only if I wish to end my career and beg for my bread, sir. No captain is permitted to leave his command in the face of the enemy,' said Clay. 'Still, it is the show of signalling that counts, rather than the substance.'

'And when do you suppose Linois will come up with us?' asked the diplomat.

'In truth, I am surprised not to have seen him sooner, sir. He must have spent some time in Batavia, but I am not in any great haste. The longer before he appears, the closer will any relief sent by Admiral Rainer be. He must have received my letter some weeks ago.'

'If he has sent any,' said Vansittart. 'No superior likes to have the error in his dispositions pointed out by a subordinate. Are you sure he will respond to you request?'

'Absolutely,' said Clay. 'In the service his reputation is as a person who values his advancement above all things. Becoming the man who ignored a warning and lost the China fleet in consequence will fit very ill with that.'

'And what if you are wrong and Linois has other plans entirely?'

'Then I shall be censured for my half-baked theory,' said Clay, holding his guest's gaze with a confidence he hardly felt. Only last night he had paced this cabin, pondering why Linois had yet to appear, and questioning his own judgement. 'But I am not wrong,' he added, as much for himself. 'No other explanation makes sense.'

Further discussion was interrupted by the bang of a cannon. Both men looked towards the *Earl Camden*. From her bow a puff of smoke was dispersing in the wind.

'And still they practice,' said Vansittart, continuing to eat.

Clay put down his knife and fork. 'Perhaps, although a windward gun is also the old signal for enemy in sight,' he said.

'Deck there!' came the voice of the *Griffin*'s lookout through the open skylight. 'Sail ho! Sail on the stern quarter!'

'Mr Sweeny, away with you aloft,' said the voice of Preston.

A long pause, while both men sat looking upwards, their food forgotten on their plates.

'Deck there!' in the shriller tone of the young midshipman. 'She has a look of a small warship. A sloop of war, perhaps, or one of those French corvettes.'

'Off you go, Mr Todd,' ordered Preston. 'My compliments to the captain, and tell him that a sail is in sight coming up from astern.'

'Did that turncoat of yours not report Linois's squadron to have such a ship?' asked Clay, crossing to his desk and flicking through his rough journal of notes. 'Yes, here is the list. *Marengo*, of course, sundry storeships, a heavy frigate named *Belle-Poule*, which is a deuced odd name, a thirty-six and here we have it. The *Berceau* of twenty-two guns. Come in!' Clay listened gravely as the midshipman delivered the message he had already heard through the skylight. 'Thank you, Mr Todd. My compliments to Mr Preston, and tell him that I shall be on deck directly.'

'Aye aye, sir.'

'My apologies, sir, but pray do not leave the table on my account,' said Clay, pulling on his uniform coat. 'Harte, some more wine for Mr Vansittart. Do excuse me.'

'If you insist,' said his guest, his eyes alight with greed as he helped himself to more pie.

Up on deck the stern rail of the frigate was lined with officers, all straining to see the sail.

'I believe I have her,' announced Corbett, making a tiny adjustment to a borrowed telescope. 'A touch of white, lifting above the horizon.'

'You must have the eyes of a hawk,' complained Macpherson. 'For I can see naught but the ocean.'

'That is because your glass is very ill directed. Over there, man! Look where I point.'

'No that's not the French. I marked that an age back, Doctor,' said Armstrong. ''Tis no more than a wisp of cloud.'

'Gentlemen, a little space, if you please,' protested Clay. 'Mr Preston is officer of the watch, I believe, and Mr Armstrong and Mr Taylor have duties that require their presence, but the rest of you will kindly go about your business.'

The crowd of officers sheepishly departed. Clay felt slightly guilty, wondering if his outburst was not partly fuelled by the knowledge that the wardroom had finished their fish pie an hour back, while his portion was congealing on a plate somewhere beneath his feet. He hardened his heart and turned to the officer of the watch. 'Mr Preston, will you signal the *Earl Camden*,' he said. '*Griffin* to commodore. Permission requested to investigate sighting.'

'Am I to understand we will be taking direction from Captain Dance, sir?' asked Taylor.

'No, but we must appear to do so,' said his captain. 'I know the French are too distant to note our signals, but the sooner we instil the practice, the better.'

'Aye aye, sir.'

The signal had to be repeated twice before it was acknowledged and a reply was received.

'The message isn't quite in the correct form, sir,' explained Midshipman Todd, 'but if I reverse the order of the flags, it could mean permission granted.'

'Thank you,' said Clay. 'Acknowledge and put the ship about, Mr Preston, if you please. I will have the topgallants on her when convenient.'

The frigate swept around, drawing an arc of white across the sapphire blue water and heading back towards the horizon. The convoy had been beating into a steady breeze, but now the *Griffin* was broad reaching, with the wind flowing in across her quarter. It was her best point of sailing, and as the lines of topmen spread along her yards added each fresh sail, the pitch of the frigate's deck increased by a couple of degrees. Soon she was flying, leaving the forest of masts that made up the convoy behind. Clay stood by the now abandoned stern rail and looked back at the China fleet, seeing them as his enemy might. The three East Indiamen with their blue ensigns and narrower buff strakes were closest. They certainly looked impressive in close formation, but did they really look like warships? He glanced from them towards the other merchant ships and back again. Their masts didn't seem to be quite massive enough for seventy-fours, but might they seem to be sixty-fours, perhaps? When masked by the smoke of their broadsides?

'I believe I can see her from the deck, sir,' said Preston. He was standing close to the mizzen shrouds, balancing his telescope on a rattling so that he could focus it with his one hand.

'Are you certain?' said Clay, joining him. 'It is not Mr Corbett's wisp of cloud, I trust?'

'No, sir,' said the officer of the watch, smiling at the joke but still keeping his eye on the sail. 'If it is only a sloop, we should be able to drive her off.'

'Perhaps, but Linois would be a fool to send a lone ship against a convoy this large,' said Clay. He focused on the sighting, her topsails clear of the horizon now as the *Griffin* rushed on.

'Deck there!' came a hail from above. 'Sail in sight beyond the first.'

'What do you make of her, Mr Sweeny?' called Clay.

'A frigate, sir, much the same size as us. And Dawson here thinks he can see another ship beyond that.'

'Mr Preston, kindly signal the *Earl Camden*. Enemy in sight. Submit squadron prepares for battle. Then clear the ship for action, if you please.'

The moment the first drum roll echoed through the frigate the men of the Griffin rushed to prepare for battle.

In the main cabin, Vansittart found his half-finished lunch whisked from beneath his nose as Harte and his assistants rushed to pack everything away. His posterior had only just begun to rise as the chair it had warmed was pulled from under him and borne off towards the hold. Bemused, he wandered across to the cabin door, only for the whole bulkhead to come down as the carpenter and his mates knocked free the wedges holding it in place.

Deep in the hold the gunner and his mate entered the copper-lined gloom of the magazine in their soft felt slippers and began stacking the charge bags for the battle ahead close to the felt screen through which they would be passed to the ship's boys. Further aft Corbett and his assistants were taking their place in the cockpit, lining up their saws and probes on a temporary operating table formed from officers' sea chests.

On deck Macpherson's most talented sharpshooters were clambering up into the tops, followed by Arkwright, the frigate's armourer, installing chain slings to hold the heaviest yards aloft. Harrison and some of the ship's more experienced sailors were assembling on the forecastle, ready to dash aloft to repair any damaged rigging. But the bulk of the crew were down on the main deck, taking their places at the guns, stripping off their shirts and rolling their neckcloths into bandanas to protect their ears from the deafening noise to come.

When Clay returned to the quarterdeck in his full dress coat and with his presentation sword around his waist, the ship had been transformed. He pulled his watch from his pocket and flipped open the cover. 'By Jove, that was swift, Mr Taylor,' he exclaimed. 'The men are eager for battle, I collect.'

'So it would seem, sir,' said the first lieutenant, touching his hat. 'The enemy is holding her position.'

'She wants to keep the convoy in view, I make no doubt,' said Clay, looking across at the *Berceau*. She was ahead of him, hull up now, and side on. She was a graceful ship, a half-sized version of the *Griffin*, with a primrose yellow strake running the length of her dark hull. A prominent tricolour flapped from her mizzen rigging. Through her masts he could see a second, much larger, ship, almost bow on, beating up towards him.

'She is not unlike my first command,' he said, returning his attention to the *Berceau*. 'Although she is bigger than the *Rush*,' he added as he counted her gunports. 'Is it not eight-pounders that their corvettes carry?'

'That's right sir,' said Taylor. 'What concerns me is the rest of their squadron. That frigate is much the size of us, and coming on very bold, and the lookout reports he can see a larger ship beyond her.'

'Let us take our fences as we reach them,' said Clay, still studying his opponents. He measured the closing gap between the *Griffin* and the *Berceau*, and then further back to the approaching frigate. The second French ship was closer, but the *Griffin,* with the wind on her quarter, was much the faster. Try as he might, he couldn't tell which would arrive first. 'Mr Armstrong, would you take your sextant and tell me if we can reach that corvette before the other fellow comes up. She will doubtless be their thirty-six. Named the *Sémillante*, I believe.'

'Aye aye, sir.'

'Deck ho! Another sail just showing on the far horizon! Proper big bugger by the look of her, this'n!'

'You mean to fight, sir,' said Taylor quietly. 'One against two, perhaps more?'

'Not in earnest, George, at least not yet,' explained Clay. 'But if we can lessen the odds a little, that will serve us well. I also want to plant the seed with Linois that he may have caught a tiger by its tail. If he believed the convoy only had the *Ganges* for company, the discovery that the *Griffin* is present may prompt him to ponder what other vessels may be on hand.'

'It will be touch and go, but we should reach her first, sir,' reported the American. 'Only if the wind holds, mind, and by five minutes at best, and only if *Berceau* doesn't turn aside.'

'Thank you, Mr Armstrong,' said Clay, continuing to watch the enemy. 'Mr Todd! Take my compliments to Mr Blake, and he can run out the starboard guns.'

'Aye aye, sir.'

The *Griffin* sailed on, the range falling all the time, and still the French ship held her course, broadside on to him and apparently waiting to do battle.

'Up ports!' ordered the voice of Blake from the main deck.

'Do you think she will stay and fight, or turn away to the protection of her fellows, sir?' asked Taylor.

'That will depend on the character of her commander,' said Clay. 'Is he a cautious man or someone wanting to appear the hero before his peers?'

'Starboards! Run out your guns!' Clay felt a rumble through his feet ending with the collective thump as the gun carriages reached the side.

'What would you do, Mr Taylor?' asked Clay.

'I would turn away. Why immediately fight a superior opponent alone, when you can do so in company with a friend soon?'

'That would be prudent,' agreed Clay. 'But are we dealing with a man of such a character?'

'Here is your answer, sir,' said Preston, pointing.

Clay watched as the corvette took in sail until only her topsails were drawing. The tiny ant-like figures of her crew flooded down her rigging again, and a little later she came up into the wind, waiting for him. Along her side a line of dark squares appeared as she ran out her guns. Clay felt a strange feeling of familiarity. The tropical sunshine, the blue water, a ship waiting broadside on as a larger opponent approached, bow on. 'It's the *Courageux* against the *Agrius*,' he muttered.

'Beg pardon, sir?' queried Preston.

'You remember, Edward! Back when you were a youngster on the old *Agrius*! When that damned big French frigate nearly raked us. We are approaching in just the same manner that the *Courageux* did!'

'Aye, and nearly ended the fight with a single blow, sir,' said the lieutenant. 'Wait, do you mean to play the same trick upon the *Berceau* as that Frenchman tried on us?'

'I do, for it is all we shall have time for. Run below and tell Mr Blake to leave the starboard guns run out, but shift the bulk of the crews across to man the larboard battery. He is to have them double shotted for good measure. Have him keep the ports shut, but be ready the run out the guns in a flash the moment I give the word.'

'Aye aye, sir,' said Preston, running off.

'Mr Taylor, the instant we have raked our opponent, I shall want to put the ship about and get clear before we become embroiled with the *Sémillante*.'

'I'll go forward and see all is ready, sir.'

Clay advanced until he stood at the front rail of the quarterdeck. Beneath him Blake could be heard reorganising his men. The bulk of them were padding barefoot across the ship to take their places at the larboard guns, and a buzz of anticipation greeted the strange order. Clay leant forward, staring ahead at his opponent. The little corvette was growing close, lying directly across the *Griffin*'s path. Faces appeared at some of the gun ports, staring back at him. He opened his telescope and focused on the ship's quarterdeck. 'Where are you, then,' he muttered as he moved between the officers clustered around the wheel. One man was standing away from the others. His uniform was a little grander and he was gesticulating towards another officer, pointing at the approaching *Griffin*. 'A young blade,' decided Clay, looking at the long blond hair that flowed from beneath his hat. 'Probably his first command, then.'

'Sir?' queried Preston, who was coming back up the companion way.

'Our opponent,' explained Clay, lowering his telescope. 'He is both very young and very animated. All of which bodes well. Is it arranged?'

'Yes, sir. Mr Blake has a man stationed at every port lid, and the guns are ready. He says he can rattle them out in a trice when you give the word.'

'Good,' said his captain, returning his attention to the enemy.

A curtain of smoke gushed up from the *Berceau*, followed a moment later by the roar of a broadside. Splashes rose all around the *Griffin* and a loud crash sounded from forward.

'I doubt if an eight-pounder ball will penetrate the bow at this range, sir,' commented Preston. 'There is a little damage aloft.'

Clay glanced up and saw that a circle of blue had appeared in the foretopsail and a halliard was swinging in the air. Harrison had already sent two of his men aloft to repair it.

'Mr Armstrong, come a touch to larboard,' ordered Clay. 'I want to persuade her we mean to fight side to side.'

'Aye aye, sir.'

'A glimpse of our starboard battery, run out and ready is it, sir?' asked Preston.

'Something of that order. Will you keep an eye on those approaching ships beyond her, if you please? The large frigate and the *Marengo* are too distant to concern us, but I wish to be away before that thirty-six can come up.'

'Aye aye, sir,' said Preston, moving a little further away to get a clear sight of the *Sémillante* through the rigging of the *Berceau*.

The corvette was growing rapidly, her masts dark against the blue sky. Clay could see soldiers up in her fighting tops. One stood watching his approach, a long musket cradled in his arms. Another blanket of smoke, glowing with inner fire, roared out as she fired again and Clay heard the ripping sound of a ball passing close above his head. More crashes from forward, and part of the forecastle rail exploded into a shower of fragments. A wooden block tumbled down from above, trailing a tail of severed line. It bounced off the main shrouds and splashed into the sea alongside.

Clay continued to stare across at his opponent. She was very close, her foretopsail pressed back against the mast, holding her in position. Her captain had his sword drawn and it glittered in the sun as he exhorted his crew. Clay watched the shrinking gap. One more broadside, he decided, and then he would make his move.

'Mr Armstrong, are you ready to lay us across the enemy's stern?' he said, glancing behind him.

'Aye, sir,' said the American. 'When you give the word.'

'Mr Taylor! We will make our turn immediately after the next broadside!' The first lieutenant raised his hat in acknowledgement from the forecastle, and then stepped back to allow a wounded sailor to be carried past him. The man writhed in his shipmates' arms, his shirt dark with blood.

'That frigate is taking in sail, sir,' reported Preston. 'She is either preparing for battle, or is perhaps a touch shy of us, but either way it will serve to slow her approach.'

'Good,' said Clay, his attention on the *Berceau*. She

seemed to fill his view ahead. He could see individual crewmen gathered on the quarterdeck, clustered around the swivel guns on each of the rail posts. A grey-haired helmsman in a leather waistcoat stood at her wheel, his hat pushed back on his head as he watched the backed foretopsail. Her captain had broken off from his sword-waving to stare at the *Griffin*, seemingly determined to ram his ship. On her main deck the first of her cannon was emerging into the light, the black 'O' of its muzzle aimed directly at Clay. 'Steady!' he called out. 'We turn the moment she is blinded by the smoke of her broadside!'

More cannons trundled out until every port was filled. A moment of calm, and then they fired.

At such close range, even the *Berceau*'s guns could do some damage. Balls thudded into the tough oak of the *Griffin*'s bow. A fan of splinters flew up as one ball clipped the bowsprit, leaving a white gash in the wood. Cut lines came snaking down all around Clay and a boiling cloud of gun smoke enveloped the frigate.

'Mr Armstrong, hard over! Mr Taylor! Head sails!' roared Clay. 'Mr Blake, run out the larboard guns! Only fire as you bear on her stern!'

'Aye aye, sir!'

Clay thanked his stars he had such a veteran crew. The frigate heeled over as the rudder bit, and she swept towards her opponent's stern, her topsails flapping in protest. Meanwhile her blank side was transformed as every port lid shot open and her gun crews rushed to heave their cannon out against the slope of the deck.

'Midships, now!' ordered Armstrong, steadying the *Griffin* on her new course, and the frigate emerged from the bank of smoke, on a heading to pass a matter of yards from the *Berceau*'s stern. Clay saw the French captain in the sunlight, his mouth wide open as they bore down on him.

'Larboard a point!' ordered Clay, having to shout as the marines lining the sides of the quarterdeck started firing, so close was the enemy. 'Square across, if you please, Mr Armstrong.'

'Aye aye, sir!'

'Where is that other frigate, Mr Preston?'

'I judge we have time for a brace of broadsides before we need depart,' reported the lieutenant.

'Fire as you bear!'

The elaborate little stern of the *Berceau* was painted deep blue, with gilded figures carved around her five window lights. Clay noticed that several were of women cradling babies. Across her counter was her name, in raised gold letters. Glass and gilding sparkled in the warm sun, but could offer no possible protection for what was to follow. The broadside started at the bow and ran down the endless side of the big frigate as each double-shotted cannon bore in turn. With every crash a fresh pair of iron balls were sent sweeping their murderous way down the length of their opponent. When the *Berceau*'s stern was level with the front of the quarterdeck, her mizzen mast gave a shudder as it was cut clean through below her deck. It leant to one side for a moment and then toppled slowly forwards until it fell with a rush over the side. By the time the eighteen-pounder in Clay's day cabin fired, accompanied by the stern most of the quarterdeck carronades, her main mast was falling too. While the crews rushed to reload their guns, Clay stared at the wrecked ship emerging from the smoke. The stern had been beaten into a shattered hole and her decks were festooned with wreckage. Her quarterdeck was dotted with downed figures, many calling out in pain. There was no sign of her young captain, but the quartermaster in the leather waistcoat remained at his station, holding the ship's wheel.

'That frigate is still coming on, sir, but time to give her another rake,' reported Preston, but Clay shook his head.
'I think not,' he said. 'She is no possible threat to us now, and that frigate will have to aid her if the survivors are to ever make port. Secure the guns, and let us return to the convoy.'

Chapter 16
The Choices of Admiral Linois

It was a wary squadron of French ships that approached the China fleet later that day. The sun was sinking towards Sumatra, a jagged line of distant peaks and scattered islands on the western horizon. A thin line of grey marked where one of its volcanos smouldered uneasily. The *Marengo* led the two frigates in a tight line as they steadily overhauled the convoy from astern. The *Berceau* was far behind. Once it was clear that she was unlikely to sink, they had left her to limp back to Batavia under a jury rig and what sail her foremast could bear.

When the British ships had grown close, Linois tucked his telescope under his arm and made his way along the starboard gangway towards the forecastle with Captain Vrignaud beside him. The *Marengo*'s boatswain shooed the forecastle hands out of the officers' way, leaving them the whole of the forward rail. Linois paused and looked back at his flagship. Just behind him was her foremast, thick as a mighty tree, soaring up into the evening air. Her long yards spread far on either side, the sails they carried huge bulging scoops of white. It was a scene of utter beauty, he decided, marred only by the pair of sailors just beneath his feet relieving themselves on the open heads. He followed the line of the bowsprit pointing to the crowd of ships ahead. He looked over at the enemy, but his mind was running free, contemplating what he should do now.

When he had left the cold waters of Brest, almost a year ago, he had been excited at the prospect of an independent command. He was newly promoted and had leapt at a chance of freedom. This time he would be able to escape the endless frustration of another long war in Europe, watching his beloved navy rotting at its moorings, confined to port by the damned English. The only slight apprehension he had felt as he slipped away from the French coast was the thickness of his package of sealed orders. It had been delivered on the eve of departure, with a note forbidding him from opening them until his squadron had passed forty degrees of latitude. Once there he had slit open the heavy canvas wrapper. The contents were as bad as he feared.

In place of clear orders, he was confronted by a menu of competing instructions. He could almost picture the committee of bewigged officials who had gathered in Paris to draft it, each one the champion of his own pet scheme. He was to do his utmost to recapture France's former Indian colony at Pondicherry, pronounced the first paragraph; but without risking his ships, cautioned the second. He was also to reinforce the garrisons of his country's islands in the Indian Ocean, presumably with the same troops the draftsman of the first paragraph would want him to have left defending Pondicherry. Then a page later he was urged to look to the defence of Batavia (a mere three thousand miles away from the document's previous objective); unless there was an opportunity to ferment a rebellion on the Malabar coast, of course. Towards the end of the dispatch were instructions about the shipwrights for Travancore, promised in a recent secret agreement made with her chief minister, which seemed to have been dropped in as an afterthought. And then there was the central importance, repeated throughout, to wage war on British commerce, but only without imperilling his command, of course.

The months spent sailing out to India had at least given him time to impose some order on what was little more than a wish list. In those long hours of thought and struggle, the gem of an idea had begun to form. What if he could use that very profusion of his instructions to his advantage? Do a little of everything, and send the poor English running from place to place, with little idea what he would do next. When all was confusion, then he would strike.

So he had appeared off Pondicherry, squared up to Admiral Rainer and then vanished in the night. He had delivered the shipwrights and a few soldiers to Travancore, and then gone. He had reinforced the French islands with the rest of his soldiers, then disappeared. All for this moment of triumph. When he would capture the greatest treasure fleet in the world and return home a hero. In his mind he had built today up into an easy victory; and then that damned frigate had appeared, killing young Halgan and laying waste to his little ship in a matter of minutes.

He opened his telescope and began to examine the convoy ahead in detail. What he had at first thought of as little more than a cluster of masts began to resolve itself into distinct parts as the *Marengo* drew nearer. There was a varied group of merchantmen to leeward, then a much straighter line of a dozen East Indiamen, and finally what looked like a squadron of warships a mile to windward. Three of them were big, with two gundecks, while leading them was the frigate that had pounced on the poor *Berceau.* Much further ahead he could see another, smaller ship.

'What do you make of them, Joseph?' he asked his captain.

'It's the China fleet, sure enough,' said Vrignaud. 'That

is clear, but I am not sure what to make of those other ships. To windward.'

'Blue ensigns,' mused the admiral. 'Just like the squadron we encountered off Pondicherry.'

'But are these warships, monsieur?' queried Vrignaud. 'They seem only a little bigger than the rest. Could they not be more East Indiamen?'

'They might. How many ships did that Dutch trader report seeing outbound last year?'

'Twelve sail of Indiamen and an armed brig, monsieur. I think I can see the brig, a few miles ahead of the rest. Then they had no other escort ships.'

'Yet now they have several,' said Linois. 'I agree, they are too small for seventy-fours. Might they be sixty-fours or even fifty-gunners? The frigate that attacked the *Berceau* was certainly a warship.'

'That puppy Halgan was a fool, monsieur!' snorted the *Marengo*'s captain. 'Why not fall back on the rest of the squadron, instead of throwing away his command? But I agree, that frigate was well handled.'

'Yes, we need to be cautious. Batavia may be able to supply a new main mast for a corvette, but the nearest replacement for the *Marengo* is in Toulon. Let us come closer, and see what the enemy does. Have the squadron cleared for action, if you please.'

*****

'They don't seem dismayed by Mr Blake's paint scheme, or the ensigns, sir,' commented Taylor, watching as the French ships relentlessly came on. 'And they have several hours in which to attack before it is dark,' he added, looking around him.

'No, they do not seem deceived at all, and it is plain to see why,' fumed Clay. 'Dance is still too much the cautious merchant captain. To pass off as a duck requires more than resemblance. On occasion some quacking is required. Give me that speaking trumpet, Mr Todd.' Clay marched to the stern rail and pointed the brass cone towards the bewigged figurehead that loomed behind the frigate. '*Earl Camden* ahoy!' he yelled.

Several sailors appeared at the bow rail, wearing a mixture of turbans and broad-brimmed straw hats, and after some discussion, one disappeared. He was replaced moments later by a western sailor with a leather boatswain's hat. '*Griffin* ahoy!' he replied, using little more than his considerable lungs to project his voice.

'I need to speak with your captain!'

The boatswain waved in acknowledgement and barked an order. One of the sailors vanished.

'Are you minded to set too with yon Frogs, sir?' called the boatswain.

'I certainly mean to try,' shouted Clay. 'Is the *Earl* ready?'

'As she'll ever be, sir. Guns be manned and loaded, and your Jacks have put some heart into the lads. So long as we don't take excessive punishment, they'll do their part.' He stepped back, touching his hat, and Dance appeared in his place.

'Good afternoon, Captain,' he called through his own speaking trumpet. 'The enemy don't seem over concerned by us.'

'I agree, which is why we must confront him with the boldness to be expected of king's ships,' replied Clay. 'Will you kindly order a turn to cut them off. After which follow my lead, and attend to the space between us. Leave no gap the enemy might sail through.'

Dance looked across at the French and stood for a moment, shifting from one foot to the other. Then the commodore levelled his speaking trumpet back towards the *Griffin*. 'Aye, let us make it so,' he replied. 'We may as well be hung for a sheep as a lamb. And I will station a reliable hand here to relay your subsequent instructions.'

'My thanks, and good luck,' replied Clay.

Dance touched his hat and then disappeared.

'Mr Taylor, is the ship ready for action?' asked Clay, although he knew the answer.

'It is, sir,' replied Taylor. 'The crew are all at their stations.'

'The *Earl Camden* is signalling, sir!' announced the midshipman of the watch. He dictated the flag numbers to the rating beside him, who chalked them on to his slate, after which there was a feverish pause as he thumbed through the signal book.

'Be ready to go about, if you please, Mr Taylor,' ordered Clay. 'Do you have that signal yet, Mr Todd?'

'Er … I think so, sir. They are asking if we have a purser on board.'

'No matter, it will serve,' said Clay. 'Kindly acknowledge. Mr Taylor! Have the ship put on the other tack. Mr Blake! Run out the larboard guns!'

'Aye aye, sir.'

The frigate turned smartly through the wind and settled on her new heading. Now she was actively challenging battle, on a line of advance that would see her steadily close with the French. Clay moved to the larboard rail, from where he could see the enemy. As he reached it the main gun battery rumbled into life beneath him and cannons appeared in the warm sunshine. 'Mr Taylor, spill some wind if you please,' he ordered. 'I do not want to leave the squadron in our wake.'

'Aye aye, sir.'

Clay looked astern, to where the *Earl Camden* had just reached the puddle of disturbed water left by the *Griffin*. Slowly she lumbered up into the wind, her head sails flapping wildly and her foretop yard strained over to push her bow across. A long moment of hesitation, and she was around, gathering pace. The *Royal George*, the middle of the three Indiamen, advanced to take her place.

'They aren't the handiest, sir,' observed Armstrong from his place by the wheel. 'Perhaps it would be safer to wear ship next time?'

'No,' said Clay. 'For nothing will shout "merchantmen" to the enemy quite like lubberly sailing. Remember, we are putting on a show for them, Jacob.'

'Aye aye, sir.'

Clay watched the French ships as they came on, seemingly unconcerned by the turn towards them. The *Marengo* was growing huge, her side a wall of oak studded with guns. A few were missing from her upper deck, he noticed, spiked, dismounted and rolled into the muddy waters of Kollam inlet, but her lower battery of huge thirty-six-pounders was intact. They could smash through even the *Griffin*'s tough sides with ease. Behind was the larger of the two frigates, her guns also run out and ready, followed closely by the third. He glanced behind him at the rest of the squadron. The *Warley* had just fallen into line behind the *Royal George* and all of them had run out what guns they had on the side towards the enemy. They certainly looked impressive, he decided, but would they truly convince the French? Was Linois consumed with anxiety as he watched them, or was he laughing and joking with his officers at the absurd attempt being made to deceive him?

'Out quoins!' he heard Blake order from the main deck. 'Handspikes! Train them around!'

The barrels just below his feet elevated to the maximum and then swung round to settle their aim on the *Marengo*. A thread of smoke drifted by from the coil of slow match smouldering beside a quarterdeck carronade.

A midshipman appeared at Clay's elbow and touched his hat. 'Mr Blake's compliments, and he believes that the enemy is in range, sir,' he announced.

Clay watched the French for any hint that they would turn aside, but still they came on. He closed his telescope with a snap and felt anxiety knot in his stomach, but when he spoke, he managed to keep his voice calm. 'My compliments to Mr Blake, and tell him that he may open fire.'

*****

On board the *Earl Camden*, following in the *Griffin*'s wake, Trevan had command of her bow twelve-pounder. He had allowed most of the men to squat around their charge as they waited, chatting in the curious mix of English, Cantonese, Tamal and Urdu that was the *lingua franca* on board. But the frigate's first broadside had an electric effect on the gun crew. They sprang to their feet in alarm and then rushed to find their positions. Two collided with each other as they jumped for the same gun tackle, and stepped back, rubbing their heads. Another pair of sailors engaged in a lively tug of war over a single handspike, ignoring a second one that lay beside them on the deck, while an English cook grabbed the linstock from its tub and held the glowing point trembling over the touchhole.

'Easy there!' roared Trevan, knocking away the cook's

arm. 'There be no call for such disorder on account of a whiff of powder! For starters, we don't go a blazing off without no word of warning, and for another, what we be aiming at, exactly?' He pointed towards the open gunport, where nothing but blue water was visible beyond the mist of gun smoke from the frigate's broadside.

The crew all stared as one along the gun barrel and then back at the Cornishman.

'Sorry mate,' said the cook, surrendering the linstock. One of the handspike men released his grip and the crew all shuffled to their places around the cannon, muttering apologies in several languages.

'That be better, shipmates,' beamed Trevan. 'It'll not be long now. See, the stern most of them Frogs be a-coming into view.' He pointed back at the gunport, where part of the *Sémillante* had just appeared. The crew turned to stare once more, this time engaging in some excited chatter, before returning to their positions. 'Mind she still be a way off,' he added. 'These shortened twelves don't have the reach of the old *Griffin*'s long eighteens.' He ran a hand over the breech of the cannon, and then smiled at the gun crew. 'But, I daresay she'll serve us well enough.'

Another broadside roared out from ahead, and fresh clouds drifted past. When they cleared, all of the sternmost French frigate was in sight, together with a little of the *Belle-Poule*.

'Have a peek outside and see what be happening, Abdul,' ordered Trevan.

The gun's loader leant forward and craned his neck out through the port, just as the rumble of a more distant broadside sounded, deeper in pitch. He quickly removed his head.

'Big Frenchie firing, Sahib,' he reported, with an

agitated bobbing of his head. 'Your ship get proper bugger now.'

'Aye, I daresay, poor lads,' said the Cornishman. 'Be we in range, yet, to aid them a touch?' he muttered, crouching down to peer along the barrel. 'Perhaps, if we fires on the up roll, like.' His gun was isolated from the others on the main deck by a mound of cargo, so he stepped back until he could see Evans, stood behind the next twelve-pounder in line.

'Game bleeders, ain't they?' commented the Londoner, indicating his crew. 'I had to collar a brace of them right sharp, just to stop them blazing off anyhow.'

'Aye, that they be. You reckon we be in range yet, Big Sam?'

Evans stooped down to look across at the French ships, just as the *Belle-Poule* vanished in a cloud of smoke. Several loud crashes sounded against the hull, followed by the rattle of falling debris on the deck overhead.

'You might be right there, Adam,' said Evans, straightening up.

'Larboard guns!' bellowed a red-faced young officer in an East India Company uniform who was stood beside the main mast. 'Open f—' He paused, as Fletcher, who was beside him, whispered in his ear. 'Er, right. See that your quoins are out!' Another hasty dialogue between them. 'Oh, and your mark is the middle ship!'

Trevan returned to his gun, glanced down to check the cannon was elevated properly, and then sighted along the barrel. The French ships were much closer, their masts rising up above the trailing smoke that lay thick on the water. From ahead he could hear the *Griffin*, firing quickly in a continuous rumble as each gun was discharged independently the moment it was loaded. 'A touch to starboard!' he ordered, gesturing to the handspike men. The gun carriage was levered around on the deck, until it was aligned with the main mast of the French frigate. Trevan raised his fist, to show his gun was ready, and then realised that no one could see it across the cluttered deck.

'Fire when you bear!' shouted the voice of the red-faced officer.

'Stand clear!' warned Trevan, glancing around him. Then he brought the linstock down. A fizz of burning powder and a moment later the twelve-pounder shot back across the deck. 'Wet swab!' he roared. 'Now the charge! Ram her home! Ball! Don't forget the wad!' The crew worked well, not as fast as the Cornishman was used to, but at the steady pace they had trained for, with little risk of skipping a step and causing a misfire, or worse.

'Good, run her up,' he urged. A ball slammed into the side of the hull just beside the gun port, dislodging a burst of splinters. One of the crew let out a shriek of pain and dropped the gun tackle. He tottered backwards, blood flowing from his arm. 'Leave him be, and run that gun up!' roared Trevan, glaring at the two crewmen who had turned towards the wounded sailor. The gun thudded back into place and the Cornishman bent forward to plunge a spike through the touchhole and into the charge. Then he poured some fine grain powder into the hole from the horn around his neck and sighted along the barrel. 'Clear!' he yelled, brought down the linstock, and the gun roared out again.

'Reload it!' he barked, before turning to the wounded crewman. Blood was dripping from a large gash above the elbow. Trevan pulled off his neckcloth and bound it tightly around the arm. 'You be all right to see your way down to the sawbones, Kabir?' he asked.

'I … I think so, Sahib,' said the sailor. 'But … but will

he cut? Like your milord Nelson?'

'Not if he can help it, lad,' said Trevan with a smile. 'Away with you, now.'

The man tottered off and the Cornishman returned to his place. 'We always serve the gun afore ourselves, lads,' he urged the crew. 'Else they'll be a deal more like Kabir this day. Wad in, Abdul? Then get her run up, and let's give them Frogs some more!'

'Yes, Trevan Sahib!' chorused the sailors.

*****

Linois looked in dismay at the blood spattered on the arm of his coat, vanishing into the cloth before his eyes as it was absorbed. The ball from the *Griffin* had scoured across the top of the mizzen chain, taking a deadeye and shroud with it before it ploughed into the crew of the quarterdeck eight-pounder beside him.

'Afterguard!' yelled the admiral, over the sound of gunfire. 'Have those men taken below!' A petty officer barked out some names, and a group of sailors came across to gather up the wounded.

'Warm work, is it not, monsieur,' said Vrignaud, coming over. 'But my men are fighting well.'

'As are the enemy,' said Linois, returning his attention to the battle. 'This is far from the action I wanted. Snapping up some fat merchantmen was my plan, not fighting a pitched battle.'

'You think the enemy is superior, monsieur? I still hold they may be East Indiamen putting on a show for us.' A ball from the *Royal George* rushed past with a tearing sound and both officers ducked instinctively.

'If they are, they are fighting better than any that I have ever heard tell of,' said Linois. 'And when did merchantmen start choosing to sail down and fight warships? No, something is wrong. I can feel it, Joseph.' He stared across at the four ships opposite him, looming shapes in a fog of gun smoke, full of dark menace. Their gun flashes had become noticeably brighter in the last few minutes. Why was that, he pondered. Were they coming closer? 'Edge away from them, Captain,' he ordered.

'But monsieur, it will be dark soon. Surely we must finish this while we still have light.'

'Dark, you say?' said Linois, looking around him. The sky above Sumatra was a wash of yellow, dotted with huge pink clouds and the sun had already dropped behind a distant mountain. 'I want no night action! Break off the fight immediately!'

'But—'

'Immediately, I say!' ordered Linois. 'Signal officer! Send this message. "Flag to squadron. Discontinue the action." Go! Run, man.'

'I had best have the ship put about and the guns secured, monsieur le comte,' said Vrignaud, saluting stiffly, his face a mask.

'Joseph, a night action is much too risky,' said Linois, taking his captain by the arm. 'Surely you must see that. And I did not say that we will run away. Time is on our side. We will still be here tomorrow, and our enemy has weeks of sailing to go before he reaches safety. Let us see what happens tonight. If, as you suspect, they are only merchantmen, then they will surely use the hours of darkness to try and make good their escape. In which case we will have our answer, and time in which to hunt them down.'

*****

The stern cabin of the *Earl Camden* took Clay aback when he was shown in by a gloved steward. It was a huge space, furnished with an opulence that only an East India Company captain with five successful voyages to his name could boast. The Persian carpets were thick and yielding underfoot and the lamps that hung from the beams were of polished silver. The cherrywood furniture was upholstered in pink watered silk, and rich hangings were draped against the bulkheads. Two doors amid the run of window lights at the rear of the cabin stood open, leading through to a balcony that ran across the back of the ship. Clay could see the other captains out there, sipping wine and laughing in the warm air. Beyond them was silky night, dotted with the lights of the rest of the convoy reflected in the dark water. As he was ushered forward, he felt a draught of air against his legs. He bent down and moved a decorous swath of damask aside to find it was draped across the jagged hole torn in the ship's side by a thirty-six-pounder from the *Marengo*. Good, he thought. At least it was not just his *Griffin* that had been battered by the French.

'Ah, here he is, gentlemen!' exclaimed Dance as Clay ducked through the door to join the others on the balcony. 'The hero of our tale! A glass for the captain, if you please, Grimshaw.'

'Some wine, sir?' murmured a servant, holding out a tray to the new arrival.

'Lieutenant Cumpston of the *Ganges* you know, of course,' continued his host. 'The gentleman beside him is Henry Wilson of the *Warley*.'

'Delighted to meet you, sir,' said the merchant captain, a tall man in his forties with a balding pate. 'I was once third in the *Hydra* under Captain Mundy.'

'A fine ship, as I recall,' said Clay, shaking Wilson's hand.

'May I also name John Timms, of the *Royal George*,' said Dance.

This last officer was an aristocratic-looking man with thick curly hair. 'Delighted, I am sure, Captain. Got to hand it to you, when Dance first laid out your proposal, I had my doubts, but when the Frogs cut and ran tonight, it was the finest deuced thing I ever heard tell of, what?'

'Slunk away like whipped curs, did they not?' added Dance, with a chuckle.

'That is kind of you to say,' said Clay, 'but I trust you gentlemen do not consider the matter to be over?'

'But why the devil not, sir?' said Timms. 'Ain't that why you asked us all to assemble here? To celebrate our victory and make plans to vanish in the night? Leave the enemy to wake on the morrow and find the birds have flown?'

'I am afraid that is the very last thing we should do,' said Clay. 'The nearest place of safety is Madras, over a thousand miles away. It is a voyage we will never complete if the enemy once suspects he has been duped. Flight is what an unprotected convoy would do. We must continue on our way in a steady fashion, as if safe in the knowledge we are under the care of a powerful squadron.'

'And when can we expect such protection?' asked Dance. 'Proper protection I mean, arriving from Admiral Rainer?'

'Not before a fortnight at the earliest, and not at all if we stray from the route we are expected upon.'

'A fortnight!' protested Timms. 'But damn it all! My *George* took a cruel battering today. I dread to think what state the cargo is in.'

'Quite apart from the crew?' queried Clay.

'Indeed, they too.'

'I am afraid Captain Clay is right, John,' said Wilson. 'To deal with a savage dog, you back away in an unhurried fashion, cudgel to hand. Turn and flee and the blighter will be on you in a flash. We have stared down the French this day, and must be prepared to do so again on the morrow.'

'Still a Royal Navy man at heart, I see,' said Timms, rounding on his colleague. 'Easy for you to say. The *Warley* was barely engaged, skulking along in the rear.'

'In the position I was assigned, sir!' bristled his fellow captain. 'I trust your remark was not meant to impugn a want of courage on my part?'

'Certainly not,' said Clay hastily. 'I saw nothing but firmness and resolve in all of your actions this day, and I daresay we can change the sailing order for tomorrow. But my hope is that when Linois wakes and sees our vessels drawn up and challenging battle once more, he will leave us to proceed on our way.'

'And what if he fails to be discouraged?' said Dance. 'Tomorrow he will have the leisure of a whole day to engage us, and my ship for one cannot long endure his attentions.'

'Then we must look to Lieutenant Cumpston and the others to aid us,' said Clay, indicating where the *Ganges*'s young commander stood on the edge of the group.

'Me, sir?' he said, his face colouring.

'You, sir,' confirmed Clay. 'I have a project in mind that involves your brig and the other East Indiamen, in particular the two swiftest.'

'What are you about?' queried Timms, intrigued in spite of himself.

'An idea I had today, to play a little further on the fears of Admiral Linois,' said Clay. 'Shall we go through to the cabin, where I can lay it out in full? After which I suggest we postpone any further celebrations until our safety is assured and return to our ships to speed any repairs still required. We have a busy day ahead.'

*****

Admiral Linois had a restless night. It was warm and humid in the Malacca Straits, and his sleeping cabin was an airless box. In addition to the normal shipboard sounds he could hear the bang of hammers, sometimes close, sometimes distant, as the crew repaired the day's damage. When he did briefly drift off, he dreamt of blank-faced undertakers leaning over him to close the coffin in which he lay with bright steel nails.

Most of the night he tossed and turned in his cot, amid the twisted sheets, playing over the events of the day. The bold squadron of ships, sailing down to give battle. The resolute wall they had offered, cutting him off from the convoy behind. They had fought well. Too well for merchantmen, and yet not quite as he would have expected Royal Navy ships to do. For one thing, they seemed reluctant to close with him. But was that just their desire to protect their charges? His flagship had suffered some damage, of course, in particular a worrying split in the foremast. But then again, the fight had only been at long range.

In frustration he threw off his sheets and padded into the stern cabin of the *Marengo*. Only a few items of his furniture had been brought up from the hold, given it would all have to be taken away again when the ship cleared for action once more. This, and the missing cannon, made the room seem strangely spacious in the faint light of the shuttered oil lanterns.

He went to his desk, which was back in its usual place against the bulkhead, and sat down. He opened the lamp that hung above it and pulled his orders out from a drawer, trying to find some guidance. He sat with a page in each hand, looking from one to the other.

'It cannot be overstated the harm that would be caused to the enemy from the loss of the China fleet,' he read aloud from the sheet in his left hand. Then he turned to the page in his right. 'It is essential that your command is preserved from harm. The longer you are at large in the East Indies, the more resources the enemy will be obliged to divert to oppose you. Therefore, you are only to engage in battle under the most favourable circumstances.'

Linois dropped both sheets on to his desk in disgust. '*Putain*!' he exclaimed. 'Who writes such bloody nonsense?'

He stared at the two sheets for a while longer, his loose hair flopping down around his face, and then came to a decision. 'Sentry!' he yelled towards the cabin door. 'Pass the word for my servant! I want to get up!'

A little while later a man arrived with a jug of steaming water. 'Apologies, monsieur,' he reported, as he laid out his master's razor and towel and opened more lamps. 'I hadn't realised you would be awake yet and the galley fire had burnt low.' He glanced towards the windows at the stern of the cabin, still black with night. 'Would you like breakfast once you are dressed?'

'Just coffee, Francois,' said the admiral, moving across to the washstand and pulling his nightshirt over his head. The face that looked back at him from the mirror was gaunt and thin, the eyes red with fatigue. What was he to do, he asked himself? What?

It was still dark when he came up on deck. The officer

of the watch turned around in surprise, and then touched his hat. 'Good morning, monsieur le comte. The captain is forward with the boatswain, fishing the foremast. Shall I send for him?'

'No, lieutenant. Just a night glass, if you please.'

Armed with the telescope, be moved across to the quarterdeck rail. He was back in the same place as yesterday. The carpenter and his mate were repairing the damaged mizzen chain. A lantern was set down on the deck beside them, ghoulishly up lighting their faces as they worked. He glanced at where the wounded sailors had fallen, but the planking had been scrubbed clean.

It was close to dawn. The eastern horizon was growing pale, although Sumatra to the west was in darkness. He could see faint points of light along the shore, where fires and lamps were being lit in villages. Over the dark sea the grey bulk of ships began to emerge from the gloom. Linois swept his night glass towards them and found his answer. Far from running, the China fleet were still there. As pink light stole across the sky, the detail became clearer. In the distance was the untidy chain of merchant ships, all sailing northward towards the Indian Ocean under easy sail. Closer to him was the straighter line of big East Indiamen and between him and them, barring the way, were the same four ships in close formation he had battled with yesterday. Their blue ensigns appeared as black flags, the buff strakes on their sides faintly visible. As the light grew, he spotted the little armed brig, a few miles further to the north and leading them all. Everything was just as it had been when the sun went down, except that they had all sailed on twelve hours. He looked from the two-decked warships, across to the line of East Indiamen and back again, searching for clues. Surely they were different, bulkier, larger ships?

As he studied the enemy, their grey sails turned by

increments to rose and then white, and it was day again.

'What orders, monsieur?' asked Vrignaud, appearing at his elbow.

Linois closed the telescope and for the first time in his career was not sure how to answer. 'How is the foremast, Joseph?' he enquired, while he decided what to do.

'She is not in any immediate danger, monsieur,' said the captain. 'If we don't meet with too many storms, she should see us home to France.'

'Or too many more blows from the enemy's shot?'

Vrignaud shrugged his shoulders. 'That too, of course, but they say lightning never strikes twice, monsieur. I see they have chosen not to flee in the night.'

'No, which might mean much or little,' mused the admiral, patting the tube of his telescope against his open palm. 'Oh, very well, give the men their breakfast, and then have the squadron cleared for action, and let us try once more.'

It took the best part of an hour to prepare a hot meal and serve it out to the six hundred men of the *Marengo*. The sun was well above the horizon and it was already uncomfortably warm when the roar of drums echoed across the three French ships as their crews went to quarters for another day of battle. Linois had stayed on deck the whole time, preferring to brood over his problems rather than go below and toy with the plate of delicacies his steward would have laid out for him. He stood aside as the crew of the eight-pounder appeared, still two men short from yesterday. They quickly went through the routine of casting off their cannon and checking over their equipment, and when all was ready, calm descended over the ship.

'Run out the starboard guns, Captain, and bear down on the enemy,' ordered Linois.

'*Oui*, monsieur le comte.'

Linois made sure that he was watching the British line as the French guns rumbled out. The ships carried serenely on, and then little dark squares appeared all over their sides as they responded in kind. The two squadrons were sailing parallel to each other, steadily northwards, just out of long cannon shot.

'A half point to starboard, quartermaster!' ordered Vrignaud. 'Trim the topsail yards!'

Now the French ships were edging towards their opponents a little, sliding ever closer. 'What will you do, English?' muttered Linois, his telescope settling on the frigate that led the British line. 'Will you fight, or turn away?' He searched her deck, looking for her captain. Then he found him, a tall man standing among the big carronades that British ships carried in place of the useless little cannon that continued to clutter most French quarterdecks. Beside him he could see a red-coated marine officer. Closer and closer they came, and still there was no sign of the enemy flinching.

'We are in range now, Admiral,' reported Vrignaud. 'Shall we begin the action?'

Shall we? Linois asked himself. The side of the frigate vanished in a wall of smoke, and moments later a series of crashes rang out as the well-aimed broadside thudded into the *Marengo*. A cry of pain from somewhere on the deck beneath him was cut off by the roar of noise as the rest of the British ships joined in. Plumes of water dotted the sea and shot tore through the rigging all along the French line. 'Very well, Joseph,' he said. 'You can open fire.'

*****

The *Griffin* was lost in a world of fire and smoke. This close to the equator the temperature and humidity was high anyway even so early in the day. Add the furnace heat of battle and the air was stifling down on the frigate's main deck.

Sedgwick had been drafted in to take O'Malley's place as gun captain of the eighteen-pounder closest to the frigate's main mast. He was stripped to the waist, and yet still the sweat ran from his skin, dripping on to the sizzling breech of the cannon, to vanish a moment after contact. He poured the stream of fine grey powder into the touch hole, snapped back the lock, and then retreated to the full length of the firing lanyard. He glanced along the barrel, checking that the gun was still aimed at the dark shadow of the *Marengo*, a ghost ship lost amid the brown haze of smoke. 'Clear!' he yelled in warning, and then jerked hard on the lanyard. A sparkle of gold and the gun thundered back in board, to be pounced on by the waiting crew.

Sedgwick stood upright, easing his aching back, and pulled his bandana off to wring the sweat from it. As it cleared his ears, the noise of battle jumped closer. The ripping of passing shot flying overhead. The groan of the wounded sailors being carried past him. The hammer blow of balls smashing into the hull. The deck was littered with debris that rattled down from aloft. The cannon next to his was out of action, the gun carriage tipped over by the huge clanging blow it had received on the barrel from the *Belle-Poule*'s first broadside, but despite that, the frigate was fighting well. All along the gun deck the remaining cannon were rumbling back and forwards, firing as quickly as their well-drilled crews could manage. Rushing among them were the ship's boys, some with a fresh charge from the magazine, others racing away to get the next. Walking steadily towards him was Lieutenant Blake, one hand behind his back, the other pointing out patches of bare planking to the boy beside him who was casting handfuls of sand from a bucket to help give the gun crews grip.

'Gun loaded!' announced the sailor with the rammer.

'Run her up, lads,' ordered Sedgwick, pulling the sopping neckcloth back over his ears and rubbing his hands dry on his trousers.

On the frigate's quarterdeck Clay was listening too. He was by the rail, his head a little on one side, his eyes narrowed. Around him the roar of battle swirled. The French ships were easiest to pick out, firing steadily, in booming broadsides that arrived like a burst of hailstones driven against a window. Nearer was the rattle from the three East Indiamen, a constant banging of individual cannon, sometimes closer, sometimes more distant. Loudest of all was the thunder of the *Griffin*'s guns firing quickly, but he could sense their pace starting to slacken as the crews tired.

'Mr Taylor's respects, sir, and we are twice holed between wind and water,' reported Midshipman Sweeny, picking his way across the crowded deck to stand before him.

'Twice, you say?' exclaimed Clay. 'Is it bad?'

'Fair gushing in down in the hold, it was, sir,' reported the youngster, holding out a sopping coat sleeve as proof. 'Chips has got one hole largely plugged and is working on the other, but says we have two feet of water in the well, and gaining. Mr Taylor requests the pumps be manned.'

'Of course,' said Clay, starting to rue his generous transfer of prime hands to the other ships. 'Where am I to take the men from?' he muttered aloud. 'I can't have the gun crews weakened any further.'

'Use my Lobsters, sir,' suggested Macpherson, indicating his sharpshooters up in the rigging. 'The enemy seems content to batter us from far beyond musket range. They can turn a pump handle as swift as the next man.'

'Perfect, Tom! Make it so!'

'Corporal Edwards!' yelled the Scot. 'Two dozen men to the pumps, if you please! Mr Sweeny here will show them their duties.'

'Aye aye, sir!'

'Hot work, is it not, sir?' said Macpherson, once the men had descended from the masts and clumped off towards the main deck.

'It is Tom, perhaps a little too hot,' said Clay, who had returned to his listening. 'Do you think the *Earl Camden* is firing less swift?'

The Scotsman listened to the ship that loomed behind them. Two guns fired close together, then a pause before a third gun fired. The gun smoke seemed to be thinning too.

'Aye, perhaps a wee bit, sir,' he conceded. 'I may not be the best man to judge it, mind. My hearing may still not be fully restored.'

'How are your eyes, then? Is it me, or do the enemy seem closer?'

'I can barely see them through the fume of battle, sir, but aye, that last broadside did appear closer.'

'Then the moment is at hand,' said Clay. He turned from the rail. 'Mr Todd! Kindly hoist a general signal. Just the word "Begin". You will find it to be 107 in the code book. Pray use the far halliard, so it is visible to the convoy and to the *Ganges*.'

'Eh, aye aye, sir,'

'And what, pray, is the significance of yon signal, sir?' asked the marine, as the row of flags broke out aloft.

'Why, it is the moment that we play our final card, Tom,' said Clay, trying to smile. 'Let us hope that it proves to be an ace.'

*****

Upon the Malabar Coast

'How long have we been fighting, Joseph?' demanded Linois, leaning close to be heard above the sound of the *Belle-Poule*'s broadside, just astern.

Vrignaud consulted the slate that hung beside the binnacle. 'Almost an hour, monsieur,' he yelled back. An eighteen-pounder ball burst through the quarterdeck rail behind him and bounded across the deck, scouring the planking but miraculously missing everyone.

'An hour?' queried the admiral. 'And you still think they are just merchantmen?'

'Perhaps not,' conceded the captain. 'But I feel we are having the best of the battle, monsieur.'

As if in answer there was a loud crack overhead, accompanied by the rending of canvas. Both men looked up to where the mizzen topsail yard had been shot through, the broken end dangling loose among a cocoon of torn sail and severed lines.

'Afterguard!' yelled Vrignaud. 'Get your men aloft, Pelous, and secure that damage before the whole yard comes down.'

'*Oui*, mon capitaine,' said the petty officer, urging his men on, and then following them up the mizzen shrouds.

'Winning?' queried Linois. 'If only I could believe that was true.' The *Marengo* roared out another full broadside, the recoil heeling the deck under his feet and blanketing the ship with a fresh wall of smoke. As the noise washed away, he heard a cry from aloft.

'Deck there!' yelled the lookout.

Linois stepped to one side, picking his way through the fallen debris and splinter fragments littering the deck, and looked up at the tiny figure stood on the main royal yard. 'What can you see?'

'The other ships! They are …' the rest of the message was lost as the *Sémillante* added her guns to the fury.

Linois strode across to the ship's side, and stared into the smoke, but could see little more than shadows in the fog, their sides flashing with fire. 'Damn all this smoke! What bloody ships?'

He stood for a moment and then marched down the gangway until he reached the main mast shrouds. Beneath him he could see the upper gun crews methodically working through the process of reloading, the stages called out by the lieutenant in the centre of the deck. It was slower than independent fire, but much safer with an inexperienced crew. He clambered up on to the main chains, gripped the thick shrouds and looked up. The two-hundred-foot mast seemed lofty as a mountain, the angle of the shrouds that of a steeple. He began to climb, and immediately realised one shroud was too slack in his hand, twisting from his grip and only held in place by the thin rattlings. Leaning back he saw where a cannon ball had cut through it. He shuffled forward until he found a place where the ropes were taut as iron, and began to ascend quickly.

Linois was still a fit man, and although he had not climbed the mast since he was a lieutenant, his hands and feet found the right places by instinct. The hardest part was when he had to hang out backwards on the futtock shrouds as he reached the main top. He heard the order to fire barked out below him just in time to tighten his grip before the shock of the broadside reached him. One foot slid free, but he was able to scramble on, his heart thundering in his chest. The hot smoke from the guns billowed past him and he was lost in a brown fog, the lines of rigging vanishing into it all around him. He paused to catch his breath, and for the smoke to clear a little, then climbed up into sunlight until he arrived at the topmast crosstrees, sweaty but triumphant. He carefully settled himself into position, with one arm securely wrapped around the thin topgallant mast, his feet dangling over the plunging void beneath him. Another thirty feet up was the lookout, sitting on the topgallant yard and staring down in disbelief at him. 'What is your name?' gasped Linois.

'B— Badeaux, mon amiral. Sorry, monsieur. I did not expect to see you up here.'

'And believe me, I never expected to climb up here when I rose this morning, Badeaux. But it is the only way I can hear you above the guns, and your hail sounded urgent. Now tell me, you spoke of other ships?'

'The other East Indiamen, monsieur. They are on the move. Look!'

Linois followed the direction the sailor was pointing. From this height the fume of battle was boiling under him, trailing away downwind and dispersing. It seemed like an ugly stain on the carpet of blue ocean that stretched out to the far rim of the horizon in all directions, except to the west where the coast of Sumatra lay beneath rain clouds. He could glimpse snatches of his own ships, in a tight line, sailing parallel to their four opponents. The upper sails of both sides stood proud of the smoke, pockmarked with holes. Further away was the convoy, the merchantmen sailing on towards the north, but the line of East Indiamen had changed direction. They were looping around, curling towards him across the sea like the vertebrae of a huge serpent. He watched topgallants appearing on some of the ships as they hastened forward.

'They mean to come up on our disengaged side!' exclaimed Linois. 'To surround us!'

'Oui, mon amiral,' agreed Badeaux, and then his

attention shifted elsewhere. 'The little brig over there, monsieur. She has fired a gun. Is she signalling?'

Linois had forgotten about the *Ganges*, stationed ahead of the convoy between it and the northern horizon. He had missed the gun firing, but could see the puff of smoke it had left.

'A gun? It must be urgent,' said Linois, focusing his telescope on the brig. Flying from its mizzen halliards was a string of coloured flags. 'Definitely a signal, but I have no idea what it says, of course.'

'No, monsieur, but a windward gun?' said Badeaux. 'That is the old signal for a sighting in every navy, no?'

'Perhaps,' said Linois, moving his attention to the other ships. 'Who is he signalling to?'

There was a loud crack and the mast jolted sharply. Linois almost dropped his telescope as he clung on. '*Mon Dieu*! What was that?'

'A ball from the English hit the mast, monsieur,' said the lookout, calmly. 'A poor shot for them, they prefer to batter our hulls.'

Linois bent forward to examine the topmast beneath him. Ten feet below was a white tear in the wood where the ball had struck a glancing blow. He carefully shifted his weight about, but apart from a few creaks the mast seemed solid.

'Ah, there, monsieur!' said Badeaux, pointing. 'That ship with the commodore's pennant. See? I just glimpsed a red flag with a white cross. That is their acknowledgement, I think.'

'Yes, and now he is signalling in turn.' Linois shifted his gaze to the brig. More flags streamed up the mast. 'What are you saying, little ship?' he pondered aloud. 'What is it you have seen?'

'Whatever it is, monsieur, it must be coming from the

north,' said the lookout, staring that way. 'That is the only direction where he could see something that is over the horizon to us.'

'But we are much higher so it should be visible soon,' said Linois, a feeling of dread settling over him. No French or Dutch ships would be coming from that direction, only fresh enemies. He scanned the horizon, left and right, searching carefully, but it was Badeaux, a little higher up the mast, who saw them first.

'There, monsieur!' he reported. 'A point to windward of the brig!'

Linois focused on the place and saw it too. A tiny square of something more solid in the haze on the edge of sea and sky, followed a little later by a second square beside it. '*Merde*! Topsails!' he cursed. 'Two ships, big ones, sailing towards us!' He closed his telescope with a snap and returned it to his pocket. Then he looked at the line of East Indiamen, still advancing to cut off his only line of retreat. 'Its a bloody ambush!' he decided. Then he did something he hadn't done since he was a midshipman twenty years before. He grabbed the back stay, wrapped his feet around it, and slid in one long glide down to the deck.

'Captain Vrignaud! Captain Vrignaud! Break off the action! Now!' he cried as he strode across to the wheel, his hands still burning from the speed of his descent. 'We are being lured into a trap. There is not a moment to lose!'

*****

'Signal from the *Ganges*, sir,' reported the signal midshipman. 'Strange sail in sight.'

'Thank you, Mr Todd,' said Clay calmly. 'Keep me

informed of any further signals, if you please.' He was aware of the faces turning towards him across the quarterdeck, but he kept his attention on his first lieutenant. 'So have the holes been plugged successfully, George?'

'For the present, sir,' said Taylor, his eyes straying across to where he could see Todd feverishly chalking down a fresh signal. 'And the pumps are holding. I was going to try and get number six gun remounted, unless you need me here?'

His eyes slid back to the signal midshipman once more as he came over. 'Another signal from the *Ganges*, sir,' Todd reported. 'Two sail in sight, bearing north by west.'

'Two sail, sir,' said Taylor. 'From that direction, they must have come from India.'

'Let us hope, so,' said Clay.

'And the other East Indiamen are sailing to join the battle, sir,' persisted Taylor. 'Things are moving in our favour, at last.'

'Perhaps they are,' said Clay, his face impassive. 'But we still have a dangerous opponent to deal with. To that end, kindly leave the dismounted gun until the battle is truly over. We cannot spare the men to remount it with the enemy still alongside.'

'Aye aye, sir.'

Clay returned his attention to the battle. He looked down at the side of his ship, scarred and battered by the bombardment it had endured. The buff strake was blackened by powder smoke, and yet the guns continued to emerge, slower than before, to spit fresh columns of fire towards the enemy and vanish again. He stepped across to look down on to the gundeck. Some of the crews were distinctly thin in numbers, with other members sporting blood-stained rags tied over light wounds. All drooped with fatigue, their bodies shining with sweat, but still they served their guns. The cries of 'loaded!' and 'clear!' lacked the panache of earlier, but he was pleased to see the gun captains pausing to sight their pieces before firing and waiting for the down roll. Blake continued to stroll up and down the deck behind the guns, a calm presence, encouraging here, reassigning a man there. It was a level of professionalism that he knew his opponents had long abandoned, if only from the dwindling number of shots now hitting the *Griffin*. But still the battle went on. Come on, he urged towards the tall shadow of the *Marengo*. Surely you must have seen what is happening?

And then the miracle began. The remorseless pounding crash of the frigate's eighteen-pounders started to falter. Gun captains began to look up from their scorching cannons, firing lanyards limp in their hands as they searched in vain for a target. All along the British line, guns fell silent, while through the thinning smoke Clay saw that the silhouette of the enemy ships had changed. A gust of wind tore apart the fog, and there was the gilded stern of the French seventy-four, huge and square, with *Marengo* in an arc of bold letters across the counter, sailing away from him. A few cannons fired, and one of the mass of windows exploded; and then the enemy was out of range, sailing away towards the south, setting ever more sail, with her two consorts beside her.

'They've cut and run!' roared Armstrong, enveloping Macpherson in an enormous bear hug and bodily lifting the marine off the ground. A storm of cheering swept across the frigate and on to the three battered East Indiamen behind her. Captain Dance appeared on the bow of the *Earl Camden.* True to his name, he shuffled out a few steps of a jig, before he flung his hat high into the air. His aim was sadly out, and there was much laughter as it tumbled down into the sea to be promptly swallowed by his ship's bow wave.

'Congratulations, sir,' smiled Taylor, taking Clay's hand and wringing it. 'That was a damned close thing.'

'Two sail in sight!' added the *Griffin*'s lookout. 'A point off the starboard bow.'

'What do you make of them?' called Armstrong.

'Big and ship-rigged, sir, and coming on fast.'

'Are they reinforcements?' queried Taylor.

'From Admiral Rainer?' supplemented Armstrong, one arm still draped around Macpherson's shoulders.

'Admiral Linois certainly believes so,' said Clay with a smile. 'Which is all that truly matters. In truth they are the *Henry Addington* and the *Cumberland*, two East Indiamen from the China fleet I dispatched to beyond the horizon during the blackest part of the night, so they might return with all haste in the midst of battle. But by the time their identity is beyond doubt, the French will be much too distant to appreciate it.'

'Well, I'll be damned!' laughed the sailing master. 'We've humbugged them, by God!'

'I trust that we have, gentlemen,' said Clay. 'But now let us get our ship restored, and this convoy on its way, before Admiral Linois has a change of heart.'

The End

Note from the author

The events portrayed in *Upon the Malabar Coast* are a blend of the truth with the fictional. These notes are for the benefit of readers who would like to understand where the boundary lies between the two. The frigates *Griffin* and *Marseillois*, the slaver *Sao Vincente* and the cutter *Curlew* are fictitious, as are the characters who crew them. All other ships mentioned are historical, and were broadly in the locations set out in my novel at the time I say. As in my previous works, I try my best to ensure that my descriptions of those ships and the lives of their crews are as accurate as I am able to make them. Any errors I have made are my own.

Polwith, Lower Staverton and their residents are all fictitious. Porto Praya, Bombay and Trivandrum, the capital of Travancore, are real. Bombay is now the city of Mumbai. Returning them to their 1803 appearance was achieved by a combination of research and imagination.

Travancore was a native state on the Malabar coast of India. It rose to prominence in the eighteenth century under two successful rulers in the way described in my novel. The state signed a treaty of perpetual alliance with the Honourable English East India Company in 1795, after the Company had come to Travancore's aid when the neighbouring state of Mysore invaded. When Dharma Raja died in 1798, he left a powerful, politically stable country to his son, the weak and vacillating teenager Balarama Varma. After several years of poor rule Velu Thampi, a powerful nobleman, became dalawa or chief minister in 1801. He was the *de facto* ruler of the state and pursued a policy of distancing Travancore from British influence. This never included the building of warships with French support. His policy brought him increasingly into conflict with Britain. Matters came to a head in 1808, when Velu Thampi ordered an open attack on the British Residency by Travancore's army. Following military intervention by East India Company forces, Velu Thampi committed suicide, and Travancore returned to being an independent state loyal to Britain. Following Indian independence in 1947, Travancore was incorporated into the modern state of Kerala. The current maharaja is a descendent of the Varma rulers of eighteenth-century Travancore and still lives in the old royal palace to this day.

Major (later Colonel) Colin Macaulay was resident in Travancore throughout this turbulent period. A tough Scottish officer, he spent thirty years in India, including two imprisoned by Tipu Sultan as one of General Sir David Bird's companions. He was a good friend of General Arthur Wellesley (later the Duke of Wellington). A committed Christian, when Macaulay eventually returned home he founded the Society for the Suppression of Vice.

Vice Admiral Peter Rainer was commander of Royal Navy forces in the East Indies, although he was generally based in Madras, rather than Bombay. A keen supporter of the expansion of British rule in India, he was a strong ally of Richard Wellesley, the governor-general, and his brother Arthur. His twelve years commanding the East Indies squadron saw him return home an immensely wealthy man.

Rear Admiral Charles-Alexandre Durand, Comte de

Linois, led an expedition to the Indian Ocean in 1803, setting out two months before war was declared. It consisted of the ships listed in my novel, a number of additional storeships and several thousand troops. It did not carry the means to set up a shipyard in Travancore. Having been prevented from taking possession of the former French colony of Pondicherry, Linois used the troops he had brought out from Europe to reinforce the French islands in the Indian Ocean and devoted his efforts to commerce raiding, culminating in his attack on the annual China fleet in February 1804. It was not to be the admiral's finest hour.

The Battle of Pulo Aura was fought as the China fleet entered the Straits of Malacca, between the Malay peninsula and the island of Sumatra. The forces on the two sides were as I describe, with the exception that the French had an additional small Dutch warship with them, and there was no Royal Navy frigate accompanying the China fleet. Realising that he could not out-fight or out-run the French squadron, the commodore of the convoy, Nathaniel Dance, organised four of the sixteen East Indiamen to fly blue ensigns and pretend to be warships. Unknown to Dance, Linois had been told by a Dutch trader to expect only twelve East Indiamen, which helped the ruse to succeed. Dance's ships acted boldly and engaged the French in a running fight over two days. When the rest of the East Indiamen moved to surround the French ships, Linois broke off the action. Clay's idea of two ships posing as reinforcements was never attempted.

Linois was roundly condemned for his failure to capture a poorly protected and highly valuable convoy, not least by Napoleon. In his defence, confusing East Indiamen with warships was surprisingly common in this period, not least because these merchantmen were often built to resemble them as a deterrent to pirates. In 1806 Linois was returning from the Indian Ocean on the *Marengo*, accompanied by the *Belle-Poule*, when he spotted what he though was another fleet of East Indiamen in the Atlantic. Perhaps with his previous failure in mind, he attacked them boldly. Unfortunately, this 'convoy' proved to be a squadron of seven Royal Navy ships of the line and two frigates under Rear Admiral Sir John Warren. After a brief but bloody fight both French ships were captured. Linois and his men were to remain as prisoners of war until 1814 because Napoleon refused to allow them to return to France under a prisoner exchange.

Other books by Philip K Allan

The Alexander Clay Series

The Captain's Nephew

A Sloop of War

On the Lee Shore

A Man of No Country

The Distant Ocean

The Turn of the Tide

In Northern Seas

Larcum Mudge

Upon the Malabar Coast

World War 2

Sea of Wolves

About the Author

Philip K Allan comes from Hertfordshire in the United Kingdom where he lives with his wife and two daughters. He has an excellent knowledge of the 18th century navy. He studied it as part of his history degree at London University, which awoke a lifelong passion for the period. A longstanding member of the Society for Nautical Research, he is also a keen sailor and writes for the US Naval Institute's magazine *Naval History*.

He is author of the Alexander Clay series of naval fiction. The first book in the series, *The Captain's Nephew*, was published in January 2018, and immediately went into the Amazon top 100 bestseller list for Sea Adventures. The sequel, *A Sloop of War*, was similarly well received, winning the Discovered Diamonds Book of the Month Award. He has since published seven further books in the series as well as *Sea of Wolves*, which was his first book set in the Second World War.

If you want to find out more about him or his books, the links below may be helpful.

Website: www.philipkallan.com

Facebook & Twitter: @philipkallan

Instagram: @philipkallanauthor

About the Cover

The cover artwork for *Upon the Malabar Coast* was commissioned from the talented marine artist Colin M Baxter. If you would like to acquire a signed reproduction of this picture or to see any of his other work, please contact Colin direct or visit him at his gallery in Gosport.

Colin M Baxter Marine Artist
Driftwood Studio and Gallery
2a North Meadow
Royal Clarence Yard
Weevil Lane
Gosport
PO12 1BP
United Kingdom

Telephone: +44 (0)2392 525014

Email: colinmbaxter@hotmail.co.uk

Website: www.colinmbaxter.co.uk